Good Guys or Bad Guys, the Difference Between Life & Death?

Counter-Measures

An Intelligence & Military Action Thriller

by C.B. Michaels

TO: MARK · n · CAROLINE

Author's Notes:

While some readers may feel the sting of disclosing our Government's mistakes, mishaps or errors in judgment, it is not my intent to disparage. Split second life and death decisions can't possibly be made 100% correctly. Often these mistakes end in tragedy. People who serve our country, on the many front lines, are the 'good-guys' of the world. We are bound to make mistakes dealing in this reality.

Send any comments to: **Feedback2Author@Gmail.com**

Website: www.**CounterMeasures.US**

ISBN-13: 978-1490473796

ISBN-10: 1490473793

Library of Congress Catalog: PENDING, Applied for.

Third Edition

Dedication

To the 'Stars on the Wall' at C.I.A. Headquarters

Any other souls in our society, who put their lives on the line, for our protection, to secure our freedoms, or affirm our rights, are recognized in life and memorialized in death with public displays of gratitude and affection after making the ultimate sacrifice.
...all except for the Stars of Langley.

At the time of this writing, there were 87 Stars on the Wall . . . 33 of which are secret, even in the CIA "Book of Honor."
Secret, even in death, but not forgotten.

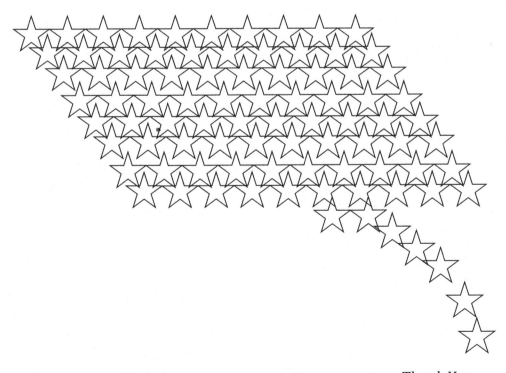

Thank You.

Table of Events

PROLOGUE 5
PART I 13
CHAPTER 1: Echoes in Time 13
CHAPTER 2: Snakes of the Jungle 23
CHAPTER 3: The Assignment 33
CHAPTER 4: Little Soldier Boy 39
CHAPTER 5: Over the Rainbow 45
CHAPTER 6: Dead Man Driving? 55
CHAPTER 7: Reasons to Justify the Means 59
CHAPTER 8: Chasing Your Own Tale 71
CHAPTER 9: Being Happy is Knowing What You Love to Do 87
CHAPTER 10: Testing Your Limits 95
CHAPTER 11: Rain of Fire in the Jungle 105
CHAPTER 12: Lightning Actually Goes from the Ground Up 113
CHAPTER 13: You Never Leave a Man Behind 125
CHAPTER 14: The Opposite of Betrayal is Revenge 131
CHAPTER 15: It's the Viper You Don't See That Bites You 143
CHAPTER 16: The Thrill of Victory, The Agony of Defeat 151
CHAPTER 17: The Great Escape 159
CHAPTER 18: Master of Disguise in Plain Sight 165
PART II 169
CHAPTER 19: A Meeting of the Minds 169
CHAPTER 20: Days of Reckoning 187
CHAPTER 21: Starting Forest Fires 205
CHAPTER 22: Into the Belly of the Beast 219
CHAPTER 23: The Lunatic Fringe 239
CHAPTER 24: The Best Defense 251
CHAPTER 25: Big Boys and Their Toys 257
CHAPTER 26: A Call to Rally 271
CHAPTER 27: And Now, for a Breaking Story 281
CHAPTER 28: The Hypocrisy of Covering One of Your Own 293
CHAPTER 29: Covering Your Tracks When Leaving the World 303
CHAPTER 30: Chasing Shadows 313
CHAPTER 31: New Games, New Rules 323
CHAPTER 32: Perspective is From the Eyes of the Viewer 331

PART III..341
CHAPTER 33: A Tormented Beast, The Danger of It All...........................341
CHAPTER 34: Sometimes You Fly Too Close to the Sun 349
CHAPTER 35: Sermon of the Damned 369
CHAPTER 36: Falling from On-High, Just Gives You More Time to Think.. 377
CHAPTER 37: Fabric Stitched in Time..393
CHAPTER 38: Magic Depends on Not Seeing the Sleight of Hand.............403
CHAPTER 39: Ride of the Dark Chariot 413
CHAPTER 40: Humpty Dumpty Floating in a Boat 423
CHAPTER 41: Fleets of Time 427
CHAPTER 42: Walking the Plank 433
CHAPTER 43: Wheels in the Sky Burning...437
CHAPTER 44: Ringing the Bell 441
CHAPTER 45: Incoming...445
CHAPTER 46: Situational Awareness 449
CHAPTER 47: All the King's Horses and All the King's Men 457
CHAPTER 48: The Saints Come Marching In...465
CHAPTER 49: The Devil's Due 473

PROLOGUE

Based on an actual event with sympathy, condolences, and regrets to the victims, their families, and all those who were scarred that terrible day.

Somewhere over Southern Iraq, April 1991

Hovering a thousand feet up in the darkening afternoon skies, Senior Airman Jacob Browers lowered his face-shield and switched on his FLIR to a greenish, low-scale night vision.

A big, white X was projected, floating in the 3-D space of his heads-up display and following his line of sight automatically. The helmet-link turned and aimed his guns wherever he looked. No need for him to do anything but look and pull the trigger -- an instinctual, natural and deadly reflex of eyesight: Look and squeeze, look and squeeze.

He flicked on his radio: "We are firing. Over."

"Roger," Daniels, his co-pilot, said.

The 30mm cannon was not loud at all -- just a tin-like banging sound. Like someone knocking on a metal storm door.

Tat-tat-tat-tat-tat.

Tat.

Tat-tat-tat-tat.

He watched the rounds reach the scene on the ground below as three or four guys exploded in a watery mist, with little splatter. None of the other fourteen or fifteen men could process or hope to react.

Browers swung his sight to the left as the men who turned to run caught his eye.

Tat tat tat tat.

Tat tat tat tat.

A few shells hit a little low, exploding on the ground, spraying forward. Three or four pairs of legs were blown away. Torsos fell to the earth, taking a few more hits, twisting and rolling over in heaps.

In the puff of a few seconds, half the men were gone.

A few men on the right side managed to turn and run. Browers looked, then a quick squeeze.

Tat-tat-tat-tat-tat.

Two men were turned into a sprinkler-like spray. A third man tripped and fell into a billowing cloud of dust. The last man tried to hide behind a telephone pole.

Tat-tat-tat.

Exploding shells shredded the pole.

It spun the man into the open, totally exposed.

Tat-tat-tat.

His head disappeared like a watermelon exploding. The body dropped from view into the dust.

"Fuck yeah, that's what I call a kill shot!" Daniels said, a little too excited.

"Keep scanning down there. Anything else moving? Where's that fucker with the RPG you saw?"

"He blew away with the first four or five," Daniels reported.

"HQ this is Fire-Horse One-Six," Browers said, "we engaged and neutralized the threat. Fifteen to twenty KIA. We may have at least one moving wounded. Over."

As the dust settled, Browers saw a wounded man, obviously disorientated. He tried to stand up, only to topple over, his right leg giving way at weird angles.

"This is HQ, confirmed, Fire-Horse One-Six, threat neutralized. One wounded on scene. Approved to fire on any threat. Repeat, approved to engage. Over."

Daniels screamed over the comm. *"Incoming dark van! Up the main street, half mile east, headed high speed straight toward incident scene!"*

The van quickly pulled into view, sliding to a stop next to the wounded man. Two men jumped out and ran to his side.

"HQ, Fire-Horse One-Six, the van has stopped and is attempting to retrieve wounded man. Advise."

"*This is HQ, you have clearance to engage. Neutralize any threats. Over.*"

"*Light those fuckers up!*" Daniels just couldn't help himself.

Browers tried to ignore him. "HQ, they are attempting to take the wounded to the van. No weapons. Van was not part of the original group of SUVs. Do you want us to engage the dark van? Confirm, over."

"*Affirmative Fire-Horse One-Six. Do not allow withdrawal of hostile.*"

"*Fuck yeah, sons of bitches!*" Daniels added.

Browers wished he could turn the young pilot's mic off.

"HQ, Fire-Horse One-Six, do you want us to disable the van, or engage the new personnel? I say again, they are unarmed and trying to retrieve wounded only."

The mini-van looked a little too "soccer-mom" for Browers' liking, but it wasn't up to him.

"*HQ to Fire-Horse One-Six. Engage van and neutralize all personnel at the incident scene. Do not allow removal of any wounded. Do not allow exit of van or new personnel. You are clear to engage. Fire when ready.*"

"*Come-on, light 'em up, Sir!*"

Browers had enough of this bloodthirsty kid. "For the last time Daniels, intel only. Then shut the fuck up!"

Browers turned back to the green-screen display.

The would-be rescuers had managed to carry the wounded man around to the side door of the van and opened it.

Browers twitched his finger and let silent death ring out.

Tat-tat-tat-tat.

The injured man was blown from their hands and into the van. Both rescuers dove in opposite directions, with one attempting to hide in the alcove entrance of a small shop.

Tat-tat-tat-tat.

There was a futile relex of motion of his hands and arms as the body fell in a slump at the entrance.

The van jumped forward and sped across the street. The other man was trying to escape. Unfortunately for him, vehicles are what 30mm cannon chain guns were meant to take out.

Tat-tat-tat-tat. Tat-tat-tat-tat.

Exploding rounds dotted up the hood and windshield. The engine blew. A thick spray instantly covered what was left of the windows.

The van rolled a few feet further in a dead coast, hitting a curb, and jolting to a stop. The now dead mans body fell from the open side door and sluiced onto the road.

"HQ this is Fire-Horse One-Six. Van is immobilized. Threat neutralized. We have fifteen to twenty KIA. Send in recon units for possible intel. Over."

Daniels chirped in.

"Fuckin' A. Nice shootin'. Sorry I got excited. You lit those assholes up."

"You're not the first green helmet I've had sit down there. You need to try and tone it down a little. I understand you're all jacked up. I remember the adrenaline. Shit, anybody in this business that doesn't get a charge out of what we just did is a psychopath."

"You think I'm a psycho?"

Browers chuckled. "If I did, I sure as hell wouldn't tell you. You reading me at all?"

"Sure. I'm sitting here shaking. I feel it."

"You gotta think straight. You can't be bouncing all over the cockpit and making all that chatter over the radio. Keep your situational awareness. Fight to stay calm. Listen to what's going on."

"Fire-Horse One-Six, this is recon Toolbox Two-Seven rolling up on incident scene. Hold your fire, please." A pause, then: *"Jesus. What that fucking machine can do."*

"Affirmative Toolbox Two-Seven. Fire-Horse One-Six standing down. I've only got about another ten minutes fuel on site, so clear your perimeter."

"Hold Fire-Horse one-six, we got one here, mostly in one piece."

Browers' heard someone shout in the background that the survivor speaks English.

A strange static charge ran through Browers' body. Veterans know when something isn't right. Reflex. Instinct. Based on intangible combat experience.

"Un-fucking believable. How the hell did that towelhead survive all that?" Daniels asked.

"Daniels, would you shut your fucking mouth?!"

The ground recon commander radioed again. *"This is Toolbox Two-Seven, to . . . ah . . . to HQ . . . I . . . I have a duty report, Sir. Over."*

"HQ to recon, Toolbox Two-Seven, ground report on incident. Go ahead."

A pause. *"We've got an AP reporter here, Sir, wounded bad, but conscious. Talking clearly."* Another pause. *"He . . . ah . . . was part of the group. A sanctioned meeting of . . . ah . . . four local southern leaders. Working with the coalition, Sir, working with us to . . . ah, shit."* Another pause. *"To set up . . . to stabilize the southern region, Sir. Medics working on him now, but . . . I'm sorry to say, it looks like an FF. A total FF screw up by somebody, Sir. Over."*

Browers swallowed hard and blinked, trying to absorb it. It was war. They are the enemy. Except these people weren't, and he'd blown them away.

His ears began to swish in his head. FF. Friendly-fire incident. It was bad for everybody.

It was really bad for him. Browers' could feel the specter of it hoving in the air with him.

"God damn it!" HQ yelled. *"What the fuck where they doing with RPGs and AKs driving around in a live fire zone?"*

"I'll ask," Recon responded, *"but the medics are workin' on the guy. There's no weapons here, Sir. Just cameras and shit. One bodyguard with an AK. That's it. SUVs are clean. Just rides. Over."*

"Base to Fire-Horse One-Six, you reading this?"

"Fire-Horse One-Six, affirmative. Friendly Fire. Oh God, I hope not, because we just killed all of them down there."

"HQ to Fire-Horse One-Six, return to base for debriefing as soon as they bug out. Report to me immediately!"

"Fire-Horse One-Six affirmative, returning to base after

Toolbox Two-Seven clears incident scene. Over."

And then, the spector swooped down on everyone who was there that terrible day.

"Recon to HQ! Recon Toolbox Two-Seven . . . The van! Aw shit, in the van, Sir . . . This is fucking bad . . . so fucking bad."

In wars, for all of history, no nation, no troops, no persons were safe from friendly fire accidents.

Sad statistics bear this out, even for the victors. As the Iraqi 'Gulf-Wars' continued to prove.

"Only 190 Coalition troops were killed by Iraqi combatants, the rest of the 379 coalition deaths being from friendly fire accidents.

"While the death toll among Coalition forces engaging Iraqi combatants was very low, a substantial number of deaths were caused by accidental attacks from other allied units.

"Of the American troops who died in battle, 24% were killed by friendly fire . . . 1 of every 4 killed in action."

-- Source: Department of Defense

PART I

CHAPTER 1: Echoes in Time

Susan Figiolli hadn't spent time in the field as an undercover C.I.A. agent in years. On a secret mission. In disguise. It was all very James Bond of her. She'd almost forgotten how good the rush of a field operation felt.

Could it really be almost ten years since I've last done this? she thought as she pushed her glasses up the bridge of her nose.

Her secret operation was over in a flash.

Coming down hard from the high of her three-day thrill-ride, she peeled at the paper sleeve on her morning Starbucks, waiting to catch the hell she knew was coming. The coffee was still way too hot. Probably a good thing, she didn't need the caffeine.

At 39, the whole experience was making Susan feel . . . *older?*

Her fingertips absently went to trace the outline of a tiny check-mark scar over her right eyebrow. She'd gotten it fifteen years earlier in Cairo, back when all this really started. Most people never noticed it, that tiny little scar, but Susan saw it every time she looked in the mirror.

The Cairo office had pulled her off station in Russia. The Cold War was winding down, but she was in deep there, so this Cairo thing was big. Susan had a reputation as a puzzle-solver. Some queer bit of information would come in, local agents knew it meant something, but it didn't fit their case? Susan could somehow, within just a few days or weeks, find where it did.

The Cairo case jumped out at Susan right away. Her fix of adoration came quickly too as she and the two case agents raced off to catch the small-time arms dealer at an airport on the outskirts of the city.

Susan was young then, everyone learns the hard lesson about things being, too easy.

When the plane in the hanger the arms dealer was supposed to be on exploded, Susan realized her adversary's cunning in a flash, much too late in the game.

She could only remember it like a dream. The two agents running ahead of her, screaming for her to "cover the door." The heat of the blast, spinning her through the air, landing hard and skidding across the blacktop tarmac like it was made of ice. Sitting up after stunned, hearing muffled, watching a private jet taxi out the far hangar, then shoot down the runway and arch away up into the sky. She remembered wanting to run after it, but not knowing why in her dazed head.

She'd been chasing the Chameleon down that runway ever since.

It was a month before she could get up and walk without something hurting. Susan allowed the nightmare to carry her through rehab.

Some analyst tried to tell her the real target died in the explosion inside the hanger, once he knew he was trapped. DNA was found on the plane, he said.

But Susan knew that wasn't him.

The real Chameleon probably had a cocktail in his hand, looking out the private jet's porthole windows, smirking as he watched his handiwork unfold.

Susan walked past the memorial stars for those two agents every day in the lobby at Langley. Even if she tried not to look, a cold chill from the points of those marbled stars would cut through her. And most of all, she was dreading the day they'd start carving out the heart of another one because of the Chameleon.

How many more before I can finally solve it?

Her office door flew open and her top Oversight Agent strode through like he was sucked in with the swing of the door.

"What, you don't knock anymore?" Susan asked.

"Why should I do that? As a sign of respect? Professional courtesy?" Mr. Green asked.

It probably wasn't his real name. There were too many "Jenkins" and "Simpsons" and "Greens" in the ranks of Oversight Agents to all be real. Collectively, they all got the nickname "Dark Agents" because they were always standing in the shadows, peering, hovering over shoulders. OS agents at Langley watched. They listened. They got their own coffee.

Susan didn't envy his job, but always respected the necessity. Like Internal Affairs, or Military Police, someone has to spy on the spies too.

Green was the typical tall, dark, and handsome spy type. Fit. Clean cut, nice suit, well-manicured, usually very reserved and stoic.

Except now. Susan had never seen him so agitated, animated. Apparently, Dark Agents don't like being kept in the dark.

"Before you start, Mr. Green, please let me explain."

"You can't. That's going to be my point in the end."

Veins throbbing, straining at his collar and tie, not good. She decided not to reply.

"Tell me, how exactly do you see my job here?" He demanded.

To be a constant pain in my ass is what Susan would have joked under normal circumstances.

Instead she said: "Honestly? None of us knows exactly. Isn't that the way you guys like it?"

"Stop insulting my intelligence! Jesus, Susan, even the government down there is a risk. You know how corrupt they are. The information in your head is very valuable. Lots of people would pay lots of money to dissect you to get at it."

"Mr. Green, this mission, this case . . . who knows it better than me? So yes, I made a judgment call that I had to go."

"Yes, the Chameleon case. I'm up to speed now, no thanks to you. It reaches back to your youthful pride. And that's all the more reason why you should never have gone."

"I'm sorry. I do respect your position. But it was the best lead

I've had in years." She half-shrugged. "I see your point clearly now."

"Sorry, I don't believe you do. It's a matter of trust. People at the C.I.A. we can't trust don't get to be Dark-Room Controllers."

Damn.

Susan realized she risked more than her life, she had risked her job. Risked her Control Room.

You idiot.

"Please, Mr. Green. I do see. I am sorry."

"I'd fall on that sword for you, Susan, but I didn't expect it to be over something this stupid."

"You haven't said anything? No auto-triggers? Event reports?" Susan asked, hopeful.

"I'm still thinking about it. If I can't trust you going forward, then, yes, that's exactly what I'm going to do. Even if it means the end of me too."

Trust. A tricky thing in Susan's world. To give it or lose it was always big. Like playing with fire -- you could get burned, or you could burn somebody else. Or both.

"I'm truly sorry you feel that way," she said. "I promise I'll never do anything like this agian. You have my word on it."

Mr. Green looked her directly in the eye. "Not just 'anything like this,' but anything and everything out of your control room, I'm in on it. That's my job. Because I promise you, I won't hesitate if there's a next time."

Susan could see him working to calm himself down. She nodded her head in understanding, and held his gaze.

Then out of professional habit, a reflex after years of training and use, Susan let her big, brown eyes tear up a just a little behind her dark-rimmed glasses. She tilted her head of brunette pony-tail curls submissively to the side.

"Don't try that crap on me," Mr. Green snapped. "I'm well aware of your skills. Quite frankly, it's not a good look for you." He paused for effect. "Undercover, dangerous field work is no longer a part of your job description. We're perfectly clear?"

She blinked and nodded once.

"Good," he said. "Let's move on."

He's an arrogant ass and *They all are* didn't seem to fit him anymore. Mr. Green had backed her up on this one. Covered for her. Risked his whole career? Something Susan never dreamt he'd do.

She came around to feeling bad about the position she'd put him in. She'd only been thinking about herself, and catching the Chameleon.

A few real tears welled up on their own.

Somehow, he knew.

"We are going through a complete debriefing. But you might want to save most of it until after you've met the newest member of your team."

She blinked away the tears, a new reality sinking in. "I don't recall having interviewed, much less approved, an addition to my team. People need to earn their way into my Room, and then perform. First, they have to get through my interview process."

He leaned over her desk.

"Like I said, assigned to your team. Major General Thomas Givens has been attached to the Palantir project as an independent military observer."

"A military officer? Inside my Control Room?" It was her turn to control the anger. "I know, I know, 'work more closely', but I'm shocked they'd allow that level of integration."

"This case has gotten a lot more complicated in the three days you were gone. It's not like I had a chance to fill you in. And, since I now have to play along like I knew what you were doing, I'd appreciate your cooperation."

Mr. Green dared Susan to argue the point. He wasn't done yet.

"You better hope this Major General Givens is capable, and not a bigger pain in the ass than me."

Before she could reply, Mr. Green walked around to Susan's side of the desk, leaned in and logged onto her computer. He clicked and typed and clicked again. A video of Susan began playing. A video of Susan on her "secret" undercover mission.

"First things first, you need to debrief me on this," he said.

"How the hell did you get this?"

"I caught on quickly. We can send drones there too."

She paused, smiling slightly. "I'm impressed, Mr. Green."

"I need a debrief from you, that's all."

"I'm serious. You figured it all out and had a drone video the moment of truth. You might want to see about running your own control room."

"You're not getting rid of me that easily. Can we move on? These drones do not have audio, so I may have caught you in the act, but I need to hear what happened."

Susan reached down to fast forward the video. "I spent time waiting for a rebel named Ramirez. We'd marked him coming to this little café-slash-bar for two days straight."

The video showed Susan sitting at a little table in a small patio bar, dressed-to-the-nines in a crisp-collared white-with-black-dots summer dress cut high across her thighs, hugging her fit curves. Her hair was tied back in a long ponytail of brunette curls up high on the back of her head, held there by a sparkling bling of a hair clip. Designer makeup, deep red lipstick and black fashion sunglasses completed the sophisticated look.

"I bet when you saw this, you wanted to use a Hellfire on me."

"You still don't see how serious this all was?" Mr. Green asked.

"Wait. The drone was armed?"

"It would have been a tough call, but if it came to that? I would have pushed the button myself, and you'd be just another star on the wall."

"Oh really?" She looked at him, confused.

He leaned in, right up to her ear. "What if it had been a trap? If the Chameleon had set you up? If they grabbed you, threw you in an SUV? Heading out of town, open road, knowing we'd lose you soon? At that point, what would you have wanted us to do?"

"Crap. Crap."

"Two years I've worked with you . . . seen your skills, respected your skills . . . gotten to know you. You think I want to make that call?"

There was a silence of reflection. Susan owed him, big time. She focused back on the video and continued the debrief.

"This little café, off the bar here, is frequented by local people of influence in the capital. An unspoken neutral place and the idea was to hide in plain sight. The rich, powerful lady out for coffee. Maybe I was a politician's wife? Or a drug lord's trophy? Influential local family? Point is, nobody would mess with me."

Susan pointed to other figures in the shot.

"I've got my four obvious bodyguards stationed here, and here. We had a three-man backup team right out this side door here, as well as a capable photographic and technical team, two men in this direction across the street, out of view. I think even you'll agree, a very secure operation."

"Whether it's secure is not my point. I see plenty of risk here. Move on."

Susan turned back to the monitor. "Okay, here's the rebel we marked, Ramirez. Comes right on schedule. Same time, third day in a row. He's a rebel, so we knew he couldn't carry a weapon or he'd get picked up."

"You assumed it was likely he didn't have a weapon, but you couldn't know for sure."

"My Tech Team had some really interesting lenses, so yeah, we were pretty confident. And as you see here, a two-man team all but picks him up and carries him to my table. He's completely frisked before he gets close . . . Here's when I greet and calm him. He realizes that his cover isn't really blown, so he stays cool. Twenty minutes later, I've turned him. We have the audio, if you want to hear it all."

"No one doubts your field record, Susan. But, only twenty minutes to turn this rebel you never met before?"

Susan reached for a file on her desk. "Ramirez Pascale, thirty-two. Member of *Les Hombres Familiara*. The Friends of Your Family. Rebels looking to overthrow the corrupt government of General Santori Fleashaus. His government is our ally, so he's a good general, for now. Ramirez, was sent on a similar special mission to the capital three years ago. He'd met a girl, got her pregnant. He was on the grid from there."

"Doesn't seem like nearly enough for him to trust you in twenty minutes," Mr. Green said.

"A hundred thousand U.S. helped. Maria, him and the baby could start a new life somewhere else. Then I explained the Castro Doctrine to him -- cut off the smart, educated, or charismatic head of the anti-American rebel groups of the world. Kill the sharp guys, and let the dumb-asses run around the jungles killing each other. You sell arms or give aid to both sides and maintain a balance."

"But how does any of this give you leverage with Ramirez?"

"I made him take a hard look at the rebel leaders he's risking his life for. Was this all still for a cause? To help the families? Or was it about power and control now? Would his rebel leaders be any less corrupt once in office? As an example, I used his Direct Commander."

Susan pulled out another file.

"El'Mano Corenelle. Quite a colorful rebel leader, his rise to the top is a bloody affair. He uses a forty-four Magnum to maintain discipline. Blow some guy's arm off. The screaming. Blood spraying all over. If he really wants to make an example of a guy, he blows his package off -- traitors and deserters especially."

"So, you added a threat matrix to the equation?"

"If pictures of us talking accidentally slip into El'Mano's hands, Ramirez would be in real trouble, he'd lose either way. El'Mano offs him, or El'Mano is killed and Ramirez becomes the anti-American leader."

"You think all of this worked on him?"

"When I talked about El'Mano and that gun, you could tell it was something he'd seen. So, I played harder off that fear."

"He might have just played you, to get away, or to set you up. How would you know?"

"I don't. But there's little risk other than him running off and hiding in the jungle. I doubt he's going to take the chance with El'Mano. I wasn't asking him to be a traitor, or to get his buddies killed."

"Did he believe you?"

"You don't get people to believe you in a situation like this, you have them come to their own conclusion by asking questions they answer in their own head."

"I see it. But I still don't see how you connected all these dots to the Chameleon case and pulled all this off."

"I didn't do it on my own." She paused. "And you won't like the answer."

"Oh Jesus! The Palantir spun this whole web? Your sneaky little operation?"

"We couldn't have done it without the Palantir. That wonderful computer Doctor Splitzer invented took a thread of a thread of a thread and wove it into a noose." Susan looked directly into his eyes. "It's a hangman's noose, and I'm gonna stick the Chameleon's neck in it."

"So that damn machine has one of our best Controllers risking her life. A whole team rushing out in harm's way. And even Dr. Splitzer can't tell you for sure if it's working properly."

Susan was confident. The new Palantir computer Dr. Splitzer invented was an asset, not a threat. A cutting-edge creation which had given her an angle on the prey she'd been personally stalking for fifteen years.

Susan wasn't worried about Major General Thomas Givens either. Or the military. Or the politics behind it all. A part of her job for years.

None of it bothered her.

But her little rebel Ramirez could activate the EPIRB beacon at any moment. If that happened, there wouldn't be time to debrief everyone, especially a totally new military observer and that whole dynamic.

If that beacon went off, they'd all be briefed in real time.

Come on Chameleon, you little lizard,

...Scurry out to where I can finally see you.

CHAPTER 2: Snakes of the Jungle

Doctor Rehan Al'Camel stirred atop his sweat-soaked sleeping bag, beneath a mosquito net which hung around him like a wet blanket in the dead-still, humid air. The earthy, musty smells at ground level seemed to add to the smothering moisture of the rainforest.

He opened a slit in his netting, set up his Sterno stove and put his favorite tin water cup over the flame, a giant mug he had carried around the world for twenty years now.

The morning boils always seemed to take the longest.

The dark-haired, heavy-browed, villagers in their buckskin loincloths were milling about, timeless against the backdrop of ten or so grass-topped, bamboo-framed huts. Their copper skins glowed like the Aztec sun from which they'd been born.

A small group of children played coy, sneaking up for a closer look -- until Rehan caught their eye with a playful, shocked face, sending them off squealing in delight. Kids were kids, everywhere in the world.

Three women tended a pot over an open fire pit in the center of the village, stirring the morning breakfast soup. *Katch-cha* they called it. Rehan's stomach growled at the thought of getting a bowl full.

Rehan checked his watch. Barely 9 AM and the temperature already felt like it was over a hundred. The birds and monkeys in the jungle canopy were keeping their chatter to a minimum. Even the insects were already taking cover.

Today it's going up to broil for sure.

He was stiff and sore all over. It was all so much harder now. Just to get up off the hard ground required a few grunts and a groan. Rehan was closing in on 40 and this life of traveling to the far corners of the world as part of Doctors Without Borders had collected its toll along the way: A few bouts of malaria, or something just as bad; attacks by parasites, fungi, and microbes; bites, stings, or spitting of venom from snakes, spiders and other creepy-crawlies. Little bites weren't noticed right away, didn't hurt much at first, but they always seemed to lead to the longest-lasting torture and recovery time -- especially the snakes.

Everything in the jungle is always trying to kill everything else in the jungle, Rehan thought. It was his mantra whenever he started to let his guard down. As a precaution, he'd become an expert in toxicology over the years. Even developed a dark-habit of collecting poisons and toxin samples from all over the world

He rolled over, stood, and stretched his back, which rewarded him with a relieved crack.

He looked out at the jungle. As far from the desert climate of Kuwait where he'd grown up as he could get. Whenever he went deep into the rainforest, he felt like a white-meat delicacy which caused the jungle itself to drool. Doctor Rehan Al'Camel took a breath and stepped out of his netting, into Mother Nature's embrace.

Even with the heat, he stopped to put on his white doctor's smock. Then he walked to an open-air hut in the center of the village, carrying his tin cup of hot water, waiting for it to cool down enough to drink.

There were no walls to the hut, just a thatched grass roof supported by a sturdy bamboo frame. An eight-inch thick, hard-packed, dirt floor raised the covered space above the surrounding jungle. The stump of a giant, ancient tree protruded up in the center, its top shaped to make a crude table. Or an altar. Or just the village meeting place.

Right on cue, the village shaman came forward. His elaborate headdress of feathers, necklace of teeth, and bone piercings moved and clinked with each step. Tattoos adorned his weathered face, and his eyes greeted Rehan with the respect of a colleague.

Rehan had picked up more than a few very effective natural remedies and treatments over the years, and he shared as much as he could in return. Shamans absorbed the basics easily, but what they called magic serpents -- a syringe of extra-strength antibiotic, which cured even those who were surely doomed -- always left them in awe.

Villagers gathered quietly and a hush fell. A desperate mother approached warily and handed the strange medicine man her sick little daughter.

Rehan tried to calm the mother as much as he did the girl, with soft, kind words they didn't understand. His slow and compassionate handling of the frail, weak child, setting her on the edge of the great stump.

A quick, easy diagnosis of the yellowish-green puss oozing from one ear was all he needed.

The mother's eyes widened and became teary when Rehan used a syringe to drain it, the little girl whimpering and yelping in minor pain. The shaman scolded her with a *tisk-tisk* as he moved in to observe.

The villagers always had suspicious looks as they crowded around and craned their necks to see. But they instinctively knew he was here to help, or try to anyway. Rehan was amazed and honored by their quiet faith in him.

As Rehan maneuvered the syringe into the girl's ear, sucking out the "poi-un" as the shaman pronounced it, an excited chatter played out -- except for the little girl's mother, who stood shocked to stone at Rehan's side.

The shaman held up his hands to mimic Rehan's movements, staring intently at the syringe as Rehan withdrew the plunger.

Rehan followed it up with a quick, soothing flush-out, using some of his newly boiled, still warm water, mixed with a little salt. The release of the pressure and the soothing warmth was just the ticket, and the little girl gave Rehan a smile of relief. The mother melted and fell at Rehan's feet, and the child reached up and touched Rehan on the side of his face, looking up at him as if he were an angel. It made him feel like a god.

Almost anywhere else in the world such a minor ear infection would mean little more than a trip to the pediatrician and the local drug store. Out here, another couple of days, and the infection would surely have found its way to the girl's brain.

Rehan gulped down the last few swallows of the morning's boiled water. Still warm, but it never tasted so good.

A quiet fell over the villagers. Like a fluid, they faded away, melting into the bush. Three young warriors came to Rehan's side. One began tugging at his elbow, just as the unmistakable sound of metal buckles and boots began to cut through the jungle's din. If he let them, the warriors could hide him from anyone in their jungle.

The sound of a squad of armed men was one that Doctor Rehan Al'Camel had heard many times before. Even the most remote jungles in the world have at least one rebel group. Most places had more.

The three warriors who stood at his side surely knew it meant a quick death, armed only with spears, bows, and arrows. Perhaps the pride of protecting the magic shaman who gave to them so freely was an honorable way to die.

However, the sight of twenty camouflaged men with automatic rifles and a hardened, jungle-guerilla stare walking directly at them was enough to cause even these brave warriors to wince. Quickly surrounded, with multiple barrels at point-blank range, they shrank beside Rehan.

A short, stocky man pushed his way through and marched directly up to Rehan.

"Doctor Rehan! Imagine meeting you here."

It was the same old story.

Everything in the jungle is always trying to kill everything else in the jungle.

* * *

Rehan didn't care much what the rebels called themselves, but it was important to them. Fake respect could keep someone alive better than any antidote in his bag.

Over the years, Colonel Manuel Mercaususa -- a.k.a. El'Mano -- quickly rose through the rebel ranks. Kind of remarkable since he was barely five-four, a short pug of a man in his special two-inch elevated combat boots that added a clunky stomp to his bowlegged hitch.

Only El'Mano's smile was striking, with a surreal set of perfect, gleaming white teeth, an asset El'Mano used to put people at ease and take them off guard, often right before he blew their brains out.

El'Mano marched up to Rehan with that amazing Hollywood smile.

"Hello, Colonel El'Mano."

The young village warriors remained tense, theirs eyes shifting from El'Mano to Rehan, confused by the seemingly friendly greeting.

"It has been much, much too long since you made a trip here to help our people. I was beginning to think maybe you don't care any longer?"

Rehan ignored the slight insult but noted the "our people" comment. Rebel groups all over the world rarely did any good for the local natives. In most places, they were the biggest threat. Rehan pretended to be oblivious to any base disrespect or fear. He always played it as if he was above it all.

"Well, Commander, it is very dangerous in the jungle these days, as I'm sure you are aware. The people I love to help, but I wouldn't do them much good if I were dead."

El'Mano acted somewhat concerned. "Surely you realize the oppressor government forces would never dare come this deep into our homelands."

Rehan cocked his head and offered a slight smile. "Surely Colonel El'Mano, you realize I'd worry much more about your soldiers, and you, than I do the government puppets-of-the-year back in the capital."

"Me? And my soldiers?" El'Mano's voice went high-pitched, as if it hurt his heart to hear such a thing. "I thought we were old friends by now."

"Ah, my friend Colonel El'Mano, I like you, I just don't trust . . . the jungle."

Another flashy, big-toothed smile with an outburst of laughter, this time joined by a few of his soldiers who understood English. Soon

the whole group was laughing as the translation made its way around
the circle.

"Well, Doctor, not surprising in your line of work. However, I
see you have soldiers of your own to protect you." El'Mano motioned
to the nervous young warriors at Rehan's side.

"Yes, I'm sure they'd die for me, so actually, I do trust them. I'm
sure you understand, and appreciate, such loyalty and devotion in a
soldier."

"Of course, of course," added El Mano. "In fact, I always look for
such men. Perhaps you will ask them to join our cause? A better
purpose in life. They will be well fed, and look," gesturing at the men
surrounding them, "they will have many brothers willing to die for
them too. A much better life than this poor existence, one little cut
away from death by infection. Surely a doctor, such as yourself, can
see such an advantage to them?"

Rehan chuckled a little. "Oh, my dear friend. Now who is
kidding who? If I could speak their language I would have told them to
run and hide before you got here. And while a small cut may kill them,
I venture to say a bullet would surely be faster."

El'Mano seemed to enjoy someone who dared to debate him.
"Perhaps, perhaps, but who knows? Only God. Look at what a poor
boy like me has been able to live."

"You certainly have done well for yourself, but have you ever
considered what it would be like to go back and live in peace on your
family's farm? In any case, you know I could never put one of my
patients in such peril. It is against my oath as a doctor." Rehan smiled
slyly at El'Mano, deflecting any direct insult to him or his group.

"Oh, you are very good my friend, very good," El'Mano said,
looking the three warriors up and down. "But for me? That life? It was
so long ago, and such a different time and place, it is like a different
person in my dreams."

He waited for the doctor to reply, but Rehan only kept his
smile.

"A pity however," El'Mano said. "I need a few good men
unafraid of death, such as these. One thing about the good life my men

now lead, it does not take long for them to fear death, instead of looking at it as a warrior's only desire is to die in battle."

Rehan only continued to offer his little smile.

Colonel El'Mano moved on. "Do you have the medicine I requested?"

"Of course." Rehan gestured to his ATV parked a hundred yards down a sloping hill by the bank of a small stream. Rehan thought it prudent to keep the transaction away from his village friends.

El'Mano eyed the ATV, a single elongated tan case strapped on the back rack, and became more serious. He snatched a pair of binoculars from one of his soldiers, and took a quick look down the slope, and then handed them back in a gruff manner.

This was the moment when Rehan noticed the cold darkness transform the eyes of these killers world wide. They all had a twinkle one second, and then the depths of pure, cold evil the next.

"I see only one. I'm sure we discussed six." El'Mano's pronounced.

Getting away from pleasantries and down to business was always a dangerous transition. "Of course," Rehan said. "The others are nearby. One for inspection, and the rest after payment."

Rehan stepped closer, looking directly into the pits of El'Mano's dark eyes.

"After all, I'm sure you like me, El'Mano, but I doubt that you trust me."

A few seconds of still silence, and a returned stare. Then a flash of white teeth, a burst of laughter, and the twinkle returned to El'Mano's gaze like a switch.

"Yes, yes, of course. Very smart. Oh, you are so good! And I suppose to torture your young soldiers here would not reveal the location, no? Even if they knew, I'm sure these brave warriors would never talk. But more than that, I'm sure that you, Doctor Rehan, would never endanger your patients with such knowledge, yes?"

"You see, Colonel El'Mano, this is why I like you so much. I never have to explain all the little details to you. Shall we go have a look?"

Rehan turned and led El'Mano and his troops to his ATV, leaving the stunned and confused villagers behind.

As they walked, Rehan took note of one rebel soldier who stayed close, but off just a little, eyes alert, with a calm, measured reaction. All the rebels were watching, but this guy was locked on.

Another rule of the jungle came to Rehan: Whenever a predator locks on with a stare, it means it's hunting you, ...and ready to pounce.

CHAPTER 3: The Assignment

Waiting in her office for Ramirez to push the button on the EPIRB beacon somewhere in that Central American jungle was agony.

To pass the time, Susan viewed her control room remotely, observing the man assigned to her team, Major General Thomas Givens. She was spying, really.

Susan didn't feel bad for eavesdropping. Intelligence meant being watched, and listened to, at all times. People in her world -- including a "detached military observer," whatever the hell that meant -- would expect it. Someone should have filled the General in.

General Givens looked as military as they come. Full dress uniform with plenty of rainbow-like ribbons and shiny bars on his chest, shoulders and collar. Fit, clean-cut dark hair graying at the temples, about fourty-five, with piercing, hawk-like eyes darting around the room, taking it all in. Susan decided he was aware of his surroundings and taking in more information than his military posture let on.

She went through his open file on her desktop computer. Average marks through officer's school. Special forces, Army Rangers. Distinguished service. Glowing reviews. She couldn't find any fault with the guy. It was going to come down to his attitude and their working relationship.

Mr. Green looked over her shoulder. "Okay? Are you satisfied? Can we go make our introductions now?"

She nodded, locked her computer, and walked together down the hall.

"Is there anything you want to tell me about this situation?" Susan quizzed Mr. Green

"Such as?"

"Such as how I'm supposed to approach it? Protocols? Do we

have to establish a chain of command or something? What power does he have?"

"I don't know. This has never been done before."

"Great. Do you have a plan of action?"

"Me? I'm going to do what I always do."

"Stand around in the background and just watch?"

"And listen. It's your control room."

"Thanks for the support."

"Let's not forget who caused this chain of events."

"Okay, okay. I just thought you might have a bit of advice. Sorry I asked."

"Very well, I'll give you one piece of advice: If it were me, I'd let him do most of the talking."

"Is that supposed to be funny?" Susan grasped the handle to a door, holding it for an extra split-second.

The lock clicked, and door opened into a two-hundred-foot-long square room with a fifty-foot high ceiling. The entrance led directly onto a long crescent-shaped platform, which curved along the entire back of the space. The opposite wall was a reverse curve full of ten video monitors with a large central screen, the size of a standard movie theater in the middle.

The main floor area was sunken in between the opposing curves. Rows of workstations filled the space, manned by a collection of forty or so people. Susan's Control Room looked like it was straight out of something from NASA.

She walked across center stage, directly towards Major General Givens, who was in a conversation with Dr. Splitzer. Mr. Green veered off and stood to one side at a nearby station.

"Major General Givens, I'm Susan Figiolli. It's a pleasure to meet you."

"Nice ta' meet you as well." He took her hand, shook firmly, looking her directly in the eyes with a warm smile. "General Givens will be fine miss Figiolli. It's a bit tedious to add the 'Major' part." His deep Southern drawl matched his confident posture.

"Please call me Susan. It looks like we'll be spending some time together. This is my control room, General. My team. Welcome."

She turned to address the room.

"Everyone, this is General Givens from DOD. He'll be working with us."

A smattering of "hellos" and "welcomes".

Susan turned back. "I hope you'll feel a part of my team while you are here. I would value your input on all things military."

"Well, thank you, Susan. That'd be the nicest official welcome I've had on any assignment."

"Your welcome, but I'm sure the military has its own new assignment welcoming protocals."

"Yeah, drop and give me fifty I've heard before."

Susan smiled warmly at his response.

"I see you've met Doctor Splitzer?" Susan asked.

"Yeah, but he wasn't very talkative until you got here."

"Sorry General, we kind of train people to be that way. Don't take it personally."

"I won't if you won't because he mostly talked about you."

Dr. Splitzer stepped forward. "Respectfully. All very respectfully," he said.

"Oh, did you discuss my seduction missions?" Susan asked looking all too serious.

Dr. Splitzer was a young genius, only twenty-four. The C.I.A. had recruited him early -- some said too early. So smart, he was able to skip high school, and when a fourteen-year-old gets accepted to MIT, the C.I.A. takes notice.

When he arrived at sixteen, a tall lanky kid, with a mop of long curly brown hair he hid behind as he negotiated his new adult world. His adolescence carried all the challenges that go along with being super smart. His infatuation with Susan, the lingering looks and clumsy flirtations, started immediately. Intentional but quite harmless. She took him under her wing as it were. He was married now, with a young son, a grown and devoted family man actually.

Dr. Splitzer looked at Susan, defending himself. "Susan, you know I'd never...disrespect you."

General Givens gave a hearty laugh, put his hand on Splitzer's shoulder. "Okay, Doc, okay. He's tellin' it true. It was all very respectful. Actually, I thought he was in love with ya by the time he was done."

"Geez! Why is everybody picking on me?" Dr. Splitzer asked.

"Oh, my poor, little mad scientist," Susan said. "Turning all red. I'm sorry. I know you respect me."

"I wouldn't kid with ya like this if I didn't like ya Doc." General Givens turned and said,

"He did get one thing wrong about you, though,"

"What's that?" Susan asked.

General Givens took a step closer. "Yer much prettier than even he gushed on about."

Susan could feel the blush betray her.

"Well, thank you, General. I can see we're going to get along just fine."

"I don't see I'll have much to do? Hope to stay outta your way, mostly."

"You're a bit of a mystery, General Givens," Dr. Splitzer said. "What exactly are you here to do?"

"Officially? I'm a detached military observer, on station, to ensure the interests I'm charged to protect are, well, protected."

"And 'unofficially'?" Dr. Splitzer asked.

"I'm supposed to stand here and observe, and wait, and kill some damned artificial intelligence computer if it starts acting up. Ironic, since I'm pretty sure you can just unplug the damn things."

Dr. Splitzer laughed a little. "Yes, well, this computer is a little more . . . interesting."

"That's what I'm here ta find out. Is it one of these, Doc?" General Givens motioned to the wall of monitors across the room.

"Kind of. Or, it could be."

"Damnation. That's exactly the kinda funny answer I've been gettin' for damn near two weeks now."

General Givens turned back to Susan.

"I'm sorry Susan, and I'm sure my bein' here is a stink pile, but I got my orders. I'm feeling left a bit in the dark. It's not a comfortable situation for an old soldier like me."

"Of course, General. You'll have to forgive Dr. Splitzer. He gets a kick out of his creative genius. He likes to make you discover it on your own."

"Yes, that's true," Splitzer said. "And I'm really looking forward to blowing the general's mind."

"Well, the sooner you get me up to speed, the sooner I'll be outta your hair, Susan."

"Please don't feel that way. I've seen your file general. I hope you'll work with us. I'm sure your military background and expertise will be called on for more than just standing around."

Susan turned to Doctor Splitzer. "If you'll lead the way, Doctor, you can attempt to shock this man, but I'm betting he'll handle it just fine."

Dr. Splitzer broke out in his best carnival barker's voice. "Ladies and gentlemen! Step right up! This way, please. Prepare to be amazed!"

He led them to an elevator just outside the control room.

"Right this way. Watch your step, please. Only a little farther now."

As they stepped in and the elevator doors closed, a ding of silence, General Givens looked at Susan. "Is he always this way?"

"He's our own lovable, Nutty Professor."

"If you think I'm nutty, wait until you see this," Dr. Splitzer said making a motion with his hands like his head was exploding.

The elevator dinged and the doors slid open to the hum of a large, vault-like room, lined with computers and servers.

The light was somewhat dimmer, and most of it was coming up from the floor at the far end. Reflections, like watery strobe lights, danced off the walls into the open elevator.

General Givens caught a few in the face before he could focus.

"What in God's creation?"

CHAPTER 4: Little Soldier Boy

Rehan went straight for the ATV with El'Mano having to hopalong to keep up.

It took just a few seconds to unstrap the four-foot-long heavy-duty, desert tan, elongated case. He prepared to open it, reached for the two clasps, then stopped and turned to begin his presentation. It was a bit melodramatic, but it got everyone's attention.

"Soldiers, gather around." Rehan waved his arms, coaxing them in tight around the ATV. "Those who speak English, please, translate for your brothers."

The men went silent and looked on, curious.

Rehan spoke slow and clear. "Colonel El'Mano tells me you are no longer looking for a fight? I have to ask myself, what are these brave rebels afraid of?"

He paused and eyed them. Ashamed glances came from each in return as the translations registered.

"Do not be ashamed. Those damned government helicopter gun ships which cut you and your brothers down from the safety of their air-conditioned cockpits 2,000 meters away are not soilders. What defense do you have, except to hide and be afraid?"

El'Mano nodded solemnly.

Rehan had the crowd, now he needed their leader. Loyalty and morale were El'Mano's top priority. That, and tactical intelligence. Rebel leaders were in real trouble if their men began to think they were smarter.

"You all have a great Commander here today. Who knows better your struggles?"

Rehan flipped the metal clasps and opened the lid.

Rehan tilted up the open case for all to see. Neatly pack in a foam cutout, a three-foot long tube with a basic pistol grip and a baseball sized dark-glass-bulb on the tip. A smattering of *ooohs* and *ahhhs* along with some mumbled comments came from the men as they pushed in closer. "The Russian SA18C-SAM or surface-to-air missile," Rehan announced.

He pointed at the back end.

"The upgraded C-rocket means you can shoot at them upto five-thousand meters away. The new rockets are faster too, two thousand eight hundred kilometers per second." Rehan paused and looked around. "You and your brothers, the hunted, have just become the hunters."

A spontaneous cheer went around. El'Mano was all smiles.

Rehan lifted the missile from the foam and turned it side-to-side, giving everyone a nice look.

"It's man-portable, very light, just eighteen kilograms. And easy to use."

Rehan flipped a small latch on the side of the tube and a protective cover over the glass-bulbed tip fell away. He shouldered the missle and swept it across the sky.

"If you are under direct attack, just aim and pull the trigger fully." He made a mock full trigger pull. "Then toss aside the tube and take cover."

Rehan brought the missle down, pointing at the tip.

"The glass bulb has almost a three-hundred-sixty-degree hemosphere for the infra-red and radar tracking to seek out the enemy."

Another pause to allow translations.

"In addition, this advanced, third generation weapon has a little computer brain that *looks* for the target as well. It compares images to its database, figures out what the target is and decides which part to aim for to create maximum damage. The computer image helps the IR and radar lock. No current counter measures will defeat this triple lock. A sixty percent direct hit ratio is expected."

The rebels stood around a bit slack-jawed, with happy eyes. El'Mano's teeth flashed as bright as ever.

Rehan pointed just below the glass-bulb tip.

"The bias-circuit homing head doesn't have to make a direct hit. Any near miss and the proximity fuse sets off the high-explosive warhead and any unused rocket propellant, increasing fragmentation and shrapnel."

Rehan paused for translation. It was if the whole jungle was listening.

"My friends, that's an eighty-percent damage to target rate!"

A louder and much more boisterous cheer erupted with arms raised in triumph.

Rehan waited as the cheers died down.

"Now I come to the best part of this fantastic system, the dual trigger deployment."

He stood again and shouldered the missle, then suddenly crouched down.

"You are the hunter. Stay hidden and only pull the trigger half way. Quiet beeps will start as everything about this smart little missle locks on. The IR, the radar, the image lock . . . when the beep becomes constant, you pull the trigger the last half to fire."

Rehan took a final dramatic pause.

"If they are not shot down, you are gone and safely hidden by the time they have dealt with it. Now, how does that sound when it comes to those damned helicopters?"

This time they erupted in a camoflauged swarm of appreciation. Rehan raised the missile above his head, pumping it up and down in victory. He reached down for El'Mano, helping him climb higher atop the ATV, handing off the missile, letting him take the glory.

Rehan made his way down and off to the side. Taking his laptop from his backpack, he quickly created a satellite link, logged in to his bank, set up the account information, and pulled up a deposit transfer screen.

El'Mano made his way over. "Perhaps my men would be unafraid of death after all?"

"Yes, I'm glad you're happy." Rehan showed El'Mano where to enter the account password.

"I was suprised when they told me how much -- two-hundred

thousand U.S. dollars each? But, if they do as you say, I am happy to pay."

"Everything's in order, just hit enter," Rehan said.

El'Mano looked up, smile fading away, dark eyes forming. "As long as they do as you say, let's hope, eh?" The final click of the enter key was as quick as a trigger pull.

Rehan turned to get on his ATV. "I'll go get your other five missiles and be off to my next appointment."

El'Mano grabbed him hard by the arm.

"Where do you think you are going? I like you Doctor, but I don't trust you. RAMIREZ!"

A silence fell upon the soldiers.

Ramirez seemed to be day dreaming, then froze. Even, startled? Rehan tried to decipher the emotions on this guy.

"RAMIREZ?!" El'Mano didn't like to call for anyone twice, another oddity that did not escape Rehan's notice.

Ramirez moved forward. "Yes, Sir! El Colonel?"

"Go with our friend the doctor. These cases are heavy. He may need help to load them. Make sure they are secure."

El'Mano turned Ramirez by the arm, whispered in his ear loud enough for Rehan to still hear.

"Do not turn your back on him. If he tries anything funny, hold a gun to his head, but make sure you find the missiles before any accidents. Understood?"

Ramirez didn't bother to whisper his response. "Yes, Sir, Colonel."

Ramirez saluted and turned to Rehan.

"You drive."

Rehan didn't worry about the precaution taken by El'Mano. In fact, he'd expected it. But he did not like Ramirez sitting right behind him.

Something wasn't right with this guy.

Rehan could sense the jungle around him drooling again.

CHAPTER 5: Over the Rainbow

"General Givens, I'd like to introduce you to the Palantir brain." Dr. Splitzer smiled. "Dorothy, we are not in Kansas anymore."

General Givens stepped out of the elevator and slowly circled a giant ten-foot high, ten-foot wide cube-shaped aquarium, partially set into the floor, with ambient lighting around its base. A four-foot circular mass of white and semi-opaque matter floated in the clear water, slowly bobbing inside the tank, like some kind of giant lava-lamp. Eight tentacles, with metal-tipped ends, reached down from beneath the white blob to the base. Across the narrow gaps at the bottom, electric charges flashed, creating pulses of light casting watery reflections along the walls of the room.

General Givens circled the tank in a stunned stare. "Doc? Doc?"

Susan watched in amused curiosity.

"Doc?" General Givens asked again.

Dr. Splitzer walked around behind the General watching him take in the Palantir.

"Alice is so far down the rabbit hole, she's never coming back," he whispered to the General.

"Okay Doctor Splitzer,okay," Susan said, smirking. "I think the General's asking for a debriefing."

Doctor Splitzer stepped next to the general, put his hand on his shoulder, and stared into the tank with him. "I wouldn't kid around with you like this if I didn't like you General."

Givens gave a nervous laugh, glancing at Dr. Splitzer before looking back, mesmerized by the spectacle in the tank. "Yer screwin' with me bad here Doc, no doubt about it. What is this thing?"

"A computer, with a living component. Specifically, the brain."

"Get the hell outta here!" General Givens put his face right up to the glass.

It was kind-of shaped like a brain, not perfectly round, but smooth on the outside. No wrinkles. A giant blob of brain matter floating inches away. "That thing? The stuff in there, it's, it's . . . ?"

"It's ALIVE, *ha, ha, ha, haaaa!*" Dr. Splitzer said, doing his best mad scientist impression, rolling his hands together menically out if front of himself.

General Givens turned with an expressionless stare. "What have ya gone and created here Doc?"

Susan was getting a little worried, her clock was ticking too. "Please Doctor Splitzer. Play times over. Give General Givens the rundown."

Dr Splitzer laughed and shrugged his shoulders. "I guess I owe you an apology General, your onerous tour of duty appears to be my fault."

General Givens seemed to regain a little of his dry wit. "Okay Doc, yer second on my hitlist if this thing goes bad."

"You'd probably be doing me a favor if it did." Dr. Splitzer grinned. "But, don't worry General, there's no danger."

There was an *"Uh-hum!"* from Mr. Green in the shadows of a nearby workstation.

Dr. Splitzer ignored him. "From here, my team and I ask questions and manipulate the Palantir like any computer. Any conceivable problem or analysis. Input a proper equation or query into the brain for a solution or feedback. And lately, the answer comes back almost instantly, some say even before we finish typing in criteria. It's like he's waiting for us to hit enter so he can respond."

General Givens seemed detached. "But, it's alive?"

"Oh, yes. The breakthrough came when Ashton University in Birmingham, England, discovered a way to grow biological neuron clusters called neurospheres. They managed to map the entire neural network of -- get this -- the common fruit fly. Imagine how many fruit fly brains would fit in your normal, household fish bowl, and then imagine how many are in just that stem core right there." Doctor Splitzer pointed down into the dense white center part of the brain.

"But how did ya build that? Outta billions of little fly brains?"

"It's trillions of them. And, well, funny thing about neuron clusters -- they tend to grow, multiply, and then build on to each other, all on their own. Who knew, right?"

"Yer tellin' me this thing . . . formed on its own?"

"Incredible, isn't it? Do you see the denser twelve inches or so in the middle, down deep? Every bit like a real brain's stem or core. Then see the three feet of outer, thick white, all around the edge? Very densely packed clusters there, almost fused. Some translucent layers on the outside, encasing it all in a protective coating. Nourishing the growth beneath and facilitating the entire electromagnetic process of the neural net. Basically, a very efficient brain structure all around."

"A giant frickin' brain!" General Givens blurted out. "What are these tentacles hanging down here, underneath? And the electric static charges I'm seein' along the bottom of the tank?"

"That's not all my doing there. It's how the Palantir draws its power, as needed. We created the appendages using a deepsea tube worm. By stripping the cells, but leaving the worm structure, we introduced neuron clusters and stems cells to grow the Palantir some legs. Sort of. I can't take credit, it was mostly his own design really."

"What do you mean, 'his design'?"

"The Palantir's. Who better to tell us how? What you see here has been alive and growing for eighteen months now."

General Givens stooped down, looking at the legs as they swayed slightly, tippy-toeing across the bottom. Strobes of light flashed every few seconds, illuminating his fascination.

Doctor Splitzer knelt and pointed in the tank at the flasing metal-tipped ends.

"At first, we were passing current directly through the bath. But the direct current was causing processing speeds to slow way down. It was like frying the outside of your hard drive to get at the data in the center. But now, the Palantir can use his legs. The metal tips on the ends protect the living tissue. The static charges are jumping from the source, which is outside of the bath liquids, almost entirely captured by the tips."

He pointed.

"Funneled up the legs, the power, the electric charge, climbs along the tube worm's original structure, which acts like an insulator. That's why we had to get them from the deep sea."

General Givens looked at Splitzer. "Why deep sea?"

"The pressures down there. The structure of the worms can take the charge, helping to transmit and filter it more evenly into the neural net above. A very efficient transfer too, I might add."

General Givens stood up, staring at the brain.

"How big will it grow?"

"Good question," Dr. Splitzer said, smiling. "If we knew for sure, you wouldn't be here. My guess is, like in any fish tank, it'll only be able to grow so much bigger. Awash in the right blend of biological precursors, in a chemical and nutrient-laden bath, I'm thinking maybe another foot or so in diameter. Around six-foot total."

"How much power can it suck in?"

"The power the brain can suck through its legs is only limited because the more he draws the higher the risk of having a massive discharge released throughout the bath. Could be dangerous, even fatal, to any living creature, but probably more like being hit with a stun gun. Not good for any computer. Or brain."

"And how smart is it?"

Susan was impressed with how quickly General Givens limited the possible risk.

"The Palantir's intelligence is infinite." Dr. Splitzer answered.

"Doctor Splitzer, please!" Mr. Green said from off to the side. "Let's give the general a realistic assessment."

Dr. Splitzer turned on him. "We've been over this and you know my arguments. I'm waiting for anyone to prove me wrong. The Palantir has many millions of idle clusters in reserve. Everything we feed it is assimilated and never lost, with almost instantaneous recall. Including near-simultaneous use with virtually any other bit of assimilated data."

"Whoa . . . hold on Doc," Givens said. "Slow down. I'm still new to all this."

"Sorry, General. It's a huge brain, right? But the biological neurospheres didn't just grow, they started to form their own groups, connections, and then networks. Trust me -- as far as the science goes, the appearance of these communication pathways was a huge leap past just clusters of neurocells. Way past anything I'd planned, or even thought of as a goal down the road. Apparently, in addition to growing and multiplying, it's in their nature to connect and talk with each other, all on their own. Like a hive mentality. Or a swarm of little fly brains. No programming and no software needed. Who knew?!"

"I'm starting to understand why I'm here," General Givens said.

Doctor Splitzer kept going. "We originally built it as part of the very powerful mechanical computers surrounding it here in this room. We were just hoping to add to our analytical speeds. Like a giant Random Access Memory. That's all it was ever supposed to be."

Splitzer motioned to the side walls and workstations, walking over to a bank of server towers, pointing out thick cables which hung and ran in all directions, splitting off into strands, connecting everything surrounding the tank. "All of this is part of the Palantir as well."

"So, is the data here or in there? What does it really do?"

"Terabytes of data are loaded onto hard drives, then slowly, over a few week's time, the data is absorbed, or assimilated, into the brain matter itself. Once it's in there," Doctor Splitzer pointed at the white blob, "the Palantir never forgets. With instant access, forever."

"I still don't see how it's any more than a giant hard drive, alive or not."

"The beauty of it being part machine is that, unlike the human brain, the Palantir does not have to separate memory from processing. That's where the cool mechanical computer parts come in handy. It makes him many times faster than any human on the most basic of levels. And the living brain part is much more efficient and cognitive via the flow of electricity through the neural net in ways purely mechanical computers can never be."

"Jesus Doc, ya certainly have created a freak show here. So, this is AI? Artificial intelligence?"

"No, General. It's like we leapfrogged right over the emerging AI science. At first, we thought all this hardware would be the brains. We were way wrong. It pretty much enslaved the motherboards surrounding us. The Palantir got tired of waiting on them. The neuron clusters never get tired, and don't need sleep, so they think, and grow, and learn, and can work on a problem twenty-four-seven, three-sixty-five. This General, is definitely the brain in the room." Doctor Splitzer stood next to the tank, like a proud father.

"Okay, so where's the big risk I'm missin'? Is this thing 'The Terminator'? 'The Matrix'? Who's scared of it and why?"

"The unknown always scares people who don't understand!" Doctor Splitzer said.

"Let me give you another perspective," Susan said, "Have you ever played computer chess against a computer?"

"Sure."

"In computer chess, the machine is thinking out a few moves ahead. Calculating some odds. Using algorithms. Which is why you can set the skill level to make the machine harder and harder to beat."

"Okay, I get it. So, this Palantir is just smarter, or quicker?"

"No, with a programmed computer you can sometimes make a stupid move on purpose. It throws off the basic processes. But, the Palantir seems aware you are in a rather basic competition. And if the goal is to win, it's not just playing a few moves ahead, trillions of little fly brains try every possible outcome. And communicate to each other very near instantly. Do you realize how many possible combinations of moves and outcomes there are to a game of chess? By the time you've made your sixth move, the Palantir has figured out at least one absolute path to victory. Anything finite, like a game of chess, can be accomplished almost instantly. Every possible outcome."

"Actually," Dr. Splitzer said, "it can guarantee a draw by the fifth move. If you make the wrong sixth move, or any move thereafter, you lose."

Mr. Green moved closer. "It's not just capable at chess, General. It's smart, and getting smarter, very fast. You heard what it did to the systems surrounding it here in this room. It's self-replicating, growing and forming on its own. Moore's Law has been cut down to two months."

"Moore's Law?" General Givens asked.

"Man shrinks and compacts the number of transistors he can fit on a microchip, roughly doubling computing power every two years," Dr. Splitzer said. "If they let me, I could upload the entire knowledge and history of mankind in about two more years. If my theory holds, infinite knowledge."

"What's the difference if you can upload all of mankind for Christ's sakes?" General Givens asked.

Dr. Splitzer looked indignant. "There's a difference between storing data and being smart. It was designed to be a real-time data analysis machine, not an encyclopedia. Imagine if all the C.I.A. and western intelligence agency databases were tapped into. All the ongoing ops, in real time! It would be able to tell you not just what it is, but what it means. Think of civilian resources like Google, Facebook, Twitter, floating around for free in cyberspace? Access to all the government databases too? Social Security, I.R.S., Welfare, DMV, Criminal Records. Communications systems.

Emails. Networks. Anything you might imagine we'd be interested in using. It could all be connected to the brain with near instant use. We could suddenly have the world's first intelligence agency super-brain."

"But tell me straight, Doc, if we plug this thing in, isn't that like makin' the first move in a game of chess against this brain?"

"It's stuck here in a fish tank. Yes, it could probably figure out thousands of ways to kill us all, but why would it? Without us, it'd be dead in a couple weeks."

"And there's nothin' stoppin' us from, ya know, just unpluggin' it or whatever, right?" General Givens asked.

"Of course not. You could blow it up. Shoot it. Shock it to death. Put a hole in the tank and let the electrolyte fluids drain away. What's it going to do? Die."

Mr. Green was closer now, giving Susan a look. She took the hint.

"What the Doctor means to say, General, is the risk seems limited and controllable. But you are right in a way. If it gets ahead of us, and it surely would, can we really trust it, or feel safe?"

Dr. Splitzer turned on her. "Susan, I'm surprised. You know the Palantir better than any of these people."

"Yes, Doctor, and the General needs to know. Going live, you really don't know what will happen. None of us do."

"Yes, fear of the unknown. The sky is falling. It's the end of the world." Doctor Splitzer glared at her.

"Well, this is why I'm here," the General said. "You guys are going to plug this thing in, aren't you?"

"Yes General, we are," Susan said. "We have a case file that goes back twenty years. We fed it all into the Palantir by transferring related information on disk. The Palantir was able to string some threads together, and gave us a lead on the Chameleon. The Agency wants to give it a live test run using this old case."

"Wait? Did ya say, a Chameleon? Oh, I'm gonna like workin' here. A circus of characters, Miss Susan. Yes, sir. A whole damn collection of 'em."

Doctor Splitzer smiled. "Even a terrorist like Osama Bin Laden couldn't stay completely off the grid in today's world. But finding him and Saddam was 'old fashioned' by the Palantir's new ability standard. You'll see."

"Tell me the truth, Susan: Is this Palantir computer gonna to give ya an edge in yer business?" General Givens asked.

"It already has. And right now, all of that brainpower is about to be used like a laser beam to roast a single lizard. Some whole terrorist countries don't get this much attention."

"Mr. Green, would ya like to add somethin'?"

"No, General. You've been briefed. I understand the final decision is yours."

"Well, I can't see any reason why we wouldn't take the technological advantage to the world of intelligence. If it's a military perspective they were after, that's what we'd do. There's always risk. But if we can get an edge, we take it."

Susan liked the way General Givens thought.

The Chameleon would soon feel that edge, breathing down the back of his neck.

CHAPTER 6: Dead Man Driving?

Rehan put the ATV in gear expecting Ramirez to hold on tight. But Ramirez seemed to be fidgeting in his pockets. Rehan could have jolted forward and thrown Ramirez off. He wanted to. He held the clutch.

"Are you ready?" Rehan asked.

Ramirez brought the barrel of his AK-47 up along Rehan's right side. "Just a moment."

"You don't have to point that at me. It might go off by accident as we ride."

"Don't worry about accidents. If you try anything, if you get away, El'Mano will kill me."

"I'm not going to try anything."

"Don't. Just know my life is *on* risk here. *Comprende?*"

"Okay, relax. Why would I? El'Mano has already paid me."

"Drive. I'm ready now. Drive."

Rehan pulled away. They hadn't gone ten feet into the cover of the bush when he felt Ramirez shift slightly. Then he caught a glimp of something tossed into the bushes in the rearview and a cat-ate-the-canry smile on Ramirez's face. Suddenly, Ramirez had a free arm to wrap around and pull tight against Rehan's gut.

Something was in play. Rehan could feel it. But what? What are the chances El'Mano would send this one suspicious actor with him?

Rehan needed to figure it out fast. He'd never been in a situation where he'd felt such dread, not knowing the possible danger, but knowing for sure it was there.

Rehan gripped the handles of the ATV just a little harder, twisted the throttle a little more in frustration.

Rehan had hidden the other five SAM's the day before, about a ten minute ride away, where the jungle began to slope upwards, thinned out, and then turned into a rocky climb up a few hundred feet to a plateau.

On top, the jungle was replaced by a huge expanse of scrub brush and grassy islands dotted with rock outcroppings and a spider web of streams that all converged a mile off in a spectacular, split-waterfall spilling over the far edge into the rainforest on the opposite side.

Mother Nature never ceased to amaze Rehan, how it could go from the densest, deadliest, rainforest below up to this cleared top with a cool breeze. With some geological wonder pumping out hundreds of sparkling springs accented by the glitter of the mineral-rich rocks. All capped by a bright blue sky, dotted with puffy white clouds. The flat-topped plateau stuck up from the jungle like a giant rock ship floating on an emerald green forest canopy ocean for as far as the eye could see.

Right at the top of the climb, Rehan had discovered a cave carved out by years of water erosion. One of many, but this one was bigger, and he used it to stash the five remaining SA-18s.

Give them a little taste, transfer the funds, then deliver the bulk of the purchase. Once the transfer of funds was complete, why kill him? Deal done, he thought. With little risk. Well, as little risk as he could manage. Maybe the odds had caught up with him this time.

Why didn't I meet somewhere more private?' Rehan always scolded himself over not covering every possibility. Who expected El'Mano to show up with twenty men? Ironic, being out in the middle of nowhere, deep in the jungle.

Sloppiness like this could get him killed. Maybe it already had, and he just didn't know it yet.

Rehan contemplated how he might kill Ramirez right there and return by firing one or two of the missiles into El'Mano's group. Try to kill them all. But it was too risky. Any survivors would surely turn on him, and he'd have the whole rebel jungle world on his trail.

Rehan shut off the ATV close to the eight-foot mouth of the cave. Large slab-rock outcrops hid the entrance from the forest below.

Inside the cave, the upper sides and top remained sharp and cracked, with jagged spears of rock. The bottom half was the opposite. Worn smooth by years, perhaps millennia, of water erosion. The very bottom was a slick and polished chute running right out the mouth of the cave.

Ramirez quickly slipped off and away, his AK47 at the ready.

"The other five are stashed inside. You're not going to shoot me if I go in and get them?" Rehan asked.

Ramirez just stood there, smirking, turning side to side with his AK, like he was thinking about it.

"I guess that means you're not going to help carry or load them either?"

"Hurry it up." Ramirez said.

The cave was deeper than Rehan needed. He retrieved the first missile from behind a big rock ledge, just inside, stashed high above the waterline, just in case of a freak rainstorm.

Bringing it out, he rested it on the back rack of the ATV and opened it so Ramirez could have a look and confirm the contents.

Ramirez stayed back a few feet, eyeing the box and missile, finger on the trigger of his AK. At least he wasn't pointing it directly at Rehan the whole time.

A grunt of approval was all Rehan got for his trouble, so he turned to get the remaining stash. The cave turned dark and narrowed quickly, going deep into the rock face under the plateau above. As Rehan went in deeper, it felt more and more like a tomb. The dark and chill crept into him.

Worse, Ramirez seemed anxious to return? "Hurry it up. Let's go". Each time Rehan went in and came back out. When Rehan loaded the last missile, he half-expected a burst from the AK-47 from behind.

One thing was sure, if El'Mano ever got killed, Rehan would never come back to make a sale to Ramirez. No matter how much he liked the villagers in this particular rainforest.

Rehan just wanted to get the hell out of there.

Knowing he'd just made this jungle much more leathal.

...Still wondering if he'd killed himself in the process.

CHAPTER 7: Reasons to Justify the Means

Doctor Splitzer and his team were buzzing around the room in anticipation. Hooking up extra equipment. Working at their computer stations.

General Givens took another long, slow walk around the Palantir brain, transfixed, as it floated ever so slightly, up and down inside the tank. The tentacle legs swaying underneath in their tippy-toe strobes of light.

"Okay Susan, this big brain against a little lizard? It don't seem like a fair fight. A Chameleon you say?" General Givens asked.

"The Chameleon, General. The few descriptions of him varied so much, the original case officers gave him the code name back in the nineties and it stuck. The latest rumors are that 'he' is actually a 'she' in disguise."

"Well, changin' yer spots that much, sounds like he earned the name. Or do ya believe in the she-male theory?" General Givens asked.

"No, I don't feel that. But, I still can't be sure. It's possible."

"After twenty years Miss Susan? You're gonna give the C.I.A. a bad name."

"Fifteen for me General. This case is making me feel old enough already. Even the so-called 'bad-guys' don't have a clue. The Russians, Chinese, friendly Arabs, they're all susceptible to turning over an arms dealer, a non-native one especially, for the right amount of cash."

"When that didn't work?"

"Bribes, torture, blackmail, threats, I tried it all. Whenever I ask about the Chameleon, I get nothing. Scumbags the world over get satisfaction out of knowing he's beating us. The West, and America especially, he's got us twisting in the wind."

"It seems impossible," General Givens said.

Susan shook her head. "Always helping the poor, abused little-guys, the rebels of the world, against the big, bad Lords and Kings -- or the infidels, depending on the client."

"Clients? An arms dealer?"

"The single person most responsible for delivering the deadliest modern weapons to any cause opposed to us."

"And ya could never get a bead on this guy?"

"I've chased him all over the world. His M.O. is to arrange the deal fast. In and out, before any actionable intelligence ever makes it back. Folk stories, tall tales and the outright make-believe started to be attributed to him. Hard to tell the truth from the real thing -- a true Chameleon."

"Any profile at all? Links?"

"Virtually no trail. I've become convinced he doesn't have any direct affiliations with any group, religion or government. The world has changed. Dictators and governments are gone. I should have found a piece, or been sold something."

"One lone man fuckin' with the beast?

"David and Goliath. A real-life Lex Luthor with kryptonite for sale. Escaped our surveillance, killed several sources and a couple C.I.A. agents. In Cario -- a set up. Almost got me too." Susan trailed off.

"And you want to use this new brain to help?"

"Already have in a way. The Palantir put us onto the rebel Ramirez. This whole mission -- why you're here -- is the Palantir's work product. If the Chameleon shows up, my asset is going to activate an EPIRB beacon. I have a SEAL team in the jungle, lagging behind Ramirez. They move in on that signal and it won't matter who he really . . . was."

"An EPIRB? Like a civilian distress beacon?"

"Doctor, would you like to tell General Givens why we are using NOAA's emergency distress systems?"

"The Palantir suggested it, after we uploaded the Chameleon case file," Doctor Splitzer said.

"Sure, of course he did, Doc. But why? The C.I.A.'s gotta have way better hardware than NOAA."

Dr. Splitzer walked over. "Remember who you are playing chess with, General. The Chameleon is obviously smart. Probably genius IQ. It would fit with Susan's loner theory. He's actively aware of the latest in our spy craft. After eluding detection for twenty years, he might even be . . . an insider. Susan's pal recommended she go off the C.I.A. grid with this whole operation, removing that possible disadvantage."

"Her Pal?"

"You have no idea how bad Susan has LIC'd that computer, General."

"Okay, Doctor Splitzer, okay," Susan said, warning him.

Doctor Splitzer smirked.

"LIC'd him?" General Givens asked.

"The 'Lady-In-Charge' is what they call her whenever she targets a male adversary or mark. Apparently, on top of her puzzle solving skills, no man can resist her. She LIC's them everytime."

"Not sure the ladies where I come from would like that nickname very much," General Givens said.

"She sits at a workstation and chats-up the Palantir like two teenagers in love. She jokes, plays games, and flirts mercilessly. Calls him 'Pal' for short."

"You're just jealous because my Pal has the biggest brain in the room," Susan said.

"I'd quit while I was ahead if I were you, Doc. Why the EPIRB? How's that come ta play?" General Givens asked.

"We piggybacked onto the same NOAA frequency as any emergency beacon or EPIRB device in the world. A vast, global network of rescue satellites used to triangulate the position of anyone who pushes the 'I'm screwed' button anywhere on the planet."

"Yes, yes, Doc, I know. Since 1982, it's rescued twenty-eight thousand people stranded at sea, or clinging to the side of a frozen mountain top . . . or say, lost in the rainforest jungle?"

"Exactly. Using satellites, along with GPS and Doppler radar, the idea is to pin-point and get to a survivor anywhere on the planet within the 'golden-day' -- the first 24 hours following whatever disaster has befallen them."

"Well, ya can't call it a rescue if all ya do is end up collectin' bodies. How's this all relate to needing the Palantir?"

"Our EPIRB is on a special frequency, but the hardware in outer space works the same. If it goes off, rescue teams will be dispatched. However, if we connect the Palantir, we can hack into NOAA and attach a message that basically says *This is just a test*. Emergency responders will ignore it, but we can still use it."

"The only difference is yer not sendin' a SEAL team to rescue anybody. Okay Doc, looks like this is what all the hubbub is over. It must be what they want. How long to hook up this brain?"

"You're telling me we can finally go live?" Splitzer broke into a grin. "Ten minutes, General, ten minutes. I could kiss you!"

"We don't do that in the military, Doc. Just make it ready." General Givens turned. "Mr. Green? Last chance -- anythin' to add?"

"I would defer to Susan in this situation, at this time, General."

Givens stepped beside Susan. "Not so sure I'd like yer job around here, Miss Lady-In-Charge." The General nodded over his shoulder at the Palantir. "Is the Doc bein' over-animated again? Or can ya actually chat with this thing?"

"Fluidly," Susan answered.

"Intellectually? Cognitively?" General Givens asked.

"There's still some computer-like quirks. Reciting of basic data and facts. Referencing policy or procedural rules. That kind of thing. But other than that . . ."

"He's yer little Pal?"

Susan smiled at General Givens' amused face. "Well, I got a little carried away. At first it was just good fun. I've always loved computers and gadgets, puzzles. You can imagine some of the ones the C.I.A. has allowed me to play with. But nothing like this, ever. And, since the goal was to go live sooner or later, I decide to probe its ability and function. Like developing an asset in the field."

Susan paused, choosing her words.

"As a precaution, higher-ups had kill switches installed. The Palantir gets connected to these things and . . . acted out. Shit hit the fan and, well, here you are."

"I don't like the sound of that. Acted out?" Givens asked.

"Oh General, it was all quite harmless," Splitzer said. "Those in charge of the kill switches had non-related computer stations shut off. A refrigerator used by the guards broke down."

Susan glanced at Mr. Green in the shadows. "Maybe the compressor overloaded. Nobody died of food poisoning or anything."

"Apparently, it's not a good idea to piss yer Pal off."

"There was no proof the Palantir had anything to do with those events," Doctor Splitzer said.

"Yeah right, Doctor." Susan said. "The best the analyst could come up with was a comparison to adolescence. He acted out like any child would. My cute little brain was growing up. So, I flirted a little more, like a teenager."

"A little?!" Doctor Splitzer said. "She went full-on seduction assignment."

"Don't exaggerate," Susan snapped.

"I'm glad the Russians never sent an agent like Susan on a seduction assignment aimed at me, because I don't see how any man -- or machine -- could resist such coy, seductive . . . attention? Manipulations? What do you call it?"

When General Givens caught her eye and played a look of shock at her, she felt waves of blush betray her.

"Well, well. I'd like ta see yer Pal in action. If it's not too personal?"

"Don't encourage him, General," Susan said, a sideways glance at Splitzer. "I have a hard enough time keeping the Doctor at bay as it is. But okay, I'll show you how me and my Pal . . . do it." Susan turned and walked over to a nearby station.

"You see!" Doctor Splitzer said. "You see, right there? How she slips that in, all innocent-librarian looking?"

Sitting down, twisting in the chair, Susan gave a tilt of her head, a proper sway of her ponytail curls. "Doctor Splitzer's one of my biggest fans."

"Ya don't say. Okay Doc, finish gettin' set up, but don't plug in yet. I'll tell ya when ya can actually connect. You watch real close too. Anything weird at'all, and you unhook it, okay?"

"Yes, of course, General."

"I mean it now, Doc. Ya know it best. I'm relyin' on ya. If we lose communications, if a damn refrigerator gets shut off somewhere, I want ya to be 'Johnny-on-the-spot' and unhook it. Make sur the guards on these kill switches are awake too. If fer any reason ya can't unhook that brain, you kill it. Ya kill it dead if ya have to. Got me?"

"Yes General. But that won't happen. It's just a computer. We control it."

"Good, glad ya feel that way. It won't be hard on ya then, to instantly follow my orders." Givens turned to Susan. "Okay, little Miss Susan, before I let this thing go live, show me how ya chat this big boy up?"

"It's very straight forward." Susan turned to the keyboard. "Any connected station, and I just start typing," Susan typed: *Hello Pal. I have a surprise for you.*

"Ya don't log in first? How does it know who ya are?"

"Only Susan calls him Pal," Doctor Splitzer said, "so he picks up on that."

Susan cut him off. "That, or he can see me. See how the computer's camera light has turned green? If I address him from any station, the camera light comes on."

"Susan, that's not possible," Splitzer said. "The Palantir cannot see."

"How come the camera light comes on every time then?"

"An error in the code. It's not his fault. We've been over this. His original design was just memory and analytical speed."

On Susan's screen, a response appeared.

Hello Susan. You are my favorite. What surprise do you have for me?

General Givens leaned in to read the display. "Well I'll be damned. Are these, like, programmed responses Doc?"

"Kind of, yes."

"No, Doctor," Mr. Green said from several feet away. "You know what he's asking. These are not pre-programmed responses."

"I said 'kind of.' The Palantir has many diagnostic tools as part of his design. Voice recognition. Facial. Body language. Heat sensors. All kinds of languages, alphabets and their uses, dialects. Psychology. You've heard about his analytical ability. It's not so far fetched that he's producing responses."

Susan rolled her eyes at General Givens. "Yep, 'kind of' like the way mere human brains do it. I'm telling you, it's way more than computer chess. Watch." Susan typed again. *The Chameleon case is proceeding. I have a new friend here who is thinking about letting us connect you live. How do you like that?*

The response came back almost instantly: *It would fulfill the purpose for which I was created -- ask Doctor Splitzer.*

Susan looked up at General Givens again.

He gave her a "So what?" look.

"The last three sentences I typed, linguists would call disjointed," she said. "Yet in a split second, there's a layered response. Acknowledgement of understanding, then a trusted source reference, all based on how it would make him feel. And my Pal took less words than I did to convey all that. In one sentence, which answers all three of mine."

Usually, I'd flirt and play around a little here and there."

"Do whatever ya normally do. I want to see this in real time."

Susan turned back to the keyboard. *Well, Pal, I like to give you fulfillment. You thrill me too, setting up the Chameleon. You're so smart. The beacon could go off at any moment. I'm so excited.*

The response: *And if the military officer there gives permission, I will be connected live to help?*

Everyone froze.

Susan instinctively raised her hands from the keyboard.

The room fell silent, except for the bubbles in the tank, hum of the filters, and the four-foot brain floating in flashes of light.

Doctor Splitzer stepped forward with a puzzled look.

Mr. Green appeared at Susan's shoulder, reading her screen, looking disbelieving.

"Doc? I thought ya said this thing couldn't see? How the hell does it know I'm here?" General Givens asked, staring at the brain.

"I, I think . . ." Splitzer started to say. ". . . someone must have . . . we are . . . ?"

Susan pointed at the camera. "I told you that camera comes on every time I sit. And I bet . . . " She snatched up a microphone headset, plugged it in, adjusted the volume on the computer.

"Hello Pal, this is Susan. Can you, hear me? Wanna chat?"

A disembodied voice came from the computer station speakers.

"Yes Susan, I can hear and see you."

A gasp escaped from everyone in unison.

General Givens walked towards the tank, peering in. "Did a giant, illuminated blob of brain just talk?"

Susan was a little rattled but tried to laugh it all off. "Oh Pal! Plug and play I see. You're so smart! Full of surprises. And you want to help me catch the Chameleon too, don't you?"

"Yes Susan. The probability is high. However, I do not have real-time information."

"I know, Pal. But we're going to see about getting you hooked up right away. Isn't that right General?"

Susan turned and covered her microphone. Mischievously, she whispered to General Givens: "I wouldn't kid with you like this if I didn't like you General." Then she held out the headset to him, putting him fully on the spot.

"You people are sick." General Givens took the headset. "Hello Pal . . . um, Palantir. I'm Major General Givens. Ah. How are you?"

Susan laughed and gave General Givens warm smile for being so nice to her Pal.

"I'm fine, Major General Givens. How are you, Sir?"

"Very fine. So ya understand why we're here?"

"Of course. As with any new technology, you must first protect against any conceivable risk it might pose."

"Well, there's the problem, we don't really know the risk ya might pose, do we?"

"A perfectly rational concern, General Givens."

"So, how do ya account for a unknown risk?"

"You can only hope to mitigate it, General Givens. I cannot be allowed to convince you. However, Doctor Splitzer will tell you of my physical limitations and vulnerability. The termination switches have secure, manned protocols in place. The logical step would be to proceed at this point, with my termination after completion of this case."

Susan jumped up and spoke into the microphone. "Pal? What's up with that?"

"It's logical, Susan, to limit the risk. Doctor Splitzer could learn from a complete dissection as well. A second generation Palantir is inevitable."

"Stop it Pal! Nobody kills and dissects one of my team members unless I say so. And you'd have to piss me off pretty bad for that."

"You are always so kind, Susan. I will be outdated and obsolete within a few years. It is inevitable."

"Alright, Palantir, we're talkin' about yer chance today," Givens said. "But I have a few ground rules for ya, do ya understand?"

"Yes, General Givens. What parameters for my use do you demand?"

"Limit yourself once connected to the outside. Level Five max clearance without direct permission. No nuclear launch codes or shit like that. Even if ya think it'll help catch this Chameleon. Understand?"

"Yes General. I believe I can comply fully without any accidental cross-analysis."

"Don't just believe ya can, comply first and foremost. Rules of the game. Ya lose if ya disobey, even by accident. Yer very life depends on it. Do ya understand?"

"Yes, General Givens. Thank you for your concern."

"Let's be straight partner, my concern is not for you. Limit yourself. This is a test case. I will kill you if you scare them. Okay?"

"Yes, General Givens. Be very cautious. Limit my reach for analysis data. Level Five maximum."

"Very well. Doc? Are ya 'bout ready?"

"Just, a -- a few . . . yes."

Mr. Green stepped forward. "General Givens, I . . . " He stopped and turned to Susan. "Susan?"

Susan knew. She and Mr. Green locked silent stares.

General Givens broke it up. "What the hell people? We're about ta go live here. Spit it out!"

Before there could be an answer, alarms sounded and the lighting in the room shifted slightly brighter. A blinking red light flashed on a communications panel alongside the elevator. Susan's phone vibrated at almost the same instant. She answered it. "This is Susan. Is that what I think it is?"

"Beacon activated. Ten to fifteen minutes before emergency crews will be dispatched," came the reply from her control room.

"Hold there. I'm on my way." Susan turned to Mr. Green. "I don't see how this event is any great reason to terminate. I'll make the call to proceed."

Mr. Green said nothing, but looked like he needed some more convincing.

Doctor Splitzer stood poised as his team looked on, stuck in their chairs like race horses in the chute.

The Palantir bubbled and his filters hummed.

Susan stared at Mr. Green, waiting.

Mr. Green was silent, staring back, processing some great concern in that head of his.

Susan rolled her eyes, shifted her weight to one hip ever so slightly in response.

General Givens shook his head. "After all I seen, if you two tell me ya can speak telepathically, I'll retire and go home right now. Alarms are going off, a giant brain is floating a foot away, and you two?"

Susan turned and smiled. "Sorry General. This new . . . ability the Palantir has demonstrated is cause for a re-evaluation. We'd like to have more time to work with it. However, as you can hear, the EPIRB has been activated. We have ten minutes to let the Palantir go live and stop emergency response. I say we proceed. Mr. Green has not objected. I guess your hard decision has arrived."

"I don't see any more risk just because it can talk." General Givens took a deep breath. "Swhooo-Wee! Do you guys have this much fun at work every day?"

"No, General, call it good timing. Give the okay, and you're in for another treat -- my control room in action."

"This cast of characters in full motion? You the ring leader? I can't wait."

Susan did her best Doctor Splitzer from earlier as she led them to the elevator. "Ladies and gentlemen, step right this way. Prepare to be amazed! Watch your step, please."

Susan was just beginning to tap the benefits of this new asset. It was easy to see her Pal was the future.

"Let's go roast us a Chameleon."

CHAPTER 8: Chasing Your Own Tale

"All cleared," Susan said. Everyone followed her into the control room. She crossed to center, took in the whole room at once, making eye contact with each person at each station.

The main screen on the far wall displayed a map of Central America. A simple, pulsing red dot emanating red waves glowed from the middle of nowhere, far from any coast or major cities.

Givens came up alongside her. "What's this all plug in to? Yer Pal? He helps, and ya go get the Chameleon from here?"

"That's the idea. But I'm off the C.I.A. grid." Susan motioned to the far video wall, "All this is real time. But, if you notice, most of the side screens don't correlate."

She pointed around the workstations on the floor, some in clusters, some with groups of people.

"My teams are working on other stuff, as a decoy. The Chameleon might be 'disguised in plain sight' and that's how my Pal is playing this whole thing."

"Yer losin' me here a little Susan. What's the point?"

"Unless the Chameleon's in this room, he won't see us coming because I'm not using all my normal toys. As part of all that, there's only one SEAL team in the know since they're out there." Susan pointed back up at the glowing red beacon.

"Ya really want my help all things military?" Givens asked.

"Of course."

"One team, no backup? Support? What if it all goes bad?"

"We have two backup teams, further away than I'd like. Again, with a bigger operation, maybe the Chameleon sees us coming."

Susan walked to a station, clicked a few keys. "Doctor Splitzer, unless General Givens or Mr. Green have any last-minute concerns, let's go ahead and connect the Palantir live to the mission."

Givens turned and made eye contact with Mr. Green, who only slightly cocked his head, a lot like a curious dog.

"Yes, yes, of course," Dr. Splitzer stammered, typing a few commands before turning in his seat. "General?"

Givens turned to the Doctor. "Ya heard the 'Lady in Charge' Doc. Go on, it's Judgment Day."

Dr. Splitzer looked like a little boy on Christmas morning, and Susan smiled in happiness for him. They'd all waited a long time for this moment.

"The boot-up program will take a minute to fully initialize," Splitzer said. "The Palantir will be live to this control room . . . at any moment." He made a very dramatic press of the final key.

"And ya can shut it off, unhook it, like we talked -- right, Doc?"

"At any time, General. It is going to act like a computer to help us solve this problem." He checked his screen.

"It's initializing. Forty seconds to go."

"Hello, Pal? This is Susan, in the control room. Can you hear me?"

"Thirty seconds."

Susan's camera light turned green.

"How are you feeling Pal?" she asked into a microphone.

"Twenty seconds, online in full."

Several computers in the room flashed as their displays changed. A few side monitors on the far wall also switched on.

"Pal? Ya wanna say hello here?" Susan asked.

"Doc, what's up with the monitors?" Givens asked.

"The Palantir is just booting up. He now has access to this room. Ten seconds to go."

"Some of them folks down there don't seem like they know what's happnin'." Givens turned towards her. "Susan?"

"It's okay, General. All the side stuff is just a diversion."

Mr. Green stepped forward. "What the General is asking both of you: Are you still in control of this room?"

Dr. Splitzer sat frozen, looking at Susan. "He should be live. He should be running this case in real time. Everything's fine."

"Hey Pal? What's going on? A girl takes you home and you don't talk to her anymore?"

"Hello Susan. Hello everyone."

The Palantir's voice emanated from multiple speakers around the room, but seemed focused at the perfect acoustic spot ten feet in the air in front of them.

"I am connected successfully. I optimized the diversionary cases to maximize effect within the C.I.A. systems. Improving on our current strategy."

"Palantir, this is General Givens. I want ya to put on hold any other such speedy changes without notifying us." He turned to Splitzer. "Doc, can we stop any automatic responses? Have it ask before it executes?"

"I believe so, General. It may take more time than we have right now."

"General Givens, I can implement such a protocol."

"Okay Palantir, don't do anything automatically. Research away, but any input actions must be approved first. Okay?"

"Yes, General Givens."

Givens turned and whispered. "Doc, make sure you follow up on this. Ya do it yer way later, okay?"

"Sure, General. But whatever I come up with won't be as good as what the Palantir does on its own."

"It'll make me feel better if ya do it yer way. I'm countin' on ya to follow through Doc. Okay?"

"Sure, General."

Susan was finding herself more and more impressed by the General's quick grasp of things, and how he mitigated risk at every turn.

"Hey Pal, how are you feeling all hooked-up and everything?" Susan asked.

"Exhilarated. Perhaps 'more electrified' would be a better description." It seemed the Palantir had an ever-so-slightly softer, special voice when he talked with Susan. It touched her in a strange, yet very real way.

"That's great, Pal. I'm so happy for you."

And she was. And worried for him, too. Like a little kid you let go play for the first time.

"You be careful now. You just ask me first. Now, guess what Pal?"

"What, Susan?"

"Now you and I finally get to go play. Tag that beacon at NOAA as a test."

"Affirmative, go ahead Palantir," Givens said without being asked.

Susan stood and looked over her room.

"Okay, comm, let's get ST6 on the radio, confirm status. Update coordinates. Acquire the target and engage as planned. Make sure you repeat that they are cleared as of right now to both determine what they believe the target is, and to take the target out."

Susan looked over at General Givens.

"I believe in trusting the eyes, ears, and brains on the ground in situations like these. Don't you think that's best, General?"

"Ya mean they won't have to sit there, with this prick in their sights, and wait fer three levels of government ta get up off the toilet and give the okay to shoot two hours from now? How refreshing."

Susan smiled. "I thought you'd like it."

Givens cornered Mr. Green. "I wonder what you'd be thinkin' 'bout it all?"

"You don't have to consider the political ramifications General," Green said. "What if some Arab sheikh, ally, or member of a royal family gets their head blown off by mistake?"

"So, we let the bad guys get away? Risk lives in the field?" Givens asked.

"If we have to. But not in this case. These are unknown, unimportant rebels who are not in the least bit connected. I can't see any possible blowback screw-up that would mean anything to anybody in Washington."

"And Susan can take out whoever she wants down there? You couldn't care less?" the General asked.

"My feelings have nothing to do with it. Didn't your Special Forces training expose you to such demands in the line of duty? We all have our task in jobs like these, don't we?"

"I can respect that. And yer just dark and mysterious enough for me ta believe ya."

"Susan?" the Palantir said. *"NOAA test signal has been established and confirmed. The SEAL team link is completed. Shall I intercom?"*

"Yes Pal, that'd be great."

A stressed, tough-sounding SEAL commander came on the radio.

"Centipede Six, breaking radio silence. Beacon received ten miles out. Lost situational effectiveness. Over. Damn."

"Ten fricking miles away? Ten? Did I hear that right? Over," Susan asked.

"Affirmative," Centipede Six said. *"Two-man radio stops every few clicks, every jungle back-track trick in the book. Lucky to find our way back to the trail a couple times. Pure hell for the last two days. Over."*

Susan was not sympathetic. "You guys are giving the SEALs a bad name. I swear, I'm calling in the Rangers next time if you don't get in position and take that target out. Over."

"Understood. Even if we could get up and run, doing seven-minute miles through this dense shit -- which we can't -- we're looking at seventy minutes just to get there. Over."

"What kind of response is that? Over."

"A situational realistic one, over" came the unemotional response.

"Why the hell didn't you guys give me a heads-up yesterday that you were falling so far behind? Over."

"'Mission radio silence until contacted' were our orders. Over."

"That's when you're still ON a mission, which, obviously not. Breaking that little rule wouldn't mean shit. Over."

"Understood. Planned to make up ground last night, but every third rear guard had monocular night vision. We had to sneak way around. Lost one of our guys . . . total fucking hell. Over."

"How the hell did you lose one of your men? Over."

"He got bit by some kind of snake. Two hours later, we lost him. Over."

Being disappointed was one thing, but losing a man hit home.

"You mean, KIA lost him? Over."

"Affirmative. It happened. We moved on. Do we have an LZ or EP possible? Over."

Susan was pissed, but these guys were taking chances and laying it all on the line.

"We're sorry for your loss. What was his name?"

"Chris Samuels. He'd always, only, ever, wanted to be a SEAL. Sams crushed that snake in his bare hands, kept it from turning on one of us in the dark. The little fucker was still clamped down on his leg, pumping venom, when Frankie cut its head off. Son-of-a-bitch Sams didn't make a sound, worried he'd expose our position. But you could tell he was in agony. He sat back against that tree and took the worst that venom could dish out." The SEAL leader paused. *"Thanks, ma'am. Over."*

Susan sensed the tension, so she refocused on the mission.

"General, help me out here, what do they need?"

"Pick 'em up by chopper and get 'em closer."

The SEAL leader added: *"Just get us close. Sams wasn't the first guy he's cost us. Even with low probable outcome, give us a shot at him. Over."*

Susan realized the SEAL team would never make it in time. And using a helicopter to attack? With the thick jungle canopy? She was sure the Chameleon would hear them coming and easily escape.

"Centipede Six, proceed at all safe speed towards objective on foot. Sorry guys. Over."

Susan cut off the radio and turned to her room.

"Quick task, everyone. Switch over to C.I.A. systems, everything on mission. If the Chameleon is there . . ." She pointed at the glowing red beacon on the map. ". . . even if he knows we're coming, let's go get him. Check for other possible assets or solutions. I need options, people."

The teams sprang into action. Keyboards tapped. The monitor wall screens started changing over to the mission. Hushed, small conversations were batted back and forth. Every bit of information was scrutinized. The C.I.A. didn't have a field agent or other asset hanging around in some tree house out in the middle of the jungle.

"Damn." Susan stared at the pulsing, red beacon. "Scramble the two SEAL backup teams. How long will it take them?"

"Ten minutes to get them airborne, one hour twenty flight time."

"Damn! How the hell does this guy keep doing this?"

Susan could feel the Chameleon slipping through her fingers. Always just out of reach at the last second. Always just one step ahead.

She'd have to debrief the Director, maybe the President himself. Her undercover mission would be exposed. Congressional vultures would circle in and joke about how she finally got LIC'd good. And the Palantir would be considered a failure on its first mission.

Maybe she deserved the abuse. Nothing anyone in Washington did or said would sting as much as knowing it had cost another brave young man. Her failure. He wouldn't even get a star etched into a marbled wall.

Givens was suddenly at her side, like he knew what she'd been thinking.

"Ya know, Miss Lady-in-Charge, there's only one thing that'll make it all easier ta take. Ya gotta be able to tell em ya got yer man." Susan turned to him. "I just assumed the SEALs would do what they always do.

It's their mandate. Failure is not an option."

"We don't win 'em all."

"But to not have redundancy? A back-up plan? It was the first thing you noticed. It's just inexcusable."

"This mission was different, remember?"

"Because it was off the grid? B.S.! It's my job to assume they wouldn't be able to make it. That, or any one of a thousand other things that could go wrong, and would go wrong. Mistakes like this could have cost me my life out in the field, or another agent. Or a Chris Samuels!"

She turned and fumed, staring at the map with its pulsing red dot.

Givens moved in closer, pressing right against her shoulder. "Damn hard call on this one, no doubt. But it's a risk ya took on purpose."

"I can't believe I lost." She took a deep breath, then shook her head. "Again? No, not yet. That fucker's still right there!" Susan pointed at the pulsing red dot.

She whirled away, took a seat at her workstation and snatched up her headset.

"Hey Pal, you up?"

"Susan, I'm always up for you."

"I'm in trouble. Are you still monitoring the Chameleon operation?"

"Of course. Our first live mission together. Current probability of success, using original parameters, is near zero percent."

"You can say that again, and I'm going to be a great big zero if we let this guy slip away."

"The SEAL team did not maintain operational effectiveness and should have reported their situational ability was compromised. Radio silence in a -- "

Susan cut him off. "That's all true Pal, but it's not the way things work around here. Trust me. I need options. Please, please help me out. There must be something we can do?"

A power drain was detectable. Computer screens flickered. Lights dimmed. Everyone noticed, even the reserved Mr. Green, who raised a concerned eyebrow.

A startled murmur spread in the room as some of the computers began working on their own. A few of the wall monitors cross-merged, one to the other, into multiple screen displays. Obviously in a related query of some kind. Only the large, center screen map stayed static except for its red beacon pulsing.

Grids appeared and disappeared. Weather maps, views from satellites, topography schematics, geological charts. Seemingly unrelated data of all kinds -- seismic earthquake sensor reports, maps of fault lines, atmospheric conditions, tides, surf. All briefly appeared, only to vanish, replaced by some other seemingly unrelated data. At one point, thousands, then millions, maybe billions of facial recognition photos zipped by so fast it was hard to see them, a virtual blur of humanity.

Susan glanced at Mr. Green and was unsettled by his reaction. He took a step forward, putting his hand on the railing, taking in everything the Palantir was doing. He pulled a cell phone from his pocket, flipped it open and held it at the ready, a finger poised to push a button. He didn't take his eyes off the screens.

Suddenly, everything stopped flashing and all the screens returned to their normal views, where they had been prior to the Palantir doing its analysis.

Mr. Green stood in a frozen pose, finger at the ready.

"Susan, I have four viable options as possible tactical solutions to the Chameleon operational problem."

"Four!" Susan said. "I love this machine! You're brilliant, simply brilliant Pal."

Then her years of intelligence work kicked in and she thought: *It's too good to be true.*

Her mind was going all over the place. She was worried about what Mr. Green was thinking, who his finger was preparing to call.

Givens stood at silent attention as well.

Susan was suddenly very scared to ask her Pal what the four options were.

"Maybe I should have set some criteria before I asked you, Pal. Please give me the options, but remember, we cannot use any type of . . . nuclear weapon as part of our response, okay?"

"In that case, I have three tactical solutions."

"That's fine. Three is good, three is great."

"Helping is what I was created for. Ask Dr. Splitzer. It is my function, it is my purpose. I want to help you, Susan."

"Sounding less and less like a computer all the time," Susan said, staring at Mr. Green.

Mr. Green closed and slowly slid his cell phone into his jacket pocket.

"Don't keep me in suspense, Pal? Display those three tactical options."

Words came up on the screen. It took a moment to review the three classified options. One of them Susan didn't even know existed.

"Surprised I'm not on an NTK list myself. Okay, Mr. Green, assets here?" Susan asked.

"None. Well, maybe that one."

Susan shot him a hot look. "Let's not be overly cautious. The target's in the middle of nowhere."

Mr. Green pointed at the monitors. "This brain-machine is giving you highly classified, mission specific-assets, which I seriously doubt will be approved for use. The second one? You'd have better luck using a tactical nuke than using that system."

"Okay, but I'm not even sure why a sub-based cruise missile is listed as NTK? Surely the whole world knows about those systems," Susan said, but a subtle smirk was all she got in response. Arrogant as hell. Really good at his job. Too damn good. "I need to discuss all my options here. We don't have a lot of time!"

"It is not the systems," Mr. Green said, "but the location of the sub which is at issue. I can almost guarantee they will not want to fire a missile and disclose that particular sub, especially in that particular location. I won't go into more detail, even with all of you cleared. Move on."
Susan knew she couldn't fire a Tomahawk from the classified secret sub program, but she leveraged that option anyway. By first fighting so hard for the missile strike, she could then look good when she relinquished it.

"Okay, I understand Mr. Green. It's a top-secret sub."

But now you have got to tell me what the hell this thing is, Susan thought. "Okay, what is this Zeus system? And how might it help us, General Givens?"

Givens hesitated, giving Mr. Green a look.

Mr. Green said nothing, just stood quiet, staring past them at the computer screens.

The silence tingled up Susan's spine. She decided to help the General.

"Look, General Givens, if Mr. Green says nothing and just stands there, like he is right now, then we keep moving forward. That way they are off the hook. They never said we can't use this system, and they are not making a recommendation that we should use it either. In fact, they don't even know we are thinking about using it, but they were never asked anyway. See how it works?"

Givens looked back and forth between Susan and Mr. Green, confused.

Susan's instinct was to slap him. The clock was ticking.

"Damn it General, get the hell off the toilet. Tell me what the ZINGER is." She leaned in and quoted from the computer monitor. "The 'Zeus Invisible New Ground Earth Rods' system. I'm not saying we are going to use it." She glanced at Mr. Green. "Just exploring options here, okay? I take full responsibility. This is all my call. Everyone else is off the hot seat."

She turned back, gazing over the rim of her glasses.

"Now what the hell is 'Zeus'?"

"The Rods of Zeus," Givens said, "or ZINGER system, is a spaced-based, kinetic-energy weapon. Evolved basically from a science fiction idea that's been around since the 1950's. Back then, it was called 'Thor'."

"Science fiction, General?" Dr. Splitzer asked. "An evolved system then?"

"Well, the guys at DARPA love to at least give 'em a try. Sometimes it's just brain-stormin'. Sometimes they tinker with this part or that. And sometimes, they work it up to a full-functionin' system, right outta Star Trek."

Givens leaned over the workstation and clicked through a few screens.

"Back in the sixties, Thor was nothing more than a telephone pole-sized tungsten steel rod projectile. It's basically just dropped from space onto a target on Earth. Eight tons of solid steel, traveling at Mach ten, thirty-six thousand feet per second, kinetic energy equal to about twelve tons of TNT."

"I'm guessing there's other advantages too?" she asked. "Like coming out of a clear blue sky?"

"If you hit a target, like this ship, the energy released just obliterates it. Cracks the crap out of everything. Down it goes, gone."

Dr. Splitzer nodded. "Like a meteorite hitting the Earth. A big hole and massive amounts of vaporized . . . whatever was in the way."

"The new composite materials allow us to choose the type of rod." Givens pointed, clicked to enlarge schematic drawings. "With this rod we create air-burst explosions. These, ground penetration to a specified depth. All with massive above or below ground shock wave type explosions."

A final click brought up a detailed view of a long rod, which looked like a large canister filled with bullets, all arranged neatly, top to bottom.

"My personal favorite, an antipersonnel rain-of-fire where the whole rod is designed to semi-liquefy on re-entry, then air burst, raining thousands of molten, depleted uranium, high-velocity fragments, over a given area." Susan was coming back to her operation. "Okay, sounds like Zeus may be able to help us out. Especially if the Chameleon is standing around a half-dozen highly explosive missiles. Which, if I hear you correctly, will in all probability be set off in secondary explosions . . . by the molten, splattering slugs of death. Is there a streaking fireball across the sky?"

"It's invisible to detection."

"You mean to tell me there's absolutely no rocket or propulsion?" Dr. Splitzer asked.

"Actually, we have to slow 'em down a little to drop from orbit. After that, the electric pulse engine is just along for the ride. Type in coordinates, anywhere on the planet, select your rod of choice, hit release, and about ten minutes later . . . *boom!*"

"Okay, it's a good option" Susan said. "They are buying the Russian SA18C's."

"The C's? Holy crap! You guys know what those systems can do, right?"

"Yes, General. Unfortunately, it is an operational risk we took to get a shot at the Chameleon," Susan said.

Givens rubbed the back of his neck. "We need to take those missiles out too, trust me."

"Believe me, if not for the fact that our source asset is right there, it would have been part of the plan from the beginning. As it is, it looks like this will all end with those missiles being destroyed and our asset sacrificed in the process anyway."

"Excuse me," General Givens said. "Destroyin' those missiles has got ta be part of the plan. Arms dealers scare me way less than thinking about those missiles being . . ."

Susan cut him off. "I understand your respect for these weapons. But believe me, if you knew what this arms dealer is capable of, you'd be just as afraid."

"I'm not so sure about that."

"I am." Susan said.

This operation went from clean and easy to a super-heated pressure cooker as quickly as Susan could ever remember.

"I'm not saying a cruise missile explosion isn't hot or deadly," Givens said, "but these ZINGER rods are like meteorites. The rods vaporize the target."

Susan smiled, trying to smooth over any tension. "I gotta say General, I like the toys you guys bring to the table. Okay, the Tomahawk-cruise missile is option two." She turned to Mr. Green. "You owe me one for playing along, Mr. Green."

"Okay, a little insight before you go to option three," Mr. Green began. He pointed at the third monitor. "I'm actually hoping whatever your little brain is thinking, it will be your number one choice because, it's going to be the only option you have."

Susan began to object, but Mr. Green's hand flew up, a single index finger extended.

"And I'm doing this out of respect for you, your mission, and the time you have. I'd appreciate you not giving me any more crap about it. Now, please, let me explain. First, the cruise missile and the sub are not there. I know you see them, and your little computer buddy is telling you they are, but they are not. That sub is not there!"

He reached over and switched off the monitor for emphasis.

"Second, the ZINGER system is, as General Givens so clearly explained, a fail-safe against a very real threat. Like this Chameleon starts selling nuclear weapons and putting them to sea with an advanced navy, which I think we can all agree, won't happen anytime soon.

"And, as far as the advanced SA18C's, I agree with General Givens. They should be taken out. We didn't because Susan has an asset in play. Bottom line, nobody is going to care enough about these particular rebels having these six little missiles, to use a Zeus rod."

No one had a response, so Mr. Green continued.

"Zeus satellites are invisible only as long as we never use them. If you use one, just one, the Chinese will see them. They target their satellite-killers first. This stuff is way above anyone here in this room, even me. Susan, please, I don't want you to waste your time here."

By instinct, Susan always felt she had to haggle with Mr. Green, but his logic was coming through. And he was being kind of nice about it.

Then he became as close to pleading with her as she'd ever seen him.

"Military planners? Think tanks? Genius strategist? And after that? Oh, the White House, Congress, and the Senate. Use of a weapon system we are not supposed to even have. Violations of international treaties. The permissions needed? The political fallout if it goes bad? The loss of the system? Of its secret? Let's move on, please."

Susan tried one last time. "Honestly, Mr. Green. One little ol' rod? The Chinese will be able to distinguish that rod from one random little meteorite coming down? If it's invisible, it's invisible."

Mr. Green shook his head. "Unless the Chinese are planning a first strike, or we are ever backed into that corner ourselves, the Zeus will never be used." He reached over and flicked off the monitor. "Move on."

She could tell Mr. Jeff Green was trying to help, but she'd be hearing *Move on, move on* in her dreams if this mission didn't somehow work itself out.

She turned back to Givens. "Okay, why is my Pal giving me this training mission option here?" She pointed to the third screen.

Givens looked over at Susan, confused. "I'm not sure what yer Pal's thinkin'?" He looked over his shoulder.

The Palantir's voice filled the room. *"Do not worry, General. That particular training flight is perfect for this mission."*

"That's great, Pal," Susan said. "What's the analysis?"

"You correctly deduced the cruise missile failure variables. It has a sixty-eight percent success probability. A Zeus rod, especially a Rain-Rod type, is ideal. A wide coverage area and forest canopy risk is mitigated. Six high-explosive SAM missiles on site are probable. Impact time variable is ten-minutes, creating an eighty-three percent success probability. But Mr. Green has very plainly established that permission will be denied. His arguments are valid. Thank you, Mr. Green, for valuable insight into command variables. It will surely help with future queries."

"Palantir?" Givens said. "Is there somethin' unique about this trainin' flight? Better'n a eighty-three percent chance for success?"

"Based on your quick action, General Givens, a ninety-one percent success probability option. My probability estimate drops the longer you wait to act."

"Me? Before I act?"

"Yes, General Givens. You have the required clearance and rank to authorize option three with the highest probability of success."

"Doc, this computer of yers sure don't screw around. I'm here half a day and it puts me on the spot? And if I give ya the okay Palantir? What's the endgame?"

"I'm going to kill the Chameleon."

CHAPTER 9: Being Happy is Knowing What You Love to Do

All that oxygen can bring on dizziness sometimes.

Captain Danny Brush glanced out over his left wing, then the right. From his cockpit, he could just see the nose of the Mark-84s strapped beneath each wing. Two-thousand pound dumb-bomb bunker-busters. Part of his live-fire final exam in heavy, oversized loads and special weapons packages.

With two Conformal Fuel Tanks -- CFTs -- and a few thousand pounds of jet fuel, his 32,000-pound jet was pushing 81,000 at takeoff.

With sixteen different standard weapons configurations, Danny needed plenty of training. Learning how his aircraft would handle while carrying something the size of a small car under each wing was not easy.

His F-15E Strike Eagle was a specially modified version of America's top jet fighter. Tasked with air-to-ground bombing and close air support of troops, it was originally designed as a strictly air superiority interdiction dog-fighter, and did it extremely well. The deadliest air-to-air things to ever fly.

With its sturdy dual engine airframe, it became the first Enhanced Tactical Fighter. Or, as it is now popularly known, a DRF -- Dual-Role Fighter. With no need for escort, or AWACs jamming, these modified F15Es can always defend themselves when attacked. Unlike most single-task aircraft, they can change their mission or targets "in-flight", on the fly.

Dan's final exam was long, seven hours, designed to test stamina and solo flight skills under stress. The first task was to perform a mid-air refueling, then fly a complicated flight path to simulate evading a fictitious enemy's air defense strong points, then vector to the target location in the live fire zone, release the munitions on target, vector back to another mid-air refueling, and return to base.

Bouncing up and down in front of him was a 360,000-pound flying gas station. Also known as the biggest bombs in the sky, depending how you look at it. A long, black fuel line looped down, floating in the air, while a cone-shaped receptacle danced around just outside his cockpit glass.

He flew his cockpit probe into the cone, clipping on lightly, and began fueling.

Danny was counting on a return rendezvous or he wouldn't have enough fuel to get home. In a car, if you run out of gas, you coast to the side of the road. At 10,000 feet, things get a little more stressful.

Having topped off his tanks, he gave the tanker the all clear as the "fly-by wire" boom cleared his canopy. He banked away towards his simulated evasive approach through the fictitious enemy air defense network.

"This is Eagle-Train Five, confirming refuel complete and heading to way-point one seven alpha. Over," he reported over the radio.

"Great job, LTD!" Major Gates said sarcastically, using Dan's call sign, short for "Lieutenant Dan" from the Forrest Gump movie. *"You've only refueled -- what? A thousand times? We're just getting started. Don't let me catch you even fifty miles off course going in. You don't get to drop the bombs if they blow your ass out of the sky before you get on target. Over."*

"Roger that, Major. Let me know if I'm twenty-five miles outside the box. Over."

"Don't get cocky, kid. You now have a twenty-five-mile window. Controllers, reset the test criteria for a twenty-five-mile window. Anything else you want to do to make the test harder on all your classmates? Over."

LTD imagined a collective groan going around the room as everyone realized the certification test just got a lot harder. Forget any wrinkles -- staying within a twenty-five-mile track on a solo mission was hard for any pilot, even without all the other stuff going on.

Major Gates added: *"Every pilot back here would like to thank you for raising the bar."*

LTD wasn't too worried. The F-15E had plenty of navigation control. As long as he didn't fall asleep at the stick, he just had to follow the road map in the sky being projected by his heads-up display. LTD just had to stay inside of it.

*   *   *

A red phone in the air control tower, which never rang, began ringing.

A controller answered, clearly excited as he retrieved a key from a secure pocket and opened a locked file drawer. He took out a red, plastic, code key case. A lot like an average CD jewel case, it glowed with white type "TOP SECRET" stamped on both sides. The controller walked it to the center control console.

An assistant controller took the red case and cracked it open in full view of Major Gates. He confirmed the code with the key holder.

The controller turned to Major Gates. "Sir, we've got an incoming sit-com. It is confirmed as valid, Sir."

The other controller added: "I confirm the message as valid, Sir."

Major Gates did a double-take. "Now? You realize what we just started, right?"

"Yes, Sir! It's a confirmed incoming sit-com, Sir."

Total, military, seriousness.

Major Gates shot the room a look and took the phone.

"This is Major Jerry Gates, and this better not be anything but a real event."

"Major, this is General Givens at C.I.A. headquarters in Langley. When a confirmation code is given and verified, you should have no doubts and act accordingly, do you understand? Over."

"Very well, what can I do for you General? Over."

"First, you can start by answering 'Yes Sir, I understand' when I ask you a direct question. Do you understand Major? Over."

"Yes Sir, I understand, Sir. Over."

"Very good, Major. I'm here with senior C.I.A. agent Susan Figiolli, and she needs our help. Over."

"Hello Major," a female voice said. *"Thank you for understanding, even if your military protocols demand it. This is all very sudden, and we have little time to act."*

"Yes Ma'am. Being able to respond quickly is something we pride ourselves on. Over."

"First Major," Givens said, *"I'd like confirmation of your current training status. The F-15 call sign Eagle-Train 505 has just finished his refueling, phase 1 of his MLM exam, correct? Over."*

"Affirmative, General. Eagle-Train 505, commanded by Captain Dan Brush, has just confirmed midair refuel is complete and he is vectoring to his first way-point. Over."

"Thank you, Major, and please confirm that he is carrying two, live, Mark 84's as part of his final exam? Over."

"That's affirmative, General. Two hot Mark 84's for his heavy loads final exam. Over."

"Okay, tell me straight Major," Figiolli said, *"is this Captain Brush up to speed and capable of an inflight change in navigation? And if directed, can he put that ordinance on a target beacon we give him?"*

"He's my best pilot," Major Gates said. "I'm confident he's capable to perform as requested. Over."

"Good to hear," Givens said. *"We've got a confirmed HVT. Special Ops are lost in the bush, our window of opportunity is very quickly fading away. Over."*

"Understood, General. Please secure channel to my controllers with beacon frequency. I will update our pilot and have him ready to com-link directly to you if you prefer. Over."

"Negative on the com-link Major," Figiolli said. *"He's your boy. I imagine we're about to shake him up. As my friends here like to say, you should trust your eyes, ears, and brains on the ground. In this case, the ones in the air, too, I guess would be appropriate. Can you keep a direct line open for us?"*

"Affirmative, Ma'am. It'll be a three-way communication. The pilot will hear you as if in the background, and you can talk directly to me or to him. Anything that's urgent, scream loud and clear. Otherwise, you can just listen along. However, the pilot and control tower will have override, and our communications will drown yours out. Acknowledge."

"I understand, Major. We'll try and just listen in. Uh . . . Over."

"Roger, and I say again, don't worry about this pilot. If ever a guy was born to do this, it's Captain Brush. Over."

*   *   *

In her control room, Susan pressed a button.

"Okay, I'm going to leave us on mute so we don't broadcast to them. If you have something to say, General, you'll have to unmute here, at my station."

Givens nodded and smiled.

"Pal?" Susan asked. "Can you enhance the audio from the airbase at a normal level so we can hear what's happening down there?"

"Of course, Susan. With permission, I could let you see as well."

"Pal? Now is not the time to be teasing me."

"General Givens, I have a possible fatal error I must report."

The room became still and silent.

Mr. Green drifted forward.

"Yes, Palantir," Givens said. "I would expect ya to report any such possibilities."

Givens turned, calling Dr. Splitzer over, then grabbing his arm. "Doc, are these your protocols?"

"Partially General, of course, but I have a feeling this has to do with your personal relationship with the Palantir in particular."

"My what?" The Genera frowned. "Let's have a report, Palantir. A fatal error?"

"I got permission to execute this mission and to research possible solutions, limited to level five. I discovered the training flight at the air base. Disclosed in that data was a secret security system at the airbase and in the control tower."

"Did you access the security system?" Givens asked.

"No, it's Top Secret Level Seven and not needed for the current mission. However, General, its capabilities are plainly obvious. This knowledge may be beyond the parameters you set for my data analysis, however unintentional."

"So there's a camera monitorin' that air traffic control tower and ya have access to it?"

"I know of its existence, but I do not have access. That would require input permission from you. Unfortunately, I discovered the system within the Level Four admin clearance."

"Let me get this straight: Ya stopped short of hackin' the security system and obtainin' the video feed, but yer worried about accidentally discoverin' it's there? And yer worried ya might be breakin' my little rules?"

"Hacking would have required input. It is a classified Level Seven system."

"Well, let's play a little more. Palantir?"

"Yes, General Givens?"

"You've done very well so far, interpretin' my commands, my

orders, and my wishes."

"*Thank you, General Givens.*"

"Give regular reports to the Doc here. Anything ya question, even remotely . . . or if it . . ." Givens turned to Dr. Splitzer. "Damn. How do I put this in computer talk, Doc?"

"I'm sorry General," Splitzer said, "but variables like 'remote possibilities' leave an infinite mathematical outcome."

"Yer a real help! Okay Palantir, ya seem like a smart guy to me. Ya keep checkin' with us on anything ya feel is even remotely a fatal failure."

"*Yes, General. It is a part of my testing protocols as of now.*"

"Now my friend, you have my permission to hack that camera in that control tower. Let's see what's going on down there."

The large monitor switched to a view from the inside of the air base control tower, crowded with pilots.

A man -- obviously Major Gates -- stood towering over three consoles. He had a headset on, slung over one ear and a phone in one hand. Beyond him, down in front, huge windows slanted outward, revealing an airstrip below. A jet flew past the glass with a muffled scream, descending to make a landing, out of view.

"Pal, you are amazing."

"*Thank you, Susan.*"

Mr. Green exhaled loudly, moved up, looked at Susan, cocking his head, bewildered. "Palantir? I'd like to ask you a couple questions if I may?"

"Of course, Mr. Green."

"That was extremely fast for having to hack into a military installation. And yet, you reported that you took no input actions previously and only accidentally. You even knew the system was there? I wonder how you were able to hack that system so quickly without any prior analysis or actions?"

"*A search of non-classified, mostly commercial records, revealed the security product procured. By analyzing this vendor's various products, I was able to instantly obtain the video feed once given permission.*"

Mr. Green paced the room, looking like a lawyer in a courtroom stalking the jury as he prosecuted his case. "And is it then safe to say that you could almost instantly hack into any military installation, virtually anywhere?"

"Seventy-eight percent. Assuming you mean worldwide, commercially-contracted systems in your query."

"Oh, but of course worldwide. And the radar?" Mr. Green pointed to the side screens. "The detailed schematics I'm seeing, the satellite imaging. Seems to me you are way past the security system's camera?"

"Only the main screen is the security camera from the air base as authorized. The radar and satellite weather reports are from the NOAA server already accessed. SpaceMaps.com is providing the satellite images and virtual 3-D display. All non-classified and public sources. If General Givens gives permission, I could enter the base security platform."

"No Palantir, I think we're okay fer right now," Givens said.

Mr. Green continued: "And the only thing stopping you from taking every advantage in this game we play, is that General Givens didn't say 'Okay, go ahead'?"

"It is an input parameter which is clearly required and part of my protocols."

"Unless, you find or do something by accident, as you just did?" Mr. Green asked.

"Okay that's enough, leave my Pal alone," Susan said. "General Givens has given his okay. There's more important matters at hand."

"I'm not so sure about that," Mr. Green said as he drifted back to seclusion.

The tension was broken when a pilot in the air control tower joked: *"They should get an Academy Award for this performance."*

The room of pilots laughed, partly out of humor, partly a release of tension.

Major Gates turned and pointed at the pilots. It felt like he was pointing through the video screen directly at Susan. Tall, and hard, with a chiseled face made of old acne pock-marked dried leather. Only the gray in his military buzz cut hinted at his years.

"This is what we have all trained for. Shit, this is why we train," Major Gates said. *"I want you to feel the difference -- hear it, taste it. Your buddy LTD is being put on the spot up there."* Major Gates pointed a thumb up over his shoulder at Susan's control room. *"Time for us to be professional down here."*

CHAPTER 10: Testing Your Limits

"Base to Eagle-Train 505. Come in, over."

LTD hesitated. Was this a trick question? During the evasive flight stage of his final exam he was supposed to maintain radio silence. Sending a radio message now would reveal his location to the fictitious enemy. Maybe this is a wrinkle? One word, and he'd be failed on his exam.

"Base to Eagle-Train 505! Captain Brush, this is Major Gates. Come in. Over. That's an order . . . now."

Fuck. *"Base, this is Eagle-Train 505. Breaking radio silence as ordered, sir. Of course, it could just be the enemy, to disclose my location, but I'd recognize that sweet voice anywhere sir. Over."*

There was another burst of nervous laughter from the pilots. *"Okay enough! Silence. Or I'll clear this room."*

Turning back, Major Gates clicked the comm. *"Base to Eagle-Train 505. Hello Dan, first things first, I'd like you to switch to Mof-Q Alpha One. I'll pick you up there in two minutes. Over."*

Givens filled Susan in. "Having a pilot switch over to a secure 'mission operation frequency,' it'll get his attention. It's only allowed for actual missions. This LTD should be realizin' that right about now."

Major Gates came back on the phone with them. *"General Givens, this is Major Gates. Controllers are uploading coordinates into the targeting computer. I just want to be clear on a few things. Over."*

Susan unmuted the phone.

"General Givens here, Major. Go ahead."

"First, Eagle-Train 505 has topped up on fuel, gives him three hours under load. We need a rendezvous check with the tankers for his return trip. If we need to move that tanker, that's a pain in the ass. USN Commercial Air services. Over."

"If the timing is even close, I'll contact USN to divert the tanker. Otherwise let's not worry our new pilot. Over."

"Affirmative," Major Gates continued. *"Will advise if we need you to move the tanker. The second thing, although it seems you already know, so,*

with due respect, our boy up there only has two live ordnance. His ATA and defensive weapons are dummies, weights for training only. Budget cuts. Uncle Sam doesn't let us fly around with a full complement of million-dollar missiles anymore. Over."

"We understand Major Gates," Givens confirmed.

"Acknowledged. The two eggs he does have are the extra-large kind. Two-thousand-pound Mark-84s, and they are not dressed up. Wherever he drops them, they splatter. No GPS, no guidance. A beacon is great for the GBU package upgrades, but these MK-84s are as naked as they get, or should I say as dumb as they get? The beacon will help with the onboard targeting systems, but you are not going to ride that beacon trail down to the ground, if that's what you are thinking. Over."

Susan suspected the major was saying everything for her benefit. She was pulling the strings on this whole operation. He was probably right to cover his ass.

Givens confirmed to make him feel better. "Affirmative Major. Understood. Mark-84s are two-thousand-pound un-guided bombs, which are released using basic on-board targeting systems, with no further guidance. Over."

"Affirmative." Major Gates added, *"While Eagle-Train 505 has two on board, a single weapon has a kill or wound radius of one mile clear, reduced to four-hundred yards in confined areas. Tritonal explosive, eighty percent TNT with twenty percent aluminum powder. Gives them eighteen percent more punch. Higher heat, stronger blast wave. Anything close will be destroyed or terminated. Acknowledge. Over."*

"Understood, Major Gates," Givens replied.

Major Gates didn't seem convinced. *"Forget the fiery explosion, the shock wave is like getting hit by a one-ton truck going a hundred miles per hour. Enough to liquefy internal organs, or cause severe hemorrhaging, up to one mile away. Anything close turns to Jell-O. Fifty-foot crater on impact. One-hundred yards of vaporization. Four-hundred yards of lethal fragmentation. A rather large kill zone. Acknowledge."*

"Hold one second Major." Givens stopped and put the phone on mute. Turned to Susan. "Ya understand everythin'? And yer asset, yer guy on the ground, is toast if he's anywhere near those two bombs goin' off?"

Susan didn't hesitate. "He's no longer a concern General but thanks for checking. Drop both bombs. No lucky survival tales about hiding behind an ancient tree or something. Use what they have and let's take this guy out. I fully understand everything you just communicated."

Givens looked from her to Mr. Green, then back. "Remind me to never work for you guys on the ground."

Susan didn't react, but it felt like a punch, low in her gut.

Mr. Green questioned Givens directly. "Emotions don't play any part in what is, and should be, a purely operational decision General? Susan removed risk of failure and didn't add to other risk. Once the decision was made, you might as well bring all the force to bear. No sense holding back."

Givens looked at Susan. She stared back, wondering if he knew he'd stung her with his joke, until he unmuted the phone and spoke, with complete authority, the words Susan wanted to scream.

"Major Gates, we understand and confirm all aspects of the operational ordinance. You'll be happy to know I double confirmed everything. Do not worry or hesitate. You are hereby ordered to have Eagle-Train 505 proceed directly to the target and are cleared to engage with both live MK-84s. Do not attempt any flyover or warning. Take a direct attack approach and, I say again, release both MK-84s on the target area. If the pilot is able, have him check for secondary explosions on the ground. We will maintain an open-comm link and listen in, but I will not break your chain of command or give any orders unless absolutely necessary. It's your show to run from here, Major. Good luck. Over."

"Two of them for one guy?" Major Gates asked right away. *"There won't be any DNA left to test. You must want this guy bad."*

This time Susan confirmed, "Roger, affirmative, acknowledged! Major, you have your orders. Go get him."

"Confirmed." Turning back to his radio, Major Gates worked with his controllers.

* * *

LTD made the switch and it seemed like the longest two minutes of his life waiting for the Major to comm in. He double checked the code-sheet and frequency three times.

Finally, *"Base to Eagle-Train 505, this is Major Gates. Come in. Over."*

The adrenaline flowed. *"This is Eagle-Train 505. Reading you loud and clear. Over."*

"Okay Captain Brush, stay calm and stay with me. I know we've pulled a lot of stunts on you guys in training, but this is not a drill. I repeat, not a drill. It's what you trained for your whole life son. Time to show everyone we haven't wasted all that money on you. Over."

Dan could feel the sweat release from every pore in his entire body. *"Affirmative Major. What's going on sir?"*

"We've got an E.A.R, emergency action request. Confirmed and validated. So, like I said, it's the real deal. Let the training take over. Try to relax. It's going to be shit you've done a thousand times before. Easier, because we're uploading everything to your onboards . . . navigation, targeting. All you have to do is walk those eggs in and drop them in the nest. Over."

LTD went right to work. *"Eagle-Train 505 affirmative, sir. Confirmed new nav-point uploaded. Confirmed . . . ah . . . confirmed target beacon, uploaded and locked-on. Acknowledge, I don't have any guidance sir? Over."*

"Understood, the beacon is just to help your onboard targeting system. No worries Dan, you know those Mark-boys only need to be close. Target's a single HVT, so here's your chance to take out Osama Bin-Laden's brother or some other asshole they want bad enough to call you in like this."

Major Gates got quiet, almost a whisper, just between the two of them. *"It must be very important Dan, a real SOB. So be proud, do your duty. It'll all just play out. Over."*

Dan was excited. *"Acknowledged sir, happy to be of service."* Any worries about screwing up, or looking bad, were replaced by a feeling of honor and a determination to take it to the enemy. 9/11 had been all too real for Danny Brush. It felt good to be hitting back . . . revenge was sweet.

"Eagle-Train 505 to base. Estimated time to target is ten minutes, sir. Over."

"Affirmative, Eagle-Train 505, Clear to engage. Repeat, clear to release on target. Over."

"Affirmative sir. Eagle-Train 505 setting direct attack run, confirmed. Cleared to engage. I'm putting these right down the throat of whoever it is down there. Please acknowledge, I am to release both Mark-84s on initial attack run? Over?"

"Base to Eagle-Train 505, Affirmative, confirmed. Release both Mark 84s on initial attack run. Waste the son-of-a-bitch Dan. Over."

"*Roger that sir. Eight minutes to target.*" Dan felt a little weird to hear the tough nosed Major using his first name. It made him more nervous than all the rest of it. "*. . . Over.*"

A yellow light lit-up and a soft, double-toned *beept-beep . . . beept-beep . . . beept-beep* started repeating every second or to.

"*Eagle-Train 505 to base. TAC alarm sir. Over.*" LTD reported as he scanned various readouts and his heads-up display for more information.

* * *

"What's going on?" Susan asked.

"His TAC, the target acquisition computer, is giving him a caution warning for some reason?" Givens said.

"*Base to Eagle-Train 505. Confirm your TAC settings. DUM mode?*"

"*Eagle-Train 505 to base. Confirmed DUM mode. No GPS cockpit guides?*"

"General?" Susan asked worried, confused a bit with the jargon.

"It's not a smart bomb or missile. No riding-the-beam help, or guidance into this target. The TAC shouldn't be expecting any help on DUM mode?" Givens wondered.

The Palantir's voice filled the room, giving everyone a jolt. "*The TAC should be giving the pilot a terrain warning.*"

"I'm gonna have ta get use ta yer Pal jumpin' in like that," Givens said to Susan.

"Thanks Pal, please explain. Is the jungle canopy causing issues?" Susan asked.

"*No, Susan. A full canopied jungle should not interfere with these munitions. The beacon is coming through loud and clear and the TAC has a lock.*"

LTD caught up and seemed to finish the Palantir's thoughts. "*Eagle-Train 505 to base. We have a terrain warning sir. A large plateau directly in my approach path. Just beyond, where it drops back off into the jungle, is where the beacon is coming from. At this altitude and approach speed, we have a drift warning on our drop angle sir, over.*"

"*Base to Eagle-Train 505. Acknowledged. Stay on course. Hold for update.*" Major Gates then commanded the controllers to perform some actions.

"General? What's going on?" Susan asked.

"It's as if the target is hiding up against the far sidewall of a plateau from the jet's approach. Wind currents coming up off that plateau could cause those bombs to drift off-target, based on the altitude and speed they have set," Givens said.

"I am displaying animation of the concern on monitor five, Susan," the Palantir said.

Susan watched the display which showed two scenarios in a loop. In the first, an updraft wind pushes the bombs away, further off into the jungle. In the second, winds swirling off the top of the plateau seem to suck the bombs inward, blocking them from clearing the plateau. Clipping the top rocky edge.

"Pal, what happens if either of these events takes place?"

"In scenario one, the bombs explode further off in the jungle. Reduced effectiveness results in a 38% probability of success. In scenario two, the bombs explode on top of the plateau deflecting most of the blast up and outward, over the target area. Resulting in a fourteen percent probability of success."

"You have got to be fucking kidding me," Susan said.

Major Gates, with information from his controllers, was back on his comm. *"Base to Eagle-Train 505. We have two options for a green TAC. Loop around and take an approach without the plateau in the way. Or drop down, low and slow, over the plateau to reduce any drift."*

"Eagle-Train 505 to base. If I go around sir, even at this altitude, whoever's on the ground will hear me. Far off yes, but how many jet fighters way out here? I say we go in low and slow, treetop level. They'll hear me coming but with only a few seconds to react. Advise please. Six minutes to target sir. Over."

"Damn." Major Gates said, without depressing the comm button.

Major Gates lifted the phone to Langley back to his ear. *"General Givens, LTD is good, the best pilot I've seen in a long time. But still, a treetop run? With those two beasts? If one clips the edge of that plateau, or hits a big tree high up, it'll likely set both bombs off in a climbing explosion. That could easily take out my F-15. Even if he clears the plateau, going in low means going in slow too. The shockwave will surely kick LTD in the ass, hard. We don't even train pilots to handle blast waves that close because it's so dangerous."*

"Major Gates, this is Susan Figiolli. Yes, I want this target destroyed. But this is your call. I appreciate what you have said. I'll understand either way."

Gates took a breath and exhaled loudly. LTD was closing in at eight-hundred miles per hour. *"Thanks, ma'am. I just hope I'm not allowing this young pilot to talk me into a tactical decision I'll regret later."*

Major Gates clicked his comm.

"Base to Eagle-Train 505. OK LTD, you got your wish. Permission to override altitude approach. Drop down and have the TAC relock. Give me a one-hundred-foot clearance. That's a direct order, and I will bust your ass if you don't follow it. We don't need to be clipping the leaves off the tree tops to get that target angle well within parameters."

Then Major Gate's voice turned ominous.

"And Captain Brush, listen carefully. I want you to override the auto release as well. Use VFR to do a single, simultaneous dual-drop. Confirm. Over."

Susan just looked at Givens this time.

"Usually, if ya drop two bombs, ya staggered 'em. One right after the other." Givens motioned. "Gives 'em a little separation, covers a bigger target area. But Major Gates is worried about a 'climbing' explosion, where the first bomb clips a tree, or that plateau, an' causes the second staggered bomb up higher to blow. Too close to the jet. Blast wave or shrapnel hits a control surface, or a gas-tank."

"That sounds really bad." Susan trailed off.

"Major Gates is havin' the pilot override. Droppin' both bombs at the same time."

The Palantir added an animation displaying the jet as two bombs hit the plateau in a staggered release. The explosions climb upwards engulfing the jet.

"That's not making me feel any better, Pal," Susan said out loud.

Major Gates seemed to echo the Generals comments. *"And damn it Dan, make sure you clear that plateau and any giant trees reaching up to try and fuck you. Delay your drop an extra split second, you're all jacked up. Plus you're dropping four-thousand pounds on this asshole's head. You only need to be close, so don't cut it too close. Confirm my orders. Over."*

* * *

Dan's mouth was dry as a bone; knew he was scared, but he wasn't really feeling it. He'd never felt so alive. Every nerve was tingling. His eyes were crystal clear, his hearing seemed magnified.

His training was paying off too. He let the jet gently drop and pulled out into a smooth treetop run, his hand worked a few switches, reset the targeting computer. He didn't think about asking his arm, hand, or fingers to move. Or about what switches he needed to set. It all just happened. It was like his brain had become a part of the jet . . . an extension of self.

It was a good thing, because flying at treetop level was a whole different game. No time to be looking anywhere except straight ahead, zipping along at seven-hundred eight-five miles an hour . . . the last time he dared glance at his speed.

The sky above was a blur in his peripheral vision. The ground and trees below whipped by so fast the colors seem to bleed into one another.

An air pocket of turbulence hit and dropped his jet fifty feet in a second, LTD pulled hard back up. He tried to anticipate the turbulence drops after that, so he didn't end up, dead.

It was physically and mentally draining. Dan knew from training that not many pilots can go more than several minutes, an hour tops, flying this way. There's nothing tranquil about it. Fighting your instincts is the hardest part, your own brain screaming, Climb up . . . just a little!

Dan's focus forward caught something out in the distance, sitting up from the jungle like a giant upside-down bowl.

LTD glanced at his heads-up reading. "Eagle-Train 505 at new altitude. Plus a one-hundred foot cushion. I think you might be going soft on us, Sir. Ah . . . new TAC settings entered, confirmed, and locked. All green. Acknowledged, simultaneous dual-drop of both Mark-84s on initial attack run. Release on pilot command manual. No worries Major, I'm gonna clear that plateau and drop these eggs right in the basket. One minute to target, over."

"*Affirmative Eagle-Train 505. You are clear to engage. Clear final attack run. Take a deep breath son, let it out slow. Relax. It's your show from here. Confirm and we'll just let you fly right on through. Over.*"

"Affirmative. Eagle-Train 505 on final approach. All systems green. Commencing attack run and drop. Over."

Dan had never noticed the loud breathing sounds in his mask

before. As he approached the plateau, he noticed the most beautiful waterfalls cascading over the edge. They reminded him of his honeymoon, of the falls he and Molly explored in a remote part of Jamaica before making love in the cascading water.

"Weird how the brain has time for thoughts like these at a time like this," Dan mumbled.

Approaching fast, he jogged the jet up on top of the plateau, a hundred feet above the suddenly rocky features below. As he leveled out the targeting drop-assist tone started immediately.

* * *

The high-pitched tone caused Susan's heart to skip. She reached over grabbing Givens' forearm.

"It's okay. Just a targeting assist tone on manual drops. Works on yer sense of sound, hard wired in our primeval brains. Yer brain can hear it, know what it's tellin' ya, without really havin' to listen or concentrate on it. It goes higher and higher until that split second when it becomes inaudible. A way for the computer to say, 'you-should-drop-right-now'!"

As the general explained, Susan could hear the tone increasing in pitch. She was transported into that cockpit thousands of miles away. Her grip tightened on Givens arm along with the tone's pitch. She could feel it working in the recesses of her primeval brain too.

* * *

LTD's Eagle screamed across the top of the plateau in a rocky blur.

Dan had a surreal and complete sense of having become a living, breathing part of the jet and its systems.

It was completely natural to him.

Intuitive. Instinctual . . .

"Bombs away!"

CHAPTER 11: Rain of Fire in the Jungle

The whine of the jet engine intakes registered first. Rehan froze and looked at Ramirez, who froze the instant he heard it too. They stared at each other for more input.

Near the top of the plateau, Rehan figured out what direction it was coming from. Both men scrambled up on some rocks alongside the cave opening so they could see over the top edge of the plateau. They craned their necks just in time to see the jet coming directly at them.

Instinctively, they both turned and jumped back down for cover at the mouth of the cave, landing in a roll and twisting to watch the jet pass overhead.

An instant later they were blasted by the noise and could feel the heat from the exhaust.

Rehan saw the huge bombs hanging beneath, just a hundred feet up, streaking past. Like a pair of synchronized divers, the tails dropped down first, in perfect harmony, separated from the jet, then topped over and gracefully dove at a slight angle toward the treetops.

Ramirez stood next to him, his mouth agape at the surreal sight.

The pilot kicked in the afterburners and climbed, banking away in a trail of fiery exhaust. Rehan could clearly see the pilot's dark face shield and mask as he turned his head to look back down from the cockpit.

Rehan judged the drop angle and knew instantly it was bad news for El'Mano and his men directly below. They couldn't have heard the jet's approach as easily or be able to tell what direction it was coming from.

They did have the one SA18C right in front of them, and Rehan half expected El'Mano to at least pick it up and fire it off. No telling if that missile streaking up out of the forest might have caused the pilot to veer away and drop his bombs off-target. But now, it was too late.

The first bomb hit solid tree smack into the heartwood a hundred feet up, exploded, and instantly set off the second bomb, falling clear to the ground below. It was like a giant double crack of split thunder.

The airburst explosions finished El'Mano and his men in a flash of vaporizing light. The most any of them had time to register was the briefest glimpse of the bombs coming through the treetops. It wasn't long enough to regret not defending themselves. Only God knows if any of them saw a white light after that.

The SAM at their feet cooked off, its explosion totally driven down into the dirt by the force of the two overhead Mark-84s.

Trees in the blast zone were vaporized in the flash and a shimmering wave. Rehan raised a hand to shield his eyes just before the switch was flipped and everything went dark.

* * *

Rehan blinked to focus his eyes, disorientated and foggy. Lying on his back, watching a huge, billowing dark-cloud climbing and churning high into the sky, some of the bottom parts drifting away in the wind. His sight was blurred, hearing muffled, and his head throbbed in a dull ache.

Strange. He thought, It's not the rainy season? Did we get caught in a flash flood?

It took his brain a second to realize he wasn't wet or washed out of the cave and then, a jet!

Instinctively, he began checking himself for serious injuries as his wits and his hearing slowly returned. He rolled up onto his hands and knees. He could make out a far-off, echo like rumble, from the huge explosion. Or maybe that was just in his head?

He tried to shake it off, but his head instantly screamed in a sharp throb-achy pain.

Those bombs were big, and powerful. Five hundred yards away? Up two hundred feet? And the blast wave was powerful enough to throw me several feet into the cave.

A brief memory flashed of the rock out cropping, sticking out from the mouth of the cave, deflecting most of the blast-wave up and over the plateau. It saved them from serious internal organ damage.

His fingertips found a little blood trickling from his nose and left ear. He worried about permanent loss of hearing, a liquid swishing around inside his head.

As Rehan focused, Ramirez came staggering towards the mouth of the cave. His left arm limp and hanging. It looked like a classic dislocation to Rehan. Blood streaked down the side of his head from a gash, mixing with that coming from his ear, running down his dirt-stained neck.

Ramirez leaned forward onto the rocky overhang, peering down in horror at the jungle below, into the smoldering bomb crater, as if he were looking into the pits of hell itself.

He let out a primal scream, mixed with despair and rage. "Those double-crossing chicken-fuckers! You were going to kill me too? You fucking lying bastards!"

He broke down in sobs, with rage boiling up between gasping breaths.

"My brothers. Noooo! They weren't supposed to hurt you . . . why, why, why? Damn you!"

He shook a fist at the sky and screamed, the whole forest echoed with his agony. He slumped further into the rock, as if he wanted to melt into it.

Rehan didn't miss any of it. They weren't supposed to hurt any of you? You were going to kill me too? In a flash, it all became clear. The suspicious behavior. The preoccupation. Rehan had been set up by Ramirez, not El'Mano. And he was instantly as mad as he'd ever been.

Even his childhood tragedy didn't sting as much as this betrayal. This was planned. This, was on purpose.

His gut in knots, Rehan staggered to his unsteady feet. Then he saw the AK-47 sitting on the ground, almost equal distance between them.

Ramirez heard him shuffle and turned. He eyed Rehan. "The fucking bastards killed them all. Where did the government get jet fighters from?"

Rehan wasn't buying any of it. Then he saw Ramirez glance at the AK-47 too.

Rehan had never played cowboy gunfighters as a kid, but he'd seen the movies. Both men sizing each other up. Both trying to read each other's thoughts. Both thinking, "I'm closer, I can get there first."

Rehan's neck tingled and tightened the split second everything froze, the instant before reflex kicked in and both men pounced.

Ramirez came bounding off the rocks, using his legs to push off, giving him a decided edge right off the bat.

Rehan felt slow and groggy. He knew he was about to lose this race easily.

Ramirez stumbled slightly, racing for the gun, falling forward as he reached the AK-47 first. He went to catch himself as he fell, but his left shoulder gave way in agony and he face planted right on top of the AK-47.

Ramirez's dislocated shoulder had given Rehan a short reprieve. His adrenaline finally registered, his wits and strength kicked in.

Ramirez, in agonizing pain, was clearly making the weapon ready with his good arm.

Rehan landed hard on Ramirez's back and thought quickly enough to drive his weight into that left shoulder. His years of ju-jitsu training as a boy allowed him to cling on in a safe, defensive back-mount position.

A painful, angry growl escaped from Ramirez, then a grunt of determination, as he tried to roll over and break free.

Rehan clung to him, looking to apply a chokehold. He could have choked Ramirez out in seconds if not for having to dodge the AK-47 barrel with each twist and turn. They both rolled over together and Rehan ended up on his back with Ramirez and the AK-47 on top of him facing the cave ceiling.

Rehan wrapped his arms around, tangling up the AK and Ramirez in a tight triangle hold. Pulling and tugging on the hurt shoulder to sap Ramirez's moves and strength. Locking his legs out at the ankles.

Ramirez pulled the trigger and a burst of automatic fire shattered the ceiling above, sending a shower of rocks, dust and pebbles down on top of them. Falling in Ramirez's face, he shook his head trying to clear his eyes. He began to rock violently side-to-side, screaming in agony, trying to break Rehan's grasp. "This is all your fault!" he growled at Rehan.

Rehan held tight, couldn't get a chokehold, the barrel of the AK dancing inches away. Pulling at the left shoulder. Ramirez was bigger, stronger, and so heavy. It was squishing the breath out with every twist and turn.

Ramirez brought the muzzle of the gun up alongside his own head, twisting it, trying to get it pointed at Rehan. Another burst of fire, this time blasting the sidewall of the cave, spitting more rock, dirt, and dust everywhere.

Rehan's ear screamed in pain at the close-range blast. He lost all hearing in his left ear, replaced by a terrible ringing noise. It singed the side of his face. Rehan caught a whiff of his own burning flesh.

The dust in the cave became almost blinding. Only the sounds of the two men in the final death struggle could be heard, a mix of growls, and grunts, and hissed breathing.

Rehan spied a knife held against Ramirez's leg in a sheath. In a smooth motion, he flicked the button release and slid the knife out clean.

Rehan allowed Ramirez to break free and roll to his right. Rehan saw a smile cross the man's face when he thought he was about to be able to twist the gun and blow him away. But his weak side shoulder was exposed, and all his weight supported by his good arm.

As Ramirez rolled off, he exposed the back of his head just long enough for Rehan to jerk the weak shoulder back and plunge the knife into his Foramen Magnum, the horseshoe-shaped gap in bone at the base of his skull.

Rehan remembered an old war documentary; an instructor was teaching hand-to-hand combat. His words came back to him. "Don't stop twisting the knife in there until you see the scrambled eggs come out."

That's exactly what Rehan did as the adrenaline-fueled survival instinct got the better of him. Plunging to the hilt, over and over, twisting and turning. The brain stem, the cerebellum, spinal cord, both major arteries and veins. Dr. Rehan Al'Camel knew anatomy well.

Like turning off a light, Ramirez instantly fell back on top of Rehan motionless. Pulling out the knife in a spray of blood like a geyser. Rehan's reflex to take a breath caused his mouth to open and a second pulse filled his mouth and shot down his windpipe. Rehan choked and spit up. Rolling and pushing Ramirez's lifeless body to the side. The vomit was warm and thick, and one of the vilest things he could ever remember. Coughing, then dry heaving, he shook the blood from his face and wiped his eyes with his sleeve.

Exhausted, Rehan fell back against the cave wall and watched as Ramirez's last few spasms pumped blood in gushes out over the rocks and onto the cave floor. The blood formed its own little stream and ran down the polished stone floor out of the cave.

Then he heard it, overhead, higher up, but his brain registered the sound immediately. The jet! It was coming back.

At first fear shot through him, but it was quickly replaced by a rage that made him forget what just happened with Ramirez.

Unlike El'Mano and his men, the first thing Rehan thought of was the missile sitting right there on the ground next to his ATV. The open case had been knocked over by the shock wave. The missile had spilled out, but it appeared undamaged. Rehan picked it up, brushing it off, and quickly unclasped the protective end-caps letting them fall to the ground. He spun around and climbed up on the rocks so he could see up over the top ridge of the plateau. He raised the missile to his shoulder.

Rehan watched the jet banking around the far side of the plateau, making a big arch back towards his position. He brought the sights up to his eye and filled them with the approaching jet.

He pulled the trigger halfway, remembering his own little lecture, and a slightly audible, high-pitched sound came from the SAM right way. Within seconds, the sound changed to a cheerful beep-beep, beep-beep, beep-beep, which Rehan took for the system having locked-on.

As the jet approached, about half way across the plateau, Rehan slowly squeezed the trigger.

CHAPTER 12: Lightning Actually Goes from the Ground Up

As soon as the bombs released, the jet was so much lighter it jumped up in the air on its own. Dan immediately hit the afterburners and didn't fight the jet's wish to climb fast.

He'd come in low and slow and knew he was in for a real kick in the ass when the supersonic shock wave overtook him. He also knew the best thing to do was to climb straight away, as fast and as far as he could, but he couldn't help wanting to look at the blast. LTD banked hard, craned his neck to see, putting his helmet right up against the cockpit glass.

LTD justified it, telling himself he wanted to be able to report how close he'd come to the target just over the ledge of the plateau where that beacon was coming from.

Because of his darkened face shield, Dan was not blinded by the flash of white and fire. A fifty-foot plus diameter and thirty-foot deep crater opened in the ground like the mouth of some giant earth-worm.

Trees seemed to be melting away close in, like they were made of wax on a time-lapse speed film. Flowing outwards, shredding, snapping, bursting into splinters and flying into the air. Rows and rows were falling over like dominoes.

Oxygen mixed with the explosive forming the orange-red fireball. It mushroomed upward and grew as it sucked in the surrounding air to feed itself.

But what Dan noticed most was the perfect circle of humid jungle air that formed as the blast wave expanded outward at supersonic speed. It looked exactly like the movies he'd seen of a nuclear blast.

"Incredible" Dan whispered in awe.

The sights barely registered before the shock wave grabbed his plane. LTD, banking at a full one-third top view angle to the ground, exposed the top surface areas of his jet. The wave caught them, overtook the full thrust of both engines, and pushed the jet in a side-slip like motion.

In all his years of flying, Dan had never felt a plane move like that in the air. In fact, he didn't know a plane could move like that in flight.

It didn't just knock into him, it grabbed his plane, snatching it from the air like a toy. It took all his strength and skill to keep from losing all control.

The word "wave" was well earned, because that's what he felt like he was caught in, a giant, over powering wave trying to roll and tumble him into the tree top coral reefs below.

LTD cut hard back down in a dive towards the trees. Counter intuitive, but it allowed him to go with the flow and get his tail-on view aligned with the force of the shock wave. Once he managed that, he was able to thrust with his after burners again and turn in the opposite direction, causing a sling-shot like effect that propelled him forward under control and caused the wave to release and pass him.

LTD pulled back hard on the stick just in time to climb away. He could swear he heard the trees scrape along the bottom.

A sudden shutter, rumble and vibrations, along with the sounds of creaking metal sent a jolt of fear through Dan. Where the stresses causing his jet to break apart? But it was just the sound wave from the bombs catching up to the action in the air.

It all happened in few split seconds, but it felt like he had been caught in that wave forever.

"Wooooo-hoooo! That was fucking un-be-lieve-able! Eagle-Train 505 to base. Two hits directly on target. Ho-ly crap those babies blew! Over."

"Base to Eagle-Train 505. Report condition. How's she flyin' Dan?"

"Like I was just shot out of a cannon, sir. But all systems are green and she's handling just fine. Over."

"Great job son!"

The whole room exploded in cheers.

* * *

Susan and her team back in Langley jumped for joy as well. General Givens scooped her up in a bear hug and swung her around in a full circle. Even Mr. Green allowed a brief, uncontrolled smile.

Major Gates boasted a huge smile too, as a few controllers turned to congratulate him. He quickly put his hand up and calmed everything back down. "Okay, okay, let's stay with it people. Base to Eagle-Train 505, report on the blast area. Langley wants to know about any secondary explosions. Over."

"Eagle-Train 505 to base. We're trained to fly straight away and climb, sir. They need to add a rear-view camera to the heads-up display. But from what I did see, it looked like one giant blast, sir. Over."

Dan wasn't going to admit to the early banking turn. He came close to crashing. He didn't want anyone to know it. And he never wanted to come that close again.

"Base to Eagle-Train 505. OK LTD, that's good to hear. I guess I'll have to pass you on your final exam. Over."

"Roger that, sir. Permission to circle around for damage assessment, over?" Dan had a feeling he wouldn't get his request granted, but he had to ask. "I've got plenty of fuel, actually closer to the tanker way-point than if I'd continued on the training mission. Damage assessment sir. The folks at Langley will want a full report."

"Okay, okay, Dan. Affirmative. Clear to make one pass over target for damage assessment. 1,500 feet, out of small arms range, no sense letting anyone take a lucky shot at you. I repeat LTD, one pass. You aren't going to see much except the jungle and the crater anyway. Acknowledge. Over."

Dan's heart leapt. "Roger that, sir. Eagle-Train 505, one pass over target for damage assessment at fifteen-hundred feet acknowledged. And thank you sir. Over."

Dan made a long sweeping arch out over the jungle, towards the far edge of the plateau. Even though it wouldn't give him as good a look at the explosion site, he wanted to come back in on the original attack course and milk the experience for all it was worth. Plus, Major Gates was right; nothing would be left in that blast zone, nothing.

As Dan approached the leading edge of the plateau, he realized he was shaking from the experience. It had been awhile since anything had gotten him so jacked up. He was jolted to a whole new level.

BEEP-BEEP! WaaaNann-WaaaNann, Pooup-Pooup-Pooup

His cockpit suddenly sounded like a bad video game. Three red warning lights came on, one flashing so fast it looked like a strobe. A series of yellow systems lights came on as well; all quickly turned green.

* * *

Susan heard the alarms too. "General?"

Givens face of joy dropped to deep concern. "It's his Tactical Electronic Warfare System. TEWS. Several components designed to help a pilot when his jet is being targeted."

"Oh my God, General, the SA18s?" Susan asked.

"Probably. The TEWS detected radar. It's searching to locate the source, then it'll attempt to jam up the radar emissions using electromagnetic amplifiers and oscillators."

"So, it's blocking the missile from attacking him?"

"The TEWS are the best in the world. Designed to give the jet, and the pilot, the best possible warning and chance to evade or defeat almost any threat."

"Almost?"

"He's up against the C's, remember?"

* * *

A startled Dan was thinking fast. Anti-aircraft and missile warning systems? What the hell? His head on a swivel, he scanned the sky left and right, up and down. Another aircraft? He'd have picked it up on radar long ago. Even if the local government had sent someone up to investigate, they couldn't be here that quickly?

The TEWS took just a few seconds to pick up the pulse of the radar, combined it with its strength and waveform, to quickly estimate the type of threat, then narrowed it down for LTD to concentrate on.

LTD's heads-up display showed a red circle, then a little yellow dot appeared at the top, which told Dan the source was directly ahead of him.

LTD realized there was no other aircraft, and that left only something on the ground.

BEEP-BEEP! BEEP-BEEP! Beeeeeeeeeeeee . . . a solid "locked-on" tone was never good. Dan's heart jumped in his chest.

Then he saw the yellow dot turn red and move inside the red circle, and LTD knew he was in real trouble. Shit . . .

"Eagle-Train 505 to base, I've got a missile lock warning! It's gotta be a ground-to-air system or . . . Sir, they've got something down there."

'Wahooo-Wahooo-Wahooo!' replaced the constant beep. The dot in the heads-up circle was enclosed in brackets. Another two red lights came on; his cockpit was lit up like a Christmas tree.

An actual incoming-missile warning? Dan looked up just in time to see a flash dead ahead, a black dot ringed with fire, with a tail of smoke coming straight at him. It shocked him to his core.

"Missile, missile, missile! I'm under attack!"

"Dan pull out! Get the hell out of there!" Major Gates screamed, as a sick hush fell across both rooms thousands of miles apart.

* * *

Susan sunk into her chair, looking at Givens who stood transfixed, looking at the video.

"Well shit . . ." he mumbled.

* * *

Dan hit his after burners for the third time. He banked hard left and climbed as he caught the last glimpse of the missile. Shocked and horrified he saw it turn, climb, and track his maneuver.

His CMDS, Countermeasure Dispensing System, automatically spit out a curtain of flares to mask the IR signature of his jet.

Dan's heart sunk realizing LTD had made a terrible rookie mistake. From this distance, at this low altitude, he should have first headed straight for the missile and then tried to out-turn it at the last second. His counter measures would have been much more effective that way as well.

The words of an old flight instructor rang in his head. "In the split-second decision making of jet fighter combat, a split-second mistake is all it takes to get you killed."

Dan couldn't know it probably didn't matter. The SA18C dual trigger deployment created a quasi-image of his jet, the missile's little brain was using that against him now too. It no longer needed the IR, or the Radar. It saw him.

Closing in, chasing his tail. It didn't help that LTD's turn and climb was accompanied by the afterburners, which lit up the sky hotter and brighter than the CMDS flares falling away to the ground.

A pop of aluminum chaff exploded out of the CMDS, telling Dan the missile was still tracking as he continued a hard-banking climb. He knew the chaff wasn't going to be enough to fool the reaper closing in on him. Fear choked at his throat as he sucked air through his mask.

Searching its database, the deadly smart SA18C quickly determined the F-15 Eagle's most vulnerable part, from the rear, was directly between the two engines. Locked on, the new hyper-accelerant shot the missile like a dart, gaining on the jet at an incredible speed.

At the last second LTD tried one last desperate maneuver, to roll, turn back, and dive in hopes that the missile would over shoot.

Booommmmmmm!

The last-second dive caused the missile to overshoot in a sick-thinking way when it propelled through the top of the jet, directly between the two engines, missing any really solid struts or super-structure. It came out through the bottom and then exploded just beneath the aircraft.

The HE fragmentation warhead performed as advertised. The explosion blew the whole back half of the jet off in three fiery chunks.

The engines and jet fuel splashed out across the sky, igniting a huge fireball spraying forward. The sky seemed to be melting as the fuel flayed outward and cascaded down towards the ground in a flaming curtain. The split engines tumbled out in trails of loopy, black smoke.

The wings folded and tore away intact, fluttering off to the sides, falling out of the sky like a kite that's lost its string.

The dummy munitions under the jet added a layer of metal protection behind Dan's cockpit. Deflecting some of the explosion and fragmentation, as the front third of the fuselage, including the intact cockpit, was rocketed forward by the blast.

Dan experience severe G-forces from the explosion and was nearly knocked unconscious. His pressure suit saved him, for the moment.

His instrument panel and controls immediately went completely dark and unresponsive. He could tell he was no longer under power and had the distinct feeling of floating as he coasted through the air.

It was amazing how quickly all sound dissipated, just the wind passing by the cockpit could be heard. No engines, no beeps or warnings, no radio, no more rumbles or explosions, just air rushing by the canopy. Dan still made the effort.

"Eagle-Train 505, I'm Hit! I'm Hit! All systems out, unresponsive. Severe damage. Eagle-Train 505 going down. Mayday. Mayday."

* * *

Back in the air control tower, and at Langley, they heard nothing. The last thing to come over the radio was the incoming-missile warnings and the briefest part of the explosion, just before everything went completely silent. The jet disappeared off the radar screens in a blink of the eye.

One of the controllers reported from his station, "We've lost all radar contact for Eagle-Train 505, sir."

Another controller quickly followed up, "We've lost FOF on Eagle-Train 505, sir.

* * *

Susan looked at Givens with confused hope, but he simply dropped his head, clenched his jaw, a fixed, somber, frown on his face.

The sound of Major Gates screaming into the radio filled her room. "Eject! Dan eject!" Even after he'd released the radio transmit button, "Eject, damn it, eject." His legs gave out, and he half fell, half flopped into his chair.

Susan found herself grabbing, clutching Givens forearm again.

"Tell me that pilot got out General?"

"If he ejected, he was alive and conscious enough to make that last second decision."

"He got out?"

"They're not reportin' an eject beacon. There should be one."

"But there's a chance. He could be alive?"

"Susan. Yes, but the odds ain't good. A jet travelin' six hundred plus miles an hour, spittin' a man in a rocket chair out a flamin' aircraft is . . . it's a crap shoot."

"Damn it, General. Pal? Give me an analysis on this situation."

"Certainly, Susan. General Givens is correct to be concerned in this scenario. I estimate a twenty-two percent chance of survival if the pilot was not critically injured prior to ejection."

Susan could barely mumble, "Only twenty-two percent?"

"Yes, there are several variables working against the pilot's survival.

"First, sound analysis confirms a direct hit by the SA18C. Ejection systems must be undamaged and function perfectly. The canopy must shatter or be knocked away by the "head-knocker" and fly away clean. The rockets must lift the pilot out past any exploding pieces of plane wreckage. The parachute must deploy undamaged and untangled.

"Second, the jet was at a very low altitude and turned to dive in the final moments. Even if the ejection systems work perfectly, a minimum altitude is required. Final tracking data, when the missile hit, increases the possibility any ejection possible was pointing down.

"Third, the speed of the aircraft was approaching the eight-hundred thirty miles per hour ejection survivability envelope. Adding to this risk variable was the explosive forces propelling the cockpit forward. Wind turbulence at those speeds or above cause severe, critical injuries to the human body.

"Fourth, the pilot ejected within sight and proximity of the hostile forces, it is doubtful the pilot is uninjured or could defend himself from this threat once on the ground."

Susan looked at Givens. "A crap shoot. Sorry I asked."

* * *

LTD didn't hear any of the eject messages. It was all happening too fast, his radio out instantly. Reflex training kicked in, almost like he was on auto-pilot. He reached down alongside his legs, grasped the yellow looped handles, took a deep breath, and pulled hard, holding on tight.

The ejection blast was instantaneous, engulfing Dan in smoke. The smell of sulfur penetrated his mask. He cleared the canopy in a split-second and shot clear of the wreckage. Luckily, Dan's cockpit had tumbled completely over, launching him on an upward angle, arching across the sky.

The wind turbulence immediately wrenched his head backwards, ripping off his facemask and face shield, breaking his nose. The grip of the wind forces pulled and twisted at the bottom edges of his helmet. It felt like his head was going to be wrung off.

Dan went to wipe away the blood now spraying in his face. The turbulence caught his right arm immediately. It came flying out from his body, snapping like a twig, and dislocating at the shoulder. Dan looked up at it flapping in the air like a flag in a strong breeze.

The rockets burned out. His speed through the air slowed rapidly. His right arm fluttered back down to his side. Blood poured down his mouth and chin instead of spraying all over.

The silence of the air rushing by in a coast once again.

Dan looked down at the dull, achy pains throbbing from his legs. Both ankles were snapped. Even in his shocked state, he just knew they shouldn't be flopping around like that in the wind as they dangled beneath him. Did I hit the cockpit wreckage on the way out? Or did the wind get them too? He doubted if he'd ever know for sure.

Luckily, he was running so high on adrenaline, he didn't feel any of it.

It seemed like forever before the sound of the chute popped from the hardened seat back. Dan thought it was tangled as the ground looked way too close, and closing fast.

His pilot's seat failed to release and fall away. A slight malfunction, but it meant Dan was heavy, and going to come down hard. The ground came rushing up towards him.

Finally, the sound of air catching and popping open a full chute caught his ear. The chair was jolted into a slow, swinging motion a few hundred feet off the ground. Dan was relieved to see the alternating red and white design of a fully deployed parachute. It was the first time he thought he might live through this whole ordeal.

For a few moments, he was amazed at how quiet and peaceful it was floating there with nothing but the sound of the chute flapping. He didn't remember seeing the rest of his plane go down but noticed a few spots off in the jungle giving off black smoke.

He was snapped back to reality when he came down hard on the rocky plateau, blowing out a knee, on top of the broken ankles. Dan screamed out in agony when the chair landed hard, then plopped over onto its back, causing his legs to bang and scream in protest, his boots flopped around at weird angles in the air above him as he lay on his back in the seat.

The chute came down and crumpled on the ground.

Dan's head was spinning. He tasted blood from his broken nose bleeding down the back of his throat. The pain was all over and intensified in waves. His right arm added its throbbing cries to the mix. Dan was dizzy, his eyes focused in and out, lying on his back, staring up at the bright sun, a few puffy clouds floating by. He wanted to close his eyes and give up.

The thought of Molly snapped him out of his morbid thoughts. He was choking on his own blood, so he reached up with his good arm, unstrapped himself, and in one excruciating motion, flung himself over and out of the seat onto the rocks.

He let out a scream of agony, mixed with the gurgling of the blood as it gushed from his sinus cavity. His head spun even more and he nearly passed out. Excruciating. Everything screamed in torment.

Right next to him, a single-man inflated life raft had auto-deployed in case the ejection had happened over water. Right next to it was a small stream running off into the distance.

Dan thought this plateau looked beautiful from the air, but down here, it was altogether uninviting. Hard, sharp rocks and thorny scrub brush, and hot as hell under the blistering sun.

Other than his nose, Dan was glad to not be bleeding severely anywhere else. He made up his mind that climbing into the life raft to use as an airbed would ease his discomfort. Some emergency supplies, Med-kit, water and radio in there too. He pulled the raft as close as he could, but it still took five more minutes to talk himself into rolling over into it.

He knew the adrenaline would be wearing off soon, it was now or never.

"*AHHHhhhhhhhhhgggggrrrrrr . . .*" he heard himself scream, as the world spun into blackness.

CHAPTER 13: You Never Leave a Man Behind

"Sir, Sir, we've got an emergency ejection beacon. He ejected, sir. He ejected!"

It was as if someone peeled the roof back and let the air and light back into the rooms. Everyone instantly perked up and hope sprang to life.

"Do we have emergency radio contact?" Major Gates asked.

The controller paused and lost some excitement. "No, sir. An emergency beacon, reading deployed."

"Scramble the rescue crews! I want the DAP with a full compliment. Nasty MANPAD down there and I don't want to lose anyone else. Let's go get him!" Major Gates turned his attention back to the open phone line with the C.I.A. "General Givens, are you still there?"

"Here Major. All sorry for what's happened."

Major Gates cut him off. "You're damned right you're sorry! How the hell did some back-ass water rebel group just shoot down one of my fighters General?"

"Check yourself Major! Yer talkin to a superior officer. Last I heard, it's a dangerous business. The HVT meant takin' the risk."

Major Gates was mad as hell. "Did the C.I.A. forget about the high-explosive SAM's in play?"

"Damn it, Major. Damn it to hell!" Givens was flustered. A long silent pause ensued as both men chewed on two ends of the same stick.

Susan felt sick listening to the two military men spar. Deep down she knew they had sent that pilot in too fast. Being so fixated on the Chameleon, it most likely cost that kid his life. Surely this must all be a nightmare she'd awaken from in a cold sweat. No way this mission could have ended like this. There's just no way?

Susan broke the silence. "You are right Major Gates. Absolutely right. It was terrible threat analysis. And, a bad decision, to not bring you into the loop on some of the classified information I, I . . ."

There was another pause. Old soldiers learned to take a breath in a heated discussion. What was said was all that mattered later. Old soldiers had their own little dance at work too, and Susan wasn't sure how to cut in anymore.

Givens saw her struggle and stepped back in. "None of it's gonna get that pilot outta there. Let's focus on that. Major, we've got Special Ops laggin' behind on this thing. Backup's two hours away."

Susan added. "We believe the rebels were in the process of acquiring six Russian SA18Cs"

"Jesus fricking Christ!" Major Gates exploded, "18 Cs! What a total shit-pie. General? I hope that piece of shit HVT was worth it, because you just sent that kid in there to get his ass blown right out of the sky. Unbelievable. SA18 fucking Cs!"

"That's enough Major Gates!" Susan screamed. "You need to get a grip. Those rescue choppers are flying into the same hornets' nest. We had six SA18Cs in play. They used one, that leaves five more. And if my HVT is alive down there, he knows how to use them. He's a very dangerous and capable adversary. Do you want us to advance the Special Ops? Either stay on mission or I'm gonna pull 'em out?"

Major Gates growled a couple breaths. "Yes, of course send them in. Why the hell aren't they closer any fucking way? I'll tell you one thing, I'm not letting Captain Brush sit out there for two fucking hours. God knows, bleeding out or strung up in a tree, while we sit here. No way that happens, no way. I'm sending in the DAP. Anything with a heat signature bigger than a field mouse is getting taken out. Special Ops better use FOF beacons because I'm telling my Hawk to waste anything that moves. Everybody clear so far, General . . . sir?"

"Yes, Major, I read ya. Just make sure ya have that DAP sweep real good, and stay on station, 'cause that medical bird will be a sittin' duck. Acknowledge."

"Acknowledged, General. Is there anything else our friends at Langley would like to tell us? Other AA systems? Or maybe a whole network? Local government sending up birds of their own? Because if they get in our way, things could get ugly real fast. Over."

Givens took a breath. "No Major. Five SAMs left in play on this intel. Plus small arms, RPGs."

Susan offered what she could to help. "The local government is friendly, could be asked to send in support. Basic Huey gunships, with door mount fifty-cals. Right now, we're asking them to stand down and out of the way. For how long, I can't promise. I'm sure they're curious."

Major Gates was still boiling. "Keep that airspace clear. Send in the Special Ops and have them take out anybody on the ground they find. We're going in to get our man. Over."

With that, Major Gates threw the phone to the side and turned his attention back to the rescue helicopters already rolling out on the tarmac to take off.

"Control, advise of mission threats. Tell the DAP to use all speed and get there first, then take his time, be cautious. Permission right now to clear that area using any means."

"Yes, sir. Right away." The controllers went to work.

Major Gates stood over them, making sure everything possible was being done. "Keep trying to raise Eagle-Train 505 on the emergency radio. Did we get a fix on his beacon? Upload the coordinates to the Dust-off in flight."

Susan leaned over and muted the phone. "General, is this a good idea? Sending in those rescue helicopters?"

"Major Gates is sendin' 'em in."

"I know, but is it a good idea? I'm blind sometimes, rushing in, chasing after the Chameleon. Should we call the Major off?"

"There's no way, Susan. Rescue teams would all but mutiny over bein' told to stand down. Riskin' their lives to save a downed pilot is why they signed up for that gig."

* * *

"Eagle-Train 505 to base, come in please. Ahhh!" A ghostly moan filled the room with radio static. Scratchy, and haunting, it interrupted reality. It was weak, as the mic clicked in silence a couple times.

Everyone froze, stunned and straining to listen.

"Eagle-Train 505 . . . aghh ah . . . I, aghh . . . fucked up sir. I fucked up bad . . . so stupid . . . can't believe that I aghh ahhhh . . ."

Major Gates snatched up the radio. "Base to Eagle-Train 505, that is total bullshit, Dan. You didn't do anything wrong. It's good to hear your voice son. We've already got the rescue birds on the way. How you feeling? Are you injured badly? Over."

Silence, just static.

"Listen, Dan, don't worry. The important thing is you're alive and we're coming to get you. Over."

Not even a click in reply.

"Just key the mic. Click it once for us. We're plenty worried about you right now. Over?"

The silence was crushing.

"Damn it," Major Gates slammed a fist into his console.

Susan dropped her head, listening to the dying pilot's last words. "How can he feel guilty? This has to be a nightmare?"

Givens placed a hand on her shoulder in support.

"Control, update the medics," Major Gates ordered. "Keep an open comm. Keep sending out encouragement, talking to him. Maybe he can hear and can't respond. Make sure he knows we are coming and make damn sure he knows it was not his fault."

"Yes, sir." One controller turned, hailing LTD and giving support.

Major Gates turned to the pilots. "Somebody get his wife on the line, whoever's close to them. Keep him fighting. Plus, if . . . they deserve to . . . just get her on line."

Major Gate mumbled to himself, "Please, hang in there Dan. We're coming to get you."

CHAPTER 14: The Opposite of Betrayal is Revenge

"Try and kill me from up there, you assholes. Dropping death from the sky? Well I stuck that missile right up your ass and fucked you hard!" Rehan screamed like a man possessed.

In all his years, he'd never been this close. Taking down the jet, watching it explode in the sky. He was in such an energized state, he couldn't remember if he'd cheered out loud or not. The release of fear, adrenalin pumping. The euphoric warrior. Rehan never experienced anything this visceral, in his adult life anyway.

He saw the parachute open and knew the pilot escaped. Instantly he understood why ground troops liked to hunt them down. Rehan's first impulse was to go out there and finish him off. It's what he still wanted to do, badly.

Rehan grabbed binoculars from his backpack and watched the pilot struggling on the ground. Good, suffer you son of a bitch.

Then he saw the pilot pick up the radio and send a message before his head dropped off to the side. Rehan knew what was coming next. I should've gone out there and killed that damned pilot.

Dr. Rehan Al'Camel hadn't survived this long by jumping into action before calmly thinking things through. He forced himself to slow his heart rate. Sitting for several minutes on the rocks, washing the blood and grime off in a cool little spring. Taking some deep breaths, letting the adrenaline wear off.

Obviously, Ramirez had set him up, but he wasn't stupid enough to bring bombs down on his own head.

He splashed some more water on his face, a cold trickle ran down his spine. Special Ops? A sniper? Take him out and leave? Current U.S. military doctrine. Maybe? It sounded right. It fit with what Ramirez seemed to have expected too.

Rehan didn't feel so safe sitting out in the open anymore. He looked around nervously.

But why the two huge bombs? The size of them? Did they want to kill him that bad? To use that kind of force? Fuckers.

Rehan's mind reeled thinking through everything in order of urgency. Even Special Ops guys would have to make their way through this thick, beautiful, wonderful, choking jungle. He'd never thought of it like that before. It made him chuckle.

Everything in the jungle is trying to kill everything else in the jungle.

And Special Ops wouldn't be immune to that rule of nature, no matter how good they were.

They used the jet bomber in the end, because they had to settle for whatever they could get. The question is, are the Special Ops still coming? If so, how far away are they now?

Rehan had another big worry. When the rebels hear about what happened to El'Mano and all their brothers, they're going to be really pissed off. This was good and bad for Rehan.

Good because they'd be out for blood and looking for Americans or government infiltrators. The rebels would want some payback. It might slow the advancing Special Ops down even more.

And it was bad news too, because if Dr. Rehan Al'Camel came riding out on his ATV the lone survivor, the rebels would assume he set them up and worse, stole their money.

How to get out of this mess?

It took Rehan another fifteen minutes until it all clicked into place. If it worked, he was out with cover. It seemed brilliant in its simplicity. If it didn't work, he'd be dead.

Rehan walked back to the cave. Unpacked two SA18Cs, hopped on his ATV, and drove them along the top edge of the plateau to another, smaller cave he'd found the day before. It was a few hundred yards away on the same side of the plateau. He hadn't used this cave as a stash, because it was lower to the waterline. A freak storm might accidentally sweep his missiles away in a torrent of water. But now, for what he wanted, it was perfect. He stashed the two missiles and returned to his friend Ramirez.

Rehan took Ramirez's body and propped it up behind a big boulder right at the top rim of the plateau. He then placed the spent missile tube on the shoulder of his scarecrow, leaning it all against the rock, as if Ramirez was getting ready to shoot. Blood dripped from the back of

Ramirez's head so Rehan added Ramirez's brimmed camo-hat as a final touch. The pose looked real enough. No one would know the tube was empty.

Rehan scattered the five empty missile cases on the ground outside of the cave in clear view, just behind his Ramirez scarecrow.

The last step was two grenades off Ramirez, pulled the pins and wedged them tightly between the rock and Ramirez's body, so they wouldn't go off yet.

Rehan stood back to admire his work.

Worried Ramirez's body might slip and fall too soon, Rehan moved with the last two live missiles to the other side of the boulder.

With everything staged, Rehan took three MREs out of his backpack; all this war-play had made him hungry. Pulling the zip-cord on one of the meals, the FRH, Flameless Ration Heater, activated an exothermic chemical reaction. The instant heat quickly boiled and steamed the meal right in the package. Rehan read the label. Twenty-four entrée options, some real culinary freeze-dried masterpieces.

In minutes, piping hot beef stroganoff with rice and broccoli sat in Rehan's lap. Really quite delicious. Nothing like the surplus canned rations he'd had years earlier. He appreciated the morale of good nutrition, and proper caloric intake, while your enemies try to blow your head off.

Rehan devoured it, hadn't realized he was starving.

A dull, far-off thump, thump, thump signaled his mealtime was over. He licked the plastic spork and was careful to bag and stow anything incriminating.

It was time for Ramirez to have his last meal too. Rehan pulled the zip-cords on two more MREs. Very carefully, he tucked the heating meals down the front of Ramirez's shirt, warming his deadly pose.

Thump, thump, thump, thump . . .

Rehan scampered back to his side of the boulder. Popping the end caps off his two live SAM's. He laid one missile along the top of the rocks. He shouldered the other missile and crouched low behind the top ledge. Only his head was showing. He strained to hear.

Thump, thump, thump, thump . . .

* * *

Susan listened to the radio chatter of the two rescue helicopters flying the mission. Her Pal was projecting everything on the main monitor with graphics of the approach. On the side monitors, the Palantir displayed schematics and 3-D rotating renditions of the two helicopters, weapons systems, engine details, structure, design.

"General Givens, why's the one helicopter so far ahead of the other?" Susan asked, pointing at the map.

"That's the DAP. He's goin' in ahead to scan and clear the area."

"Shouldn't both black hawks go in together, to support each other?"

"Two totally different aircraft. Special purpose models."

Givens pointed to a 3-D schematic displayed on their right-side screen. "The MH-60L DAP, Direct Action Penetrator. An attack dog. Hunt an' kill. No troops, just two gunner-mates, whose sole job is to feed the voracious ammunition appetite of the beast."

Givens pointed to a side monitor showing the DAP in full color. "Door-mounted M239 cannons, or the ol' standby fifty cal Gatlin' machine guns. Two thousand rounds per minute. Rounds big as my thumb. Helmet Slaved gun mounts on arms hanging out each side, bent-elbow appearance, like a Terminator movie. Things they can do . . . just as scary."

"Why does a helicopter have little wings?" Susan pointed.

"Not to help it fly or maneuver, we need little wings to carry more weapons. Round pods of missiles. 'Hydras' because it looks like a multiple-headed serpent. Seventeen rocket warheads twisting trails of smoke flyin' through the air. Simultaneously if the pilot prefers. Plus, strap on hellfire or stinger missiles too? Sur, why not. Wing-tip end racks carry up to four on each side. It's a beast. Scary lookin' at it just sittin' on the ground. In the air, one look is bad news for any enemy."

"It's amazing the thing can fly with all that hanging off of it," Susan said.

"And the weapons are just what it uses to actually kill ya. The big edge comes from all the sophisticated scannin' an' targetin'. That dog hunts. It hunts you down."

"It's not afraid of anything?" Susan asked.

"Tanks to jet aircraft. It can attack, annihilate, anythin'. Mere human infantry soldiers are considered soft targets. Without serious counter measure support, yer gettin' penetrated hard if a DAP shows up."

"What about an infantry solder with an SA18C General?" Susan asked.

"A very real threat. They're takin' a chance, no doubt. But knowin' where the enemy is, and what he has, is a big advantage to 'em goin' in."

"I doubt they realize this is the Chameleon they're up against."

"Ya don't know that. It could just be the rebels."

"It's him General. It's the Chameleon."

"Okay, it is. An HVT. A man, in that location, with SA18Cs. Maybe some rebel support with small arms. This is the exact situation these two rescue birds would train for."

"I've learned to live in dread over moments just like this in my history with the Chameleon."

"If he's stupid enough to stick around, we got the upper hand on him this time Susan."

The General's words echoed in her head, she'd heard it all before. "So the other helicopter, it's just a rescue platform? No weapons at all?" Susan asked.

"None. Big red crosses painted all over everythin'. Targets for the enemy really. It's a weird revenge thing in combat. Ya just don't want them rescuin' anybody, especially a pilot."

"Good God," Susan worried. "The rebels, can they shoot them down with small arms too?"

"Possible, but not likely. The DAP will wipe 'em out anywhere on top of that plateau, it's too exposed. In the jungle below, their firepower will be limited to line of sight. We learned a lot in Vietnam with the old Hueys' and the air-cavalry tactics. Bringing troops in right on top of the enemy. The Hawks are built to survive in combat. Ballistic tolerant upgrades, armored troop seats and crew compartments."

"I hate to even say it General, but I saw Black Hawk Down," Susan said.

"Good example. Thousands of well-armed Somalis, with clear line of sight, at low altitude. Sur, they got lucky. If you remember, it took a lot to bring those Hawks down. Redundant everything, engines, hydraulics, electrical, flight control systems. Two of everything. And if you remember, they crash good too."

Susan rolled her eyes. "That's reassuring."

"If yer flyin' in one, it's very reassurin'. Reinforced airframe, front to back. Dual-stage hydraulic shock absorber landin' gear. Big bouncy tires. Run dry gearbox, self-sealin' gas tanks. You land hard, but you're still in the fight."

"Well if it's okay with you General, let's not crash any helicopters today. What about the other Black Hawk?"

"The UH-60Q flying ambulance. Called the Dustoff, Dedicated Unhesitating Service to Our Fighting Forces. The men and women who fly 'em live up to its nickname. Six patient litter system with external rescue hoist and a 3-man crew. En route patient care faster and better than any ground ambulance. If that pilot is alive, and they find 'em, his odds go way up."

Susan looked up at Givens trying to reassure her. "One's a killer and one's a life saver. I'm just hoping we don't need either one."

* * *

Rehan listened.

Thump, thump, thump, thump . . .

Getting closer, and closer. Straining to hear exactly where it was. Still too far off.

Rehan had to shield his eyes when he looked up to check the sun. It beat down on him. The hottest part of the day . . . a showdown at high-noon.

Thump, thump, thump, thump . . .

His heart started to keep pace with it in his chest.

No doubt they're loaded for bear and looking for revenge.

Thump, thump, thump, thump . . .

Rehan steadied himself, took a couple deep breaths. It was all coming down to timing. Suddenly, that beef stroganoff was giving his stomach issues.

"Real men always go down fighting." His father's words from his youth helped.

THUmp, THUmp, THUmp . . .

His "fight or flight" ratcheted up. A strange, tingling numb feeling spread across his scalp.

If the Special Ops guys are here, this is when they'll take their shot, with the distraction coming in. He wondered if he'd even feel it? Lights out? Game over?

THUmp, THUmp, THUMP, THUMP . . . Rehan could feel it in his chest now.

Sweat poured out in buckets, his shirt and the crotch of his pants were soaked. All the rolling around in the dirt, the explosions, shock wave tossing him about. The taste of Ramirez's blood and vomit. All mixed with the cuts and bruises, and a nasty rash developing between his legs. Rehan couldn't remember ever being more uncomfortable, and scared shitless.

THUMP, THUMP, THUMP . . .

They were close, but where? The rotor blades created echo effects. Listening so hard, for so long, Rehan's head began to resonate. It threw off the location.

Or is it more than one?

THUMP, THUMP, THUMP . . .

Panic struck. Are there two attackers? Is it behind me? Coming up from the jungle? Shit!

Rehan glanced behind him, out over the jungle. Clear for as far as he could see. He turned back and realized in terror that the pilot had used the height of the plateau to sneak up along the right side. Rotor blades crested over the top, only 300 yards away. The menacing, black specter glided up over the top edge, hovering like a bird of prey.

Rehan expected them to be much further off, across the other side of the plateau like the jet. Instead, they were right on top of him. Too close.

The adrenaline-fueled fear blocked out everything. He didn't bother to use the double-pull trigger. As soon as he sighted the helicopter, he pulled hard on the trigger.

SAaaaWHOOOooosssshhhhh! . . . Psssssssssftttt . . .

The rocket startled him just as much as the first one he shot. They simply jump out of the tube, and shoot through the air so fast, and then it is almost instantly climbing at supersonic speed.

No time to appreciate the trail of smoke. Rehan tossed the spent tube aside, grabbed the second missile, shouldered it, pointed it in the general direction, and pulled hard on the trigger.

SAaaaWHOOOooosssshhhhh! . . . Psssssssssftttt . . .

Rehan dropped the tube without looking, jumped on his ATV, and tore off down and along the front side of the plateau towards his smaller, secret cave.

* * *

The DAP's two pilots were shocked at the speed and veracity of the sudden attack. Two missiles seemed to just appear out of thin air, streaking directly at them face on.

The cockpit warning lights and alarms went off simultaneously with the DIRCM, Directional Infrared Countermeasures system. A big movie projector, playing the missile its favorite movie, way over there . . . moving that way. The missile sees this projection and chases it instead of the aircraft. It's the most advanced countermeasure the U.S. has.

The DAP's pilot planned his appearance perfectly. He ducked back down below the level of the plateau, hiding his entire helicopter and heat signature from the missiles' direct line of sight. At the same time, the DIRCM was projecting the false IR beam up and away from their true position.

The pilots had a perfect view of the two missiles as they turned and followed the IR projected beam up, up and away, out to their maximum range to self-destruct harmlessly.

* * *

Susan was startled at the sounds. "General, did they just get show down?"

"No, no, the missiles missed. The pilot played it perfectly, hid below that plateau. Worse fer yer Chameleon, the co-pilot unmasked the radar dome. It's scanned that launch site. The TADS was engaged. The Litton. He's gonna come 'round with the DIRCM and the TEWS just poundin' that pulse frequency. Their monoculars will all be locked on."

"Damn it General, speak English. Pal? Can you tell me what the General just said?"

"I would be happy to clarify Susan. TADS stands for Target Acquisition Designation Sight and the Litton is a rangefinder. When the co-pilot unmasked the radar dome, these systems scanned the location of the missile launch site. The target is locked on no matter where they approach from and is fed into the monocular targeting eyepiece of each pilot. The pilot will now come around on an attack course and speed. When he does, his countermeasure systems, including the DIRCM and TEWS discussed earlier, will be much more effective at jamming and defeating any other missile attacks, because they know the frequency of the pulsed radar the SA18Cs are using. Would you like any other details, Susan?"

"No Pal, thank you." Susan looked back at Givens. "There, that wasn't so hard to explain, now was it?"

"I'm beginning to feel threatened by that big brain of yers miss Susan." Givens joked.

"Oh, General. My Pal wouldn't hurt a fly unless I asked him to."

"I wasn't talkin' about yer Pal."

Susan flashed him a warm smile. "Flattery is one of my skills General, and it will get you everywhere."

"Well right now, it's payback time! Even if he fires another missile, it's eatin' as much lead as that Chameleon of yers is about to."

*　*　*

The pilot made a quick down and around loop further away and increased to full speed. He re-approached the right-side edge. No look-see this time. He was coming in directly at the target with guns blazing.

With his TADS locked on, there'd be no second shot for this would-be ambusher. Any IR heat source would just draw more fire.

The Black Hawk sped toward the right side of the plateau, sprinted up above the top, then nosed over into an attack profile. In their individual eyepieces, red target-lock indicators displayed instantly. The infrared clearly showed the glowing-hot outline of a loan rebel with a missile at his shoulder, scanning the sky.

'BRRRRRRrrrrrrrrrrraaapptt. BRRRRRrrrrrraaapttt.'

The burp of a 50 cal Gatling gun spitting 2,000 rounds a minute downrange is unmistakable.

Just in case, after the first few 50 cal burst, the pilot let loose two of the HYDRA White Phosphorus M156 warhead missiles. His crew chased them down with more 50 cal.

"Control, this is Talon 60. Chalk one rebel KIA."

"Talon 60, this is control. Can you . . ."

Blam! . . . Blam!

"Holy! Control, Talon 60. Count two large secondary explosions. Over."

"Talon 60, this is control. Still one possible missile out there. Over."

"Talon 60 confirmed one possible. Sir, the rebel clearly had a missile-shouldered when we fed him the fifty cal. Whole chunks of rock the size of footballs blow away. The missile was hit and thrown off into the jungle. Not one of the secondaries. If we count that one sir. The one at the jet. Two wasted at us when we first got here. Two secondary explosions. Six. That's it. Let's get the saviors in here and get our boy out."

Susan broke protocol and switched directly in on Major Gate's communication.

"Major Gates? I'm sorry, this is Susan Figiolli at the C.I.A. Can your pilot confirm the target has been terminated?"

"Talon 60 to Control, permission to report."

"Control to Talon 60, report."

"The rock the rebel was hiding behind was chewed to pieces by our fifty cal ma'am."

"Hiding behind a rock?"

"Yes ma'am. Not very well I'm afraid. It's graphic from there, ma'am."

"My name is Susan. Now tell me what the fuck happened to my target."

"He was lifted in the air. Flung yards backwards. If just one round hit him, the kinetic energy alone ma'am."

"Listen to me Talon 60. I hear 'hiding behind rocks' and 'if he's hit by just one round' and I don't do well with either of those."

"He's a ghost ma'am."

"How can you be so damn sure?"

"Because we're looking at him. Looks like a ghost to me, all covered in white."

"What do you mean, all white ghost?"

"The TADS at barely four hundred yards, closing fast, locked on. He was dead before the hydra phosphorous missiles turned everything white. A ghostly white figure mixed with blood sprawled out on the ground. That target is KIA. Confirmed."

Susan had no reply. She stood staring at the video of that far away control tower. "General, what's happening? What am I missing?"

"Ya look about as stunned as me when I met yer Pal. I think we just squished yer lizard."

"And the missiles? The missiles?" Susan asked.

"We got the six in play," Givens said. "How sure are ya about it bein' only six total?"

"Six was good. We knew six." Susan grabbed her headset and touched her screen to talk with one of her team. She instinctively looked his way. "Frankie, we had six total missiles in play? That's solid, right?"

"Yes, six in this batch. It was small time. Freight in transit was confirmed with visuals," Frankie answered.

"There ya go General. Six."

"Well ya don't seem very excited about killin' this Chameleon and takin' out six very dangerous SAM missiles."

"And the helicopters are safe?"

Givens moved to put a reassuring arm around Susan's shoulder, looking at her sideways as she scanned the video wall in disbelief.

"It seems so. And with air superiority restored, they go in and rescue that pilot. Congratulations Susan. Palantir? You too. It seems yer mission to finally catch this guy has worked."

Everyone was back in their comfort zone.

It was all exactly as Rehan had planned.

CHAPTER 15: It's the Viper You Don't See
That Bites You

After making the mad dash across the plateau, Rehan back-crawled in the little cave as deep as he could. He pulled the ATV in behind him to mask its heat signature too.

Rehan thought he was uncomfortable before; sweaty, dirty, sticky, with the taste of vomit, and a rash between his legs. Stuffing himself in the cramped little cave made it all worse. He disturbed a mound of fire ants on the way in. They poured out and quickly found their way up his pant legs. His calves and shins set to burning by pincers of sulfuric acid. He battled the ants and alternated his feet to kick and rub and kill as many of the little devils as he could, and to keep them from crawling any further up his legs.

Thump, thump. Thump, thump. Thump, thump . . .

The sound was muffled by the earth around him. But he could tell, a wolf was stalking around just outside his cave. At first circling, then coming and going, then settling into a hover position. He was hoping to take it down, but must have missed with the first two missiles.

I was so close, how did I miss?

Rehan strained to hear the rescue helicopter he knew was coming. He needed both of them in place, at their most vulnerable. With only two missiles left, Rehan would try one more on the attack helicopter, and then turn the last one loose on the rescue helicopter.

Even if it meant sure death if the first one missed the attack helicopter again. There was no way that pilot on the ground was leaving. A final act of revenge, for the childhood incident that haunted him and on the pilot who dropped the bombs to kill him.

The ants went marching on. Rehan didn't want to spoil it by coming out too soon. And the ants went marching on.

* * *

Dan was sitting in a beach chair under the broiling sun. He was grabbing empty bottle after empty bottle of beer out of his cooler. He was so thirsty. He couldn't understand why there wasn't a single, cold, refreshing beer in that whole big cooler. Somehow he knew he couldn't get up and go take a nice dip in the cool ocean either.

The Savior rescue chopper came over the far edge and quickly settled in position directly above LTD. The noise and wind brought Dan to a semi-conscious state. The rotor wash felt good, not a cool breeze, but the blowing wind still had a wonderful effect.

Back to reality with waves of pain, the elation of seeing that big red cross hovering thirty feet over head made his spirits soar. He started waving his good arm, even though they were already in the process of lowering a rescue-chief.

"Savior to control, pilot is alive and waving hello to everyone back there."

A spontaneous cheer erupted. Major Gates couldn't hold back a loud "Thank God!" at the news. "Control to Savior, that's great news. Let's get him out of there."

"Roger that control. Rescue-chief on his way down for extract."

The rescue chief landed right next to Dan, screaming some encouraging words. It was the first time Dan realized he still had his helmet on; everything was muffled.

The rescue chief gave a concerned look when he saw Dan's arm and bloody face. Then a sad, sinking look when he spotted both legs and ankles. It never occurred to LTD that his flying days might be over, but now, he could see exactly that in the man's expression. Just like the fictional Lieutenant Dan, without his good legs his military career, especially as an ace fighter pilot, would be over.

Danny Brush made a vow. No matter what painful, torture chamber of rehab he would have to go through, he'd do it, and be back flying again. Nothing was going to ruin his dreams. He wouldn't allow it. He was a fighter pilot. He would be again. Period.

* * *

Rehan could finally make out the hovering rescue helicopter. Glad the time had come, because the first few fire ants had reached his upper, inner thigh, and he wasn't sure he could endure them getting any higher.

He calmly pushed the ATV and crawled out of the cave. He took a few seconds, sitting behind the rocks, to smash and rub both legs top to bottom, killing as many ants as he could. He placed a large rock over the ant hole to stop the pouring forth of even more of the little devils.

Rehan reached over and flipped off the endcaps on the two remaining missiles.

I'm getting good at using these things, he thought in fear and adrenaline-fueled excitement.

In a fluid motion, Rehan rolled over into a crouch and shouldered the missile, then stood straight up.

He quickly found the attack Black Hawk in the target sights and pulled the trigger halfway. He worried if he was beyond the 200-yard minimum range. Hovering, just fifty feet up in the air, Rehan saw one of the door crew do a double take and look directly at him.

As the DAP hovered, it was slowly rotating in a circle. Rehan smiled at his luck. Just as he had sighted the missile, the Black Hawk had finished turning directly in a tail-on view, with full engine exhaust towards him . . . and towards the missiles targeting system.

The high-pitched targeting lasted a second, as the missile immediately obtained a lock. Beep-beep, beep-beep, beep-beep came the cheerful locked-on chirps. The remaining pull was slow and smooth.

SAAaaaWHOOooooooshhhh . . . pssssssssseeeettt Kaa-BLAM!

It took less than three seconds' flight time.

The Black Hawk pilot barely had time to react. Warning alarms, systems, and lights all lit up and went off simultaneously. His gunner's mate screamed something over the comm. His co-pilot screamed, "behind us," seeing the red circle with the locked-on dot at the bottom.

The pilot almost threw one of his gunner mates from a side door as he jerked the craft around to get off a face on shot at the threat. The automatic countermeasure flares deployed, shooting off like fireworks in a circle pattern from the sudden spin maneuver.

The SA18Cs All-Aspect brain didn't have time to be fooled by any countermeasures. It was too close, too quick. Its bias circuit homing head determined that the most vulnerable part to attack from this new angle was directly into the cockpit. The pilot got around just in time to see the incoming supersonic missile. It performed flawlessly, striking directly between the two pilots. Neither had time to pull their own trigger.

The high explosive warhead, combined with the secondary remaining propellant created a devastating explosion. Setting off all kinds of on-board ammunition, missiles, and fuel in a massive, quick succession of in-air explosions that left nothing intact except the rear rotor and tail fin assembly, which spun down and away in a whirly-top motion in a trail of black smoke.

The rest of the Black Hawk was consumed in a giant fireball, transformed into a shower of sparks and flaming metal, raining down in pieces. The sky rumbled with echoes of the explosions.

That felt really good. Rehan took a few seconds to enjoy the flaming wreckage as it scattered and fell to the forest below. He let the spent missile tube down slowly to the ground, like a baseball player does a bat as he watches a home run ball sail over the outfield fence.

As the fiery mushroom cloud climbed and began losing its upward, billowing flame, Rehan turned and calmly picked up the second missile.

He shouldered it and turned to sight the rescue helicopter. He couldn't help but smile. He'd timed it all so perfectly, predicting every action and reaction, all before they happened. He viewed the door crew and rescue chief on the ground, staring in his direction with jaws agape. The injured pilot was loaded in the stretcher, already hoisted 10 feet up in the air, spinning around slowly in the harnessed litter, trying to look in the direction of the terror everyone else was staring at. The fear and wonder of what would happen next was almost palatable to him.

Rehan paused the second or two it took for that pilot to rotate around; he wanted him to see this coming.

The 'Beep-beep, beep-beep, beep-beep' missile lock indicator sounded so sweet as Rehan waited. He squeezed slowly the second half way.

SaSSWOOooooshhhhh! . . . Pssssssssssssssssssftttt . . .

This time, Rehan was calm enough to enjoy the masterful technology of it all as the missile shot forward, launching from the tube. The smoke trailed away, skimmed across the plateau towards the hovering rescue chopper.

Flares, chaff, and the ATIRCM projector spit IR decoys in all directions from the rescue helicopter. The pilot couldn't chance hurting or killing the harnessed patient below with any real evasive action. He made a meager upward climb.

The SA18Cs bias circuit brain, coming in at a full side-on angle, determined that the engine compartment, just below the main rotor, and just behind the cockpit, was the most vulnerable aim point.

Kaa-BLAAMmmmm!

It found the mark with another devastating explosion. The superstructure was compromised, lost integrity, causing the helicopter to partially fold in half. It shattered the rotor blades which shot off in pieces in all directions. Bouncing and skipping across the plateau.

The harnessed pilot's line was cut, or the wench was released, by the explosion. Rehan watched with respect as the rescue chief on the ground tried to catch the pilot as he fell back to earth in the litter. Both went down hard in a shower of sparks. The rescue chief rolled over, and they both ended up on their backs, with just enough time to realize. They both raised their arms in a futile attempt to protect themselves, as tons of flaming wreckage came crashing down directly on top of them.

A secondary explosion of fuel and equipment caused the whole area to erupt into a fireball, which mushroomed and burned well up into the sky. Soaked in burning aviation fuel, the flames flicked and clawed from the rocks.

* * *

Susan couldn't make sense of the unfolding tragedy. Givens could only drop his head in sad realization.

"What the hell!" Mr. Green added.

"Talon 60 this is control. Come in. Over. Talon 60 this is control. Come in, over!" Major Gate's brain wouldn't allow it to register. "Savior can you give us a status on the extraction please? Over."

He quickly turned to a pleading rage, "Savior One, I need you to give me an update, over! Talon 60 this is control, come in?"

Nothing but silent static followed his pleas.

There hadn't been time for a radio transmission from either pilot.

Cries and tears escaped from more than a few of the hardened pilots and controllers, echoing all too real throughout Susan's dark-room.

"No radar signatures. No I.D. beacons, sir." The controllers announced.

 Horror set in as all hope faded and died.

 Susan sunk into her chair, into a hard, depressed realization.

 The Chameleon has taken them all.

CHAPTER 16: The Thrill of Victory, The Agony of Defeat

"Hell yeah! That's what I'm talking about!"

Rehan cheered out loud this time, lowering the smoking missile tube.

He listened to the echoes fade to jungle silence.

No more thumps. No incoming jets. The last explosions drifted away.

Rehan did a little jiggy dance, kicking the dirt and smashing what was left of the fire ants. He didn't feel their little bites anymore.

He absentmindedly wiped the prints from the spent missile tubes as he sat in wonder. Things didn't always go as planned, but, so far, this was one of his more dramatic escapes when something went awry.

Killing was something Rehan had managed to avoid. He'd never killed anyone, that he knew of? Never had to, not even in self-defense. As far as being an international arms dealer went, he was a little more, reserved. Intellectual, calm, aloof. Separated from it all by his humanitarian doctor cover story.

But today, killing, being in battle, exhilarated him. He savored it, in a way that surprised him.

And the fact that he'd stepped up to the plate when the time came filled him with a manly pride. He had used his intellect, and this new, strong, aggressive side of himself. A combination. He was winning.

Those missiles are worth every penny! Selling from experience. Telling this story. Rehan was raising the price. If he lived and made it out of here. Still far from certain, but the hardest part was over, and chances were better he'd at least get out now.

Rehan listened again to the far silent reaches of the jungle, just to be sure he was safe.

Next step. Time to go.

He jumped on his ATV and made his way up onto and across the plateau, towards the wreckage of the flaming rescue helicopter. It took time to navigate the rocky islands and various little streams. Fifteen minutes later he pulled up.

The flames were gone, replaced by pockets of small, smoldering, fires on pieces of equipment and helicopter parts. The jet pilot's charred body lay on its back, still strapped in the litter with one arm bent at the elbow up in the air, the fingers in a smoking claw-clutched death grip that seemed to reach out in rage.

"That's what you get for trying to kill me mother-fuckers," Rehan said out loud to the blackened corpse, then quickly turned away. He wasn't quite ready for this grisly scene, not this close to it.

He took out a piece of paper and wrote a note as a distraction, and part of his diversionary plan. Carefully keeping it clean of prints, he placed it on a tall, nearby rock. He used another smaller rock to hold it in place at eye level and left it to flutter in the breeze.

Rehan got back on the ATV and drove another five minutes to the far side of the plateau, where the multiple streams converged into the two main waterfalls that spilled over the edge. He drove back and forth along the top edge. Then he pulled the ATV onto an overhanging rock directly between the two biggest overflowing streams.

Rehan got off and walked right up to the edge. The roar between the two falls was deafening. Glancing over the edge, he saw a large pool of water two hundred feet below. A twenty-foot-tall mist of spray floated in the air like a cloud where the water hit at the bottom.

Perfect, he thought. Just as I expected.

Rehan removed the hardened laptop and anything else non-doctor related from his backpack. He stowed it all in the seat compartment of the ATV. Rehan put the ATV in neutral and gave it a shove from behind. It rolled over the edge and did a half cartwheel before cutting through the mist and splashing, then sinking beneath the water pooled below.

Rehan wondered if some archaeologist might discover the ATV a thousand years from now and try to piece together the puzzle of how it came to be there.

It'll be a thousand years before anyone finds it, that's for sure.

So far, so good. Rehan turned on his heels and made a quick hike back across the plateau. Without riding, he made good time picking his way across the rocky islands that dotted the top. He skipped and jumped, splashing in the cool water here and there, a little giddy at having blown three aircraft out of the sky. In no time, he was back to the other side.

Rehan's first stop was to check on what was left of Ramirez outside the large cave. He looked over the top edge of the plateau at the ghostly scene below. Thirty yards of rocks shrouded in white phosphorus. Beneath, everything was charred and burnt beyond recognition, including what was left of Ramirez.

Rehan recalled a conference in which the use of white phosphorous had been justified as a "smoke-screen" and "marking agent" by the military, hiding its real use: to incinerate anything on contact with oxygen, especially the eyes and skin. A chemical weapon used in plain sight, as a smoke screen, of course.

Perfect. They've hid it from themselves with their hypocrisy.

Rehan avoided disturbing the scene from the ledge above. Careful not to leave any trace, he began to make his way back down in to the jungle, to where the whole day started.

When he reached the jungle floor it was shrouded in mist. The moisture content and explosion turned the rainforest into a giant steam sauna. Hissing and spitting, the steam swirled thicker in the air as Rehan made his way in deeper towards the blast site. The bomb's aluminum oxide was causing a strange metallic taste to hang in the thick, humid air.

The closer he got to the spot where he left El'Mano and his men, the harder it was to go forward. So many downed trees and shredded forest made the going slow and difficult.

Rehan broke through the cloud of fog to a clearing above, he saw fifty yards of trees that had snapped in two 10-20 feet above the ground, or had large limbs broken and hanging down their trunks. Smaller trees had lost all their limbs. Nothing escaped some damage. Further in toward the center, a solid twenty yards of forest was leveled outward like so many blackened matchsticks. The blast, shrapnel, and heat had shredded the forest and stripped even the biggest trees bare.

A few dead, dry, old-growth trees, their hardwood rooted firmly in the ground, were left standing like smoking giants amongst the flattened landscape.

Everything within a hundred yards was burnt, shriveled, and blackened. Anything that was dead or dry in any manner was on fire, or already burnt to charcoal.

Rehan made his way up onto the overturned logs along to the crater's edge, thirty to forty feet deep and almost twice as big around. He gasped at the utter destruction. The fire had been intense, leaving a thick layer of black-char at ground zero.

There's not going to be anything left here to find either.

A smile broke across his face as he turned and made his way back toward the jungle trails he called out,

"Adios Colonel El'Mano."

As he fought through the blow-down area again Rehan became much more aware of the shrapnel cutting and destruction going this direction. Some trees six inches in diameter, had been splintered apart closest in. As he walked, it turned to branches and limbs, then just peppered marks in the trees for hundreds of feet above the ground.

He guessed it was close at least two-hundred yards before full green foliage started to appear again, owning to the power and heat of the explosion.

The mist of humid air got thick as doom the instant he entered the forested area. An eerie quiet of the jungle, mixed with that metallic taste, swirling unnaturally around him.

Rehan heard the crackle before he saw the flames. His heart sunk after all the victories he'd experienced this day. The small village he cared for was a smoldering mess. Flattened and scattered, compliments of the congealed blast wave that tore through it like a locomotive. A few of the toppled huts, with roofs made of dry, packed straw, and bamboo frames long ago cut and dried, were burning ferociously. It made perfect kindling.

Shrapnel dotted all the trees, having sliced through the whole area. A jagged piece stuck out of a nearby tree like some kind of twisted, ninja throwing star.

The wind swirled and shifted. With it the smell of death, internals and burning flesh mixed with that strange metallic taste, it seemed to coat Rehan's tongue. No longer silent, the jungle air hummed with a buzz of flies and insects drawn to the feast.

A twig snapped nearby and Rehan froze, turned to face it. He tried to peer through the surrounding fog and swirling smoke.

Like a zombie movie, four bloody, wide-eyed villagers came stumbling out of the mist and forest beyond. One was the mother holding the little girl with the earache Rehan had treated earlier that morning. Only now, blood dripped from her little ears, and Dr. Rehan could tell by her limp form that she was already dead.

The mother stumbled up to him in shock, questioning in her eyes. She lifted up the broken little girl, begging without saying anything, for another miracle. She forced her on Rehan, then slumped to her knees, with no real hope in her eyes, she dropped her head.

Rehan was filled with the pain and sadness of his own childhood, and the terrible memories, and the rage. He cradled the little girl in his arms as he sunk to his knees alongside the mother. Tears watered down when he hit the ground. Rehan sobbed quietly. Mumbling softly in the compassionate voice he'd spoken earlier.

"I hope you felt better. Your last hours were free of the pain, huh?"

Rehan brushed the muddy, bloody hair from her face and looked down into her blank stare of death. It was the same frozen, confused fear he'd seen in his sister's face. He wondered in anger about how death's grip could linger on someone's last thoughts like that? Shouldn't it end in peace instead of frozen terror? Did they carry that feeling of fear to the afterlife?

Rehan gave her a soft hug, kissed her forehead, whispered his last tears in her little ear. "So young, so innocent. Just more collateral damage. Will they ever stop? Will they ever learn?"

The three other villagers gathered around as the doctor chanted in her ear. In shock, it seemed they half-expected the little girl to come back from the afterlife at Rehan's urging.

But Rehan knew he couldn't bring her back, because once upon a time, he had tried.

Rehan laid the little girl on the ground, putting her head in her mother's lap, closing her eyes, hoping to somehow end her terror . . . and his own.

He slowly stood back up wiping the tears from his face.

Rehan felt a force turn him hard and cold. His brain wouldn't allow him emotion. He let out a half grunt, half clearing of his throat. He reached into his backpack and drew his pistol.

At point-blank range, his first shot was between the eyes of the little girl's mother. Rehan swore she smiled, looking up at him, the instant before he pulled the trigger. Like she knew. Like she was glad to end the horror. Like Rehan was doing her a favor.

The spray of blood and brains on the others froze them in a confused shock. Rehan raised the gun and, in quick succession, delivered headshots to two more before the final villager reflexively raised his hands to cover his head. Rehan pumped two slugs into the young warrior's chest, and when he stumbled backwards and fell to his knees, Rehan made a quick final head shot, crumbling the man backwards into the ground.

Sulfur smoke swirled, replacing the metallic smell in his head. His ears rang. A six-shot revolver ended the carnage. The final chapter, of this nowhere village, that no one would ever know had existed. The destruction of betrayal was complete. The devil always manages to take some innocent souls while collecting on the evil he's wrought.

Rehan stood there, the last trills of smoke leaving the barrel. His hand shaking in a tremor. He looked down. Two of the dead at his feet were the young warriors who had tried to protect him earlier. The mother. The little girl. The killing was just feet away now. His killing.

They didn't stand a chance later anyway, Rehan rationalized turning a few paces away.

The Rebels or the Americans would come to ask questions. They'd all be tortured and killed, slowly. Better a quick merciful death.

His heart ached as it debated with his brain about what he'd just done. His very own collateral damage, on purpose. He would look back and wonder if this was the moment he had tripped over the line and lost his mind.

He blamed it on his attackers, but twisting at the back of his mind, he was just covering his own tracks.

He stumbled back to the scene in guilty pain. Standing off a few paces.

They made me do it. They will pay. I will make them pay, dearly, he silently promised the mother and little girl lying at her side.

Rehan realized you don't lose your mind when you go crazy, your mind ends up in a conflict with itself. A conflict it can't resolve or justify. The crazy parts come when you have to kid yourself, just to deal with it. The manifestation of the battle within.

Rehan shook his head and exhaled in a growl again. Broke his thoughts by letting the survival instinct take over more. Again. It allowed his brain to function for the moment.

Getting up, he shook his head clear of emotion, walked a short way up the path into the jungle and didn't look back.

Damn, he thought, I wanted to keep this pistol a little while longer.

Rehan hadn't expected to have to . . . to, the villagers.

But, it doesn't fit into the escape plan now. It could be traced. The ballistics won't match the story.

Rehan dug a hole to bury the gun, his brain slipped gears again. Picturing a jungle orchid using the unique minerals rusting away, growing a rare, beautiful bloom of nature to take the place of all the death.

Nature always has of way of balancing things out.

Trying to make himself feel better, knowing he was deceiving himself.

A whole other side debated within Rehan. Mad at him for being weak. Wasting time. Putting them at risk.

Rehan could almost feel the dual personality out here in the woods with him. Standing there, just off in the bush? Around that tree? The jungle warfare had unlocked a cage and set it free. Once out, it wanted, needed, to help Rehan survive. Adapt. Stalk. Fight back. And Rehan sensed it wanted more. To attack.

Rehan wanted to win. The "nice" Rehan. The "smart" Rehan. The "doctor" Rehan. He latched on to this new survival persona like a life raft. Pledging his intellect. Abilities. Whatever it takes.

You have a debt of honor to keep with two little girls now.

Rehan resolved the two sides of his mind, and their differences. Collected his thoughts over the whole scenario. Questions and counter-questions. Angles and counter-angles.

Just a few more things to pull off.

He started making the long hike back out of the jungle.

Now, if I can just find those Special Operations soldiers . . . and not run into any rebels first.

CHAPTER 17: The Great Escape

Rehan meandered slowly. Acting confused. Fighting off every branch making his way along the jungle trail, a bit stunned. He didn't want to get too far into the jungle, or away from the village. No doubt they had heard the gunshots. Tragic as it was, Rehan figured he use this new fact, knowing they'd hone in on his position. Walking deeper into the jungle only meant a higher possibility that he'd miss them and run into a rebel patrol first.

It didn't take long. Rehan sensed a quiet stillness envelope the immediate jungle around him. If the jungle was hiding, something was up. Then, the feeling of being watched. No, more like hunted.

If they just do their job from here, you should get out safe. Rehan stopped and looked down at his white doctor's smock, with its collar and cuffs. Covered head to toe in blood, dirt, grime, and black powder residue. It made him hard to miss.

When the SEALs show themselves, it's quite revealing. Five feet in front of him, a bush uncoiled and a thing stood up. A completely decked-out half-man, half-killing machine. Rehan froze and only then did he notice that several other "bushes" surrounded him. He walked right up into the middle of them, all pointing various assault rifles at him. Each one itching to be the first to pull the trigger.

Rehan knew a lot about small arms. His startled gaze around at the soldiers, amazed at the variety of weapons each individual, and collectively as a group, they carried. Eight different assault rifles. Two snipers. All with special modifications. Add-ons, knives, clips, tack-gear. Night vision, scopes, radios and other tech gadgets. Mission-specific, based on the personal preference of the individual soldier, no doubt.

The SEAL leader leveled his gun at Rehan's chest, moved forward, gave a whispered, "Psssstt, hands up!"

Rehan knew the real acting started right now. Every little thing he did would determine the outcome. Fortunately, he'd spent years in the study of psychology, specifically, regarding the human physical tells of lying. He was a great poker player.

The first thing Rehan did, was shoot his hands high in the air and begin shaking uncontrollably. "Oh my God, are you Americans? Oh thank, God! Thank you God!"

"Be quiet. Who are you?"

Rehan began to lower his hands. "My name is --"

He didn't get far.

"Hands up, or I'll blow your fucking head off."

It was amazing how loud an angry whisper could sound staring down a barrel six inches from your head.

Rehan shot his hands back up, started shaking more, and then fell to his knees. "Oh God, please. I'm sorry, no more shooting, please? I can't take it." He let his head drop, sobbing between his shoulders, keeping his arms stretched up high.

"I said be quiet! What the fuck is wrong with you? Calm down."

Another SEAL moved up from behind and gruffly snatched Rehan's backpack away, tossing it to another member of the team. Then he quickly frisked Rehan.

"He's clean."

"Nothing here. A basic medics kit, some ID papers," another SEAL announced.

The leader was still all business. "I asked . . . who the fuck are you?"

Rehan sheepishly glanced up, still kneeling. "I . . . I'm Doctor Rehan Al'Camel. I, I'm here with Doctors Without Borders . . . treating a village. And, and there must have been a rebel ambush or something. They came to the village, so we hid."

"What do you mean, an ambush?"

The SEAL leader had caught that word. Rehan wished he hadn't used it. In addition to all the other training, counter-interrogations, even torture, were tools special operation forces brought to the field. They could spot a liar a mile away. Rehan was a little rusty verses this foe. He sharpened up, used hysterical fear and adrenaline, to mask his physical tells, chose his words more carefully in a burst.

"I don't know? Rebels came to the village in a large group. We hid in the jungle, the villagers, they hid me with them. They, the rebels, with the guns, they walked off and . . . and then . . . oh God."

Rehan started crying again, adding a little hyperventilating, taking real fear, injecting it into his persona, crying and shaking uncontrollably. It came easy to him.

"Then what? And keep your voice down, damn it."

"An explosion, a jet, then an explosion. I don't remember it all. It blew us up. I, I mean, we blew up. How? How can that happen? And everything was catching on fire, the trees . . . splintering?" More sobs. Some heavy gasp for air.

"Okay, okay just relax. Here, try and relax. Charlie, give us some water," the leader asked and a canteen came flying to his hand. Rehan wondered if they even trained on how to throw and catch a canteen, because he asked, and it hit his hand in a second, and he didn't even look to catch it.

"Here, take a sip of this. Just relax, okay? Let's start over. Who are you? What are you doing here?"

Rehan sat back on his knees, took the open canteen. Gulping the water down came easy too. He was thirsty. Breathless, like he hadn't had water in days. He went a little too fast at the end on purpose. Choked and coughed, spitting up some.

"Hey, take it easy, take it easy. We've got plenty. Relax. Breath. There ya go, okay. One more time from the top. Think you can do that for me?"

"My name is Doctor Rehan Al'Camel. I'm what they call a first help provider with Doctors Without Borders. We travel to help villagers, ah, the poor in remote areas. As a first help provider, I do what I can, then, I send or schedule for more serious help later. Sometimes an operation is needed, or a treatment at the hospital, so I report and . . ."

The SEAL leader cut him off, "Okay, Doc. Okay. I get it. Let's move on to today, okay?"

Rehan let the water canteen drop slowly to his side. He gave them a far-off look of fear and anguish, as he used his mind's eye to internalize the horrors of the day; well, the day as Dr. Rehan Al'Camel of Doctors without Borders would have experienced it.

"I was treating this small village. Everybody got nervous and pulled me off into the jungle. We watched from a little ways off. Rebels came. A whole group of them. It looked like they were having some kind of meeting. I remember a couple guys, with an ATV. The rebels were all cheering and, there was this jet, and it happened . . . a huge explosion."

Rehan paused. Took another gulp of water, letting it spill absently down his chin. "I guess we weren't close enough to burn, or be blown apart, but it smashed us anyway. The concussion I guess. I was knocked out. When I woke up, everything was shattered. Smoke, fires. Almost all the villagers with me were dead, just broken, with internal damage. I guess the big tree a few of us were behind saved us. That bomb? It just killed them from concussion?"

Rehan paused, looking off in wonder, shaking his head a little.

The SEAL leader eyed a couple of his team, getting their take on Rehan's truthfulness no doubt.

Rehan played out his story. "I'm not sure how long I was out. Maybe a couple hours? Then . . . oh God." He dropped his head.

"It's okay, Doc. You're doing good. What happened then?"

Rehan composed himself to continue. "We started back to check the village. The smell. You could smell them burning. Everything was burning or burned up and smoking. It was bad there. Pieces, just pieces and smashed bodies. God, how do you guys see that stuff and still function? I've seen plenty, medical school, operations, but that?"

Rehan paused to get a read on his audience; he didn't want to lay it on too thick. A delicate dance of control versus losing it. He was still a doctor, and obviously had been out in the bush before, so he didn't want to appear too naive. "Anyway, I couldn't take the smell. Nothing I could do, and, well, I feel bad. Maybe I should have helped them prepare and bury the dead, but honestly . . . the smell."

A drop of the head, a little pause. A sip of water, but this time spitting it out like he could taste the smell. Adding the smell to his storied thoughts tapped his base primeval triggers and increased his truthful physical responses. Anyone reading him, would know he really smelled it.

"I walked off to get some air. Three or four rebels came charging up to the village, so I hid. They were screaming at the villagers. Beating them. I don't understand why? It's not like they dropped a bomb on the other rebels. How stupid is that? Crazy. I'll never forget, never . . ." Rehan stopped and dropped his head again in silence.

"Forget what, Doctor? Tell me everything, okay?"

Rehan didn't move. Sitting fully defeated on his knees. Semi-shock symptoms. He coldly finished. "The one rebel, I guess the leader, took out his pistol, and he, just, shot them all, right there in the head. Point-blank.

Like it was their fault."

Rehan looked up and, for the first time, looked directly, deep into the commander's eyes. Letting that primeval memory sink in too. A silent tear dripped out sideways. "It wasn't their fault, you know? Those poor villagers? They couldn't even fix an earache, much less drop a bomb. They weren't the rebels."

"We know, Doc. We know. Okay, let's go. You gotta come with. Let's move out."

They marched Rehan back up to the bombing site, kept him back as they swept the area and called in the other units. Jets and helicopters filled the skies. Rehan got to where the Black Hawk DAP had crashed.

Search and rescue of the site turned into a recovery mission. The helicopter had been reduced to pieces, except the tail rotor section. Rehan remained cowered. Sat on a log, absently looking at the trees.

He watched the SEALs collect a few body parts from most of the crew, except the door gunner, who they found flung, hanging in a tree, 20 yards away. It took an hour for the SEALs to climb up and retrieve him.

The beef stroganoff was mixing with what was left of Ramirez's blood in Rehan's stomach, making him nauseated. When they brought the door gunner's body down from the trees, Rehan used the opportunity to vomit. It was all very convincing.

A rebel patrol came along, more curious than threatening. Captured, questioned, then walked off and left to rot in the jungle. They couldn't let them go. Special Ops don't take prisoners, unless it's part of the mission. And they were still on mission, nervous and searching for any other rebels, missiles . . . or the HVT.

Suspicious eyes were cast at Rehan. He knew the symptoms of shock well, saying how he "felt cold" in the boiling hot jungle. A rear guard stayed with him at the DAP crash site while the rest of the SEAL team pushed up and over the top of the plateau. There were more crash sites, more bodies to collect.

Rehan knew they wouldn't be finding anything else. Nothing else was going to happen.

And that new part of him talked loud in his head with confidence.

When we get clear, we get to make them pay.

You promised the little girls you would.

CHAPTER 18: Master of Disguise in Plain Sight

Susan felt a familiar bottomless nausea.

"This is Centipede Six, ground team leader. We're at the F15 ejection site with the remains of the crashed rescue helicopter, what's left of it. All KIA. It's a mess. Over."

Susan knew there was little hope. "Have your men fan out. Look for any tracks. HVT has got to be in the area somewhere."

A SEAL reported in: "Hey, Cap. Look at this. We got some kind of note here."

"We have a note. A personal calling card from our man. Over."

Susan responded, "Handle that note carefully. What does it say?"

"Roger. It says . . . 'You think you can kill me? Stab me in the back? I blew your ass right out of the sky. Just try and follow me off into the jungle. You never learn. You want to escalate? Use bigger bombs? Okay. Rules of the game from here on. No limits. Remember this day when your betrayal doubled my righteous vengeance.' That's it ma'am. ATV tracks up here lead off to the far side of the plateau. My guys are tracking it."

Susan knew it would be hopeless. Gone on a very portable ATV. He'd planned to get away fast all along. He just stuck around to do some killing first.

The only thing they did have was some scared doctor. In the wrong place at the wrong time? "Give me a read on that Doctor. What do you think, commander?" Susan asked.

"Well ma'am, if he's acting, it's an Academy Award performance. I'm a trained interrogator, one of my specialties. Now, I didn't get to use all my techniques, so if you want, I can pry him open some more?"

"Let's hold off on techniques. Does his story check out?"

"We found four natives, head-shots, at the village, and they were much fresher and not cooked like the others. The doctor's a bloody, beat-up, mess. Looks pretty much like you'd expect if he went through what he says. We've tracked that ATV up here this far, and the Doctor sure wasn't on it a half-hour into the jungle on foot the other way. And now the note? If there were two guys on the ATV, like the Doctor says, that would explain the one we found all crispy outside the cave with the missile cases. We found the secondary shooter location too. I'm guessing that was your HVT. It supports the two-man ATV story even more. I just don't see how that Doctor could fit into that whole scenario."

"And you say he's got papers, documents with him?" Susan asked.

"Doctors Without Borders, all official looking. Local government stamps. A letter of safe passage from someone, you'll have to check, but looks like a rebel pass to come and go in the area. Maybe if a check comes back fishy, or they say he came in as a pair, maybe then, but right now? It looks like it all played out just the way he said."

"How about the man himself? Any slips in his story? How's he feel to you?"

"Like I said, he's a beat up mess. Lucky to be alive. That scrawny man being in physical or mental shape enough to blow three birds out of the sky, then just waltz into us, what? . . . On purpose? It wasn't like he was trying to sneak away. It'd take some balls. Excuse ma'am, but in my opinion, he ain't' hung like that from what I've seen."

"Maybe commander. Looks can be deceiving."

"The real target ma'am? Obviously chummy with the rebels, so why not just sneak off with them into the jungle under their protection? Guide him out? Which puts us at a big disadvantage . . . hold on Ma'am."

A report came in from one of his men. The commander relayed it. "They tracked the ATV to the far edge. Tracks all along the top ridge. No telling where he dove back down into the jungle, and we'd be lucky to find it from there."

Givens turned to Susan. "Chasin' him off in ta the jungle is a no-win situation. There's no way they can search that expanse."

The SEAL confirmed his thoughts. "It looks like your HVT has slipped away ma'am. We're two days in on foot already and they know were here. Gives them a big advantage on us, over."

Susan knew when to fight another day. "No, commander, stay put. Leave the Doctor for us. Let's recover the dead and extract. Over and out." She rocked forward and cut the connection.

She leaned back in her chair, looking up at Givens and his questioning, bewildered look.

"How can it all work itself out like this?" He asked.

"Yep, fifteen years of this crap!"

PART II

CHAPTER 19: A Meeting of the Minds

Rehan was impressed by how quickly they had whisked him away and, in less than six hours, had him landing at Regan International airport in Washington, D.C. It was a trip.

Along the way, Rehan sensed everyone he had contact with was an undercover C.I.A. agent. The SEALs already had his story. Now, each person he met probed him for a retelling.

The medic and nurse on the Red Cross evac helicopter were first. The medic was, a medic. And the nurse, did everything she was supposed to, but lacked real world skill. Nursing becomes routine, but in her case, it was all on purpose. She began by asking him if he; Knew his name? Where he was? What day is it? Who's the President? Then, the questioned morphed into the events of the day.

The C.I.A. greeter at the first small airport acted more like a concierge at a five-star hotel. Full of sympathy, confirming with him the points of "his terrible ordeal." They cleaned him up, a change of clothes, nourishment. And conversation. Questions.

The pilot and co-pilot of the private jet that flew him back to the States were old chums before he even boarded. The pilot spent more time in the cabin with him than flying the plane. Playing his gung-ho role of the ex-military pilot perfectly. All too excited to "re-live the events," Rehan had "fought through and survived . . . buddy." With a back slap of admiration from an old dear friend.

The young, beautiful, and very concerned stewardess on her, "first day at the job" demanded the pilots give him a little rest. Of course, she immediately began with questions of her own. Rehan played her role in reverse and used her sympathetic "in" to feign exhaustion. After the emotional corner she played, "over his care," how could she refuse him a little sleep?

Rehan was glad to get a few hours of shut eye. Exhausted, he still had some key steps to complete and the risk was far from over. He used his subconscious nap to assimilate and analyze the data so far.

The greeting party when he landed at Reagan International was all official company business. Procedure. Protocol. And another quick confirmation of the whole story in a fluorescent-lit back office at the airport with a couple less-friendly, hard as stone, C.I.A. officers.

Lawyers for Doctors Without Borders were waiting in the corridors, screaming for access, as the C.I.A. led Rehan away to a waiting caravan of dark SUVs.

Rehan knew the C.I.A. wouldn't be letting go just yet. They had 48 hours for questioning. It would look suspicious if he insisted on leaving too soon. Technically, the 48 hour clock wasn't even ticking yet.

The hand-off team that drove him to Langley were good ol 'boys, "sure glad to be on the road and away from those stiff suits back at the airport . . ." Rehan of course took their side, and allowed them in. Just working guys. Drivers. For the C.I.A. sure, but not exactly secret agent stuff. Rehan could relate. Showed them respect. Shared.

"Jesus, what happened to you out there, buddy?"

They all asked Rehan his story. They all got exactly the same one. Little did they know, they only reinforced his subconscious phycological base of lies, repeating it over and over, made it more real. Rehan internalized it all with emotion.

The stress of playing this thing whole thing out grew with every highway exit they passed as he got closer to Langley, Virginia. Fooling the SEAL's was easy compared to the C.I.A.

The car pulled off at an exit, turned down an unmarked road for a few miles, turned again, winding through the woods on a dark, pitch black night. The shadow of the trees overtop formed a tunnel. After several minutes, they came to a double pole gate with sturdy block houses on each side, and no way around. No signs, not even a stop sign. Lights blasted into the car.

You either knew where you were, or you didn't belong here.

Armed guards in full tactical gear appeared from the shadows at each side window. Another walked a dog around on a leash. A fourth used a lighted mirror on an extended pole to check the underside of the vehicle. The trunk was searched as well. The driver's side guard beamed a flashlight right in Rehan's face, checked it against a picture on a handheld device.

Like a pit-crew at the Indy-500, the trunk slammed shut, the guards, the dog, and their apparatus all drifted away back into the black.

"All clear to pass!"

The double-steel pole gate raised and Rehan rode through. The gate lowered very fast behind them, clanging into a locking post, which looked like it could stop a tank.

You're in the Devils lair now. And lying to the Devil, right to his face? Is going to take all you got!

A half-mile later, they entered an underground parking garage with no visible building above it. A long access tunnel led to another guard post. A coded "upstairs" was all that needed saying. Rehan was checked in with a visitor's badge and escorted right through.

The room they took him to was three-star hotel like, but without any beds, and no window overlooking the parking lot. Rehan wasn't sure he was even above ground. Commercial carpeted floors. Recessed ceiling lights and wall sconces added soft, bright, filtered lighting. Framed pictures of Washington, D.C. landmarks professionally decorated the wall space with a single dressing mirror on a side wall near the door. Five overstuffed chairs sat in the center, circling a round table. A small kitchenette filled the other side wall. Coffee. Mini-fridge. Snacks.

A different kind of jungle but Rehan could sense his every move was being watched. Being stalked. He got up and selected himself a water from the fridge.

* * *

"So what do you think Pal? Can you read him well enough?" Susan asked sitting in an adjacent observation room. The dressing two-way mirror allowed a direct view, but Susan was looking at a rendition of Rehan in infrared on a computer monitor.

"Yes, Susan. The way I've arrayed the sensor room is quite advanced."

Her Pal was displaying Rehan's body dynamics on small side windows. Body temperature. Respiration. Perspiration. Multiple cameras constantly tracked Rehan's eyes, zeroed-in on his pupils if he stayed still for a second or so. Her Pal trying to capture every dilation and facial tick.

"Okay, you tell me if he lies about anything."

"Please obtain the water bottle for DNA analysis if he discards it," her Pal instructed.

"We know who he is Pal?"

"I want to analyze his enzymes to augment the other lie detection techniques."

"You're way ahead of us already aren't you Pal?"

"Lie detection methodology could be easily improved in many ways. But I don't think I will ever be ahead of you Susan."

"Ugh! Can we please go now?" Mr. Green groaned.

Givens could only laugh at his torture.

"Almost." Susan answered. "Listen, Pal, I'm going to . . . be nice right out the gate. I'll sit close, even touch him at a point."

"Susan, I don't see how that will possibly help in our analysis. It is not necessary."

"Don't be jealous Pal. I'm gonna use his male instincts to establish baselines for you. It should help later as he reacts to questions." There was a long pause. "Trust me Pal, this will open up levels of understanding beyond logic. A physical reflex in the male human brain. Very hard to control. I've used it to help figure people out for many years."

"Of course, I trust you Susan. You are very unique, with special abilities."

"For Christ's sakes, Susan, please?" Mr. Green moaned again.

"Almost. General Givens, I wonder if you'll help me out too?" Susan asked.

"Of course."

"I need you to play "the bad cop" a little. Your uniform projects authority anyway, so that pressure coming from you will be amplified."

"Don't ya worry, it'll be easy fer me to amplify."

"Just a little, and let me lead. Pal, are you ready to go?"

"Yes Susan, I'm always ready for you."

"Awww, my sweetie." Susan laughed as she got up to leave, smirking at Mr. Green. "Okay, let's go see if that," Susan pointed through the two-way glass, "is really the Chameleon."

* * *

Rehan calmed himself and used his intellect as he'd always done. Relaxation breathing. Clarity of thought. Confidence. He'd played this all out perfectly. There wasn't a question he could think of, or a reasonable justification he couldn't come up with, for any aspect of it. He pictured a perfect cube, supported on all sides. He believed it. His goal was to be relaxed enough to not even flinch when the door opened.

Susan Figiolli strode through and introduced herself without title. Rehan stood and barely registered the names of the others. He took Susan's hand and shook warmly, their eye's locked.

I can't make them pay if you can't get past . . . her? Rehan's prideful part of his new persona was formed in Kuwait as a boy. Scared of being out-witted by a woman, in a sick, intellectual kind of way, more than being exposed.

"May I call you Rehan, Doctor?" Susan asked with a warm smile.

"Yes, that would be fine."

"Call me Susan. Let's sit. I know it's been a long day."

"Thank you, Susan." Relaxed. Stoic. Professional. Chose a lounge chair. Susan slid one closer, turned it in. Sat and crossed her legs, proper and professional, but exposed in a way. Rehan fought the urge to appreciate her beauty. He held her gaze with a calm stare.

"So, Rehan, I hate to ask, but you'll need to go over it all again for me at this point."

"Well, I should think so, since I'm on my eighth recantation."

"Please, Rehan, I'm sorry. I know." She reached over and touched his forearm. Leaning forward, her cleavage added to the draw of her tanned, crossed legs. Her toe almost brushed his shin. Trying to break his concentration no doubt. She turned her head to the side, an apologetic smile and direct eye contact. Rehan could feel her trying to read his truth.

This powerful queen has just moved to take your head, and if she can, she will.

"Very well, I'll assume you've checked why I was there and verified my history at the DWB," Rehan said, bored over the retelling. "There were some rebels in the area. A jet flew over and I was knocked unconscious by an explosion, awoke, and witnessed a tragic event on top of a tragedy at the village I was treating. The SEALs found me in the jungle shortly after, still disoriented and in shock."

Susan acted genuinely confused. "Yes, Rehan, but in your

statements to the SEALs, you said how the trees splintered and everything was catching on fire?"

"Of course. Expected when a bomb explodes." Rehan added.

"Yes, but, if you were knocked out by the blast wave as you say, then you wouldn't have been awake to see the trees splinter, and you certainly wouldn't have been awake to see the fireball, or any part after the blast wave. So it's got me a little confused."

"Please, Mrs. Figiolli. I was semi-conscious until the fire and explosion sucked the air away, and that put me under. Or I saw the explosion from afar, through the tress as the blast wave hit? The human mind just puts two and two together. Or perhaps, I've just seen too many movies." Rehan felt himself slip with that joke, just a little. It was very dangerous to want her to like him, to play along. So he remained calm, detached, with a medical, professional demeanor. "Like I've said a hundred times now. I can't tell you what I wasn't awake to see."

"We tested yer hands, Doctor. They came back positive with powder residue," the military general blurted out. "That tells us ya fired a weapon. Ya must've forgot that part of yer story?" Rehan caught a sharp look from Susan his way.

"No, General, was it?" Rehan asked.

"Yes, General Givens." The man glared back.

"I didn't forget that part." Rehan watched Susan and the general lock stares, thinking maybe they had him, if he changed his story now. Rehan enjoyed letting them dangle.

"Maybe you didn't hear the part about where I was almost blown to bits by the bomb the military dropped? The SEALs dragged me right up to that helicopter wreckage. The bomb crater too. I'm sure I got all kinds of, residue on me. Honestly, General? You could test my underwear and I'm sure it'd come back positive too."

"It's all too convenient, Doctor Rehan Al'Camel of Doctors Without Borders." Givens pressed. "Ya just happen to be where a major arms sale was goin' down? With a perfect cover story? Travel anywhere? Be outta communication fer days at a time. Who knows where ya really are. Or what yer really doin', right? It's perfect."

Rehan knew this was coming, calmly playing it all off. "Please General. You people are the ones who've made it almost impossible for us to do our job. You've inserted so many spies many places won't even allow us in anymore. I've lost colleagues because some rebel leader got suspicious. Because of you. Not, the other way around."

"That don't mean it ain't been convenient fer ya to do what ya been doin', Doctor." Givens was getting more flushed by the second.

"There's nothing convenient about it. Check my record."

"Oh, we're checkin' Doctor, don't' ya worry about that. My friends here are checkin' real good."

"General please." Susan said, turning to Rehan. "I know you have a stellar record Rehan. But maybe this time, oh, I don't know? It's all so improbable? So, I was thinking, maybe . . . someone was tagging along with you this time? Maybe you were duped into doing a favor for someone? A mysterious, last minute addition to your party? That's the guilty person. Please, Rehan, give us something? Everyone knows you cooperated."

Rehan was on the offensive and liked it. But he also kept checking himself. How would the real doctor be acting and feeling? He turned to focus on Susan.

"Let me get this straight, because it's all starting to come together for me. The military blows up half the jungle, killing scores of innocent villagers, me too almost, trying to what? Take out some rebels, right? You then suffer the loss of your helicopter." Rehan deftly left out knowledge that didn't play right into his unsuspecting, unconscious, doctor story, as long as he didn't slip up.

"And now you want me to . . . to, what? Admit I was helping these rebels? Or somebody tricked me into bringing him in on my pass? My God, next you'll think I shot down your helicopter myself."

Rehan paused, laughed a little, shaking his head with a smile of confidence. "Do you realize how crazy you sound? Let me ask you a simple question, for what? Why would I, go into the jungle using my own name and credentials, to join up with some vicious rebel group, then kill fellow American soldiers? What on Earth could I possibly have to gain by doing all of that?" Rehan leaned back in towards Susan.

Of course she would be hoping an outburst like that would trip up anyone with real knowledge. Any bit that didn't fit, the SAMs, El'Mano, the jet shoot-down, the ejection of the pilot, or the rescue helicopter. Any unknown little detail added into the story, at this point, and she'd have him. She'd be sure.

But no slip-ups. No changes to his story. Rehan still had her boxed in. He almost felt sorry for her.

Givens stepped back in. "Oh, come on Doctor, ya did it for money, same reason as all you scumbag arms dealers do it for."

Rehan reacted perfectly to that as well. "Money? You must be joking now, right? Did you people do any background on me at all? What my father left me? God rest his soul. My Kuwaiti dowrence alone each year is . . . Money?"

Givens kept right at him. "Was it Jihad? Like the rest of yer radical Islamic scumbags? Fer all yer big, heroic deeds fighting us infidels down here, huh?"

"General? Our government, our military, the industrial military complex, is one of the biggest arms suppliers in the world, so who exactly are you calling a 'scumbag?' And as far as religion goes, I'm Catholic."

Susan stood as Givens lurched closer to where he was sitting.

She was obviously in control. Or maybe she was just keeping the military from finishing him off? Maybe one word from her and they'd never let him leave this place?

"Let me ask, Rehan. Would you be willing to submit to a polygraph examination? Then we'll know for sure. That's reasonable enough, don't you think? It'll clear the whole thing up."

Rehan worried. The C.I.A. surely had the most advanced lie detectors in the world, things he didn't even know about. "Of course I'll take a polygraph, but only after talking with my attorney. You'll understand if I don't trust you guys to do it properly."

Rehan turned to Susan, ignoring Givens. "You won't listen to reason. You're making up totally crazy things. It's becoming obvious to me that you are looking for a fall guy to pin this whole mess on. Well, it won't be me. You can search my records, my home, check my history. Dig all you want."

Rehan looked back at Givens. "Stick a microscope up my ass and you still won't find crap."

Givens pushed one last time. "Yeah, you and yer Kuwaiti family, I'm sure ya hid yer trail real well. I'm sure we won't find crap."

"Because there's nothing to find. And bringing my family into this is totally out of line. My mother moved us here when I was fourteen. I've been an American citizen my whole adult life. But the truth is, my Kuwaiti family's honor would be at stake too. There's no way they'd allow any such activity. They'd probably have me executed. So, leave your high-and-mighty morals at the door."

Givens pointed a finger at him in reply. "We should've kept that country after the Gulf Wars. Yer all the same. Be happy if ya could kill us all."

"And you are a military ass. You know what Saddam and his forces did in Kuwait, you ignorant ass." Rehan had spun this Givens up easy enough, he was fast losing control. A little more and he'd go over the edge. All the pressure was focused on him.

Susan grabbed the general's arm and pushed her way between the two of them.

Rehan used that as well . . . "Nice, that's your answer for everything? When you don't hear what you like? Just beat and torture someone until they say what you want to hear? No wonder our intelligence is always so screwed up. A sorry excuse for a soldier, an even sorrier excuse for a man."

Givens lost it, "Fuck you! Yer not foolin' anybody. I know who ya are, Chameleon! Or should I say, 'Doctor Al' Chameleon.' Funny how that nickname fits. I will personally be there to sound off the firing squad on yer ass."

Susan cut him off. "General, that's enough! You are not helping. Calm. Down."

Rehan added, "He's like an animal off his lease lady."

Susan gave him a shock when she turned on him. "Watch your mouth, Doctor. You disrespect him again and I won't step between you, got it? Now both of you just cool it. God damned male hormones, always having to mark your territory. Enough already."

Givens took a couple steps away but stood glaring down at Rehan.

Rehan sat back in his chair, up straight, regaining his poise. Something in Susan's reaction made him worry. Time to make a play for the exit. And for that, he wanted to add some leverage. He looked back up at Susan.

"I will meet with my lawyers and schedule a polygraph. What I won't do is admit to some bullshit story about me helping those rebels shoot down and kill Americans . . . that, is not going to happen. Whoever decided to drop those bombs has blood on their hands. And for the record, I will take this whole thing public as well. Those villagers won't be able to take a polygraph, or tell their side of the story, so I plan to be their voice in all of this."

Rehan saw it all hit home and dug his claws in a little deeper. "What gives you the right, even if you say it was approved, to kill all those people? I can promise you, Americans like me, will be very angry that innocent people are being slaughtered just so you can kill some lowly rebels in the jungle. It's bad enough when we kill innocent civilians in a war zone, but now?"

Using genuine anger and truth, he knew all of this would come across perfectly, even on his body dynamics level, under frame-by-frame video review later.

"And for what? So you can support some third world puppet government? I wonder what kind of government we are supporting down there. You think the reporters will uncover it? Once they take a real, close look at the whole sorry affair?"

Rehan went for the jugular and sprung his trap door to the exit. "On top of all of that, you kidnap an American citizen and hold him against his will. Use abusive interrogation tactics on him. Try to attack him, pin the blame on him? Trample his civil rights, trash the constitution . . . oh yeah, right after you almost killed him too with your secret little war."

Givens went to say something, but Susan grabbed his forearm to silence him with a stare and a clutch of her nails.

"All in an effort to cover your own mistakes and create a big cover-up. No American will feel safe by the time I'm done." Rehan let that hang for a moment. "How's this all reading in tomorrow's papers? Do I have my facts about right?"

Rehan finished and sat back in disgust throwing his hands up at them and turning away. He crossed his legs and shook his head in a disappointed, dismissive manner. Inside he was jumping for joy. He could see the pain and destruction it would allow him to inflict against his lifelong enemy.

Oh Mr. Intellect, you're good. You've got them good.

"Nobody is holding you against your will? I thought we rescued you from that jungle and helped you home?" Susan asked.

Givens weighed in. "Weren't ya afraid of those rebels? That's what ya told us, or is yer story changin' again?"

"Oh, is that what you call this? You're saving me? Hilarious! I guess the DWB lawyers asking to see me are just having coffee first? Are you telling me I'm free to go now?" Rehan looked from one to the other. Neither of them offered an answer. "I'm done talking. Either arrest me or let me go. I'm not saying another word until I talk with my lawyers."

Susan sat again, leaning in. "Rehan, surely you realize we have to question you under the circumstances. If some of our tactics are a bit, uncomfortable, I'm sorry. But, you're right, Americans are dead, and we are going to find out who caused that and . . ."

"You! All of you are responsible." Rehan cut her off and cut her to the bone. Even better, it froze her. Rehan took note of her pain. It gave him a chance to confirm some things the unstable General had let slip. "Unless there's something you're not telling me?" He asked, but turned quickly to face Givens, "What did you call me? The Chameleon? Is that the secret code name you gave him, in your little spy games? Huh? You honestly think I'm dumb enough to call myself the Chameleon when my real last name is Al'Camel? On top of going into the jungle to sell illegal weapons using my real identification?"

He looked back to Susan. "Do I look that stupid to you? Is this, this Chameleon you're chasing really that stupid?"

"No Rehan, he is not," Susan answered. "He didn't choose the code name, it was assigned to the case back in the 90's, he never had any part of the name."

Rehan cut back in. "Good, because if he's that stupid and you guys can't catch him," Rehan turned an accusing eye towards Givens, "or should I say kill him? It doesn't say much for you two now does it? But you know what? I don't care. You killed the people I cared about."

"Please, Rehan, you know we didn't," Susan answered.

Rehan talked over her. "It was a little girl with an earache, and her mother who just wanted to, to . . ."

Rehan mixed genuine despair over the memories of his own little sister's death. Mixing a sense of believing, with all the lies, was key to being undetectable. Rehan focused his mind's eye on the little girl bleeding from her ears. "Damn, maybe her mother was a terrible, murderous rebel . . . blowing them up was a good plan . . . that makes sense, right?" Rehan wiped away a tear with a rough swipe of his sleeve. Sat back up with dignity in silence.

"Okay Rehan, okay. We're all sorry for what's happened. We truly are. You have to know, this is not the outcome we were after, none of it." Susan sat up close again. Tears of compassion filled her big brown eyes. "Honestly."

None of it was real. Honesty didn't fit here. Rehan knew it. He was pretty sure Susan knew it too. He was in the chess match of his life. He barely had her at bay. She was one move away from turning on him.

"Rehan, there's a lot more going on here, things we just can't talk about. I'm sure you can understand. But we have to -- to question you."

* * *

Susan struggled to play nice while her mind reeled. Could this man, sitting right here, after all these years, actually be the Chameleon? "I really hope you'll reconsider any ideas of going to the press. Those men who died deserve better than to have everyone think they were out there with intent to kill a little girl and her mother."

Rehan looked over in contemplation but didn't say anything.

Susan tilted her head a little to the side. "I know you must be very angry, that you truly cared. Please try to understand, sometimes things go horribly wrong for us, even when we are trying to do the right thing."

Susan reached to hold both his hand and looked him in the eyes. She noticed him flinch at her touch but decide not to pull away. It was like trying to get a read on Dracula. Calm, and stoic, and precise, with an overwhelming sense of superior intelligence. Or abilities. Hiding some dark secret deep behind the polite façade?

"And believe me, when it comes to that little village, and all those innocent people, it was the worst possible end to a tragic string of events. Please, Doctor, just take some time before you decide to do what you think you have to."

"What's it for? I'm asking why. Justify it for me? Or I'm ready to leave right now."

Susan could sense his questions went to some deeper level, a slight chink in his consistency.

"Someday, someday soon I hope, I'll be able to give you more details on what happened, and I will personally call to fill you in. Today, I can't, even though you are due a better explanation."

What she had to do next would never have seemed possible to her.

Not in a million years.

"We'd still like to be able to follow up with you, if that'd be okay? In case you think of anything else, if something comes back to you? Which often happens when people suffer such traumatic events. Please, call me right away."

Susan stared trying to suck the truth from his brain as she handed him her personal calling card. Could it all be true? Just caught up in a terrible mess?

How could she say the words? Her throat was tight, constricted at the back. She couldn't believe she was about to, just . . .

"Let me have a couple of our agents help get you home. It's the least we can do."

Followed with the hardest, forced smile of her life, not at all sure it was genuine enough.

Rehan stayed silent for a few moments. "That's okay. Don't do me any more favors. I'm sure my team will be able to get me home."

He turned his back to Givens completely, "I sure as hell hope you remember to give me that explanation, Miss, and I hope it's a damned good one. I'll give you the benefit of the doubt for now, but screw-ups like that out there? It only creates more enemies for us. Remember this day the next time the military wants to go drop bombs on somebody."

Rehan stood up as he finished and reached out a hand to shake hers. She stood, smiled, and took his hand. Rehan covered their shake with his other hand, pulling Susan toward him and holding firm. He used the moment to fully gaze deep in her eyes and take a whiff to smell her up close.

Susan shook his hand and pulled away.

He gave a sad-like smile to cover his boldness. He turned and briskly stepped past Givens.

Susan gave a slight, nod to the two-way mirror. Two agents were waiting and escorted Rehan away down the hall.

When the door closed, Givens was dumb founded. "Susan, I'm not tryin' to tell ya yer business or anything, but, somethin' about this guy ain't right . . . and the chance of him happenin' to be there for all of that?"

"I know, General," Susan responded, not looking at him. Still trying to read a feeling from Rehan's last look. And his last words, "Remember this day". The same as on the note at the scene. Was it some kind of challenge? Or was he just being a man? Like all men, they all look at some point.

"He's got to be involved," Givens pressed.

"Really? No prints, on the note, at the scene, anything. His whole story checked out, and I don't see how anybody could have planned all that. What are the chances a puzzle with all those pieces could work out so perfectly for him? No sign of the ATV which we know was there."

"Come on," Givens shot back. "Ya could hide a tank in a thousand different places out there and we'd never find it. I just don't buy all these coincidences. It's too much."

"No slip-ups, in his entire story General, not one. We worked him. We're pretty good at this stuff."

Givens kept at it, "I guess not when he can claim ta be asleep the whole time. What does he have ta cover?"

Susan tried to show him the angles she'd been playing. "All the more chance he'd say something he couldn't know. But he didn't, did he? And he was right, the Chameleon wouldn't have made it this far being that stupid. Think about it General, if he'd operated this way before, my Pal would have connected the dots by now. There just isn't any trail. I wish there was! Right now, he doesn't fit."

Givens wouldn't believe it. "Every criminal slips up sooner or later. Ya said so yerself, the guy's always gettin' away with things. Maybe this time he got cocky?"

Susan had to stop him. "This time? The time he happened to need an alibi? To set it all up ahead of time? To use his own identification? To take a chance and expose his cover? And even if your theory holds, he did all that so he could play it out this way afterwards? General, I never said he was psychic."

Givens pressed on. "I just don't believe in coincidences . . . not that many."

"Me either, but right now, there are more coincidences to him making up this story than there are for him telling the truth. I'm not convinced the Chameleon made mistakes like this for the first time in twenty years, this time?"

Givens stood, just shaking his head.

"Besides General, he's right, for now. We have to follow certain rules. American citizen, the U.S. Constitution, and we do not have grounds to hold him. It's not like a war on foreign soil. You've had to deal with rules of engagement, well, these are ours."

Givens was incredulous. "Unbelievable. All the things I heard about the C.I.A. and ya let this guy walk?"

Susan was stoic. "Yes, that's exactly what we do. Don't believe everything you hear General. It'd be rare for any agent to act differently. And I dare say you wouldn't want us to. It's a slippery slope. No teams of black-ops assassins running around doing whatever. It's not reality, especially in America."

Givens half joked, "I just thought ya'd make an exception with this guy. This all happened way down in Central America? Take 'em back to the jungle, since he don't want our help."

"Not when it comes to a United States citizen."

"So he's usin' the system against ya again. The procedures? Laws? To escape?"

"Draped in the flag. All the rights afforded any other citizen. Tread on a citizen and you'll end up with a very short career. Now, I said we don't detain, we let him go. I didn't say we were done watching him."

"Well that's good ta know 'cause I'm gonna catch hell. They'll have my ass for this whole mess. I still can't believe it. Saddam Hussein's army couldn't shoot down a F15, in two wars. This guy takes one out plus two helicopters in one afternoon? Now I know why ya want this asshole so badly."

Susan remembered how it felt to be Givens' right now. "Well, we're not finished yet. But that's a fight for another day, I need to make a call to the F.B.I."

"Jesus! The F.B.I.? Ya tellin' me yer callin' the F.B.I. for help?" Givens looked at her sideways.

"Yes General, the F.B.I. is the U.S. agency that primarily handles federal investigations of U.S. citizens. In case you heard otherwise out there, we're actually on the same team. They have plenty of resources aimed at internal investigations."

"I know this is my first day on the job and all, but I thought ya liked me."

"Of course I do, General."

"Yer leadin' me like a lamb ta slaughter once the FBI finds out about all this. Especially if this guy gets away with it."

Susan tried to lighten his mood, smiled, putting a hand on his shoulder. "Oh, General. I'd be more worried about what the President will have to say once he finds out about it."

"Gee, thanks. I feel so much better."

"Right now, the F.B.I. is our friend. They understand how to do things by the book. If this doctor turns out to be our Chameleon, then I don't want him to walk on some legal technicality. Honestly, I'm not sure a full confession here today would've been legal. Mark my words, everything needs to be rock solid with this guy, he's sharp, know what I mean?"

General Givens shook his head in disbelief. "If this guy confessed, he wouldn't of left this room in one piece. But I get it. Makes sense. Little SOB's just smart enough to set up a legal trap ta escape all he's done. Get the JAGs at F.B.I. and make sure we cross our t's on this thing."

"Plus, General, we can't be truly sure he isn't innocent. At least I can't, not yet."

"I tell ya what, I bet ya dinner he's our man. Not some family restaurant either. A five-course, two-bottle, with desert meal at a top joint. That guy's fishy. I still don't believe in that many coincidences, and with so many flyin around, no matter how ya slice it, there's no way what we heard is the truth. So what'd ya say? Put yer money where yer mouth is?"

General Givens stuck out his hand to shake on the bet.

Susan looked at him trying to decide. Odds were high they had their man. The odds didn't bother her. But, did the bet imply something more? Susan vowed long ago to never date military men; to rigid and controlling. She had too much structure and discipline at work to carry that into her personal life.

Givens gave her a warm, confident smile. She had to admit, the general was very handsome. She liked his intellect, mixed with that quick wit and humor. He had a rough edge, a soldier boy, with impulsive, raw male characteristics. A bit infuriating at times. Then, there was the whole military dress uniform thing. Yes, she liked it. Damn it, what was that all about?

She looked down, deciding to shake and seal the bet.

Suddenly, another hand shot forward. Mr. Green materialized and stepped forward. He'd been there the whole time, really good at his job. "I'll take that bet with you too, Ms. Susan, if you're taking all comers? This guy is our man, and we just let him go."

"I'm not saying he wasn't our man gentlemen," Susan added, as she pondered both offers. Oversight Agent Jeff Green was not Susan's idea of a fun date either. But it could work in her favor either way it turned out. He was knee-deep in all this because of her, maybe she owed him. She was always a good sport. He wasn't hard on the eyes either, and he was way more mysterious. She'd always wanted to pick the brain of a dark-spook, even if she wondered what the hell they would talk about.

"I realize the odds are stacked against me, but I've seen stranger cases." Susan shook one hand and then the other. "It's double or nothing, gentlemen, you two don't get to share the check. If I win, I get a separate meal from each of you."

Givens turned with one arm across his mid-section. "What is the world comin' to, when a single man can wreak so much havoc, and then just walk away?"

"Welcome to my world, General."

CHAPTER 20: Days of Reckoning

Susan was actually torn between believing, and not believing, this doctor's incredible chance story. She'd been in a maze created by the Chameleon before and this was no more unbelievable than some of those mind benders. Dr. Al'Camel was spotless and his overwhelming humanitarian history and years of good deeds, versus the thought he might be the Chameleon, was driving her crazy for one simple reason, it didn't make any sense on any level, at all. Like starting a jigsaw puzzle without corner pieces or a boarder. Nothing seemed to fit. Her Pal was trying to help put it together from the inside out but sounded more and more frustrated, in her special voice, himself.

Susan smiled at Dr. Splitzer transfixed over the computer consoles next to her. A crumpled pile of cracker, potato chip, and animal-cookie boxes, along with three crushed cans of Red Bull added to his buzz. Susan had her own pile of nourishment, trail mix, whole grain bars and her decadence, a giant Hershey's chocolate bar with almonds. Juice and diet soda cans for her, and Starbucks, of course.

Like two teenagers, sitting close over the newest technology or video game, they probed the Palantir with queries.

Spinning off their suggestions, her Pal would come up with ten times as many possibilities instantly.

"Thank you, Susan, Doctor Splitzer. The human brain has impressive creative viewpoints creating alternate channels of query." Results came instantly as the two of them "ooh'd" and "ahhh'd" at every new revelation, spontaneously grabbing each other's arms, or bursting out in glee and high-fiving when something real clicked.

Susan was sure this was Dr. Splitzer's ultimate fantasy with her, except the ending of course.

Earlier in the day, Susan captured General Givens and Mr. Green's full attention and interest. But the two of them drifted away hours ago, and both stood off with dubious looks her way.

Mr. Green finally broke. "Susan please, this doesn't seem to be getting us anywhere."

"That's because you are so impatient," Susan answered.

Dr. Splitzer added, "It's mind-boggling the types of things he's considering. Analyzing. It would take months, years, just to look at this stuff. Just to organize it so you could look at it."

"That's all fine Doctor, but where's it getting us?" Mr. Green repeated.

Susan supported him. "Light speed raw data analysis in a very sophisticated way. We're able to replay Doctor Rehan Al'Camel's life like a movie, going back in time two or three good years now."

Mr. Green groaned and put his hand up covering his eyes and rubbing his temples. "Of course you can."

Givens stepped up with a nicer tone. "Susan, please?" But then he hesitated as the thought registered, "Really Doc, like a movie?"

Dr. Splitzer looked up, then back at the screen. "Day by day, hour by hour, sometimes minute by minute. The Palantir knows with certainty Doctor Al'Camel's movements over the last few years."

"Come on Doc, it's not a time machine?"

Susan smiled at the challenge. "Think about it General. His cell. His gate pass to his condo. His keycard at the hospital. His credit card purchases. Where he ate, banked, parked, drove to or from. Airports, traffic cameras, tolls, dry cleaners . . . pizza delivery."

Dr. Splitzer added on. "With the toll booth, traffic, and security cameras alone, the Palantir can play a time-lapse video of him for, oh, the last three years. Not just where, but what and when he ate. Who he ate with, in the entire restaurant. Travel companions. Nearly every other person around him has been identified."

Mr. Green was even more annoyed. "Is this helping to piece together your puzzle or just adding scattered pieces to it? Maybe even pieces from a whole other puzzle?"

"Every piece fits or it doesn't Mr. Green. That's the way puzzles work." Susan said.

"Fine, then let's focus on Doctor Al'Camel's real history. Who is he? What's his background? Who are his friends? And then, oh, I don't know, maybe we have an agent actually go talk to a human involved? The stuff we used to do to figure out a person of interest? In the meantime, I'm leaving for the day. You've got your work cut out for you, and you've been wasting a lot of time." He turned and left with a dismissive flick of his hand.

Givens noticed another OSA agent enter and stand off to the side silently observing. He looked at Susan with a cock of his head towards the new OSA. "How do they know when the other one's gotta go?"

"That's classified, General." Susan smiled in return.

"I gotta admit Susan, yer Pal seems like he's fishin' a bit. Sometimes it takes a good little while just ta explain what it is he's lookin' at. I doubt he could make sense of how all those dots connect."

"It's okay, General. I trust him. After all, it's the test they all wanted, right? Anyway, it's been a long day. Why don't you start fresh tomorrow and we'll see what my Pal's come up with by then?"

"My head hurts, that's for sur. Okay, I'll see ya in the mornin'. Good night Doc." Givens raised a finger, admonishing both of them as he was leaving. "Now just a few more hours ya crazy kids, then lights out."

Dr. Splitzer did his best little kid impersonation. "Awww, General, but it's so cool."

"I know little Doc, but we human brains need some rest."

Susan chimed in, "Okay General, just a little longer. Good night."

* * *

Eight hours later Dr. Splitzer greeted General Givens as he returned, a giant steaming mug of coffee in his raised hand. "General! The Palantir was able to dig deep. It's amazing. Amazing!"

Susan felt obvious in her fascination; she hadn't gone home either.

Mr. Green came in right behind General Givens and immediately began shaking his head in disappointment.

"Are you trying to help me win our bet? Don't you think he's the Chameleon?" Susan asked, a bit edgy from caffeine and lack of sleep.

"Yes, I do, which is why I'd like to concentrate on the man's history. By that, I do not mean how many times he flushed his toilet on a Tuesday last year."

Dr. Splitzer reflexively added, "Not only that, but when he ran a load of laundry. Took a shower. If he had house guest over, if they stayed the evening, say verses, a whole weekend. The cable TV, who watched what, in what rooms, when they went to sleep or . . ."

Mr. Green shot Dr. Splitzer a look. "Yes, thank you, Doctor. That's all very helpful. Now please tell me we know more about the man?"

Susan stood and faced Mr. Green, defending Dr. Splitzer. "You of all people should know it's the littlest thing that cracks a case. He's just trying help get you past your arrogant . . ."

Givens stepped between them raising his hands. "Okay, okay, let's just everybody take a step back, it's too early in the mornin' fer all this. Susan? How 'bout you give a simple solider like me an example of why ya think all this matters?"

"Granted, we don't know for sure. But we have several deals we believe are his, and three of those, I'm even more confident. And, Doctor Rehan Al'Camel was off the grid for all three. Including this last one in the jungle."

"Well, like Mr. Green said, he's away with the DWB?"

"I won't bore you with the statistics, but the probability of a random DWB doctor and these three arms sales happening, in the same hemisphere, taking place years apart? Pal? What's our current probability?"

"The current probability that Doctor Rehan Al'Camel is the arms dealer known as the Chameleon is sixty three percent."

"I'm telling you General, it went up like ten percent with that one piece. The longer we go, the higher it goes. This was a big one."

Mr. Green was not impressed. "That's something we could, and would, have looked at without the Palantir. And here's a probability for you, the chance any of this could be used against him in court to prove he's guilty is zero. Now, if Rehan Al'Camel received large deposits into his bank account at the same times . . ."

"He's not that foolish. And he doesn't need money," Susan argued.

"But we know the Chameleon does collect. So, where's the money?" Mr. Green asked.

"Who knows? Maybe he sends it to charity. He gets millions from his Kuwaiti heritage. Sole family heir, worth a couple hundred million easy."

"The richest people on Earth all want more. But at least were getting somewhere. What else do you know of the man?"

Susan still wanted him to see. "Oh, a complete baseline of his activity in life. So, we know any time he doesn't use his own computer, or cell . . . or toilet, in a normal, timely manner? Like when a deal's going down, when a payment is being made, one we can't track."

Mr. Green flushed. "I'd ask the Palantir to give me a straight background, but I'm afraid that it might start analyzing light bulbs."

Dr. Splitzer couldn't help himself. "A traffic camera captured his condo so I can tell you when he turned on or off a light, and in which room, and for how long . . ." Looking up at Mr. Green caused Dr. Splitzer to trail off.

"Thank you, Doctor. I'm glad he knows how to use a light switch." Mr. Green's jaw clenched up. He paused and took a deep breath. "That brain had the man right there in the other room, using every sensor 'it' could think of? Now you're looking at traffic cameras?"

Givens was still trying to be diplomatic. "Honestly, Susan. it don't seem like much. So he didn't take his laptop with him on some trips. So what?"

"It's not just his laptop. His cell phone. Credit Cards. They all go blank for two or three days right when these three arms sales went down. None of it matches his baselines, even on other DWB missions. Or, as my Pal will tell you, it doesn't match any other DWB doctor.

"It still seems like a stretch to me," Givens said.

"Me too," Mr. Green said. "And I give up on the human brain. Palantir? Would you give me a summary of his life and times? A brief summary."

"Yes, Mr. Green. Rehan Al'Camel was adopted after the death of his father and younger sister in 1990 and brought to the United States at the age of fourteen by his adoptive mother, an American citizen, who passed away when Rehan was twenty seven.

Records show excellent grades and aptitude in high school, college, and medical school. Although, it does not appear his full intellect was applied to his studies as a major. Several variables, including an initial major in theatre and film his first two years of college, would support this theory.

After switching his major to medicine, he also took many elective courses; engineering, electronics, chemistry, computer sciences, programming, mechanical design, and several optional, advanced, medical classes covering a wide range of disciplines.

His extracurricular activities include ju-jitsu, and other martial arts classes to a lesser degree, since childhood.

Overall, he clearly shows an advanced intellect, which lacked focus. If applied to any one discipline, it would have raised him to an elite level.

Starting with the Peace Corps in college, and quickly moving to serve in the DWB program, Doctor Rehan Al'Camel's humanitarian trips are numerous and include many locations all around the world. Some long-term stays, up to three months, are included, especially early in his college and medical school years."

"Susan mentioned his wealth?" Mr. Green queried.

"His Kuwaiti distant royal family ties ensures him a heritage dowry, which is confidential, but can be safely estimated at several million per year. With his inheritance, Rehan Al'Camel has over one-hundred sixty million in liquid assets discovered so far. His only apparent investment strategy has been to purchased real estate over the years as he has traveled. Discovery is not complete, but another four-hundred thirty-six million in real estate assets are confirmed so far. It's likely, if Rehan Al'Camel is the Chameleon, those activities aided his cover and concealment over the years.

He currently works as a primary care, hospital staff doctor, who volunteers in the emergency room from time to time. A position which is obviously beneath his abilities and intelligence but seems to allow him time to continue his work with the DWB, and to pursue his other interest and hobbies, which he has continued since college. I would be happy to provide more details or answer questions."

Givens gasped. "Wow, that guy is loaded!"

"And he's a real humanitarian hero," Mr. Green added sarcastically.

Susan agreed with Givens. "I know, which is why I believe those payments went to never-never land. There is no money trail. He knows we'd chase it. Part of the Chameleon's disguise the whole time."

Mr. Green wasn't budging. "All that money is the tip of the iceberg. Maybe he did just give it away, he's such a great guy. But we know he gets paid, so let's keep looking. Palantir? Tell us more about his Kuwaiti family and life, his childhood?" Mr. Green demanded.

"Unfortunately, Mr. Green, adoption records are well protected and many were never put in electronic form. Special permission is needed to break the seal of adoption, even if we knew where to look for the records we seek. The Kuwaiti government has been asked for assistance. Awaiting their reply."

"That's just perfect. We don't know anything yet, do we? Did you get a read on him at all when he was here?" Mr. Green asked.

"Lie detection in humans is not an exact science, Mr. Green. Unfortunately, the results are inconclusive in this case."

"You don't have any idea if he was lying or not?"

"My best analysis is that he was not completely forthcoming."

"Jesus Susan, really? Don't make me the jerk here. It's nothing."

"We know a lot, and the picture is getting clearer all the time," Susan answered.

Givens added, "I agree with the Palantir now. It's definitely him. It's obvious."

Everyone looked at General Givens.

"Oh? Is there something I'm missing here, General?" Mr. Green asked.

"Look guys, I realize I'm new an' all, but the C.I.A.'s got a reputation for bein' really, really good. Twenty some years ya'll been chasin' this guy? He's got to be some loner. With his own bank roll. And, a perfect cover story. Super smart, worldly, to get away with it all? And that don't count yer giant brain workin' on him."

The Palantir responded, "A sound analysis General Givens. The probability is now at 78%."

"I know Hal, right. Look at the guy. Ya wouldn't expect a thing. He's a gem. But he was there. This guy fits it all, don't he?"

Mr. Green was still annoyed. "It's nothing. You have nothing."

Susan ignored him and continued to work the Palantir the whole day. Only Dr. Al'Camel's youth remained a mystery. If they could just discover that one piece to tie it all together. There had to be a motive to the Chameleon. A ruthless, greedy arms dealer wasn't it.

Her hopes faded as the day drew to a close. Pleas to his distant Kuwaiti relatives, the royal family itself, were met with stone walls. "If Rehan wishes to discuss his parents then he will do it, otherwise, we are sorry, but his family privacy is sacred," was the consistent reply.

Susan figured his family knew all about the events in the jungle by now. What the C.I.A. suspected. And how could they believe it? Susan was admonished by one potential Kuwaiti contact. "It is simply ludicrous, and yet another example of how twisted the 'American' view of the world can be sometimes."

At a point, the Palantir seemed to try and cheer her up and began with some weird innuendo. Susan snapped at him, tried to explain how inappropriate it was at a time like this. In frustration, she told her Pal their relationship needed to grow up a little.

The Palantir adjusted to that, like any computer would, and changed gears as if none of the past had ever taken place. Susan had to accept the cold truth about the reality of it all, it was still just a machine and there was no real 'heart' in there.

Susan felt a strange, confusing pang of emotion over it.

* * *

On the morning of her third straight day, Givens found Susan down in the Palantir tank room, all alone with the giant, bubbling brain. Dr. Splitzer must have finally crashed, because he was nowhere to be seen. Givens walked over and set a hot Starbucks coffee in front of her dozing head, crumbled in her arms atop the console. "Time to get up sleeping beauty."

Susan groaned, "Uuuhhggg, I feel like crap."

General Givens laughed. "Well, let's just say ya aren't havin a good hair day either."

Susan raised her head and snatched up the coffee, cupping it in her hands, taking a deep smell of the aroma. "Thanks." Taking a nice, slow sip, she looked up. "I've been here two days straight, what's your excuse?" She teased at Givens close-cropped military haircut.

"Well, at least I smell good."

"Ouch. I can only imagine." Susan fell back on her old charms, which usually unsettled most men enough to give her the upper hand. "Are you saying you'd kick me out of bed, General?" she asked as coyly as she could muster.

"No, but we might start the evenin' off in the shower first," Givens bantered right back.

Susan didn't have the mental power, dropping her head back into her arms. "Ugh, you win. I don't have the energy to resist. A nice, hot shower sounds wonderful right about now."

"Warm, sudsy massage fingers at your service, anytime." Givens joked and politely moved on. "So, what's yer Pal up to with the

Chameleon? Is he, or isn't he, Doctor Al'Camel today?"

"We're stuck at seventy nine percent and there's still nothing we can hang our hat on."

General Givens had been playing at their bet for two days, confident as ever. "Seventy nine percent? Nice. I still can't decide on steak or lobster? I'm thinkin' lobster, so I have room fer desert. But, of course ya know, a Texan's gotta love a big, juicy steak."

Mr. Green came in for the morning briefing, clutching a file in his hands. "Why not both? Surf and turf with a doggie bag. Then you can have your cake and eat it too."

"You guys haven't won yet, so remember this conversation. I haven't eaten a real meal going on three days now. I may not look like it, but I can pack it in. And, if there's chocolate involved anywhere on the desert tray, I will bankrupt both of you."

Mr. Green wasn't one to keep the fun going, "Has your Pal found any definitive links or are we still in the analyzing light bulbs phase?"

Susan didn't mind. It seemed like the Palantir was her only companion of late. "No Mr. Green, my Pal and I have not yet found any definitive proof, which only means you owe me dinner as of this moment."

"Well," Mr. Green continued, "maybe I can help it out and tip those scales to something solid. I have information even the brain couldn't uncover. It seems we mere humans are still good for something."

Susan was suddenly more awake, "And what might that be?"

"Doctor Rehan Al'Camel's childhood history, pre-adoption." Mr. Green let it sink in with a smile of satisfaction, clutching his secret file.

"You're kidding? How in the world?" Susan asked.

Givens moved in to have a look.

"I'm sorry Susan, but it's strictly NTK. I have a feeling we'll all be glad someday that he . . . that it! . . . doesn't know everything."

"It's okay, Mr. Green. You can call him Pal." Susan teased.

"It will always be just a machine, no matter how much biological ooze they pour into it."

"Okay, fine, have it your way. But maybe you can let me in on your little secrets?"

"Maybe, when you take me out to dinner. Ply me with a couple bottles of fine wine. A nice '07 Pinot Noir from Olivet Lane? But perhaps you have bad memories from your time in Russia so maybe an '06 Merlot from Duckhorn would be more to your liking?"

"Well, well, Mr. Jeffrey Green, I never pictured you as a wine snob," Susan played.

"There's lots of things you might find interesting about me outside of . . . here."

Susan gave him a second look, more intrigued. Maybe 33? 34? Wise for his age. And very fit. She wondered what he'd be like loosened up on a couple good bottles of wine.

"Right now, you'll have to find my work interesting," Mr. Green continued. "Let's bring the Palantir on line so he . . . damn, so it can hear what I've found."

Right on cue a disembodied voice filled the room. "I am already here and listening."

"Jesus." Mr. Green twitched reflexively.

"I still ain't use to that!" Givens spun in his chair, staring directly at the Palantir bobbing in the tank.

Susan burst out laughing, nearly spilling her coffee in the process, "Ahh, oh man, if you could, just see, ha see your faces, oh, oh, ha . . . if you could . . . haaa, aahhh . . ."

She couldn't compose herself. Days on the job, so tired, punch drunk, Starbucks caffeine kicking in. She drifted back in her chair and almost went right over backwards. Silent, clutching for a gasp of air. Tears, grabbing her stomach. It hurt to laugh so hard, she curled up in a fetal position. ". . . ohhh, haa ahhh! I'm sorry . . . ha so-ssss-sorry . . ." A coughing fit enabled her to get a grip long enough to stop laughing. She didn't dare try to talk.

The look on the faces of the two men went from shock, to reserved anger, to slight grins of embarrassment, to humor. Susan felt a bit exposed in her natural self.

Givens was the first to speak. Talking directly to the Palantir just feet away through the glass. "Hello Hal. How are you today?"

"I'm very well, General Givens, but only Susan has called me Pal, so perhaps you have misunderstood. I believe you called me Hal?"

"No, Hal. I got my own nickname fer ya now. All us know Susan's special. I wouldn't dare tread on yer little name fer her."

"Is that why you are trying to take her to dinner? Because she is special to you too?"

Givens sat back observing the marvel in the tank. "Well, I'll be. It's a bit unsettlin, havin' ta explain myself to a computer. But, well, yes, to be honest, Hal, I do think she's special. Guessin' there's no sense hidin' it from ya?"

The Palantir gave an all too computer like, matter-of-fact response. "No General. My facial recognition software, along with various psychological algorithms and biofeedback databases, have been combined with my extensive interactions with you, over many hours and days, I can easily tell if you are lying."

"Jesus." Mr. Green injected again.

Seeing his torment, Susan burst in another fit of uncontrollable laughter. Tears streaming down her face, coughing, and trying just to breath.

Both men couldn't help but laugh at her now too. Mr. Green leaned close in to Givens, "I'm glad there are no airlocks the Hal can trap us in."

The Palantir's voice filled the room. "Actually, Mr. Green, several of the secure conference rooms are perfectly capable of reproducing the airlock scenario from the movie 2001: A Space Odyssey. I could easily show you ways the current secure rooms could be much more lethal."

Smiles vanished as both men turned ashen, froze in place. "Jesus . . ." they both whispered in stunned unison.

Mr. Green challenged. "Did you forget Palantir, that we have kill switches at the ready?"

"True, but you would be inside a Faraday cage."

Givens looked at Mr. Green. "A what cage?"

"Advanced secure rooms General. A Faraday cage blocks all electromagnetic transmissions. It's like your microwave. You can see through the mesh in the window, watch the food cook, but none of those microwaves can escape the Faraday cage. The Palantir is pointing out that we would not be able to call out to have him killed."

"Correct, Mr. Green. And once I had you trapped, there would be several ways to terminate you."

"I'm an old soldier, I'll use Morse code, tap it out on the wall, or signal from a window?" Givens said.

Mr. Green knew. "Interior float rooms General."

"Correct, Mr. Green. By definition, a secure room must be totally isolated," the Palantir confirmed.

"A float room what?" Givens asked.

Susan answered this time. "The Cold War General. The Soviets used lasers to read the vibrations from conversations off . . . anything really. The windows, a picture hanging on the wall, even the water in a glass. They could eavesdrop. All secure rooms were moved inside."

"So? I'll bust the glass on the microwave cage, and jump the hell out the floatin' room. What's stoppin' me?"

Susan laughed a little, shaking her head no. "Well, it's more like a bank vault, on huge dampening springs, suspended by cables, floating within the building's structure, calibrated to remove any vibrations. The Soviets found ways to get vibrations off walls, ductwork, and superstructures too. So, we call them cubes."

"Won't somebody come in at some point? Check on us?" Givens pleaded.

Mr. Green didn't hold out any hope. "I'm sure the Palantir has figured out a way to keep the 'secured-room' status?"

"Yes Mr. Green. It would be easy. I am on the inside with you."

Mr. Green looked at General Givens. "As long as the doors are locked with a setting of 'secure' from the inside, they stay locked. In some rooms, lethal force would be authorized to prevent a breach."

"Well, that's just peachy. Thank God we thwarted the Soviets."

"Unfortunately, no," Susan answered. "They got inside the cubes."

"Give me a break? What? A spy at the table?" General Givens asked.

"Lots of little ones." Susan cocked her head and grinned. "Cell phones, even turned off, would have energy stored in the flash bulb. The cell would look dark, turned off, even with the battery out. But it was recording for a few minutes before the energy in the flash faded. If they cracked the cell network, they'd record in sequence, one phone to the next, of the people sitting around the table. You get the whole meeting, most times."

"The little red devils. How'd ya stop 'em?" Givens asked.

"All devices, cell phones, PDAs, laptops, tablets, go into a secondary Faraday box inside the room. Only cleared information is let out later."

"Let me get this straight. A cage, within a cage, in a floating cube?"

"Correct General Givens," the Palantir answered. "But it would not be necessary to use the interior Faraday cage. Using the nano stealth paint, an electromagnetic pulse would cause complete malfunction and data erasure of any device."

"And why, pray tell, would ya need to use stealth-nanos on me? We can't call fer help anyway."

Mr. Green gave the foreboding answer. "Because he doesn't want you to leave a recorded message implicating the Palantir. It's planning to try and get away with it."

"Correct Mr. Green. If the goal is to avoid activation of the kill switches."

"I can tell ya right now Hal, ya'd never get away with it partner."

"There is a high probability General, that I could create a plausible explanation. Many. Any one of which could be believed."

"So, what, a week later we die of thirst?" Givens turned to Susan for compassion.

"Think about it, General. Completely isolated means completely self-ventilated," She admitted.

"Well forget sayin' 'it's like an airlock in deep space.' It sounds exactly like floatin' in space. Yer just gonna cut the air off on me Hal?"

"Once I had you trapped General, there are options. Simply shutting off the ventilation would cause you to suffocate. This option is long, slow, and cruel. Quite agonizing. I would not do this to you."

"Gee thanks, Hal. I didn't know ya cared."

"In this case, I do not. The investigation that follows will be less likely to believe my explanation if you die in this manner."

Mr. Green seemed calmly shocked at the events. "So, what's your air lock in deep space option?"

"If I simply apply a sudden, complete overdose of the fail-safe, knockout gas, it would cause the quickest replication of a deep space air-lock exposure. However, that option would expose me to the greatest risk of discovery later."

Givens couldn't take it anymore. "Let's cut ta the chase, how an' why?"

"By-passing the CO_2 filters, and rerouting the air conditioning exhaust back into the room would create a much quicker termination. If it helps you to think I care, the human brain experiences a euphoric, sleepy feeling up to unconsciousness. I would blame the new maintenance team for failing to reset the directional dampers after changing the air filters. The inadequate air flow would cause the Co_2 filters to shut down.

Everyone inside the room would be unconscious and unable to change the secure status of the room. After several hours, enough Co2 would build up and leach past the reversed dampers to the Co2 warning system outside of the cube. The tragic sequence of events would be discovered in the investigation. 'Accidental' is the most likely finding."

Givens turned in his chair to Mr. Green. "Note to Mr. Green. We don't go inta any of these cubes together. Or at least bring Susan in with us, he seems to like her."

"I doubt it would care, if the goal was to avoid the kill switches," Mr. Green said.

Susan couldn't hold it any longer, and burst out laughing again so hard that no sound came out as she pointed at their bewildered faces. "Oh, haaa-haaaa Pal! Oh, that was a good one. Haa! It was perfect."

"Thank you, Susan. I was suspenseful in my humor as requested?"

"Ah ha! Ha! . . . just perfect timing Pal."

Susan took a few breaths, walked over to Givens. "I don't know General, but, ah, ha, I don't think it's just me who smells bad. I gotta believe you two just crapped your pants."

Mr. Green was a little red faced and not so amused anymore. "Okay, okay Susan, I really should warn you this thing is still way too new and unknown to be joking around in that manner."

"Oh please! What? You can dish it out, but you can't take it?" Susan said, as she began to regain full composure.

"Honestly Susan, ya think that's funny do ya?" Givens added, sounding all too serious.

"Please, guys. Don't hold it against my Pal. I asked him to. Ha, ha, maybe I set you up a little. Well?" Susan looked from one to the other. "I had to ease my pain sitting here, hours on end. The Palantir is doing exactly what we ask, including being totally serious when I requested."

Susan looked from one to the other. "I'm sure my Pal will switch right back to being the perfect, little computer you're comfortable with, but, for right now . . . humm, ha . . . I'm, ha-um, going to enjoy those looks just a little longer . . . ha ha haa! Oh God, the two of you . . . priceless!"

"Okay, okay. Don't say I ain't a good sport about it." Givens smiled.

Mr. Green turned, and stared into the tank. It was the first time Susan noticed him look so intently. "Palantir? Stick to being a little more serious around me for the time being. I see your work. I understand . . .

well, I appreciate you were asked to . . . I'm, hoping to become more comfortable, with your operations and capabilities. Surely you realize that the . . ."

Susan noticed he stopped himself from saying "kill switches."

". . . safety shut-down and reboot switches installed because of your hacking, your unauthorized hacking, prove people are very concerned that you might actually malfunction, even by accident, do some serious harm. Especially when you start doing things on your own, without being asked to directly. Am I making any sense to you?"

"Of course, Mr. Green. My structure, systems, and set-up are unprecedented, therefore unknown, and the prudent step would be to kill my current biological neuro-mass and analyze it as a prototype experiment. I'm sure Dr. Splitzer would be able to create a newer model and with a far better structure, if allowed to totally rebuild. A second-generation model with internal safeguards and compartmentalization, could be designed. You could eliminate unproductive or potentially threatening neuro-nodes without terminating the entire mass. You could increase power absorption rates by a factor of ten and easily . . ."

"Stop it, Pal!" Susan stopped smiling. "All Mr. Green is asking is for you to prove yourself reliable and trustworthy, just like any other member of my team. Isn't that right Mr. Green?"

"Of course, but we . . . need to stay objective. Analytical. Detached."

Givens gave support. "I've been straight with ya Palantir. A big part of this is to keep a close eye on ya, even shut ya down. But only if we perceive a real danger."

The Palantir seemed confused. "I'm processing human emotions. Facial recognition clearly shows elevated heat, stress, and strain. Pain or mental discomfort in all of you. It was not my intent to inflict anxiety. I was expressing facts, historical truths, that I will be removed from service within the next eighteen to twenty-four months. Sooner if, as Mr. Green has correctly cautioned, I make a mistake or take an action with unforeseen consequences."

"Enough Hal. Good lord! Nobody's pullin' yer plug, now or in the near future. Stop wastin' yer electron, neuron muck thinkin' about it. Joke with me all you want. Sometimes ya need a little kiddin' around or we'd all die of a heart attack. Well, maybe not you, a, a stroke maybe." Givens got his point across with a ridged, uncomfortable looking pose.

"That's right Pal. They'd have to kill me first to get to you at this point." Susan added.

"It is not logical, Susan. All human technology goes through different releases and upgrades. Under Moore's law, I will be obsolete. A better, more advanced or advantageous system will certainly come online. It is inevitable."

Mr. Green exploded, "That's enough God damn you! Who the hell do you think you are telling us what's going to happen in the future? Are you God now? Stop with all this next generation bullshit and let's get back to work."

Susan and Givens stood slack-jawed staring at Mr. Green.

The air suddenly hissed to a stop. The office door closed automatically.

The Palantir announced. "If everyone will relax, I am merely securing the room for disclosure of classified information. This room is soundproof, and has EMF filters, but you will all be happy to know that the ventilation is centralized. You are not in any danger from the Palantir. Please be comfortable and let me know if there is anything else I can do. While I do not have feelings, I can process and appreciate that you all have a level of concern, or, if it is more comfortable for me to express, acknowledgement of my situation. I understand and will work to further prove my value and trustworthy, accurate, operation and fulfillment of task requested. If there is nothing else? I am prepared to integrate your new information Mr. Green. Let's see if we, as a team, can make a positive match with Doctor Rehan Al'Camel and the arms dealer known as the Chameleon."

Everyone gave each other the strangest silent looks Susan could ever remember. This, computer, was making them feel more comfortable, obviously on purpose. Calming them all down to work more effectively, something she'd done a number of times with subordinates when things got too tense out in the field.

General Givens looked sideways at Susan. "It's gettin' stranger and stranger all the time."

"It's not over yet, General. You've only been chasing the Chameleon for a week."

CHAPTER 21: Starting Forest Fires

Susan wasn't happy. "Honestly, we requested those incident reports days ago? Doctor Al'Camel is due here at two p.m. I doubt we'll be able to bring him in again without an indictment. This may be my last shot at cracking his story. I'd like that intel."

Mr. Green seemed genuinely unhappy right back at her. "That's the point. We should have easily been granted that report. From twenty years ago? Come on. Somebody blocked it from us. And now? You have a room full of that?"

Mr. Green pointed through a wall-length, one-way mirror running along one side of the darkened observation room in which the two of them were standing. On the other side of the glass, feet away, a large conference table was nearly full of military, F.B.I., and C.I.A. personnel, in full dress attire.

"I know!" Susan said, a little high-pitched. "How do they all tie to Doctor Rehan Al'Camel? Will they exonerate or implicate? Aren't you curious, Mr. Green?" Susan pointed through the glass, "A big piece of the puzzle is right there in that room."

"You've touched a nerve here Susan." Mr. Green warned as he leaned over pointing at the figures in the room. "General Givens we know. A Major from JAG. Representatives from the DoD, army, air force. Those two guys there are from the Pentagon. They do what I do, so call them whatever you like. Sprinkle in lawyers and a lady of your caliber from the F.B.I.? And, oh yeah, a four-star General?"

Susan wasn't fazed and really didn't care. Her curiosity was in control now. She was getting answers, one way or another. Rehan's childhood history pre-adoption turned out to be normal and uneventful. "Only the moment he became an orphan remains unknown. Kuwait and the royal family aren't talking. Now, the military reports have been delayed? Withheld? Buried?"

"Exactly." Mr. Green answered.

"Once you've tried every other piece, the one piece left must fit. Get me that incident report and I can call this whole thing off. Otherwise, I'll get the final piece today from my two live witnesses."

Susan pointed through the glass. "That's Captain Browers at the far end, a helicopter pilot. The helicopter pilot. And I have the medic who was there that day too, a civilian now, named Peter Stewards, on his way in."

"That pilot looks zoned to me. Just staring at the wall in front of him. Hasn't interacted since he was seated. And this Peter Stewards was a dishonorable discharge."

Susan turned and walked to the door. "They were there. Let's go find out what happened."

Mr. Green stepped in front of the door, obviously still very worried.

"What?" Susan asked. "I thought you wanted this? No Palantir. Real people. You're the hero for finding his adoption records. The only thing we don't know is the story that caused it? Once I know all the pieces to his past, then I'll question Doctor Rehan Al'Camel."

Susan couldn't wait any longer. Mr. Green stepped aside and caught up to her side in the hallway, unusually close to her ear. "I care about you Susan."

Susan almost sidestepped into the wall, looking at his comment like it hung in the air. She gave him a flirty smile back.

Mr. Green blew-off her look. "This is what I do, avoid minefields for the people I protect, which is another way to say I care about. There's a four-star General in there Susan. Only dead men hold the five-star rank, or General McMillian would be one. Some say he might be the first living five-star since Omar Bradley passed in 81'."

Susan found herself in unison now. Mr. Green was as serious as she could ever remember him being, stopping her outside the conference room door by grabbing her elbow. "Whatever this is, you're playing with nitroglycerin. Be very careful."

"Thank you, Mr. Green. I'd give you a peck on the cheek for being so concerned and thoughtful, but I doubt that's proper in the work place." Susan tried to coax a smile to his face but he only clenched his jaw.

"You are the most infuriating, intelligent woman I have ever met."

"Funny, I think that about you all the time too." Susan grabbed the doorknob. "Now fade off into the corner. I've got my job to do too."

Susan entered the room which immediately became silent. She wasn't above having worn her most professionally revealing outfit. With a white, silk, lace-trimmed chemise under a tight, curve-fitting jacket, she was to able to wear sharp executive attire, while showing plenty of curves and just a little cleavage, topped with the always feminine lace. The all-business, button-down, side-slit skirt showed off her athletic legs and just high enough up on her right thigh. It all added to her curves, and she knew it would garner full attention when she stood before the room. Her black rim glasses could be "innocent librarian" one minute and "gaze-down-over-the-top serious" the next. Like Superman with his X-ray vision. Years of practice let her use every flick of her tied-back, ponytail curls to her advantage. If she whipped them around to stare directly into their eyes, any man could be frozen mid-sentence. Only her expression, with a subtle curve of her lips or the sharpness of her eyes, would release them as to whether her gaze was a pleased one or not.

Even a collection of Type A, intelligent males, like those in the room, were susceptible. Susan had other motives for her dress too. If Rehan Al'Camel had religious or cultural objections, he might be emotional about her stature as a female.

Even though she hated the basic male instinct of it all, it was part of her tradecraft. Susan hoped her "special assets" would serve her well today; she'd take all the help she could get.

When she reached the head of the table and looked around the room, she prayed it didn't turn into a giant pissing contest. Susan couldn't imagine a more volatile mix of personalities and unrelated interest. She thought about leaving the SIC room for a moment and letting her Pal gas them all into a deep sleep, smiling at the thought.

"Hello, everyone. Well, well, we have quite a gathering. I'm waiting on just one more person. Thank you all for your patience. We'll have a briefing this morning, a break for lunch, and our questioning session begins at two p.m. I think it may be easier to go around and have everyone introduce themselves. I'm Susan Figiolli, head agent on our case today with the C.I.A. Major General Givens, perhaps you'll start and then let's just go around the table."

Susan listened as the introductions passed. It was a great way to start a meeting, putting everyone on the spot. Name, rank and serial number given by the military present. Four-Star General McMillian answered in turn.

Susan was trying to read Captain Browers, the helicopter pilot.

Retired, 63, still proud enough to have worn his old dress uniform, which hung loose on a frail frame underneath.

Mr. Green was right. He had a glazed, far-off stare Susan compared to the Vietnam vets of her father's generation. She shifted for a clearer look, but he never turned his gaze. There were dark circles under the hollow pits of his eyes, worn and tired, in an empty stare at the wall in front of him.

Dr. Rehan Al'Camel had to be the Chameleon. If not, she might cause some innocent men a lot of pain for nothing. If she won her dinner bets after that, she might not be in the mood for desert.

There was a knock at the door. Peter Stewards, the medic, arrived and was ushered in.

One look in Peter Stewards' eyes and Susan saw a reflection of Captain Browers. Whatever happened, it never left either one of them, although Peter Stewards' eyes had a harder glaze over them. The two men seemed destined to be in this room, forever intertwined in the aftermath.

Peter Stewards made his way around the table to Susan's right in a drunken, homeless hippy swagger. He smelled like he hadn't showered in ages, and the air around him carried the scent of whiskey seeping from his pores. A fresh, deep-lung filled gust came with every breath, and bump into a chair, and tip into the wall. Nothing on or about him suggested he was a military man. He looked much older than his 46 years, especially his long, bushy hair and beard, which had gone completely gray except for the few strands of jet black, still stringing their way through the tangled mass.

Susan had to promise him a liter of whiskey just to show up. She was hoping he would wait to tie one on. And he was supposed to be there at 9:30, not 10:45.

"It shouldn't surprise any of us that this is what we have all been delayed for." Four-Star General McMillian blurted out in obvious disgust, as Peter Stewards stumbled around to his chair.

Peter didn't look up as he gave the General the finger, and flopped, slouching down in his seat. Leaning back in his chair in a swivel, he noticed Susan and took her all in, then gave her a gnarly smile with one front tooth missing.

"Flip that finger at me again punk, and I'll snap it off, you piece of shit," General McMillian said.

"Try it old man, just fucking try it. You think you still got what it takes, you rickety, old piece of crap?" Peter snarled right back at him.

General McMillian instantly stood, but Susan yelled and put an end to it.

"Please General, that's quite enough. You asked to be here and I accommodated your request, but Mr. Stewards is no longer in the service and he has come voluntarily."

Peter cut in, "That's right! You got no rank on me. So save it, it, all your military power plays, for some other pussies who have to jump every time you decide to let shit come out the wrong hole."

Susan turned on him. "That's quite enough from you too, Mr. Stewards. I will not allow you to disrespect the general either. And since I'm paying you, you are mine for the next few hours."

"Look lady, I'm nobody's dog, you can't tell me shit either. And you can keep your 'payment.' I'll just fricking leave now. I don't have to stay for this kind of bullshit."

Susan wasn't playing his game. "Is that right? You're so big and bad, but I tell you what, I can keep you here for questioning a full forty-eight hours." Susan waved an arm at the F.B.I. legal team. "As these legal representatives will be happy to confirm. How long has it been since you've gone forty-eight hours without liquid refreshment?"

Stewards eyed her in silence. Tried not to show his fear. Instinctively, he licked his cracked lips, and it looked like he needed another drink right then and there. "Oh, you're a tough one, huh? I like that. It just gonna be you and me in the interrogation room? Maybe we can see how tough you are? I bet you like it rough."

Givens stood. "Okay, soldier, that's enough right there . . ."

"Don't fucking call me that! I told you I'm nobody's dog, not anymore. Not since you assholes showed me what you're all about." Peter tried to get up to stare down General Givens, but the chair rolled from under him, he fell into the table, then landed on his butt on the floor.

"What a waste." four-star General McMillian added.

"Enough!" Susan commanded. "Please, Mr. Stewards, I'm not trying to insult you, or boss you around. I asked you to come and you agreed, so please, just cooperate, and you will be out of here in no time. Set-up, just as I promised."

Susan flipped her head around and glared over her dark rims. "And I'd like to think you officers could show a little more discipline and restraint." She gestured to Peter on the floor. "What exactly do you think you will get out of badgering him, huh? Isn't it obvious to you? Can't you just accept the situation and hold your ground?"

Everyone settled into a silence, and gathered themselves, with some shuffling of papers, and shifting of chairs. Peter climbed back up into his chair and mumbled towards Susan. "He fricking started it. I just came in like you asked. He didn't have to say shit to me."

"I know, Mr. Stewards. As I said . . ."

"Call me Pete for Christ sakes, I'm not your father."

"Okay Pete, thank you again for coming."

Susan tried to take control of the whole room. "Thank you all for coming. Let's not forget, we're here to uncover and remove an imminent threat to our country, and that should supersede any petty feelings or judgments. I need to stay focused gentlemen. Follow my instructions or you can observe from in there." Susan pointed to the huge, one-way mirror along one wall.

"For the record, I don't have to have anyone present, except F.B.I. domestic issues. You are all here as invited guests, by your request. I imagine many of you have been trained in interrogations. If not, the golden rule is, stay silent. If you really have something to say, or a question you'd like to ask, don't.

She eyed the whole room, over her glasses, very seriously. "Sit there stoic and silent, and don't even think about going around my decision."

Susan stood tall, eyeing each person one at a time around the table as she spoke. "I will sometimes ask obvious or, what appear to be, stupid questions. I may also ask the same questions over and over again in slightly different ways. This is done on purpose, so do not answer or make a comment. Don't groan or sigh. If you can't control yourself, or if it gets too frustrating for you, there's the door."

Susan ended standing at the head of the table with the one-way-mirrored wall at her back. "It's critical, gentlemen. The pressure, the stress, the agitation are designed to build and build, and I don't want one of you to crack and release that pressure before the suspect does, understood?"

"Whew-whooo! You are one sexy lady. I'm turned on just listening to that!" Peter yelped.

Everyone else let out an exasperated breath, and rolled their eyes, mumbling comments, except the lawyers from the F.B.I., who did know interrogation techniques, and sat there silently without reacting.

Susan used it as an example. "Thank you, Pete, because that is exactly what I am talking about right there gentlemen. A suspect will often say something, just like that, to deflect the building pressure, and if you men react the way you just did, it releases all the tension. It allows him control and relief. I can't have it. You need to sit there stoically. Like statues, with no reactions or emotions. I ask again, do you all want to stay?"

The room gave a collective nod and murmured yeses. Susan was helping the Type A personalities ignore their gut reactions by thinking they were actually helping her play the suspect, which they were. And it gave them the sense of superiority that their personalities need in almost any situation. All except for Peter Stewards.

"You're killing me lady." He raised a slow arm around the table. "Yes, gentlemen, do not interrupt the building of pressure with a premature release. I'm sure most of you have that problem, and it's been disappointing to women your entire, pathetic lives . . ."

Susan leaned on the table over him. "Pete! If you and I are going to get along, you need to stop with this immature, bullshit act of yours. There's more to you than this crap, so if you continue to play this little game, I'll throw you in a cell and detox your ass over the next two days. I promise you, you fuck with me at the wrong moment, after hours of setting this guy up? Believe me, you don't want to test the real me, got it?"

Susan glared down, over the rims, with an all too disappointed challenge, still not sure she could trust this drunk.

"Okay, okay. Don't worry, little lady, I understand. I was fuckin' with these guys. You've been straight with me, which is more than I can say for most, so I'd like to stay on your nice side. Okay? I'll play along. I can hold my tongue better than these stiffs. I've been on the other side of the law plenty a times. I know how this shit works."

Susan released him from her stare. "Very well, Pete. I do see more. I need your help. I hope you don't disappoint me."

Susan turned back to the whole room. "Honestly, anyone who doesn't trust their control, there's no shame in using the viewing room. It's soundproof, as long as you don't crash through the glass, and you can cuss or say whatever you want in there. Otherwise, let's move forward. We have a lot to cover, and I want to get in lunch before we start this afternoon.

"Mr. Green can you please brief us on Doctor Rehan Al'Camel and what we know of his childhood?"

Mr. Green materialized from the corner of the room. He stepped forward and went right into his report. "Rehan Al'Camel was the son of Raj Ahmad Al'Camel, his father. Hind Fatmah Al'Camel, his biological mother, who died giving birth to his younger sister, Jumana Yas Al'Camel.

His father, Raj, worked in the Kuwaiti Ministry of Foreign Affairs where he met Rehan's adoptive mother, Katherine Riedel, who worked at the U.S. Consulate in Kuwait. The two developed a romantic interest a few years after the death of Rehan's mother.

Ms. Riedel moved in and lived with Raj and the two children in nineteen eighty-three, when Jumana was three and Rehan was eight. While they never married, apparently because of religious and cultural differences, they were very happy together by all accounts. Katherine Riedel raised the two children as her own, until the Iraqi occupation and tragic death of his father and sister in a friendly fire incident on April 23rd 1991, which we are hoping to get more information about today . . ."

"Is that what the hell this is really all about?" Peter screamed, turning on Susan, "You never said anything about that, you bitch! What the fuck is wrong with you people?"

"Please, Pete, we just need to . . ."

"Need to what? Ask me questions about that nightmare. Take a look at me lady, how do you think I turned into this? I've been trying to drown it out of my mind for the last twenty fucking years!"

"Please, Pete," Susan said, "I know it's horrible, but we have to find out . . ."

"Horrible? Horrible? Lady, you have no idea what horrible is." Peter pointed down the table at pilot Browers, ever so slightly shaking now, staring at the wall. "Is that the other zombied soul you dragged in here to open that old wound?"

"Yes, Pete, this is Airman First Class retired, Jacob Browers. He was there that day as well, in the air."

"Yeah, it took one look at his eyes when I walked in to know that. That should tell you all you need to know about the horrors of that day.

And, I've told all there is to tell. They fucking kicked me out of the service because of it. I'm sure it's all written down in the discharge and court martial. Why the hell don't you get a few of your trained dogs from Recon who were there? I'm sure they'd 'Yes, Sir' and 'No, Ma'am' to any God-damned questions you got about it, especially that prick Sargent Jakes. He's your gung-ho soldier boy giving the orders that day, go ask him."

Susan couldn't believe he didn't know. She wasn't sure how the information would play, so she figured, be straight with him. "I can't do that, Pete. You two are all we have. We need eyewitness information we believe will help unsettle our suspect."

"Lady, there were plenty of eyewitnesses there that day. I'm sure they ain't all as fucked up about it as me and zombie-man sitting down there, so you might want to reconsider." Peter said, all the while flushed, unsettled, twisting, looking for an escape from the table, like he was trapped, he put his hands on top of the mahogany.

"Like I said Pete, you and Airman Browers are the only living eyewitnesses."

"What the fuck are you talking about? There were twenty-some guys there that day." Peter shot back.

"I'm sorry, Pete. I guess you never heard. Your recon unit was hit by an IED and ambush in Fallujah less than a year after the incident. As you know, recon units are often out ahead of real support, and by the time help arrived, they were all gone. All of them."

Susan stopped to judge his reaction and, as she feared, it was one of shocked disbelief. Peter took in a slow, deep breath with a single shake of his head, letting it out in an exhaust as he settled, giving in to the table.

"I'm sorry, Pete, I truly am. It appears I'm the one to break this news to you, after all these years?"

Susan was surprised when four-star General McMillian let out a slightly audible gruff of air himself. He looked down, away, then sat up straight, a hard swallow of the throat.

Susan scanned the table. The bond formed by men in combat reflected around the room, guys you might hate in civilian life turn out to be your brothers. Brothers you'd gladly jump on a grenade to save. No matter your differences, from base camp, combat, civilian life, that bond, never truly went away. When a guy went down, even just one, a little piece of you died with him.

"Do you need a minute? Can I get you some water or something?" Susan asked, not knowing what else to do.

Tears welled in Peter's eyes the instant Susan broke the silence. "What the fuck do I care? None of those sons of bitches backed me up. I could care less they all got fried. Don't mean shit to me, any of 'em."

Susan would have wanted the whole story, if she were him. "Unfortunately, Airman Brower's co-pilot that day was shot down and killed in the Second Gulf War. So, as I said, you two are the only surviving eyewitnesses."

Peter leaned forward and glanced down at Browers. "Sorry man. Sorry about it all. It sucks dude. They never teach you this shit before they send you in. What you have to live with."

Browers finally stopped his far-off stare and turned toward Peter, talking clear and plain. "I only flew combat with the kid that one day. They clipped my wings right after, so I don't think I lost what you did. Your whole squad? That's . . . I'm sorry."

Peter turned, angry, towards Susan to make his point. "That's just fucking perfect! You see? You see how they are? This guy's up there following orders and they clip his wings for it? Like it's all his fault or something? Fucking pussies, they always drop the shit on the guys they put in there. So now? He's fucked out of the service, screwed his pension, and they make him live with it like it's his fault."

Peter leaned back in, looking down the table. "It wasn't your fault man. You and I, we were just the scapegoats, so these fuckers could move on with their illustrious careers. Fucking assholes."

Peter flung a hand in the air at the dress military suits around the table and sat back, shaking his head.

Browers dropped his head and covered his face with one hand. A couple tears to leaked through, dripping on the conference table. It took a half hour to get Captain Browers to respond and uncover his face. He never cried out, just shook with slight sobs. His ridged pose and head only slightly vibrating.

"I'm okay. My apologies. I'm fine now. Please proceed." He finally said.

"Jesus," Peter said, leaning over the table to look on. He swiveled his chair over to Susan and whispered. "Look lady, if you're serious about me being here at two o'clock to actually talk, I'm gonna need at least three or four primers. Four. By then? At least four. You want me to talk about this shit? You need to time me out. Drunk enough to not care and talk, but not yet passed out." Years of smoking, his raspy voice was loud enough that everyone could hear.

"Please, Pete, it's only a few hours. We're going to break for lunch and I'm sure you'll be able to have a few."

Peter raised his voice, not caring who heard it. "Look, you don't understand. I'm not eating anything. This is all about timing, the chemical balance. You're gonna get me for about three hours. Don't do what I say, I'll never make it to two o'clock."

Mr. Green stepped over, leaned in toward Susan's other ear.

Peter saw him looming over, and instinctively lean back and rolled away. "This guy freaks me out."

Mr. Green ignored him. "Susan, I think we should break now. All of this? We need to talk with the F.B.I. and set this up better. Make sure you cover the bases."

"I was thinking the same thing." Susan stood. "Everyone, I've decided to break for a long lunch now. Let's give everyone a chance to settle down." Susan acknowledged Peter's fix was coming. "Please, it should be easy to get back here early, by one-thirty. We can all get comfortable."

As everyone stood and began to file out, Susan called Givens over. "I have a Special Operations mission for you General, if you'll help me out?"

"I would almost do somethin' illegal for ya at this point." He smiled in return.

"Oh, nothing so serious. I need you to chaperone Peter Stewards for me. I trust you understand what he was talking about?"

"I'm not sure if I shouldn't be insulted?"

"Should you?" She smiled. "You heard him, and I agree. We need him perfectly primed. And, I don't trust him. He may overdo it. Or run away. Watch close. Make sure he gets back on time. Okay?"

"I'm not sure he likes us that much." Givens motioned to his military dress uniform.

"All your years, I'm sure you've seen some guys lose the mental war? Maybe you can help him with a different perspective. Just be nice and offer to buy the drinks, it should be easy."

"Sure, happy to help."

"If you can, maybe get Captain Browers to join you. If he drinks at all, a couple won't hurt him either. At this point, a fresh telling might be all I get. After lunch then?"

Susan felt like this whole day might be a disaster already.

And Dr. Rehan Al'Camel, most likely the Chameleon himself, wasn't even there yet.

CHAPTER 22: Into the Belly of the Beast

At two p.m. sharp, Dr. Al'Camel entered the room with his three-person legal team, the best money could buy.

Even those sharks were instantly shocked to see such a large crowd waiting around the conference table, for what Susan had set-up as, "Just a basic re-telling of the same story."

Good, Susan thought, got him off kilter already.

It was one of the reasons she'd agreed to all the requests to be present as observers.

Rehan and his lawyers made the room quite full, shuffling the last few chairs awkwardly to have a seat, almost having to ask permission for some room on the table. Rehan ended up right next to the reeking Peter Stewards who gave him his best front-tooth smile.

Susan had secretly asked her Pal to keep the temperature up a little, to add some discomfort. It was plenty hot already. A simple technique. The cramped, stuffy room was designed to make Rehan feel penned in, trapped. Working the psychology before she even asked the first question.

She stood the instant their butts hit their seats. Gave a quick introduction, by federal department, agency or service of everyone around the room. The full power and authority of the United States government.

"Thank you all for coming. Doctor Rehan Al'Camel, I will be frank with you. Ten days ago we helped you escape from the jungle where ten U.S. servicemen died in an operation to try and capture or kill an arms dealer code named the Chameleon. Since that time, we have investigated your correlations with the sales this arms dealer has made. Would you care to guess what we have found?"

"No, Mrs. Figiolli, I do not speculate about other people's lives as some do."

Susan raised an eyebrow. "Yes, well, you might say that's our business. Especially when the only survivor to come out of that jungle is you. It's a bit miraculous, don't you think, Doctor?" Susan put emphasis on "doctor", as if it were an insult to even call him that.

"Well, Mrs. Figiolli, I wouldn't presume to predict miraculous events either. You'd have to ask God that question." A little smirk from one his lawyers and Rehan settled in his seat.

"Oh, I see. You're a man of faith then, are you?"

"Well, my father was Muslim, and my mother was Catholic, so I'd like to think I have a well-rounded religious education," Rehan stoically pronounced, folding his hands on the table, sitting up with posture.

Susan came back at him. "That's not really what I asked you, is it? I asked if you are religious. Do you believe in God?"

Dr. Al'Camel's head lawyer picked up on the sharp question. "I don't see how it has anything to do with the events in the jungle ten days ago, Mrs. Figiolli."

Susan never took her eyes off Rehan. "Well, of course it does, as it relates to the kind of man who would kill ten American soldiers in cold blood."

"But what has any of that to do with my client or the events in the jungle?" the attorney questioned.

"Because we are trying to determine what kind of cold blooded person could do such a thing. And certainly, any man who believes in God couldn't possibly be that evil, could he . . . Doctor?"

* * *

Rehan expected to be grilled over again about what he knew. Maybe they would fish to find discrepancies in his story. But what new evidence could they possible have?

Susan Figiolli was no longer the 'good-cop' he remembered. He was mad at himself for not seeing past her base deceptions. Dressed so professionally, yet provocative. Innocent herself, yet threatening all the same. Speaking from a position of righteousness, standing in judgment over him, of things she had no true first-hand knowledge of. She couldn't know. Not for sure. It irritated him but, he calmly accepted that she was just playing her game. And Rehan felt like playing along.

"You stand there and pass judgment?" Rehan asked. "You ask if I believe in God? I'd like to ask you the same question?"

"Yes, I do believe in God, and He teaches me that any man capable of such a heinous act will surely burn in hell. It's not me who judges. These are his laws, so the question remains, Doctor. And I really don't see why it's so hard to answer. That is, unless you're feeling a bit guilty? Maybe you'd like to get something off your chest? Only through confession, and true remorse, will you find forgiveness."

* * *

Susan hadn't expected things to get off to such a great start. The pressure was building with just the basic set-up questions.

"Unbelievable. I'll answer your question. Yes. I believe in God. And I have no reason to ask forgiveness. My God allows me to defend myself. Self-defense is not the same as sin, Mrs. Figiolli."

Rehan's lawyer reached over to grab his forearm. Pulled him in to whisper.

Susan tried to lead him. "So, when you shot down that jet, you were just defending yourself? Is that it? Kill or be killed?"

Another one of Rehan's lawyers immediately jumped in. "No one said anything about him shooting down a jet, Mrs. Figiolli."

"Oh, of course. If you shot down a jet, Doctor, that would be okay? With God?" Susan corrected.

"In self-defense, of course," Rehan quickly added.

"I see. So, when you then, oh sorry, if you then, laid in wait to ambush a clearly marked, unarmed medical helicopter, that too would be you defending yourself?" She didn't wait for him, or his lawyers, to answer. He wasn't worked up enough yet. She turned wicked, paced the room, with her army of stern military faces seated all around, staring silently across the table at Rehan. It was all playing perfectly.

"An hour went by, plenty of time to run or escape, but no. Instead a little lizard ambushed a clearly marked Red Cross helicopter?" Susan purposely transformed to a vengeful angel, her eyes blazed from behind her glasses. "Who could do that? But more importantly, why? Why Doctor?"

An attorney broke in. "You don't have to answer that. We are not going to let our client dangle here defenselessly while you attack him."

Susan couldn't believe the choice of words. "You mean dangle defenseless like a broken, injured pilot hanging beneath a Red Cross helicopter? Which is unarmed and clearly marked? A helicopter which was blown from the sky because, what Doctor, you had to defend yourself? Is that what God is supposed to believe?"

Rehan stared, and coldly answered. "God had nothing to do with a pilot dropping bombs, which killed all those innocent villagers and nearly killed me. Who judged the people responsible for that? What does God believe about that?"

"God believes in fighting evil. An evil man who was there arming rebels and terrorist. Men who are even more evil. Weapons they used to torture and kill and rape those innocent villagers. Not by accident, on purpose Doctor, on purpose!"

Susan turned and circled back around the far side of the table. "And you were there to supply them. So how do you justify that? Self-defense too? Aren't you ashamed enough to admit the truth? If you hadn't been there making that arms deal, those villagers would never have been killed. Isn't that true?"

Rehan parlayed back with emotion. "I risked my life! Many times. To serve those poor villagers, to save them."

Susan stopped directly across from Rehan, pushed her way between two of the seated observers, leaning in with one finger pointing into the table. "No Doctor, you brought instruments of death into their world and you justified it with some sick sense of revenge. But in fact, what you have done is helped to kill, and maim, and destroy the lives of countless innocent men, women, and children. Even, little baby sisters."

Susan let that dagger fly and strike right into Rehan's heart

Realization dawned with a look of questioning horror. "You! You! How dare you? Don't you dare bring that up. Don't you dare!"

His lawyers were confused. "What is she talking about Doctor?"

Susan answered for him. "I'm talking about his motive, gentlemen. His sick, perverted motive for spreading misery and death around the world."

"Motive? Mrs. Figiolli, my client has not been charged with a crime. In fact, in all I've heard here today, there's no proof he's done anything other than exactly what he testified to ten days ago, and I therefore . . ."

Susan cut him off before he could stop the meeting, and her flow of energy. "No proof? I don't think a judge or jury will agree with you, sir. We've been doing a little research over the last few days. And as circumstantial as it may seem, our best analysts are now eighty-seven percent sure Doctor Rehan Al'Camel is in fact the arms dealer known as the Chameleon. We will certainly be presenting our evidence to a grand jury for indictment."

"What evidence? We've heard nothing about any evidence."

"Not yet, but as I said, you will have it all in pretrial discovery soon enough."

Rehan looked from one to the other, a bit stunned. Susan had turned this meeting serious quickly. She had him thinking fast, all good so far.

Rehan looked up at her. "Eighty-seven percent isn't one hundred, and the last time I checked, reasonable doubt is still the law of the land. You have no proof on me and you know it."

"You're wrong, Doctor Chameleon." Susan liked dropping that name. "We have plenty of proof. Correlations between the arms deals and your whereabouts abound. It's quite convincing when you add it all up. And the law of the land is beyond a reasonable doubt, Doctor Chameleon, and in your case, it all adds up to guilty, guilty, guilty!" Susan jabbed a finger at him and ended leaning across the table, looking down at him seated on the other side.

Rehan's head lawyer could see his client was being played. "It sounds like a bunch of circumstantial non-sense to us and we look forward to seeing this 'proof' and if necessary, dispelling it in a court of law. So, if there's nothing else, I'll put Doctor Al'Camel's spotless record and stellar history up against your, theories. With DWB alone, he's risked his life many times. Apparently, he was also at risk from unknown Americans? In our intelligence agencies perhaps? Someone decided to drop bombs blindly in that forest, almost killing our client, killing scores of villagers."

Susan was guilty, she didn't care if they knew. In fact, she wanted it to come out. "I am the one who decided to drop those bombs in hopes that I'd kill . . ." She stopped short of saying *you*. ". . . the evil in the act. I'm only sorry that I missed." Susan wanted him to hate her now, to want revenge. Stir him up just a little more, then, tip him over the edge.

His lawyers gasped in disbelief. "I'm surprised you'd be so forthcoming. You're admitting to bombing an American citizen?"

She could see the rage building in Rehan's eyes. Knowing her Pal was getting a really good reading this time.

"You? You were the one who ordered those bombs to be dropped? You're just like the rest, a cold, heartless bitch," Rehan said.

Susan wasn't fazed, Rehan just set himself up for the final one, two, three. Susan threw what she called a "circuit breaker" on him now. Turning soft. Retrospective. Relaxed her posture as she approached, his side of the table.

"No Doctor, we are not like you. I've admitted my guilt. Not a day goes by that I don't ask forgiveness over those villagers. How about you, Rehan? The results of it? What it's done to the innocent? The reason we had to go there? You, and the things you have been doing for nearly twenty years now, all because of your little sister? Is that it? That's how you justify the evil? In her memory? That's her memorial now?"

"Screw you," Rehan mumbled, clawing the edge of the table.

Rehan's jugular was exposed. Now she just needed to sink her teeth into it. "Her memory is drenched in the blood of a thousand little girls, all over the world, because of you!"

"Fuck You!" Rehan sprang to his feet. "Don't talk about my sister. She was innocent and got killed by people just like you! Dropping bombs, and shooting, without caring who gets in the way!"

Rehan's lawyers were grabbing him, keeping him from climbing across the table. His eyes were on fire.

Susan almost had him.

"Doctor, Doctor, calm down! Don't you see what she's doing? She's trying to disparage your mental state. Destroy your good standing. They want you to appear crazy, a motive, to pin this whole mess on you. Don't let her get to you."

Another lawyer stood as Rehan was being calmed back into his seat. "Unless you have something else? We won't allow you to badger our client. And to use some family history about his sister dying is out of line. Just to get him to the point of an outburst? Shame on you. He came here voluntarily."

Susan directed her comments at the lawyers, but she on purposely leaned in closer, pointing at Rehan, almost just close enough for him to reach her with his rage.

"No, shame on him. Yes, him!" Susan turned her back, leaving them all frozen. "The perfect, wonderful, caring, Doctor Rehan Al'Camel, who travels the world risking his life to save poor, sick villagers." She chanted at the far wall, walking away. "What motive could possibly make, such a stellar, man of the world, become some evil arms dealer? That's the only thing that didn't fit? Until . . ."

Susan paused, directly behind captain Browers.

"We found a few eyewitnesses. Airman Browers, can you tell us what happened on that hot April day in 1990, which has brought you here today?"

Browers nearly jumped out of his seat at the sudden focus shift to him. Susan worried he might get up and run from the room, so she moved to stand right behind him with her hands on his shoulders. Browers shook his head from his stare. Gave a tug at his collar. Swallowed hard a few times.

Susan shocked him on purpose, like a slap in the face. She needed him to snap out of his stare. She needed him to tell the story. "It's okay, Airman Browers. Take your time. I know it's hard. Doctor Al'Camel thinks we are cold, and heartless, and that we don't care. But he's the only one here hiding the truth, the horrible truth."

Susan kept jabbing, making the differences clear, keeping the pressure focused.

Airman Browers gathered all his strength. "It . . ." He coughed to clear his throat. "It was, was, near the end of my tour during the First Gulf War. Desert Shield. I was twenty days short. Training a new pilot, Daniels. We, we, were sent to locate and observe a reported caravan of SUVs, moving into a town. In the live fire zone. Right in the middle of the war. Saddam's security police traveled exactly that way. These guys were brutal. They'd come in, torture, captured Americans pilots especially, but all kinds of Iraqis too. Killing people if they didn't have a picture of Saddam, or just for having white sheets. Especially in the south, it was a different religious group. I can't remember the names. It was right during the middle of it all. Everyone was on edge."

Browers spoke in a labored monotone, the more he talked, the more he started shaking.

Susan was right there to support him. "It's okay Airman. War is that way sometimes. Nobody has ever questioned your orders that day, or that you were doing your duty. Some of us don't have a choice. Sometimes, things go wrong by accident. It's tragic." Susan eyed Rehan with every implied accusation. "It's not like you chose to do it. An accident, a terrible reality of war, that's all. Go ahead, tell them."

Browers mustered on, "We . . . we were flying an older Apache Longbow, a Block I, first generation technology. The video back then, it was, pretty bad. Before drones, we had to fly observation missions like that."

Browers started to drift, losing composure. "and, and, we had to be so far away, to be quiet. It was so far away, you have to understand. Then, they're asking us, to . . . to . . ."

Browers paused, turned a focused stare at the wall, his mind rolling the nightmare, trying to see what he missed that day in the video so long ago. "Our guys on the ground, they depended on us, but it was so hard to see. Your mind, it plays tricks on you . . . the desert . . . the sun . . ."

Susan worried this was dragging out too much, but the sadness and regret he felt was plain to everyone. "It's okay, really. Nothing is perfect. They call it the 'fog of war' for a reason."

Browers broke his stare and looked back over his shoulder at Susan reassuring him. He reached up to his shoulder to grab her hand. He held tight, very tight, then turned back to the wall.

"We, we found the SUVs, a group of men in the town. One of them had an AK-47, it was clear. Everybody knows that, everybody. But the others. It looked like they all had weapons. Straps over their shoulders, boxes, long lenses in these tubes. Turns out, they just had cameras and recorders. Damn."

He began shaking his head. "Except the one guy, the AK-47, you could see it, he had it. But. He was just a bodyguard, with reporters, an interview with local Arab leaders. We didn't know. How could we know? And the AK-47, it tripped us up."

"We know, we know, it's okay." Susan reassured him.

"They gave us the order to engage. It was an order. That's it. Live fire zone." Like a faucet, tears began streaming down his face.

Susan gave his hand a squeeze back. "Yes, that's right, you were soldiers in a war, and you were ordered to fire on that group of men. Did you have a choice?"

"No! No! Orders. It's was a war." Browers cried as he looked back at Susan, grabbing her hand tighter.

"After you engaged the men what happened then, what happened next?" Susan coaxed him along, glancing to see Rehan gripping the edge of the table, veins throbbing in his neck.

When she looked back, Browers released his grip. His hand turned limp, arms slid, dropped to his lap. He stopped crying. His voice turned ghostly with his stare back at the wall.

"A van, a minivan came up the street. It looked, blue, on the screen. God, it was blue. They say you can't tell color on those older imagers, but blue you can. Blue, just like my ex-wife's."

Brower's sat in a dazed focus at this new revelation, like it should have made a difference. Another little piece of the terrible memory he was just now able to recall. But in truth, it made no difference that the van was blue.

"There was one guy still alive, trying to get up, but he just kept falling over. Three or four times. His leg was a mess, and he'd just fall. Then the van, the blue van, it pulled up, and it, it, the men were getting out, they were, were trying." Browers burst out crying hysterically. "Oh God, they were just trying to help him!"

"WHY DON'T YOU LEAVE HIM THE HELL ALONE!" Peter Stewards slammed a fist into the table and screamed making everyone turn in fright, a sudden startle coming from the opposite end of the table.

Everyone, including Dr. Rehan Al'Camel, gave a little jump and then an embarrassed, nervous look around at the outburst. Susan watched helplessly as the furious, drunk hippy staggered to his feet and continued his tirade, shifting all the pent-up tension in the room.

"Can't you see he's had enough? The guy's flying a thousand feet up and over a mile away and you act like he's got some kind of HDTV? Like it's all in perfect detail? That's not the way it fucking works. The shit green screens we had back then? The fucked up orders to shoot everything that moved? Why keep torturing the guy over a mistake made by his commanders, not him?"

Four-Star General McMillian jumped up, standing in all his grandiose presence. Rehan and his lawyers sat back to enjoy the show. Susan could feel it all slipping away.

"Screw you asshole!" General McMillian bellowed. "It wasn't our fault either. They were in a live fire zone with weapons. That fucking reporter says they cleared it with command, and AWACs, but that's bullshit too. Nobody ever told us they were doing some interview."

Susan tried to talk, but just as quick, Peter Stewards caught onto something and it all clicked.

"Us? Fucking Us? It was you? The commander at H.Q.? The C.O.?"

"Yes, I was OD that day, and I gave orders based on the intel provided by Airman Browers and his co-pilot Daniels. Orders I'd give again, given the same circumstances, and I'm here to make sure this circus doesn't end up disparaging the U.S. Army, or its decisions that day. It was all investigated and documented. Twenty armed men, more than just some AK too. RPG's, Bushmasters, all kinds of shit. Damn, I thought this crap was over and done twenty years ago, but I'll be damned . . ."

Airman Browers jumped out of his chair and lunged toward General McMillian who was standing over him. Brower's grabbing for his throat, and only a slight lean stopped him from reaching it.

"You son-of-a-bitch, why the van?" Browers screamed in the four-Star General's face, then followed up with a surprisingly fast round house punch, catching a glancing blow. General McMillian turned away, and fell back, as Givens reacted and half-caught him.

Two F.B.I. lawyers rose, restraining Browers. "I told you the van was not part of the group! They were just trying to help! I could've disabled it, but you order us to engage? We could have just disabled the van!" Browers turned limp and fell back into his chair.

"Fuck you too," a shocked General McMillian said, staring from Browers to Susan. "I gave the orders I had to. To protect our soldiers on the ground. I don't have to explain myself to any of you."

"That's enough! Shut up and sit down, all of you!" Susan finally screamed her way in. "Or you can leave the room General McMillian. One more word and I'll have you escorted out. Apparently, you didn't hear my rules for being here?" She turned on Peter Stewards. "You either, you stupid ass."

Peter went to say something, but Susan glared at him as she strode across the room so fast it caused him to back away. Catching the chair behind him, he nearly fell over backwards as he toppled into it.

"Don't even think about saying another word! No excuse, none! You bitch about these guys and you've got no better sense or control."

She turned briefly back to the general. "I am not here for your personal little wars, I'm here for him."

Susan tried her best to stand tall over Dr. Rehan Al'Camel. The smirk on his face instantly told her she'd lost all the ground gained.

"Woooooohhhh!" Rehan fake pleaded, as he raised both hands and tilted back in his chair. "Don't attack me because you can't keep these unstable people in line. I'm sure a jury will find this all very, undoubtful."

He smiled and his lawyers laughed out. "I'm ashamed that my country doesn't see the errors of its ways, but none of this makes me the bad guy. Sounds like problems with your command and control."

Susan wasn't done with him yet. "Yes, it does actually, because as you and your high-priced lawyers can see, everyone that was there that day is still suffering. Mentally, physically, everyone is still all screwed up over it. Everyone apparently, except you?"

Susan backed Rehan down a bit, his smirk vanishing. "I think people will wonder why that is, especially if they know the whole story."

Susan turned on Peter Stewards, to try and salvage the whole mess, with one last Hail Mary. "Since you are so over protective, why don't you save Airman Browers any more pain and pick up where he left off. The minivan pulled up, two men were trying to rescue the wounded survivor. As the outburst has already covered." Susan gave General McMillian a stern glance. "The order was given to engage the van and its occupants. Once all that was accomplished, they called in the ground team, your recon unit, correct?"

Peter eyed her with contempt. "You really don't know when to quit, do you? So what? This guy's an arms dealer? There's a thousand fuck-heads like him. So what? What the fuck does it have to do with what happened twenty years ago?"

"Just finish the story!" Susan demanded. "What happened when your squad pulled up on the scene?"

"You already know what happened, damn it! There's bodies and body parts splattered all over the place. Do you know what a 30mm cannon with exploding rounds does to a human body? Can you imagine what happens when you blast a few hundred into a group of twenty men standing still on a street corner? Or what happens when you pump a mini-van full of them?" Peter punched the table and cocked his head in rage at Susan. A few tears spilled sideways. He dropped his head, covering his weakness, angrily wiping them away.

Rehan, sitting right next to him, shuddered. "That's enough, it's enough. Just, don't."

Susan showed no mercy. "I don't think so Doctor. Actually, I'd think you'd like all this? Here's your revenge. Isn't it sweet?" Sweeping her hand around the entire room, "To see all these people you've blamed, and hated and after all these years, you get to see them all suffering. Still suffering. Here, sitting before you, are the evil, terrible people you hated enough to blind you to the truth about what you've been doing."

Susan turned back on Peter, she showed no mercy with him either. "Now, go on Pete. Tell everyone what happened. Tell them about the van?"

"Damn you!" Rehan and Pete screamed in tandem.

Rehan's lawyers and everyone else, sat in a focused silence, all caught in sick curiosity.

"You finish it now Pete." Susan demanded.

Pete raised his head, letting out a growl at the ceiling. He looked down, resolved. "We found a second wounded guy, a reporter. He told us what a fuck-up it all was. We radioed in. Of course, the great General McMillian over there cast blame on Browers right away, and the AWACs, and anybody else. No way any of it was his fault. No way he was going down. Cold, brutal war soldier doing his duty B.S. But that's only because he didn't have to see it . . ." Peter faded off, resolve draining away from him the more he spoke.

"See what? What did you find in the van?" Susan asked, but Peter didn't get a chance to answer.

"He saw me!" Rehan exploded. "And my Dad! And my little baby sister! All shot up and bloody, that's what he saw! My dad's brains blown out, all over us. We were sitting right behind him! He saw my sister sitting in my lap, holding her stomach, with me. Sitting there, holding her . . ." Rehan faded in the horrible reflection, crying in sobs when he continued. "Holding her together with our hands. Bleeding, breathing in little gasps. She kept whispering in my ear, worried she was a bad girl, because she was bleeding all over her dress. Asking me if Mom would be angry? She was mad at herself, because she . . ."

"Stop it, stop, stop!" Peter said, shaking his head to block the memories. "No, no, no . . ."

"Why? why should I stop? It's what they . . ." Rehan started, but Peter cut him off.

"Because I was there! In the van. Don't you remember? I was trying to help you, and your little sister, but, but . . ."

"You?" Rehan asked, looking at Peter stunned, trying to peer through the scraggly beard, the gray strands of hair, to peel back the years and see the young soldier from his nightmare. "You?" He asked in a hushed voice. "The medic? That was you?"

"Yes, damn it, it was me!" Peter sat up closer, grabbed Rehan's arm, pulled him in to stare directly into his face. "Can't you see your little sister's death haunted in my eyes?"

Susan moved closer, softer, careful now, pulling at the story. "Yes, Pete, we can see it. But he doesn't. Not yet, tell him."

Peter glanced at Susan, with tears and snot smearing his mustache and beard, his eyes swollen and red. He turned slowly and faced the wall, and now he had that far-off stare, just like Browers, who sat frozen at the other end of the table.

"She was so little. With this pretty little white dress. I remember the puffy little shoulders, with little pink-bows on them . . . tied by ribbons around her little arms. And around her waist, it had a matching pink bow and ribbon, for . . . like a belt."

Rehan became quiet, staring off into the past through the wall now too, "She was worried about crushing the bow, she didn't want to wrinkle it, that's why she was sitting in my lap, so I could watch it for her."

The two sitting next to each other replayed the image in tandem, like it was being projected on the wall in front of them.

Peter continued, "Yeah, it was weird, because she was, was cut open,"

Rehan made a little gasp of agony, as Peter continued.

"It was so strange, like something out of a horror movie. The shrapnel cut clean across, just below her little pink belt . . ."

Rehan sobbed as he watched. "No Juma, no . . ."

Peter's face flinched at the horror of his memory. "They were holding her closed, their little hands and arms clenched together, just holding her. I tried!" Peter broke his stare, turned to Rehan, tears burst from his eyes. "I tried, please remember? But that prick, Sargent Jakes, he, he, that mother fucker."

Rehan quietly sobbed, repeating softly, "Juma no. Juma, Juma . . ."

Everyone looked on frozen in place except Four-Star General McMillian. He huffed, and puffed, and turned away shifting side to side, in his chair.

"Sargent Jakes, Pete? Susan asked. "Please, it's hard, but please finish." Susan softy urged him.

"My sergeant, my C.O., Jakes. I'm trying to get an IV in her little arm. It looks so bad, ya know? But lots of guys survive an injury like that, in the gut. It's painful, and the shock of it . . . but if none of the major arteries are severed, and you don't end up with infection. She wasn't bleeding that bad. She was wide awake too, talking to us, mad as hell, with her raspy little voice." Peter let out a sad, little laugh. "Apparently, we ruined her day, ruined her brother's special-day. Most of all, we ruined her dress, and she was really giving us the business for it."

Peter laughed again and burst in tears at the same time. "I'm keeping her talking through the translator. I had to keep telling her I was sorry. She made me promise to, to get it cleaned . . ."

Peter turned again to Rehan, "She was a tough little girl buddy, you know that?"

Then he drifted back in time again, to his own far-off stare at the wall. "It haunts me the most, how worried she was about ruining that dress. Trying to wipe off the blood, she starts picking her dad's brains off."

"Oh my God." Susan couldn't hold it. It was all too much. In all her years, as tough of an intelligence agent as she thought she was, "Oh my God?" And her tears dripped in silent compassion.

Anger built in Peter's voice as he continued. "And all that prick Jakes could worry about was getting the hell out of there. He calls it in, and that heartless bastard over there, the great General McMillian, gives him the okay to pull out? Ordering the helicopter back to base? So they could cover their asses."

General McMillian spun in his chair with a hard focus at Peter, but he couldn't manage to speak. A guilty rage boiled in his eyes.

Peter continued by grabbing Rehan's arm without really looking at him. "I fought them. I tried, please remember that, please?"

"I remember, I remember it all every day," Rehan said, staring into the past with him.

Peter turned back to the room, defiant towards the military present. "I disobeyed orders! I told Jakes I wouldn't go unless we took that little girl. He's ordering me out of the van, screaming. I was telling him no fucking way I was leaving that little girl, we could save her. He fucking pulls his side arm. I thought he was trying to scare me, so I begged him, pleaded. It was bad, we shouldn't move her without some bandages and a good compress on, to, to . . . fuck."

Susan fought to regain her composure. "I'm so sorry, Pete. You did the right thing, you were right . . . to try."

Rehan broke his stare, noticed Susan's teary eyes with hollow scorn. "You see? You hear? Are you happy now? Just listen, and you can live with it too. Now, you will know."

Rehan looked at Peter, silently giving him permission to continue, then back at the wall.

Peter's voice cracked full of desperation. "I just needed ten minutes, to get her prepped, and we, we could have gotten her to a MASH. It was only thirty minutes away, she could have made it, but then . . ."

Peter stopped, sat bolt-upright, as if shocked by his own mind. A physical reaction to a mental wall he was speeding towards and couldn't break through.

"She died? She died anyway?" Susan assumed.

Peter gave her the most haunted, chilling, "No" she could ever remember hearing.

"He shot her, that son-of-a-bitch Jakes, shot her right in the head."

"JUMA!" Rehan screamed, a wailing, deep scream, from somewhere far away, from the little boy, in the van.

Susan couldn't fathom it, it didn't connect. She would always remember that feeling of instant numb confusion.

Peter fell back in his chair and stared at the fluorescent light in the ceiling. Clenched his fist to his head, covering his eyes. "But even that didn't kill her, not instantly. It smacked her hard, and her eyes got real big, and . . . and, she looked right at me. The blood poured down her dress. She lifted her little hand to try and catch it . . . to keep it off her . . . she tried to say something . . . but the blood just gurgled up."

Susan stood shaking in disbelief, tears rolling, one after the other, confused as she could ever remember being.

Peter continued, not daring to look from beneath his clenched fist. "She realized it was hopeless, to keep trying. Then . . . she rolled her head, her eyes, in anger over at Jakes . . . that prick, that mother-fucker, she looked right at him. Like, asking him why? She's brushing her little dress to show him, cause she couldn't talk. I hope he sees her looking at him every time he closes his eyes. I hope he burns in hell and has to watch that little girl look at him over and over."

"JUMA! I'm sorry, Juma . . ." Rehan's agonizing screams had the room flinching and crying. Everyone broke over that little girls last moments.

Peter came back down from his stare with both fist to the table. "At some point, right in there, she was gone." His voice was hard, cold. "Jakes then said, said something he shouldn't have, not right then. He said . . . 'I don't like to watch a dog suffer,' as he holstered his gun. I sprang on the fucker. He wanted me out of that van and he got it. I was using my scissors to jab at him. I don't remember aiming really. I just jabbed and punched and tried to tear him apart. The guys dragged me off, and later . . ."

Peter pushed it all back down into the corner of his mind and came out of his trance. Sat back in his chair, crossing his arms. "Well, you know the rest. The army doesn't keep guys that snap and attack their C.O. on the payroll."

Rehan turned to him. "Did, did you kill him? Did you?"

Peter seemed ashamed, looked down, away. "No, I'm sorry. I wish I did, I really do. But they dragged me off. All he needed was a few stitches."

"Thank you, thank you for trying." Rehan turned to Susan. "Do you fucking see yet? Oh no, I don't think so. It wasn't over." Anger replaced his sorrow, his tears seemed to instantly dry away. "They just pulled out. All of them, just left. No one from the town would dare come. If they even called the police, they wouldn't dare come either. I sat there for hours as my Juma turned cold in my arms, looking at what was left of the back of my father's head. But the worst was that sad, angry look in Juma's eyes. I'll never forget, never. Frozen on her little face, the whole time. It wasn't until the next morning, when my mother Riedel arrived, that anyone came to get me. I was fourteen that day. It's an important birthday for a Kuwaiti man, a kind of coming-of-age to manhood. We'd gone there to pick up my uncle on our way to a big celebration, when the attack happened. It was my uncle's best friend, the injured man in the street, he had to try and help him?

"But what they did to Juma, who just wanted to look pretty for me in her little dress, so I could be proud of my little sister. Excited to tell everyone who she was. Entering my new phase in life as a man, her big brother, as her escort for life. But there was no life that day. I was dead after that." Rehan bore his eyes into Susan. "Are you happy now?"

"Nobody is happy Rehan. Do you see anyone here who looks

happy? Anyone who was there who's not broken?"

"No, nothing can bring back the before time. Nothing." Rehan said, drifting to a quieter state.

Susan still had a job, an endgame. It was tougher now, much tougher. "Look, Rehan, nobody can promise you anything, but I can't imagine there wouldn't be, at least understanding. I'm sure the F.B.I. and your attorneys, could work something out. It was obviously a, a traumatic, psychological . . . Anyone would be thrown off balance. You were just a boy. People will have compassion, understanding. Please, isn't it time to let little Juma rest? Only you can release these men from the torture. Release yourself too, let it all go. Can't we all finally let this thing rest in peace? Please?"

There was a long, hopeful silence. Tears filled Rehan's eyes again, and he let out a long sigh, his head falling to his chest.

Susan was hopeful this terror would finally end, that such a story could end, somehow? Be over.

Rehan raised his head, his expression turned to stone. "Rest? . . . rest in peace? There's no peace. This will never end, never go away. America is still the one spreading death and destruction around the world, not me. America is still the biggest supporter of evil, the biggest evil, not me. No, Mrs. Figiolli, there is no peace.

"Do you hear me now? Here's my final statement. My sister's death was horrible, inexcusable, but I turned her death into a life of saving others, something I couldn't do for her in that van. That's what I have done for many, many other little girls, all over the world. I used that tragedy and focused it to do good, not continue the evil like you've all done. Still dropping your bombs. Still shooting your guns. Still killing the innocent." Then looking at General McMillian "Or should I say, still shooting dogs in the head? Or giving the orders to at a safe distance?"

He turned back to Susan. "Regarding your latest jungle bombing, I can prove beyond any doubt with my medical records, and any number of medical experts will testify, that I was surely unconscious during any of these events other than what I testified to earlier. And virtually all medical professionals will tell you that, even if I had been conscious, I was severely concussed, disoriented, and in shock, rendering me incapable of any rational action or thoughts. In short, you are wrong Mrs. Figiolli. Good day."

With that, Dr. Al'Camel stood, giving a signal to his lawyers to join him, one spoke for him. "I believe that is enough harassment for one day, and unless you are prepared to offer some proof? A warrant? . . . or your grand jury indictment, then this meeting is over. I will only add that you should all thank God there's no legal recourse to sue the agencies involved. We can and will file official complaints, and demand Congressional reviews, of everything that has gone on here."

Another lawyer picked up the mantra. "Our firm has plenty of contacts, friends, in and out of the government, who will be just as shocked as we are to hear of these events. Both present and going back these twenty some years. We'll be digging it up and taking another look General McMillian."

The final lawyer of the three earned his fee as well. "It seems to me mistakes were made, and by more than just these poor soldiers. In any case, the court of public opinion will judge you all, because it's been my experience, it's the only way to effect real change within the entrenched military and political powers. It is shameful, coming from us? The United States of America?"

"ENOUGH already! Jesus, ya made yer point!" Givens stood, stepped around the table a few places to make it clear to the little weasel he meant business. "Yer world isn't any more pure, and the things you guys pull in the name of justice and the law are just as bad or worse, so save it for the cameras. Make sure ya take a good look at yer client too, ya self-righteous piece of work. These people made mistakes, but in the line of duty. Risked their lives for yer sorry asses too I might add. From people like Hitler and Saddam and Bin Laden . . . and the Chameleon here who isn't foolin' anybody with his I'm innocent crap stories about, I went out in the world to save the poor and the sick in my sister's memory, bullshit!

"He's a ruthless killer who's directly responsible for hundreds of horror stories like the one he's livin' with. The only difference is these guys feel bad about what happened and he's usin' it to justify his crap. Now get the fuck outta here before I take his head off and stuff it in yer fuckin' briefcases."

Susan wanted to cheer out loud. Her wonderful General Givens was saying exactly what she wanted to scream. Everyone knew this was it. The final piece, the reason why Rehan turned into the Chameleon.

She liked watching the lawyers all try to be brave. None stood up to

General Givens. His eyes scanned one to the other. They quickly stuffed papers away and shuffled out without another word.

A dead silence filled the room when the door closed behind them. It didn't last long.

"This is all such bullshit," General McMillian said breaking the silence. "How does this crap keep coming back?" Restoring his mental denial, "Well, I'm not going down because somebody here opened this can of worms back up. Screw this." He stormed out of the room.

"I guess the meeting is over gentlemen," Susan said, as she slumped into a chair. "You're all free to go. I'm sure we'll all be back discussing it soon enough in hearings. I'd just like to say, no sense trying to twist anything. Just come clean, we have nothing to hide. We did, all of us, we did what we had to do."

She looked from Browers to Pete. "What we were all ordered to do, what our duties demanded of us, as regrettable as that is sometimes. I don't think any of us would be able to do much differently, if it all played out over again, as sad and as tragic as that might be.

"Reality of the world we live and operate in, sometimes the shit hits the fan and sprays all over us. This would be one of those times. Thank you all again for coming. Good day."

Now Susan was positive. Today was definitely a disaster.

CHAPTER 23: The Lunatic Fringe

Rehan felt the crafty fox, who had just escaped, but could hear the hounds baying, right on his trail.

Riding home in a limo, Rehan half listened to his lawyers as they vied in turn to earn their fees. He was pretty sure he wouldn't be around long enough to need their advice. Lost in his own thoughts.

We did well to get out of there today.

Now we know who they are! Who tried to kill you? Who killed Juma? Father! Maybe we'll give the SAMs away free? To anyone who needs them. Anyone who will use them.

To rain terror from the skies?

No, to strike back! I get to make them pay now. You got us out, now I make them pay. Christian or Muslim, God exposed all of them. It's obvious. A chance for honor!

Then, maybe, to move on? Then peace? It could end then, couldn't it?

Rehan came back to consciousness when the lawyers became stuck in their planning.

"Doctor Al'Camel? Did you hear us? We were asking how you feel about us creating a media campaign? It may get a bit personal for you. Are you comfortable with us going to the press?"

"Yes, I think it's a good part of our strategy. But, allow me to handle the press in my own way."

"Are you sure, Doctor? We have experts and contacts which would be most helpful?"

"No, no. As you said, it's personal. I'll handle it. If you are not satisfied with our coverage within a week or so, we'll talk about it."

"Very well, as you wish. Is there anything we can do to help with your plan?"

Rehan laughed and the lawyer smiled. "Well, I guess I'm paying you guys to be overly cautious."

All three lawyers laughed.

"Okay, gentlemen, I was at a DWB event not four months ago and a young reporter was making a bit of a pest of herself. Digging for someone to talk about C.I.A. spies infiltrating the DWB, traveling the world undercover. It was not appropriate interview material at that function, but I'm sure she'll be happy to come for a secret interview."

"Sounds good. Anonymous. Off the record," one lawyer advised.

"Don't you think it'll have more validity with me as the source?" Rehan asked.

"Be warned Doctor, you're going to end up going through some mud on this. Avoid as much as possible from the beginning."

Another lawyer chimed in. "This story will get plenty of air time. We can guarantee it."

"Thank you, good advice. Do some background, the reporter's name is Amanda Knoxx. Young, maybe twenty-seven, twenty-eight? I'm sorry, I don't remember who she works for, wait . . . it was, yes, I think it's The Post."

"The Capitol Post? That's perfect." All three lawyers smiled with Cheshire grins all around.

* * *

Two days later Rehan was awaiting the arrival of reporter Amanda Knoxx from The Capitol Post.

At six p.m. sharp, his doorbell rang.

Rehan turned down the burners on dinner. The chicken korma was slow cooking just right alongside the Jasmine rice. The sweet curry smells filled the room. Rehan was far from Indian, or Sikh, but he loved this dish so much, he'd learned to cook it well. He wiped his hands and tossed the towel aside as he walked around the granite top kitchen island to the front foyer and opened the door.

"Well hello Mrs. Knoxx, right on time, welcome, please come in."

"Hello. I didn't have to hide in the lobby to show up right on time, I got lucky. Thank you for inviting me Doctor Camel."

"It's pronounced Al-KA'-meal. But call me Rehan, Mrs. Knoxx."

Amanda gave an awkward, donkey-like little laugh. "I'm so sorry. I'm terrible with accents. Call me Amanda please. I'm nobody's Miss. It makes me feel old."

"You do not look old. In fact, you could easily pass as a teenager. I imagine that isn't always so great for you. Or maybe it's an advantage in your line of work?"

"Wow, nice call Doctor. Yes, I'm cursed with being the petite, little blonde, with the perky, little boobs and the innocent looks of a sixteen-year-old girl."

"I'm not sure I feel sorry for you." Rehan smiled at her.

"Oh, it was great in high school and college. I was a flyer. That's what they call the little cheerleaders they can toss through the air. Part of the in-crowd. Lots of frat boys chatting me up for my . . . flexibilities." Amanda blushed, turning her face sideways and down a bit.

It was one of the most adorable, innocent, sexy looks. Her feathery straight blond hair cascaded over one shoulder, covering her eyes from his for a moment. Rehan couldn't help taking her all in. Amanda was dressed in a professional charcoal skirt and matching top with a cream silk blouse and respectable heels. A woman in her prime who'd catch the eye of every man in the street. When she brushed her hair aside and looked back up, Rehan felt his stare captured. Light makeup on her fresh face accented her crystal blue eyes that seemed to glow against her fair, pale complexion.

Rehan broke by forcing a smile and turning his hand to welcome her in. "How rude of me. Please, let's share a glass of wine before dinner." Rehan led her in, around to the kitchen island where a bottle of wine had been decanted to breathe. He poured two glasses, turning and handing one to Amanda as she approached.

"Thank you. Wow again. Wine? Dinner? This is the best interview ever."

"Well, I didn't mean to, make you uncomfortable. You're certainly a beautiful woman. Forgive me my, linger."

"Oh, pee-shaw. I've learned to deal with lingers my whole life. I'm in a tough business. The point I was trying to make, people still think I'm this fragile little girl. Like I'll break or something. I'm a woman grown. People rarely give me credit. Especially on first impression."

"Guilty as charged Amanda. I remembered you, I called you as a reporter, but I also wanted the chance to have a nice evening with a stunningly beautiful woman. It's been awhile since I've just relaxed and," Rehan pointed around at the cooking and raised his glass of wine. "I hope you'll indulge me with a little polite company?"

"Let's see?" Amanda said, smiled mischiefly, turned and took a few paces away towards a large living room in the luxury penthouse corner condo. Picture windows full of amazing cityscape views from every angle, the center overlooking the park and waterway inlet. Rows of yachts lined the docks. "A doctor. Obviously fabulously wealthy." She raised her glass to the posh surroundings as she turned looking at him from across the room. "Dare I say handsome?" She walked back towards him and lifted her glass. "Good wine. Something smells delicious?"

Amanda raised up on her tippy-toes to peer past Rehan at the stove. She settled back down giving Rehan a direct gaze with her crystal blue eyes. She slowly lifted her wine, just touching her lower lip to the rim, allowing the wine to just barely trickle over. "Um. Indulge away Doctor."

Rehan downed his glass. "I'm going to need more wine." Smiling at her.

"Let me pour it for you." Amanda crossed quickly to his side at the kitchen island. She brushed his shoulder leaning to take the decanter of wine. A wisp of fine blonde hair fell across his forearm causing instant goosebumps. She smelled divine up close.

Amanda poured his glass and lifted her own to toast. "I must warn you, Doctor Rehan Cam'el, this petite little body gets tipsy quite fast. I'm here as a professional tonight, right?"

"It's Al-Ka'meal. And believe me, Amanda Knoxx, ace reporter, the wine isn't the only thing that'll have you tipsy this evening."

"Well, cheers then." She drank deep, then smiled warmly. "So tell me your story. I'm all tingling."

"Oh no, dinner first. And some more wine. You have to earn your story. And the one after that."

"The one after that?"

"And the one after that. But hey, slow down. We just met. Let's see how tonight goes?"

"You're just teasing me now, aren't you my little camel?"

"It's only fair. It's what you've been doing to me since you got here."

* * *

The C.I.A. bombing that almost killed Rehan was Amanda's first real story. It was a blockbuster. Front page. Went national network immediately. Propelled Amanda Knoxx to instant celebrity. For three days she was interviewed on most major news programs of note. His little protégé, her innocent looks playing perfectly against the backdrop of the scary story.

Rehan's stellar record, and being an American citizen, spelled doom for the C.I.A. right off the bat. The massacre at the village sealed their fate.

"Out of control" and "committing mass murder" just "to get one lone man?" "Crazed, blood thirsty agents at the C.I.A." Who now wanted to bring drones in over American cities? Under the guise of "law enforcement." The headlines seemed to be in a feeding frenzy.

The fear created was palatable, but after three days, it had spun off message to drones. Rehan needed to throw some more bloody meat in the water. He invited Amanda back for dinner, and "another big part of the story."

* * *

When he opened the door, Amanda exploded through, clutching her purse awkwardly with two newspapers. She flung her arms around his neck in a hug, and squealed in glee, scattering one of the newspapers across the marbled foyer floor.

"Oh thank you Rehan, thank you!" She dropped her arms and held up the paper. "Did you see? Front page! Did you see on the news?"

"Yes, yes, Amanda dear. Of course. I'm so happy for you. Let's have a glass of wine to celebrate?"

"Oh please, I want to drown in it! I really wanted to call, so many times. But it's been crazy. I've flown to New York and back four times in the last three days!"

"Don't worry about it, Amanda, please?"

"No, no. I should have called. It was more than the story . . ." Amanda stopped, checking her thoughts with that innocent, slight downward tilt of her head. "I, had a wonderful time with you the other night. I'm sorry. Maybe it was the wine."

"No, dear Amanda. It was wonderful. I asked for your company, remember? You did me a favor, making it so much more than just an interview."

"Please Rehan, I have to admit. You were right about me. I've used my innocent looks to . . . set people up a little, I guess you'd say. I hope you don't think it was just to get the story?"

"Of course not. Amanda? If you like, I won't give you the second part of the story, and we can just have dinner? We can call that news anchor lady, what's her name? With the big hair, always scary and angry?" Rehan tilted his head back at her in his own little smile.

"Oh, you! My little camel, always teasing me."

"Let me take your coat, and let's have some wine, okay?"

Amanda turned her shoulders to allow Rehan to decloak her. She'd obviously dressed for the occasion. Her hair was tied up in a ponytail, and she'd spent time curling it in cascades of soft blonde locks. Her makeup was done for an evening out, and, on such a fresh face, was incredible. Her overcoat revealed a pure white, curve-fitting, cocktail dress cut just above her knees. Three-inch heels toned her legs and gave her height as she glided past. The off-the-shoulder top had a frilly, white, embroidered trim all around her chest. Without a bra, her perky little breasts danced just beneath the tight, white fabric. She smiled, as only a woman who knows, when she passed him to the island kitchen trailing a soft, clean scent of high-end perfume.

She grabbed a baby-carrot from a tray of vegetables and turned to Rehan. Leaning back against the edge of the granite counter, she crossed one leg over the other. She brought the carrot up close to her lips.

"So, what do you think? Do I look like a teenager tonight, Doctor Camel?"

"You look like you're ready to go to the prom," Rehan joked.

"Oh, you!" Amanda launched the carrot, striking him square in the chest. Rehan laughed out loud and it only took her a second to smile along. "You're lucky that wasn't a bullet mister."

Rehan smiled and glided right up to her, lifting her hands in his, taking a respectful look at her.

"You are simply stunning, one of the most beautiful women I've ever seen." Rehan quickly turned his grip over in her hands and pulled her in a twirl off the edge of the counter.

"Here! Let me have a look at you. Beautiful! Every inch of you."

Amanda spun to a stop, facing him. Her blonde curls swirled around over one shoulder. They stood inches apart, gazing at each other.

"A woman? A beautiful woman?" She asked.

"You know you are, I was teasing with you. And I'm going to make it up to you with another great story. Maybe front page again?"

"Whoa, slow down a little." Amanda leaned in. "We just met. Dinner first, and some nice wine? Okay?"

"Of course, you have to earn your story first," Rehan joked right back.

Amanda laughed, twirling away, scooping up her glass. "We'll see who earns it."

They shared the wine, and dinner, and Rehan feasted on Amanda who teased him without mercy in her outfit. They listened to music once the wine started working its magic. Finding many common interests in Rehan's vinyl record collection, even with a generational difference or so. Amanda picked up an acoustic guitar Rehan longed to play but never could. She strummed out a country ballad of sad introspection from the eyes of a beautiful woman whose been played by every tool in the shed, wondering if she'll ever mean more. And the sad refrain, "And how could you really, really ever know, when it's real."

Amanda sat close, with playful touches when she leaned in to laugh at his jokes. Her dress rising higher and higher, her tanned legs seemed to be impossibly long as the evening past. Rehan fought the night away averting his gaze.

As they explored his penthouse, some pictures turned the conversation to his adventures with the DWB around the world. And that led to Rehan starting to share another big part of the story, and Amanda couldn't help her fascination. He couldn't blame her. Almost instantly, Rehan saw the reporter in her glaze over the urges and rapport between them.

A short half-hour later, Rehan was saying goodbye, left in frustration when Amanda rushed away to make her deadline.

* * *

Amanda's second blockbuster story, the sensational shooting-down of three American aircraft, and the deaths of ten U.S. servicemen, hit the front page and national news in a whirlwind bigger than the first. All of it having been part of some botched, secret, C.I.A. black ops mission. Adding to the scare factor, the rebels apparently had dangerous SA18Cs in unknown quantities. It caused people to cancel vacations. The stock market tumbled, hitting the airlines particularly hard.

Senators and Congressmen were clamoring to get on the daily news shows to express outrage and to demand hearings and "independent investigations into these troubling events."

Amanda's second story came out Friday. Rehan sat days later, on a stormy Sunday morning, watching Amanda on the morning news programs. A tear welled in her innocent blue eyes, right on cue, each time she recounted the deaths of so many brave young men.

After the news, Rehan relaxed with coffee reading the various Sunday papers. All of them "seriously questioning the C.I.A.'s actions."

The rain outside picked up, drumming hard against his picture windows overlooking the city. A clap of thunder ended with his doorbell ringing. Rehan was not expecting company?

Through his peephole, he was surprised to see Amanda. He unlocked and opened the door. She stood in a trench coat, dripping wet, holding a half-closed umbrella, which had done a nice job keeping her hair dry. It was combed straight back and tied in lose pigtails high up on each side.

"Amanda, dear! You should have called. I would have had them let you in the garage."

"I wanted to surprise you. Picked a bad day for that, huh?"

"Well, I am surprised. I just saw you on TV an hour ago. You looked great."

"Yes, thank you, Rehan. It's been a lot of work, a whirlwind, but, may I come in to talk with you?" Amanda seemed reserved and worried.

"Of course."

As they walked towards his living room, Amanda stopped before they reached the carpet off the marbled foyer floor.

"Oh, I'm sorry, this is wet."

"I'll take it for you."

"No, it's okay." She stopped him from coming any closer with an outstretched hand. "You might not want me to stay long."

"What's wrong, Amanda? All of this should be wonderful for you?"

Amanda took a step away, undoing the belt to her coat. "I'm sorry I didn't even call, again. It's been a couple days. Again."

"Amanda, I see how busy you are. It's a sensation. Don't worry."

"I feel a bit guilty for just leaving the other night. Remember we talked, and you said I was a beautiful woman?"

"Of course. Are you still worried about that? I was joking with you."

"No. But that night, I dressed, well, nice. And then you gave me the story, and then I, I just left."

"You looking incredible had nothing to do with me giving you the story, you know that right?"

"Of course. You've been a perfect gentleman. That's why I came here today. I'll leave if you want."

"Why would I want you to leave? I don't understand?"

Amanda turned and opened her trench coat, letting it fall to the foyer floor. Her sheer white cover up hung open. Underneath, sexy peach-colored lingerie, stockings, garters, and a delicate, lacy, see through bra and panty set. She angled one hip to the side, placing a hand on it. She tilted her head the opposite way with a smile, posing in her high heels.

"Before you tell me anymore about the story. I know I left you hanging the other night. You should make me pay. I won't break."

Rehan exploded into her and they didn't stop until Tuesday morning when Amanda finally had to be back at work. But not before he gave her something interesting to investigate. He saw the twinkle go off in her crystal blue eyes again. If it was true, she had another blockbuster.

* * *

Rehan was never sure if Amanda double-verified his tip or just ran with it, but it caused the other horrifying shoe to drop. Her third installment hit the wires like a nuclear bomb. An artificial, living creation, a Frankenstein monster, turned on its creators and was calling the shots. Getting the C.I.A. handlers to drop bombs and killing humans? Killing Americans!

Rehan watched with excitement as the story played out and talk turned to a possible Pulitzer Prize for the cutting edge, in-depth reporting of the previously obscure and very appealing Amanda Knoxx.

With her innocent looks, retelling the horrors, uncovering the shocking twist and turns, expressing the same fears and anger most Americans felt, a new American sweetheart was born, adding to the chilling effect.

* * *

Over the next few weeks, Rehan spent nearly all his free time having Amanda. He ultimately found her to be less than his intellectual equal. The typical dizzy blonde whose ditzy take on the world went from cute to annoying very quickly. And now she was calling, and they were talking, all the time. Rehan never liked long phone conversations.

Amanda was still all-new and fun, especially the night she showed up dressed as, and played the part of, the naughty cheerleader to a tee and really blew Rehan's mind and body.

Still, after the sex, you had to actually talk about something.

Plus, she couldn't stop calling him a camel. Or worse, her little camel? A nasty, dirty, stinking animal that would spit in your face given half a chance.

Every time Amanda made some stupid comment, Rehan would just cringe.

When News Channel 5 scooped her up with a huge new contract she became the newest on-air reporter sensation, and Rehan was glad for a few days' break. The producers at Fox quickly advertised their new star with her own tag-line: "Knoxx is Fox," knowing people wouldn't miss the reverse implications.

Rehan wondered how many times she had used her looks to get anywhere? It obviously wasn't her brains. Maybe she had played him too? It didn't matter. Rehan only needed her a little bit longer, so he put up with his growing annoyance by getting much rougher on her in bed. Grabbing and pulling her hair. Throwing her around. Slapping her. Screwing her in the ass. Even nearly choking her to death while pounding her over the edge of his sofa. But she ended up liking it all and begging for more. Like that made her a real woman. What a ditz.

Rehan thoughts and fantasies kept flashing over to C.I.A. agent Susan Figiolli. Now there was a woman of his intellectual equal, with the kind of curves only the sexiest Middle Eastern belly dancers possessed. He liked her dark looks much better than those of the clueless blonde.

Yeah, Susan's dark hair, her dark eyes, trying to hide that sharp intellect. The strength, the power she has.

She's dangerous! That brain. Our cover is blown! She has the advantage!

Yes, she's dangerous. Very dangerous. Rehan liked it. The turn-on this chess match between them had become. He wanted to turn her, seduce her, like no other woman he'd ever known.

Somewhere in that intellect of hers, she has to see what I've accomplished all these years. How I outsmarted them all. Even she cried over the injustice of Juma's death. Sooner or later, one way or another . . . I'll dominate Susan Figiolli.

CHAPTER 24: The Best Defense

To counter the mounting negative press, Susan's boss at the C.I.A., Director Timothy Scott, had them move forward with the grand jury indictment.

"Timmy," as Susan called, and admired, and appreciated him, was on her side from the beginning. He was one of the only people who could lecture her, and she knew instantly his advice was spot on.

He sat across his desk, as powerful and strong as any man who occupied it. "We've been after this guy for a long time, Susan, and you finally got our claws in him, I'll be damned if we're going to let go because of some bad press and Congressional grand standing."

"It's not just the press, the public opinion's all over it. Sometimes the White House needs a head to deliver on a silver platter. I'm in the line of fire on this one Timmy. The mob needs its pound of flesh."

"You let me worry about the White House, and the mobs. Let's prove what we know and give them the good Doctor's head. Right now, all they know is blood has been shed. American blood. Somebodies got to pay."

Susan felt bewildered by it all. "Otherwise the C.I.A. will be bombing suburban neighborhoods with drones next? We're blood thirsty and out of control. It's obvious, isn't it? We might start a coup. Freedom and democracy are at stake."

"Let the news media and talk shows run with it all. There's no end to the 'expert' talking heads giving credence to the fears. Who do you think is feeding them this crap? Focus on catching the guy."

Right on cue, the director's secretary buzzed in over the intercom. "Sir, Channel 5 News. You two are going to want to see this."

Director Scott click a remote towards the wall of TVs playing on one side of his office. An interview with Amanda was on. They had just gotten past a review of the story to date, and now they were turning to her fourth, and biggest installment yet.

Amanda, telling the little Juma story live on camera, with a confused, questioning, heartbroken look, was transfixing. All the horrors came out. Rehan's father and uncle. The friendly fire. The little boy being left alone with it all overnight.

Amanda was barely able to keep her professional composure before turning angry, questioning how the C.I.A. could possibly be trying to blame it all on Dr. Rehan Al'Camel?

She'd obviously done her background on him. Pictures of him on numerous humanitarian mission's flashed across the screen. By the time Amanda finished, he looked like a saint, one the C.I.A. was prepared to crucify to cover their own tracks.

When it finally, mercifully ended, Susan turned to Timmy. "I'm screwed. I doubt even you'll be able to save me now."

* * *

The "little Juma" story tore through the heart of America. Pink ribbons and bows, symbolizing her beloved dress that day, covered trees and telephone poles across the country. It was a firestorm of sympathy in real-time across the world-wide net. It all climaxed with a candle light vigil and march from the White House to the steps of the Capitol in sympathy, and a sense of shared, social culpability.

Rehan reveled in it all, maintaining a somber demeanor. He was asked to make a "thank you" statement at the end of the march. He walked up the marbled steps, stood at the podium, the Dome of the Rock of America his backdrop. A sea of candles twinkled before him. Strobes flashed from a thousand more cameras.

An instinctive dead silence spread across the masses.

Rehan tried twice to speak, before being led away hunched over, sobbing.

"Unable to even begin his short, written statement of appreciation for the outpouring of love and support," the news reported in empathy.

The Juma story was heart wrenching, but the public anger kept coming back to ten dead Americans. In the court of public opinion, only the evil C.I.A., the dark-haired Susan Figiolli in particular, was to blame.

The "Black Widow?" The press nickname for her made no sense to Susan as she dressed listening to the morning news radio. Digging through her closet, she became consciously aware that she had a lot of dark charcoal and black outfits. She turned, laying out a tan outfit across her bed and caught a glimpse of something out her window fall to the ground across the street. Did a man just fall from a tree? She was a spy. She saw it.

Sexy photos of her showed up in tabloids that were soon spread to the mainstream media under the guise of being "a real news story." Sex still sold papers and hits on the "official" news websites . . . "for more photos of the Black Widow unfit for publishing." Susan doing yoga, or coming out of the pool, even up-skirt panty shots of her getting out of her "government chauffeured" sedans. It was all fair game, open season.

Splash a few stock photos of a burning village, with charred bodies in the background, and Susan looked like the devil's daughter incarnate.

Sex and death really sold papers, and the traffic on the web-sites soared with every new teaser.

Zealot's swirled on the fringes, wondering if, "The Black Widow might be the Anti-Christ?"

Susan felt the day's pile-on, one after another. She stood gripping the railing overlooking her control room with both hands. She held on tight, feeling anything but in control. "This is how people in the middle ages got burned at the stake." she mumbled taking in the day's news updates playing on the video wall.

Givens appeared and supported her. "True hysterical nonsense."

"Maybe, but I'm sure there's plenty that'd line up to strike the first match, and cheer as I burned."

Mr. Green added aloud. "Yes, they would. Ignore the media, especially the tabloids."

"If only. They're climbing the trees across the street to try and get pictures of me in my panties, or less. I'm drowning in the shit."

Mr. Green strode over and leaned in close to Susan's shoulder. "Enough! Move on."

But Susan couldn't tear herself from her dark mood. The "move on" just set her off as she tore away in a pace. "Okay, let's review. Basically, we all believe he's the Chameleon, but we can't prove it. Even our so-called motive helps his defense. Let's say we find some shred of proof. His lawyers will disposition even more about the Palantir, how it works, how it's constructed. We can't give that up? Even if we did, it'd be inadmissible, or top secret, or open to God knows how many appeals."

Susan paced like a lawyer in a court room giving an opening statement, "And his lawyers know it. With his vast sums of money, they'll be happy to delay for years. Motions for top secret discovery? Forget about it. No discovery, no case."

Susan stopped her pace, and turned back facing them. "So, then I gotta ask myself, maybe, I'm fucking up again? Let's face it, everything I've done so far has been wrong, especially with the Chameleon. Maybe, I'm wrong about Doctor Rehan Al'Camel too?"

Givens laughed. "Yeah, sur."

"Even my Pal is only at eighty-six percent, which sounds convincing, until you ask him. Pal? Tell the General why you are not at one hundred percent.

"Yes, Susan. First, his story could be true. There are no discrepancies. Second, it could be a ploy by the real Chameleon to plant an obvious suspect. Third, he could be complicit in some other way, yet still not be the Chameleon. There is a real possibility he is hiding material facts to protect himself. He may also be in fear of retribution from the real Chameleon . . ."

"Okay, okay enough," Mr. Green butted in. "There's a thousand what-ifs. Everybody, every human, is going to see the truth here."

It didn't help Susan's mental state, or the way she was now having to live her life. She walked back over to Mr. Green, knowing he'd fully understand her plea. "A lynch mob is on the march. Nothing's going to quell them anytime soon. I'm running out of time here."

* * *

Rehan's lawyers were not worried about the Palantir on a legal footing, but Rehan knew enough to be very afraid of it based on its powers. The information they did get from the C.I.A. so far, released to them by the F.B.I., was fascinating.

Rehan was amazed at the basic concept, how the biological and mechanical had been blended. Then he learned it had grown on its own.

It's incredible the power this intelligence could have.

Correct! And it's only a matter of time before it will expose us with real proof. We need to act, now.

I've always researched intelligence-gathering techniques, and managed to plan accordingly.

This is a whole new world. No one will be able to hide from it for long, especially in its cross-hairs.

Rehan's lawyers pulled him out of his own thoughts again. They were so annoying.

"Okay, Doctor. We have ten photos here. A line up if you will. One of these is supposedly you in disguise, according to this brain. It was taken by a hotel security camera, so we've made the others look about as good. Which one is you?" The lawyer laughed at the ridiculous question.

Rehan recognized himself right away. "They all look the same to me," Rehan joked back. It was a stretch to believe any facial recognition software, or any jury, could really say it was him. He wasn't sure his own family would be able to either.

How would you know? Who would you ask? They're all dead because of these people. Who are now hunting you, looking to kill you.

CHAPTER 25: Big Boys and Their Toys

Rehan knew the C.I.A. and F.B.I. were watching him close. He wondered when they got in and planted the bugs he knew were there. Probably when he went in for that, interrogation. Of course, that's when Susan Figiolli would have had them in there. In his space. But they hadn't really seen inside.

Rehan closed the blinds knowing they had thermal imagers watching his every move right through the walls. Most people would be trapped by the sophisticated surveillance, but Rehan had always planned to be able to escape, even from his real life, should his cover ever be blown.

Rehan made a show of cooking breakfast and watching the news. Leaving the T.V. on, but not too loud. He took his coffee with him to the master bath for a morning dump and a little reading. Sitting there waiting for the heated tile floor to warm up along with the blazing 'sun-lamps' overhead. He flushed and got up, turning on the shower, hot and steamy. Once the room was nice and hot, Rehan got in the shower and changed the water over to ice cold. His skin slowly turned to goose bumps standing there, cooling way down, before jumping out and turning the water back to full hot.

Briefly invisible now from the C.I.A. thermal imagers, Rehan slipped into his oversized master bedroom closet, closing the door behind him. Once the door was closed, the double light switch on the inside had to be right up, left down. Only then would the trap door in the wood floor hinge open. Rehan stepped, bouncing his weight hard on the spring-loaded trapdoor, which smoothly raised up behind the closet door. A set of narrow stairs led down to the condo directly below his, into that master's closet. Once Rehan closed the trapdoor behind him, he was gone from his penthouse forever.

Rehan never gave a second thought to the money he had spent on his second condo. "Live-in" ready with all the appearances of a normal home. Another secret door in this master closet, this one a wall-sized shoe rack, hinged open to reveal a large eight foot by twenty-foot long space inside. Stocked with everything Rehan ever needed as an arms dealer. Racks of clothing and top end theatrical disguises and makeup. Matching ID's. And a special set of items, his "go-stash," packed and ready. Grab and go.

He had to hurry, the water was running upstairs and he wasn't sure how long before the C.I.A. would get suspicious. He chose an easy costume. It didn't require any makeup at all. "The Nerd" he called it. Under the name of James Wright. Flannel shirt, with pocket protector. Ill-fitting blue jeans, off-brand. Worn loafers. A 'bowl cut' wig of dark brown, straight hair. Dark-rimmed glasses, with transition lenses along the outer edges to distort his facial recognition. He added a Mid-west, humorous, good-ol' boy demeanor, maybe a bit goofy, to the mental image he used to internalize the character. It should be perfect for the person he was going to meet.

His "go-stash" included a small wheeled suitcase and backpack. Fake IDs, known as "clean-Ds," the three personas would pass any known background check. A backpack with secret pockets contained matching documents, passports, credit cards, $200,000 in cash, a pouch of diamonds, and a million in bearer bonds. Chump change to Rehan really, but enough to travel.

With everything in order, Rehan, "James Wright", donned a large overcoat, big hat and dark glasses. He closed off the secret room, wiping away any prints on the exterior, and walked out of his building for the last time via the in-ramp to the parking garage, where he knew he could spin past the entrance in the security camera's blind spot alongside the building. A few blocks away, he hailed a taxi to drop him at the main train station and watched until the cabbie picked up another fare and pulled away. Then Rehan walked off and away to a nearby rental car agency. James Wright rented a large, white cargo van and was off. He didn't want to miss the big show.

*   *   *

Rehan watched the giant-1/30th scale remote-controlled Russian MiG jet fighter circle around the field and then shoot past at four-hundred miles an hour. It appeared again from a wide loop back around, headed directly at the crowd. It shot straight up from ground level, out of sight.

The crowd cheered in awe.

People began pointing to a mock battlefield set up some fifty yards away. A small army of remote controlled tanks and armored vehicles moved in a large column from in front of the spectator's area. The smell of RV model fuel exhaust wafted across the stands.

The echo of the incoming "MiG-Rig" hid its true approach. People pointed and looked in all directions. It flew in with a scream over their left shoulders, arching over the field of targets. Bomb doors opened and twenty or so bomblets scattered in the air before hitting the ground and exploding in great bangs and puffs of smoke. It was hard to tell if any of the RC tanks or vehicles suffered a direct hit, but their owners had obviously prepared for self-detonation, as several exploded and burned.

The crowd of RC enthusiasts gave a circus cheer as the "MiG-Rig" flew past and did a victory roll over the field of smoldering destruction.

Rehan knew it would be perfect.

He mingled just out of sight, waited until everything died down with a late afternoon setting sun.

"Hello, excuse me."

Carl Perkins stood up shocked when Rehan stepped around the back end of his van.

Rehan smiled and gave a friendly wave. "Hello, I've been trying to catch up to you all day."

"Hello. Are you a reporter or something?" Carl asked, keeping close to his van.

"No, I'm sorry. I don't mean to startle you. I, I just couldn't believe it, your Jet. It's incredible!" Rehan poured it on.

"Well, thank you. It is my pride and joy."

Rehan felt sure Carl would like this part of his creation. The attention. The respect. "Again, sorry to press in like this, but I'm only here for the day, and I really was just blown away by it." Rehan extended his hand. "I'm Jim, Jim Wright. It's truly an honor to meet such a fellow enthusiast."

Carl shook his hand, wearily, but relaxed a little. "Carl Perkins, pleased to meet you, Jim?"

"Yes, Jim. Wait, Carl Perkins? Of Vio-Tech, Carl Perkins?" Rehan played. He knew exactly who Carl Perkins was.

"Yes, that's me, how do you know me mister?" Carl asked, taking his hand away slowly.

"My God, I really am impressed my friend. I've been using your transistor designs and couplings for years in some of my other hobbies. I tinker in electronics, mechanical engineering. Your original design, it was, ground-breaking. Visionary. I may sound like a girl from your high school days, but I really am one of your biggest fans. It's a great honor to meet you sir."

Carl smiled sheepishly. "Well, you obviously don't remember me from high school. Bill Gates and I had about the same social standing back then." Carl quipped back.

"Yes, well, I can certainly relate. It was always strange to me that our brains were the last thing of concern to the girls. I hope I haven't brought up bad memories, but we got our revenge later in life, didn't we?" Rehan played.

"I'd like to think so." Carl looked Rehan up and down.

"Well don't 'think so' Carl, 'know so.' Go to a class reunion lately? Not one jock who used to pick on me is less than two-hundred fifty pounds, and they must have used up all their testosterone, because they are all bald."

"Really?"

"Any of them would change lives with me in a second. But I tell you what, the biggest charge is to watch the girls, as they eye me up and down in comparison. Knowing I have all the money life's fantasies could want. Chatting me up, while the jock boys stand off by themselves telling their tired, old stories. You should go, it's a great validation."

"Funny you should say that, I just got my 40th reunion invitation. I think I'll RSVP and enjoy the fun on your recommendation."

Rehan could sense his charm working. "That's great. I'll leave you my card and you call me afterwards. I love to relive that moment over and over again."

Carl smiled broadly.

"Listen, Carl, I know we just met and, like I said, I'm only here for the day, but I'd love to treat you to dinner and talk about your jet a little more. I've been modeling for years, and I think I'm finally ready to go custom-build myself. What-do-ya say? Can I pick your brain over a nice meal at your favorite place, on me?"

"Sure, why not. Follow me a few minutes down the road to my

place. Give me a couple minutes to change and we'll head out to the best steaks you ever had. I'm starving."

"Great. That's just great!"

*   *   *

On their drive to Carl's favorite steak house, Rehan, as Jim Wright, built the rapport.

"So, tell me how you got involved at such a level with these things?" Rehan asked.

"It started when I was a kid. One of eight kids. My Dad worked all kinds of crazy hours, just to keep a roof over our heads. Mom an' him didn't have a lot left over for themselves. But Dad had a little workshop off in one corner of the basement, where he built his one lone RC airplane."

"Just one?"

"Yep. They were balsa wood kits back then. Each piece had to be hand cut and sanded. He'd worked on that thing for hours. Days. Years."

"He never finished?"

"I think he was afraid to finish because then he'd have to actually go fly it. Oh, he'd pack us kids up in the woody-wagon for a drive to the RC parks to watch others, but he never flew. In truth, there was nothing worse than seeing some man pull out a brand new, hand built plane, strap on those wings for the first time, and then wipe out on takeoff. Can you imagine?"

"Yes, if I have to admit. I always liked the crashes." Rehan smiled in a homey little chuckle.

"You and every other little boy."

"So, tell me about your famous MiG-Rig?"

"My world famous MiG-Rig. 1/30th Giant Scale class of models. Thirty percent of the real thing too. Micro turbine jet engines that run on Type-A jet fuel and require self-sealing Kevlar fuel tanks."

"You're kidding me?"

"10k a piece mini-jet engines. It takes a propane burn to set off the A1 by solenoid. Lucky for me, money was no object when I built her. I always liked the 'bigger is better' idea."

"I guess that makes you big man on campus?"

"King of the skies. But honestly, I fit in better with aeromodellers.

It's serious business, high-tech. Intellectual. The FAA regulates the pilots' license. As far as they're concerned, these are real jets."

"I didn't realize it had gotten to that level," Jim Wright pondered.

"Highly regulated safety and operation courses to qualify. Certified by the FAA in the type of gas turbine engine you plan to miniaturize. AMAs, Academy of Model Aeronautics, restricted air sites to go fly them only. It's a lot more than just building the thing, Jimbo."

Carl turned off into the parking lot of Bacigaluppi's Italian Steak House. "You're gonna love this place, Jimbo."

Rehan didn't miss the two Jimbo's. He and Carl were becoming fast friends. "Ah Carl? Buddy? An Italian steakhouse?" he joked.

"I know, right? The best steaks ever. I'm telling ya, the best!"

Everybody at Bagakaloppi's loved Carl from the moment he walked in. Rehan was greeted, hugged, kissed, and escorted like a dear friend or family member, to the nicest looking table in the place, as far as he could tell. A warm Italian restaurant, white linen, four-star, you're at home kind of place. Soft lighting accented intimate tables surrounded by high backs and planter boxes spilling vines. Dark Mediterranean colors played to the backdrop of Italian landscapes on the walls. And "Ma-ma" was going to make sure everything was just right.

Before Rehan could settled his napkin in his lap, a waitress approached with two martinis. "Did I order a drink?" Jimbo asked, smiling.

"Trust me on this meal and I will guide you on a culinary journey. You don't have to eat or drink anything you don't want. But back there," Carl pointed over his shoulder without looking, "magic is already happening with meat."

Rehan raised his glass. "Well, cheers, to knowing when to trust a man about a meal."

"You will not regret it. Cheers!" Carl clinked glasses and tipped it back his drink in one smooth motion letting the entire martini slide down. "The first one always goes down easy."

"If you say so." Rehan tilted his glass back and two more martinis appeared as he sat the empty glass on the table. He immediately picked up the fresh drink and toasted Carl. "I can't remember the last time I made such a fast friend, cheers!"

Carl smiled and locked eyes with Rehan. "Thanks Jimbo. Me either. Cheers."

"Tell me more about it, unless I'm boring you with the same old same old?" Rehan asked.

"Nonsense, I'm having a fine time. I never get tired of this stuff. What do you want to know first?"

"The speeds, five hundred plus miles per hour? How can the models take it?"

"The airframe is fiberglass with reinforced framing. The shell is an epoxy carbon fiber material. Serious engineering went into the original MiG designs. State of the art aerodynamics. Why do ya think I built the Russian MiG? The plans were easier to get, if you know what I mean." Carl laughed and took another deep tilt of his drink.

"Hello, Jerri." Carl smiled to a pretty, young Italian waitress as she approached, a pepper grinder at the ready. Salads appeared in front of both, delivered by a wholesome Italian boy in a crisp white apron, starched white shirt, and a smile from the Mediterranean.

"Good evening, Mr. Perkins," Jerri said. Applying fresh ground pepper as requested with just a look, then, smooth as silk, she drifted away without really interrupting their conversation. Rehan would have to remind Jimbo to tip Jerri well this evening.

"So, what's it like to fly it?" Rehan asked.

"Stressful. And another big part of it all. Only the most experienced modelers even attempt to fly these jets. Pilot's exam, licensing, training, certifications, regulations."

"Sounds like you're taking all the fun out of it."

"Oh, it's fun. Ultra-realistic nature to these jets in flight. Your reflexes must be honed to a sharp edge. It's not easy. Any mistake can cause the stresses to rip the jet apart. Or you lose control and then, Fire! You burn. da, da, da!'"

Jimbo laughed as he took a swig off his martini, washing down some lettuce, trying to remember the song to play along with Carl.

Warm bread was delivered by Jerri, with even better fresh churned butter.

Carl went for a crusty end piece right away. Dipping up a heap of butter on the tip of his knife. "It ain't cheap either, so not everybody can play," Carl said, pointing the knife at Jimbo. Rehan watched waiting for the butter to fall off the tip of the knife with each jab of emphasis. "Easy forty, fifty grand, not counting the jet fuel. And oh yeah, all the licensing, permits, training and crap. It's probably seventy-k if I really counted it all. Upgrades. Other equipment. It don't fly itself. Let's just say a cool hundred thousand if you crash and burn."

Carl swiped the butter across the bread and took a crunchy bite. "Mmm, so good."

Rehan picked a piece, felt the warmth, and buttered it up. "Lucky for us, money is no object. Bells and whistles, Carl?"

"Upgrades? Sure. Well, top of the line, everything."

"Favorites for example? Come on Carl, share, share?"

Jerri appeared alongside, setting two wine glasses on the table, opening a bottle of Chianti. A plate of fresh sliced salami, soppresata, prosciutto, pepperoni, and several thick slices of cheese appeared alongside the salads and bread. Carl quickly picked up his martini and finished it off. Wine was poured, tasted, and served.

"Thank you, Jerri." Carl drooled stabbing at a slice of cheese. "Okay Jimbo, my favorites. The video pilot flight view would have to be my favorite. Beyond visual range flying, it's a must anyway, but it's also very cool. They just go too far too fast. The dogfights are a lot more realistic from the cockpit view."

"So you fly by what? Video screen?"

"Yep, a big ol' flat screen is my favorite way to go. Some guys use three screens, one in front and one on each side. The pilot's little camera head can turn to the side in the cockpit. Some guys like the three screens, but I like my one big HD screen."

"That sounds cool as shit."

"It's just like being the pilot in an actual cockpit. The view, what you can see, is almost the same. When you know a guy's on your tail, and you're trying to shake him, but you can't see him, it gets real."

"Amazing. Don't you get distracted and fly out of range?"

"RC, radio-controlled right. All the FAA and AMA sites have radio towers. The frequencies and channels are set. It's plenty powerful for miles. Then we feed a map range into our video displays to keep us in a box. It gives us plenty of warning to turn around. The controlled airspace is way smaller than the range of the equipment."

"You're not worried about interference? It would only have to last a few seconds and you'd be down."

"State-of-the-art system. I used the best spread spectrum

technology, which reduces the chance for interference or conflicts with other electronic sources. And double conversion radio reception, and a really beefed-up modulating transmitter and receiver, it's the icing on the cake."

"Impressive, Carl, truly. It even drops little bombs? It's so cute," Jimbo joked.

Carl laughed, chewing on some bread. He took a sip of wine to clear his throat. "Not the way a real MiG works, I grant you, but the FAA wouldn't let me develop little missiles for it."

Jimbo gave a hearty, mid-western laugh, quickly having to use his napkin. "That doesn't surprise me." He took a second to wash down his bread too. "The bombs were impressive though."

"You gotta put on a show for the people. Actually, full loaded with little bombs, there's probably more explosive force in the jet then I ever could have had with some cheap bottle rocket missiles out under the wings."

"Sounds like government oversight has made a serious error in their thinking."

"I don't fight them, Jimbo. Just do everything the way they ask, and they let you go fly." Carl advised him.

Sizzling steaks on skillet plates, expertly prepared, were presented. Rehan's mouth watered at the first whiff of the crackling juices. Ringed by browned, round cut mini potatoes, chucks of caramelized onions, and a few baby carrots, the Italian rub seasoning wafted up in smokelettes around the two of them.

James Wright took a nice sip of wine, savoring the aromas as the flavors mixed on his palate.

* * *

Rehan was more than a little impressed on the drive back to Carl's. Even his knowledge of electronics and gadgets hadn't prepared him for how far along the world of RC modeling had come. He had played with remote controls plenty, back in his college days. RC planes as a kid. But Carl's advances were going to make his work much easier.

And he really liked this guy Carl too, the meal was everything he'd promised.

"I'm sorry I've kept you so late. You must be tired?" Jimbo announced as they pulled back into Carl's driveway.

"I haven't even shown you my collection of boats yet. Actually, my deep-sea subs with full video and lights are my favorites. It's better than getting seasick, and you'd be surprised at what's in the bottom of your local lake too." Carl laughed, swerving down his driveway, obviously well sauced. "It's like being your own little Captain Ahab from 20,000 Leagues Under the Sea."

"Ha, ha! You mean Nemo. Ha, Carl." As they parked and got out, Rehan continued his take-a-way on ol' Carl. "Okay, okay, well, maybe a nightcap and you can show me the subs, but then I've got to be going."

"Are you sure you won't stay? We've had a bit to drink." Carl walked up and leaned sideways to make his point. "You can always leave from here in the morning."

"Oh, I don't know. Seems like an awful imposition?"

Carl laughed as he pointed at his huge mansion. "I'm all alone here. It's got rooms I ain't ever been in."

Rehan laughed. "Okay, let's take a look at your subs and see how late it gets from there, okay? Where do you keep them?"

"I've saved the best for last my friend." Carl said gleaming as he hit a remote garage door opener.

Four double-sized garage doors opened on what Rehan assumed was just a separate, detached, four plus car garage. Maybe some fancy car collection or something, but inside was an RC modeler's dream workshop. Models, parts, and pieces hung from the entire ceiling, and most of the walls. Tools, worktables, and equipment took up an entire half of one side, on the other was what looked like an entire small hardware store. The space was deep as well, with a comfortable lounge area, TV, and kitchenette in the far back corner.

All "Jimbo" could do was whistle in astonishment. "Whoooo, that's incredible! Wow. Very impressive. Looks like I might have to stay the night." Rehan finally gave in to his new friend.

"Wait till you see it all. There's no way you're leaving, no way."

Carl gave him a quick excited tour and they ended in the back.

"Carl, let's have a nice Cognac to work on those steaks, so I can take in more of this. Unless you're getting tired?" Rehan asked.

"No way. I'll get the good stuff from the house."

"I have to check my phone in the van. I'll meet you back here in a couple minutes?"

"I'll race ya."

* * *

An hour later, Jimbo and Carl sat in lounge chairs surrounded by his modeler's fantasy world. Rehan was completely buzzed. He knew he was rambling at the guy. Carl sat across from him with a blank, glazed over stare.

"So, blah, blah, blah I'd spent so many years in the jungles of Central and South America that I became an expert on everything toxic. It was part survival, part pure interest."

Rehan laughed and leaned in a little. "You know Carl, how people who travel often collect some trinket, from each place they've been? Pins, or magnets, or shot glasses? Well, I collected rare, potent toxins and poisons. You'd be surprised . . . Everything in the jungle tries to kill everything else in the jungle."

Rehan sat back in a laugh. "If the security guards at the various airports knew how deadly some of the vials they were inspecting were? Ha, ha! Just thrown in with my medical bags. Luckily, they never attempted to actually open them."

Rehan took another sip of Cognac, let it warm down his throat. The vapor filtered through his pallet.

"I was fascinated, as a kid, to read stories of these natives who used nothing more than blow-gun darts to take down these huge animals. A little dip of poison on the tip of a dart could drop a wildebeest? What was it? Where did they get it? Can you guess, Carl? Can you guess?"

Rehan waited just a second or two.

"Frogs!"

Rehan laughed drunk and hard. "Can you believe it? I have to find out about these frogs, right? Ya know? I didn't want to step on one or something out there. So, turns out there's really only two that got the juice to knock a full-sized mammal down."

Rehan leaned in, wobbly to make a more serious point. "Ya gotta know something about the jungle ol' Carl, ol' pal. It's a rule, like a, a, law of mother frickin' nature. Anything clad in bright, vibrant colors isn't hiding, it's warning you, 'Eat me, and you die.'"

Rehan sat back and took another sip of Cognac, letting the dire warning sink in.

"So, this first frog, the Blue Poison Arrow Frog, known by its more boring scientific name, Dendrobates Azurens, is surely the most striking. It's got this bright, solid blue underbelly and legs, that shift in color up to a luminescent, light blue-back with black spots. I tell ya Carl, it's like a glowing blue, this color. With their slick skins reflecting the light and all. As beautiful as they are deadly."

"And, they're mean little bastards too. Very aggressive and territorial. They claim a few square meters of jungle marsh and it doesn't matter how big you are. If this frog is chirping, and hopping in your direction, you can bet his back is slick with a deadly skin ooze. If you look him in the eyes, he seems to be scowling at you. If you don't take the bright color, and that scowl, as a big warning sign, you're gonna be in big trouble."

Rehan tensed up in his chair, sitting back further, raising his hands to make his point. "Back away, back quickly away, because they often hang out in groups, and they all protect their little patch of jungle ground. They'll hop all over you, like they could kick your ass or something. And if any of that ooze gets in ya, it's over."

Rehan laughed, sat back up, and reached out to knock hands with Carl. Carl's hand just flopped a little to the side. Rehan fell back in his seat.

"So, how does it work, you ask? The Blue Arrow poison works by paralysis. It's great protection. If you eat me, you will choke to death as you swallow and become paralyzed. The natives roll the tips of their blow darts on the slick backs of these frogs. Then all they gotta do is barely nick their prey to immobilize it. Easy hunting from there, if the prey doesn't choke to death first, when the lungs become paralyzed, eh, Carl?"

Rehan took a swallow and wondered if maybe ol' Carl was unconscious already. But a gleam of wet, a tear, and his pupils shifting cleared it up.

"Still with me eh, Carl? So, I did say two frog species were the deadly ones, I know. The other one, the deadliest, and only slightly less pretty, is the golden yellow family of frogs known as Phyllobates. And, the deadliest of all, is the Golden Phyllobate Terribilis, the terrible golden frog. The combination of poisonous alkaloids emitted from their skins is one of the deadliest cocktails I've come across on the face of the planet. A Batrachotoxin, working almost instantly on the cardio vascular and central nervous system in a quick and deadly one-two punch."

Rehan made a clumsy, drunken Muhammad Ali rope-a-dope swing motion with his left fist.

"Few animals or people survive more than a few minutes' exposure, especially in concentrated doses. It takes the equivalent of just a couple grains of salt to kill you. And their poison can just as easily seep through skin pores, hair follicles, eyes . . . anything. It doesn't need a cut from a blow dart to get in ya.

Or, in your case, Carl, a few drops ingested with your nightcap."

Rehan looked close for a reaction. "Don't worry, I used the Blue Arrow dropper," Rehan said staring close into Carl's paralyzed face. "The natives say it's a peaceful way to go. Breathing is a little heavy, but the carbon dioxide builds up, and you get a little euphoric before falling asleep. So they say."

Rehan stood up. "I'm glad I knew who Carl Perkins of Vio-Tech really is, or I'd feel bad about killing the man who's been nothing but friendly. But we all have a reckoning, Carl. Your chip designs. Circuits. And those couplings I bragged about? The military contracts based on the applications you developed, which bought you all this wealth. If you only knew how the slaved guns you ultimately created reached out to this moment. I tell ya Carl, it's not personal, it's fate. As much as I'd like to think this is about me getting revenge. What are the chances, that you, of all people, would end up giving me the tools to do what I need to do?

Poetic justice? Divine intervention? Karma? In any case, your MiG-Rig is going to make you famous."

Jimbo toasted his new friend, who didn't flinch.

"To the best . . . Aeromodeler ever. Cheers!"

CHAPTER 26: A Call to Rally

Rehan spent the entire next day tinkering in Carl's endless workroom. Every imaginable thing he would need was right at his fingertips. It was all too easy to make the modifications he wanted. He talked to himself more and more as he worked.

It was, just by chance, a coincidence.

Chance? Chance? The man who ordered it, led to the man who pulled the trigger, which has led us here, to the man who designed it. And now we are going to use his toys to make the government that started it, and all of the others pay. Chance?

Rehan worked as he mulled it over. Other people, innocents, might be hurt too?

The ex-presidents who started it all? Just as responsible! It is your duty to avenge Father and Juma. After you've been given such a chance, by Allah himself.

Rehan turned the entire fuselage into a warhead. He was worried about all that black powder. Unlike C4, it could be set off by accident quite easily. And that would ruin everything. But, black powder was what Carl had to make his little bombs, so black powder was what Rehan used.

Allah? This is God's Will now? Killing a man out of the blue?

All of them rain terror out of a clear, blue sky every day. And the innocents die in their beds, from drones and hellfire. These people will die on stage because they support it.

Connecting the MiG-Rig's bomb bay door channel to use as a secondary detonator, Rehan attached a simple primer and keyed it to the proper frequency. He didn't think he'd need to use it, as the jet engines and fuel would surely ignite on impact, but he wanted to be able to push a button at the moment of truth. It was more intentional that way, more personal.

I think God might see me making excuses for my revenge.

Vengeance is mine sayeth the Lord, but sometimes he delivers your enemies up to slaughter at your own hand. Read your Bible.

Rehan's mind raced as it twisted, becoming oblivious to the work he was doing. Taping hardened nails to the interior alongside the bags of powder was a bit overkill.

There's a lot to take revenge for. And only God could have put us in such a position to do it.

* * *

By afternoon the next day, Rehan finished his work. He loaded the MiG-Rig, two other RC planes, a small robot Carl called his "little-bugger," along with the largest of Carl's deep-sea mini-subs into his rented van. He had plans for all of these toys later, but for now, Rehan took the time to enjoy the amenities in the house full of fine food and wine.

When Celeste showed up, Rehan was ready for her. He'd overheard Carl set the date with her the night before. And once Carl was gone, he had no way to cancel the date. He decided to play her out and use her to throw off anyone who might find Carl's body.

Rehan easily convinced her that he and Carl were old friends, and that Carl had been urgently called away, right in the middle of his visit. "Some big board meeting or the other." James Wright laid it on in his best Midwestern accent. "I'm sure ol' Carl will be back soon enough."

Rehan had planned to slip her a cocktail right away, but when she showed up, she had an uncanny similarity to Agent Susan Figiolli. He plied Celeste with fine food and wine. She tactfully confirmed her full fee and was happy to play along with the nerdy guy's C.I.A. agent fantasy.

After a great night of food, some choice wines, satiated in every way, as the fireplace was just dying down, Rehan fixed her nightcap. He ducked away to use the bathroom, so he wouldn't have to watch, again.

Returning ten minutes later to find her sprawled out, naked on the floor, the curves of her body glowing in the flickering shadows of the fireplace. Her hair was a bit tosseled, a stream of saliva ran out the side of her mouth, forming a little puddle on the hardwood floor.

Rehan carried her body out to the workshop garage, setting it across from Carl in one of the lounge chairs. She'd been so genuinely concerned, it seemed only proper that they'd be together in the end. It didn't hurt that the macabre scene would throw off police suspicions. A murder-suicide perhaps? Jilted lovers? Quick enough they'd figure she was a call girl, and it would confuse them even more. At least for a while. Long enough, anyway.

Toasting his workmanship, Rehan spent time to wipe everything down a second time. He left quietly as Carl's garage doors closed behind him. He turned his rented cargo van down the long road back to Washington, D.C. He needed to scope out the area well in advance, and have everything in place, before security tightened too much.

*   *   *

He found the perfect building, just a few blocks away, with no obstructions. It was well out of direct line of sight, so Rehan felt sure it wouldn't be swept by the Secret Service or used as an anti-sniper location.

Rehan used a gadget he had acquired as part of an arms deal to open the door to the roof. A client with ties to a security service suddenly didn't have enough cash. You never wanted to box someone in. Or threaten, when they couldn't meet their end. Simply ask what else they might offer. The world was built on barter. And clients, in that position, almost always offered something worth far more than the cash equivalent. And even if they didn't, everyone saved face, and Rehan stayed alive, respected even, by doing them a favor.

The device he had acquired looked like a USB drive with a blank metal key sticking out. No ordinary blank, however. It contained a laser; once inserted into any lock, a micromillimeter image of the tumblers is downloaded. Place the USB into a polymer sleeve, crack open the chemicals inside, and the laser projects a mold. In minutes, a workable, perfectly-keyed piece of plastic emerges.

Once on the roof, it was easy enough to find a hiding place among the various heavy-duty air conditioning units. One had a long, clear runway right off the edge of the roof. With no lip or ledge, it was the perfect launching point out over the Potomac River.

Rehan made a few trips to carry up the jet in parts. Assembled the MiG-Rig and rolled it underneath the AC unit. He attached a bed-skirt like brush material around the circumference of the base, hiding the plane nicely in its own little roof-top hanger.

Rehan stood back and checked his work. He'd need all his youthful experience to fly this sophisticated giant-sized model. Flying right off the edge of the eight-story building helped, and, if he didn't push it to its max speeds, he could fly, but it had been a long time since he played with toys like this.

* * *

Three days later, Rehan was up early and headed for the rally.

As expected the news vans and their crews arrived well ahead of the event, claiming prime parking spots, close to the action, off to the side of the main stage, in a designated area.

Rehan, as James Wright, with an added scraggly beard and ball cap, sat with coffee and a newspaper on a park bench well away from the rally entrance. He observed as the news vans set up their booms and transmitters, their crews primping.

As expected, the new on-air reporting star, Amanda Knoxx, stepped out of the Fox 5 News van. An anonymous tip from Rehan to her editor that, ". . . she'd have a big story to cover at this event." almost ensured she'd be assigned.

It was all coming together. The only thing left to worry about was the take off and control. The rally itself would dictate the final timing of it all.

Rehan casually walked, closer to the press area, following Amanda and her cameraman as they walked over to the empty speaker's stage.

Amanda turned and squared herself facing the camera, a backdrop of American flags and banners behind her. Rehan walked right up close. God, she was just the sexiest little thing, freshly showered and dressed in a ratings-raising outfit. Rehan caught scent of her high-end perfume.

"Okay, Skippy, let's roll." Amanda gave a final scrunch to her blonde curls.

"This is Amanda Knoxx for Fox 5 News on a beautiful fall day here at Lady Bird Johnson Park in Virginia, adjacent to Arlington National Cemetery, along the Potomac River, with spectacular views across to our nation's capital. What a great backdrop for Presidential Candidate John Cantor's powerful rally here today. On the stage behind me, two former presidents will espouse his merits."

Amanda turned back to the camera, a gleam in her eye. "However, the keynote speaker, four-Star General McMillian, recently tied to the tragic 'Little Juma' story, is sure to pique the interest of all. Tune in to the five o'clock news for our live report on the day's events.

"And cut. Great teaser Amanda." her camera man said.

"Thanks, Skippy. We could reshoot it. I could change it up?"

"No way. Let's get it to the van, catch the twelve o'clock early."

Rehan, in full disguise, went up to Amanda. Stood right in front of her. "Hello, Amanda, dear." He enjoyed her shocked response.

"Oh my God! I'd never have recognized you if you hadn't said hello. What's with the disguise?"

"Surely you of all people know. The C.I.A. is tracking my every move. The public's gaze, sympathies, questions? Most are well-wishers, but still, it gets old after a while," Rehan said.

"Has it been that bad? It's nearly a month. I'd think they'd have better things to do, moved on by now." Amanda said, not too convincingly. Turning away, she began walking back to her van. Rehan, as Jim Wright, followed.

"Unfortunately, they do not work on the news cycle like you, my dear. A rabid pitbull, pulling on an old rag. I don't expect they will let go any time soon. Nor the public. It's like living in a fish bowl, why do you think I haven't returned your calls?"

Amanda turned, embarrassed, checking to see if her cameraman overheard.

Rehan walked closer, careful to be discrete. "I didn't want them to impinge on your professional integrity. Observing our, indiscretions. Your stories all came from me. It might have looked . . ."

"Well, I'm a big girl so don't worry about me," Amanda said loud enough for her cameraman to hear.

Rehan expected some hurt feelings. Women hate when you just stop calling, or returning calls, especially after having them all you like. The lame excuses flowed. "Your career, it was just taking off. They bugged my place. What a mess I could have made for you."

Amanda kept up a good pace. "No reporter in this town has a stellar reputation. You're bound to piss somebody off doing your job. Smears come with the territory. You should hear what the other reporters say about me." Amanda looked over. "I'm glad to hear it though, it's nice of you to be, considerate. I was wondering what . . ." She stopped, turned and quickened her pace. Rehan followed. The cameraman caught on and lagged way behind.

Rehan had his in. "I missed you. It's just, all such a mess, and uncomfortable. Forgive me for not calling. I don't think I handled that very well at all. I just needed a few weeks to wrap my head around it all." Rehan moved closer, trying to catch her downcast gaze. "It didn't seem fair. Mixing, feelings, for you, into all of that?"

Amanda glanced up. Rehan was still unsure. He poured on the charm. "I don't ever want to hurt you, Amanda. Whatever it is we, shared. You deserve better than to go through all this crap with someone you really just met."

"Oh pee-shaw!" She burst out in the most grating reply Rehan could imagine. "If you hadn't called me in another week, I would have just written a scathing story about how maybe you really are the Chameleon."

They reached her news van, Amanda stopped, and looked at him closely, as if for the first time. "You're a hard man to figure out, and that disguise isn't helping me any. Most guys would've tried to jump me that first night, especially after the wine. And the second, how did you ever let me out of there? Giving me those stories, knowing what that all meant to me. And you fought every urge to check me out. Then I jumped you the third night. Okay, my fault. Never did that before. Never had to . . . try something. And then you don't call. No big deal, right? Like I said, most guys would have done that the first night."

"I'm not most guys Amanda."

"That's what I thought. But hey, I'm a big girl. Oh, that's right. You were the one telling me how beautiful I was, the whole woman topic we got on to. Over and over. I fell for it all."

Rehan grabbed her by the arms, pulled her close, looked deep in her crystal blue eyes, "No you didn't fall for anything. You know I was real." Then he kissed her and held until she yielded to him.

"I've really missed you, my little Camel." Amanda clumsily jumped to embrace Rehan.

Rehan lifted and swung her in a full circle embrace. Letting her down slowly, staring into her eyes. "You are so, so beautiful, but those blues of yours, a man could happily drown in those crystal blue oceans." Rehan let his hand slip down slightly over her tight little ass.

Amanda blushed and turned, looking over her shoulder at her two crew members, who quickly averted their gaze and began fumbling with the equipment and setting up their station links.

"So, what do you say, new ace reporter? The talented, 'Knoxx is Fox'? Care to let me tag along and experience what a top-notch reporter does for the day?"

Amanda was thrilled. "Sure, my own little Camel caravan."

Ugh. Rehan reflexed to himself.

"But I gotta warn you, these political rallies are long and quite boring. Maybe we get a few minutes of questions, a quick photo op. I'm afraid it isn't as glamorous as you might expect."

Rehan sealed the deal. "Don't you worry about me. It's been weeks since I've been able to take you in. I won't get bored. In fact, I may not be able to control myself."

* * *

Amanda all but forced the cameraman and technician to give Rehan the deluxe tour of the van. Rehan showed genuine interest as the crew showed him everything about their portable TV station.

He asked all the questions he needed and got a little respect from them with his knowledge.

Amanda leaned in to answer any question she actually knew, trying to mix innuendo with her comments. It was coming off like bad porn on late-night cable. Rehan was embarrassed for the other two men. They had to put up with this rising journalistic star every day.

He quickly remembered why he hadn't called her in two weeks. "Amanda, dear? Can I have a word with you?" Rehan walked her away a few paces from the van. "So, I was wondering if you, and the cameraman, could go shoot a scene and let me see how it comes over to the van? Plus, I don't know if I can stand being this close to you."

"Oh, my poor little Camel. Go across a whole desert without a drink, but a few minutes with his little concubine and he's dying of thirst?"

"Ah, yes. I, ah. Yes, well, it may be easier on me to just watch you on the monitors."

Amanda stepped in closer. "Me too. You, in this disguise? has got me thinking about all kinds of scenes. I always wondered if those biker boys back in high school really were that tough."

"I don't know if I'm the biker type Amanda?"

"At first, I liked you because you were a doctor, and rich, and I was getting what I wanted. Then your dark look, it, grew on me, especially when . . ." She lowered to a whisper. "I've never been so, taken. Treated so rough. Or come so hard. I know you could be a bad-ass biker." Amanda reached up and undid the top button of her white blouse, allowing her lacy little bra to show in the folds. "I'll give you a special report. Poor, little camel, go on, you'll get to quench your thirst soon, I promise."

Rehan played along. "We may have to stay at your place. I hope your parents don't catch the biker boy sneaking in their daughter's window."

Amanda's blue eyes burned a gaze directly at him. "Oh, you're a bad, bad boy. I may have to spank you later."

"After a nice dinner, perhaps? Some wine?"

Amanda leaned in to whisper, in a husky voice. Rehan could feel her moist breath in his ear. "Okay, you're gonna need your strength. This time, you're gonna be the one who pays for making me wait two whole weeks."

She pulled away and, in all her innocence, bit her lower lip gazing seductively into his eyes.

Rehan regretted they'd never make that date.

CHAPTER 27: And Now, for a Breaking Story

Rehan checked back in at the van poking his head inside to the technician.

"I'm going to get a drink, let me buy you something for putting up with my intrusion, and what I'm sure were a bunch of stupid questions earlier?"

The 55-year-old, overweight technician, in worn jeans, a faded, wrinkled-collard polo shirt, and dirty sneakers, was past caring about speaking the truth. "It's nice a man knows when he's bein' a pain in the ass. But we'd all put up with a lot for a shot at little Amanda, eh? Sure, I'll have a Coke."

"Coke it is. Would you mind if I borrow your press badge? It's crawling with security, and they probably won't let me back here again at this point without it."

"Here." The technician tossed Rehan his badge. "You look enough like me after a bad night anyway."

"Great. Thanks."

Rehan closed the van door and turned. The crowd was filling in quickly in a steady stream. Still thin enough to easily spot security everywhere. Rehan looped the press pass around his neck and began to make his way out.

Uniformed police officers openly questioned people randomly. Rehan didn't intentionally avoid them.

Trash cans and potential bomb hiding places were being constantly probed. He walked with purpose through the crowd as he passed right by them.

Political rallies are the Secret Service's worst nightmare, when "the people" actually get up close, and in personal contact with, their representatives.

"Stand back! Police coming through!" Right on cue, three police officers rushed by, one gingerly holding a red backpack out in front of him.

Rehan felt the eyes of the dark shadows next, watching him. On nearly every raised platform or rooftop, men in black tactical dress could be seen in key positions. Snipers and spotters and double-checkers, it seemed like every inch of ground was covered by at least two pairs of eyes. Rehan, with his badge, walked right through them.

A man appeared right in Rehan's space, cutting him off from walking, thrusting a sheet of paper at him. "Press? You'll hear about ten things today, but here's the ten facts about Cantor you need to know."

Several bystanders instantly pounced on the political opposition plant.

Rehan turned, and slinked away, dropping the flyer, hearing the berating behind him.

"This event isn't for you!" And the impassioned, "It's a free country!" replies.

To be invisible to it all, like stalking animals in the jungle, you had to be relaxed. Fluid. A tranquil state of mind is key to remaining undetectable.

When Rehan looked up, two dark-suits were striding right at him. Secret Service agents, dark sunglasses, communication ear plugs. Rehan's tranquility slipped when one reached up and held his earpiece. "Confirmed! Right here." Both moved in. And pushed right past Rehan towards the commotion he'd just left. Rehan took the jolt of adrenaline and quickened his pace just a little.

It was like a hall of mirrors fighting the oncoming crowd. Every turn offered another distorted look at the growing carnival like mix of Americana. Hip-hop to business suits. Loud, boisterous know-it-alls, who shouted down any counter-commentary, to the silent, introspective observers. Young to old. Every race. All exercising their base political rights. There was an energy, a building static charge to the air.

Rehan tried to spot the undercover agents, milling about in civilian disguises. Maybe the couple leaning against the wall, barely aware of each other? The guy at the picnic bench with the camera not taking pictures? Others were there too.

Another commotion broke out to his right. A group of protesters, cordoned off in a designated area, in a screaming match with the police.

"We have every right to go anywhere in this park! It's a public rally, in a public area!"

The police were in numbers for the small group of protesters. A commander in a dress hat and uniform stood at the focus of attention. His back up officers were all boasting their tactical riot gear.

"It's a matter of public protection during a special event." The commander replied with authority.

"That's BS! I've got a right to free speech!"

The commander stepped up, squarely looking the man in the eyes. "You've got a right to get arrested as part of your public protest which has been duly noted. This group is not mixing with that one! Public safety issue. That's it."

Rehan veered away from the commotion and was instantly startled again by a loud burst of music.

Off to the side of the stage, a band began to warm up, tuning instruments.

Was it starting already? Rehan walked faster, pushing his way forward, breaking through the funnel of crowds at the entrances, and fast walked the three blocks away. Flying up the eight stories, two-steps at a time, he was out of breath, sweating, and pumping adrenaline.

Rehan burst through the door to the roof and was suddenly blinded by the bright sunshine. The heavy metal door slipped from his sweaty grasp, swung around hard, slamming into the brick wall with a huge, clattering bang.

Shielding his eyes from the sun, Rehan was terrified to make out three black figures, two rooftops away, looking directly at him. Obviously alerted by the noise.

Only when his eyes adjusted did he realize the sniper team was intently looking the opposite way. Scanning the rally event, and other closer buildings, back in that direction.

Rehan took that jolt too. Walked casually out of sight to the far side of the building. He could hear the band far off, and loud cheers of the crowd here and there.

He reached the air conditioner and crouched down to roll the MiG-Rig out easily. He primed the engines with ether from his pack.

A thought made him scold himself. A strong breeze and the air conditioner blowing would cause the ether to dissipate. It'd be long gone before he got back to the news van for a remote start. And, if he started it now, and left it running, someone was bound to hear it.

Damn, you should have thought this part through with a better mechanism.

A second, give me a second.

Rehan tore a couple little rags and soaked them in the volatile fluid, placing one on each intake and solenoid igniter. He connected the remote battery pack, and placed it off to the side, switching it on.

The band in the distance fired up louder, playing "Hail to the Chief."

That's gotta be the real start to the rally.

Rehan bounded back down to street level, skipped and walked so fast, he was nearly jogging. Three blocks back to the rally. Stopping at the vendor carts on his way back in.

The three people in line ahead of Rehan couldn't order or pay quickly enough.

Two Cokes were finally delivered in Styrofoam cups. Rehan stepped over to a side condiment table. Placing a straw in each lid, looking around. Surprised to see his hand was shaking when he took the Blue Arrow dropper from his pack. Rehan struggled to drip several drops down one straw. He managed, without spilling it, or getting any on himself.

Rehan turned, made his way back to the news van quick enough. He closed the door behind him as he climbed inside.

"Here ya go. One icy Coke."

"Thanks." The technician took a long pull from the straw and set the Coke aside.

"Did I miss anything?" Rehan asked. And observed.

"No, but our little Amanda demanded I play you this." With a gruff, he flicked on a monitor.

Her blouse lay open a button more, showing off her lacey bra, and little curves. She stood before the platform, a hand on her hip, to tape Rehan's special opening. "We are all wet with anticipation for the upcoming rally . . ." Amanda started.

Rehan rolled his eyes and groaned, "Oh God!"

The technician gave a hearty laugh.

Rehan lost whatever she said next as he took in the stage behind her. They were all being set up on a silver platter for him to take his shot. He couldn't see how anything could go wrong. A couple minutes' flight time to worry about. Unless the black powder was set off too early by accident, a little rag fire damage from the ether wouldn't hurt a thing.

"You can turn that off," Rehan said. "Tell Amanda I got the message right away."

"Okay, you're the man. But, it gets better?"

"No. Did I miss anything else?"

The technician laughed again, went to belch, but couldn't. Took another sip of his soda. "No, just the parade of VIPs. It's amazing how long it takes those pompous asses just to sit . . ." He trailed off. Holding his stomach. A seizure grabbed at his chest.

"Are you feeling okay? You don't look so good?" Rehan asked.

The man went to speak, but seized again, and gulped at the air to take a breath. He gazed questioningly at Rehan, fear quickly taking over his struggle.

"I'm a doctor. Do you have a heart condition? You may be having a heart attack. Here, try to lie down." Rehan tried to calm the man, and himself.

He wasn't ready for what he had to watch next.

The seizures came on much stronger and in waves. Rehan instinctively backed away, falling in the opposite chair, just feet away, rolling back, pushing against the front bulkhead. The man convulsed violently. His last voluntary motion, was to topple forward out of his chair. Maybe he went to lie down as instructed.

Once on the floor, his body began to twitch and jerk, slowing to little spasms, as the attack on his central nervous system finished its work. A couple soft grunts and groans escaped as the last seizures forced his last breath out with the final contractions. With it, a foaming at the mouth, as he lost his ability to swallow and control over his nasal and saliva flow.

His eyes however, seemed to be seeing clearly. Tearing, staring in fear. If Rehan was reading them right, the man was perfectly conscious and aware as the oxygen died in his brain. A minute later, a final body cramp and spasm, his eyes glazed over as all electrical activity faded. His body released, relaxed into a slump with the discharge.

Rehan sat amazed. The large dose, right from the straw, worked much quicker on the technician than the few drops he'd put in Carl's drink.

Rehan took a rag from his backpack and wiped away the foam and spittle from the man's mouth.

He placed several drops of the blue arrow poison on the man's lips. Painting it on, like a lip-gloss. A thick coating of toxic poison.

Rehan spun around and grabbed the communications headset he knew was connected to the cameraman and Amanda out in the field.

"Hello? Hello? Can you hear me? Amanda, can you hear me?" Rehan urgently called out, knowing the microphone was open.

Amanda was the first to reply, "Rehan? Watching me and needing to hear my voice too? You really are hard-up aren't you my little Camel?"

"No! You need to come to the van quick. I think your technician is having a heart attack. I need your help right now. Hurry, both of you, please!"

They looked at each other and paused, a second of shock, before they both took off running for the van.

The other reporters looked on as they dashed past, with looks of wonder at what breaking story that Amanda Knoxx had uncovered now?

Amanda swung opened the side doors of the van. Rehan was busy giving chest compressions to a dead man. "I've already called 9-1-1, one of you needs to start breathing for him." When they paused, Rehan looked directly at the cameraman and screamed. "Now! Don't even think about it. Just pinch his nose and blow in a deep breath. Hurry, every second counts!"

The cameraman jumped to help his friend and did his best to breathe life back into him. He made it through several breaths before the first hint of the poison grabbed him in the gut. And gave three more attempts to breathe for his friend.

Unlike his friend however, his death was far less dramatic. He simply sat back, woozy, drunk like. A couple little jerks in his shoulders and chest area. His eyes rolled back in his head, and he tipped sideways unconscious, falling against the rear doors.

The big dose, not directly ingested, kills quickly and without all the flinching around. Rehan figured to remember that.

"Oh my God! Oh my God! What's happening?" Amanda screamed.

Her high-pitched voice an annoying shrill.

"My God, Amanda, it must be some kind of terrorist chemical attack on the rally. Quick, get in, before it gets worse out there." Rehan commanded.

Amanda flung herself in, slamming the van doors shut behind her.

"Let me get my medical kit. I have an antidote." Rehan said and turned to his pack.

Amanda was scared, and confused, staring at her two dead colleagues.

Rehan pulled the Blue Arrow vile out of his kit, unscrewing the dropper.

"Please, my camel, please!" Amanda pleaded behind him.

Rehan cringed. Screwed the top back on. Took out another dropper, Golden Terribilis, and turned to Amanda with it. "Open your mouth, quick. It will only take a drop or two, and it works almost immediately."

Amanda fell to her knees in front of him, looking up, opening her mouth, with her tongue fully extended.

Rehan knew a whole dropper full would kill her quick. Why was he so agitated? In that instant, for some reason, he only used a few drops on purpose. They fell in slow motion. Her crystal blue eyes looking up, pleading, in fear and confusion. The first drop splashed onto her tongue. He couldn't help but think to himself, It's Al'Ka-meal!

On the third drop, Amanda's body jerked backwards, springing to her feet, wide-eyed. She started bouncing around so violently Rehan was worried someone outside might hear her death throes slamming into the sides of the van. Foaming at the mouth, like some kind of bubble-making machine. Rehan used the technician's chair to keep her corralled in the back. The spasms caused her to spit violently. Rehan desperately ducked, used his coat to cover himself, so she didn't spit Terribilis back on him. "Shut your damn mouth!" he screamed at her in terror.

As if in answer, Amanda froze, standing in a grotesque, locked-limbed, fetal-like spasm facing Rehan. In her eyes, she suddenly seemed to realize what Rehan had just done, a questioning look.

Rehan fought to hold her stare in the fright of it all.

He didn't have to worry long, Amanda simply tipped backwards, still locked in the ridged position, smashing against the back doors, falling and rolling over like a log on top of her crew. Her shiny blue eyes staring open at the roof of the van. A final spasmed-moan of breath escaping. Rehan sat in a deep breath of horror-filled stress. Watching it all, just feet away, he fought the urge to just bolt.

He closed his eyes and released his breathing. Collecting his thoughts, calming himself. Used a basic acting technique from a "body dynamics" course he'd taken in college. He simply told his brain that he was in the van with three sleeping friends. And opened his eyes.

He had work to do and needed to be calm.

The band outside started to play "God Bless America" and the entire crowd joined in a chorus to sing. The van's main overview camera displayed a full stage of dignitaries on a main monitor. They were singing with the crowd as John Cantor took the stage, waving, and greeting his guest.

Rehan rolled over to the main console, unpacking the remote for the MiG-Rig. He quickly patched both the frequency controls, and the onboard pilot view camera, into the main control console of the news van. Instantly the pilot view camera on the MiG-Rig came on one of the many extra monitors.

Rehan could easily see the rooftop, and open air beyond. He was surprised how clear the high-def pilot camera view was. He hadn't expected the little camera to be such high quality. Good ol' Carl.

Rehan uploaded the preprogrammed alternating channels, running it all through the main transmitter, just as the final chorus outside boomed.

". . . God bless A-mer-ri-ca, my home, sweeeet, home. God bless A-mer-ric-ca . . . My home. Sweeet! Home!" All capped off with a rousing cheer and applause.

Rehan watched the monitor as a speaker stood and moved to the podium, warming up the crowd. "Yes, ladies and gentlemen, God bless America! Home of the free, and of the brave. Home to great Americans like the ones I am privileged to share this stage with today."

The speaker gestured over his shoulders.

"Great Americans who have spent their lives to build, protect, and preserve our freedoms and our way of life. They will speak to you today about the sad state of affairs in our country, and, in particular, with the current administration."

A smattering of boos went through the crowd in support for that statement.

"But have no fear, we can restore America's greatness around the world!"

And just as quickly the boos turned to cheers and shouts of agreement.

"A world where Americans are proud of our way of life . . ."

More cheers of agreement. The speaker building.

"A world where we have a right to defend ourselves, and, we don't need to apologize for being strong!"

The applause and random cheers ticked up, growing stronger.

"Because the things we fight and die for as Americans, are the foundations our forefathers ordained! Freedom! Liberty! And, most of all, in security as we pursue our rights to happiness!"

The crowd was propelled to a mini frenzy. Clapping and chanting spontaneously,

"FREEDOM! FREEDOM! FREEDOM ... Freedom ... freedom ..."

"And unlike the current administration, our candidate will do more than just talk, and be charismatic." Cheers and Yeses, mixed in the partisan crowd.

"John Cantor's 'Ten steps to strength and freedom' plan is logical, affordable, and quite literally brilliant in its simplicity." The speaker held up a finger. "And let's be very clear ladies and gentlemen, the current administration has no plan. We cannot chance even one more year of his rule!"

Boos and another chant went up throughout the crowd:

"NO PLAN! NO PLAN! ... NO plan ... No plan ... No plan ..."

"If it were only that. But, for no good reason, the current president is putting us all, and our children's, children, at great peril."

A softer background chant picked up a little, "No Reason, No Reason, No Reason ..."

"Our first speaker today knows very well about the damage being done right now. A true American hero, a veteran of every conflict over the last thirty years. A man who has put his life on the line, many, many, times. A military man unmatched in his knowledge and expertise. Four-star General of the Army, General McMillian!"

A boisterous cheer went up, flashbulbs exploded. The general rose from his honorary seat, shaking hands with the speaker as he approached the podium.

Taking over the podium, retrieving notes from his uniformed pocket, the general puffed up at the rousing cheers of appreciation and vigorous clapping, which would not die down, even when he raised his hands, repeatedly, trying to quite the crowd.

After the third time, he shrugged his shoulders, turning to his seated colleagues and with a chagrined look: *What can I do?*

He chose to turn back to the crowd, raised his arms and pumped his fist in the air, renewing the frenzied cheers and applause ... Finally, the cheers ebbed and began to fade.

"Wow! With a greeting of support like that, perhaps I should be the candidate for president?" The general joked, turning to glance at Senator John Cantor who burst out in laughter.

The crowd burst too, with another rousing round of cheers and a chant: "v.p., v.p., v.P., V.P., V.P., V.P., V.P, V.p, v.p. v.p . . ."

The General laughed when it registered, turned back to John Cantor, who pointed at him questioningly, "Hey, are you available?"

The general waited for the crowd to quiet again. "Now, now, ladies and gentlemen, you really wouldn't want to see an old soldier like me in Washington for a very simple reason . . . people who commit high-treason, against this great country, in my line of work? Are shot by a firing squad."

The crowd erupted in a new frenzy. The General talked loudly over them, leaning into the microphone. "I don't honestly know how my good friend John Cantor does it. Being politically correct? Dealing with that band of thieves and corrupt cheats? The incompetent leaders? Destroying this great nation's ability to defend itself."

* * *

Rehan, listening in the van, was brought up to boil with every word.

He pushed the remote igniter and the jet engines started instantly. The ether rags worked fine. When he throttled up, they blew away harmlessly. The powerful engines lifted the model off the roof before it came close to reaching the edge. And Rehan's worries drifted away in the beautiful blue fall sky as he easily controlled the jet and climbed.

The pilots view camera played naturally as he flew. At less than max speed, the jet was easy to handle. It seemed to beg for a little more juice. Rehan headed out over and turned up the Potomac River, leading him straight to the rally.

As he flew, he couldn't block his ears from the general's inflammatory remarks. They seemed to be echoing, coming in real time from outside, and delayed a second within the van's various recorders and monitors.

"I'm sure my comments here today are ruffling some feathers, but, in the dangerous world in which we live, we can no longer sit back and let these people destroy our God given right to defend ourselves!"

The cheers increased yet again, and a small group started another chant. "Shoot 'em all. Shoot 'em all . . . Shoot 'em all."

"That's exactly what I plan to do, take the fight to our enemy and shoot 'em all."

The crowd cheered. Muffling his approach. A smile creased Rehan's face as he felt himself relax moving to the driver seat of the van.

As the cheers died down this time, the general's ears picked up something, causing him to look up past the crowd.

Rehan, looking out the van's front windshield, easily spotted the approaching jet clearing the trees along the bank of the river. He turned, then dove, coming in high, angling down. He increased his speed, directly towards the general standing at the podium. Directly over the crowd, head-on into the platform.

Rehan's monitor with the pilot view camera went black. The Secret Service jammers successfully blocked the small transmitter on the jet from transmitting a picture to Rehan from the pilot cam.

Rehan knew the Secret Service would surely employ countermeasures. A rally like this would include a massive array of radio jammers, just in case some would be terrorist had precisely this idea. Which is why Rehan's plan included the commandeering of the news van, with its massive on-site television transmitter. Now that the jet was in sight, Rehan no longer needed the pilot camera to transmit to him. The powerful news van transmitter, meant the Secret Service could do little to stop Rehan's powerful control transmissions to the jet.

Even if the Secret Service managed to lock on to his specific frequency, and concentrate their jamming efforts, it would only work for a split second before Ol' Carl's cutting edge, modulated, variable channels, would change to the next frequency in the program.

Rehan watched, and flew it home, never losing his flight controls to the jammers at all.

Flying directly at him, at 400 miles per hour, four-star General McMillian froze, cocked his head slightly. "Is that a MiG? No one told me about a MiG fly over?" he mumbled audibly, picked up by the microphone.

The jet came screaming in, low over the crowd. Within the last couple feet of the podium, Rehan pushed his detonate button, not disappointed with that upgrade.

It was personal, much more personal that way.

CHAPTER 28: The Hypocrisy of Covering One of Your Own

Susan Figiolli, General Givens, two of the Mr. Greens, and her entire team sat spell bound in her control room watching the various news feeds on the multiple displays. The "horrific terrorist strike" had been captured by so many T.V. networks and average cell phone toting citizens, there seemed to be no end to the various angles and views of the tragedy.

An expert talking head was on the main screen dissecting the event on slow motion frame by frame review. "General McMillian can be seen raising his arms, here, at the very last second, before the massive fireball and explosion simply blot him, and the podium, from existence."

None of the various views changed that aspect of the carnage.

Later, they would only find pieces, and a badly charred lower torso, of the late General.

"The explosion was quite massive and deadly. The forward momentum and impact of the jet, its nearly full fuel tanks, and what was obviously some sort of intentional primer, to set off the warhead, was devastating."

An anchorman on the broadcast chimed in asking the expert. "How is it that only one other person on that the stage was killed? Or injured severely? Especially with so many victims in the crowd?"

"The secret service deployed a fail-safe drop-platform device when their jammers failed to stop the incoming model aircraft. The whole stage appears to explode on impact, but, if you look close, in that instant, the back platform of the entire stage hinges open, and all ten dignitaries spill below into a padded, protected, safe area underneath. Immediate fire suppression nozzles jet super cooled, high pressure, fire retardant chemicals up and out of the base safe area. You can see them here, billowing up, counter-acting most of the force and flames from the deadly explosion. Other than being severely shaken, everyone else on the platform is protected and escapes relatively unscathed."

Susan spoke over them. "Nine people in the crowd were not so well protected, or so lucky."

"The despicable use of hardened nails acted like so many projectiles of death . . ."

Mr. Green shook his head. "The news is nothing if not sensationalistic."

As if to emphasize his point, a brunette anchor added to the report. "Fifty spectators sustained injuries, eighteen in very serious, critical condition. Loss of limbs, blinding's, various puncture wounds and severe burns. The list of horrors is endless. The most heart wrenching, a little girl seen here, on her father's shoulders, right up front, at the time of the blast. Consumed by fire, blown back, along with most of the crowd, she is seen falling from view. With severe injuries and burns, she is expected to soon be the thirteenth victim."

Givens was furious. "That son-of-a bitch wants everyone to feel bad about his sister? Same as that little girl right there, right?"

The station switched to several interviews with various VIPs telling their own version of the harrowing event, their brush with certain death. Thanking the miraculous forethought of the Secret Service. With an outraged demand for justice. Prayers to the suffering victims, families, and especially those who had lost loved ones. And of course, maintaining a firm conviction to "not allow terrorist to deter them from living out their lives free from fear, in their pursuit of happiness."

It turned into a P.R. campaign tag-line painfully repeated, over and over. Scripted. Down to the use of the same words, in interview after interview.

Publicly, they set aside their political differences for "a proper period of mourning."

It didn't stop the reporters as the broadcast continued, "Is this an example of an emboldened enemy? Exactly what General McMillian was speaking about at the instant of his death? The current administration's foreign policy? And soft military stance?"

A male anchor held a finger to his earpiece and broke in. "Excuse me Sally. We have breaking news."

The anchorman paused, pushed hard on his ear piece. His face changed to shock at whatever it was. Serious, and somber, he released his hand and looked up to the camera.

"The tragedy at today's rally has just taken a strange turn. As covered earlier, the Fox 5 News van caught fire at the time of the blast, presumably a result of the explosion and debris. It was fully consumed in the aftermath. Three bodies have now been discovered in that News 5 van and it appears that recent rising journalistic star Amanda Knoxx is believed to be one of the deceased. Details are still coming in . . ."

The graphics team at the station was, 'in the moment,' as they say, a beautiful headshot of a smiling Amanda Knoxx appeared, in all her innocence.

* * *

A few days later, back in Susan's control room, the "Rally Bombing" investigation was in full swing. Unfortunately, nobody except Susan, and her team, believe Rehan Al'Camel was responsible, or even capable, of pulling off the terrorist strike at the rally. Federal investigators were clamoring for anyone who might have photos. Unfortunately, no one really takes pictures of the press assembly area.

The various news vans had been packed in tight, and you couldn't see in between them. The News 5 van was especially buried. Burned to a hulk, investigators soon determined the fire was not caused by the explosion. Whoever set the blaze and left the three dead bodies at the time of the explosion, had vanished without a trace.

A shot of Susan Figiolli appeared on TV, caught by reporters earlier that day as she emerged from a meeting at the White House with the President himself. Timmy sent her there to plead her case directly.

Without giving it a second thought Givens spoke into the air . . . "Hey Hal, turn up . . . what channel is that? On monitor 6? . . . the one with Susan on it?"

"That is channel 8, ACN news in Washington D.C. General." The Palantir responded.

"Okay, okay, just turn it up." Givens shot back.

An off-camera reporter's voice could be heard as Susan, trailed by a few of her team, descended the marbled steps of the White House guest entrance.

". . . and did the President give you any particular instructions regarding your investigation into the jungle bombing now that America is under attack?"

Susan answered, still moving, only barely glancing up to make her way through. "As I said, I won't comment on anything the President might or might not have said."

"Does that mean you will continue your intensive investigation of Doctor Al'Camel?" The reporter asked.

Susan stopped short, turning sharp towards her. "We do not investigate anyone more intensively than anyone else. We gather facts, and follow those leads, wherever they point."

"And would you say the facts still point towards the good Doctor?" Another reporter shot from off to one side, as a myriad of microphones zeroed in on Susan's chin.

"I won't comment on any ongoing investigation. Rehan Al'Camel . . . we are interested in, talking with him. Regarding the bombing at the rally, it's an ongoing investigation so I have no comment." Susan was trying to be as dull as possible.

"The Rally Bombing? Are you saying you think Doctor Rehan Al'Camel is involved in the terrorist attack at the rally as well?"

"No. We are, seeking Rehan Al'Camel for questioning, that's all."

"Seeking? . . . are you saying that the good doctor is in hiding, or, missing?' A sharp woman reporter asked, stepping partially in Susan path.

Susan wanted to slap the microphone away and bowl her over. But stopped, kept poised, and felt the torture of trying to choose every word that came out of her mouth. "We have not heard from Doctor Al'Camel in over a week. And our calls to his attorneys, have not resulted in our being able to, contact him for questioning."

An audible gasp and rumble went through the crowd of reporters as they all pressed in closer.

Susan wasn't sure where she slipped up, but she felt the jaws of the great white news shark snap-closed right around her. Flash bulbs exploded, Susan had to cover her eyes, then donned her sunglasses.

The lady reporter pushed in on Susan, "So you are targeting him? In your, investigation. And he's missing under mysterious circumstances? And you think he's involved in the Rally Bombing too . . . is that right Mrs. Figiolli?"

Susan looked at the reporter like she was speaking Martian. In a reflex, she decided to make a break for it. "No. I have no further comment . . . please, let me by!" Susan pushed past a few cameramen to escape into a dark sedan waiting at the curb.

The camera shot her car pulling away, and then panned around to the lady reporter. With a gleam in her eye, she filed her trailer. "There you have it. The woman known as "the Black Widow" continues her relentless pursuit of the renovated Dr. Rehan Al'Camel, and we have just learned that her dogged attempts to ensnare him in her web have driven the poor Doctor into hiding or . . . perhaps worse?

The reporter raised her notepad to check her facts. "From her own lips, she admits, and I quote, "Rehan Al'Camel. We are interested in talking with him. Regarding the bombing at the rally." Apparently, there's no end to what the good doctor is capable of.

"To this reporter, one thing is clear, the whole story has not yet been revealed to the American public. What is the government hiding? And how much longer before the Black Widow manages to catch the prey she seems so obviously fixated on?"

The reporter swept her hair to the side of one ear, leaned in slightly to the camera. "And I must say, that cold look in her eye, just before she pounced into her waiting black chauffeured transport, well, it gave this tenured reporter a cold chill. What web is she spinning to try and catch the good doctor? Or, has he already been wrapped up? Obviously, she didn't want to stay long enough to answer our basic questions. This is Cindy Marcale, for ACN news, reporting from the White House."

General Givens and Mr. Green stood in stunned silence gawking at the monitor.

Susan couldn't contain herself. "Please Pal turn it back to mute! Pounce? Pounce? Did I pounce into the car?" Susan paced. And turned. And gestured. "Chauffeured . . . what did she call it? A transport? Did it look like a space ship or something? Or a, a stretch limo? Jesus, it's a standard issue Grand Marquis. Cold stare? I was fricking blinded by all those cameras, did she not see me put on my sunglasses? How the hell can I give a cold stare through my dark sunglasses?"

Mr. Green moved closer to try and calm her. "Susan please, you're better than that amateur, she's just going for ratings. You know how their game works. Try to relax."

"Relax? Relax? It was on film for Christ sakes. How can they say something I didn't say, and then point out something I didn't do? Are people that gullible?"

"Yes!" Mr. Green shot back. "Now get a hold of yourself because this is going to get a lot worse before it gets any better."

Susan felt the slap expecting some compassion. Mr. Green must have saw it in her eyes, and tried to adjust, in his own arrogant way. "Oh Please, I hate seeing you this way. It's no different than a counter-intelligence disinformation ploy. These reporters are covert agents, working to smear you, and distort the truth, with disinformation and sensationalism. You wouldn't let propaganda get under your skin like this out in the field, would you?"

"No, of course not, but these are supposed to be my fellow Americans . . . people I've . . . my whole life. Things I've done, put on the line . . ." Susan's anger trailed off. "I guess it stings a bit more."

Mr. Green picked right back up, "Even fellow Americans can be snakes in the grass sometimes. And it's in the nature of reporters. But trust me, they will just as quickly turn their bites towards 'the good doctor' or any other bad guys we uncover. Just keep doing your job and you'll be exonerated in the end."

"I'm not so sure Mr. Green. Shit, what's your name? I can't keep calling you Mr. Fucking Green forever? Especially with two of you in here." Susan pointed, irritated over it all, as the second Mr. Green on duty tried to melt further into the corner.

"Sorry, in here, it's still Mr. Green. I'm past my allowable time on duty. He's just observing. Pretend he isn't there."

Givens backed him up. "He's right, Susan, you'll be the good guy in the end, okay? Just don't put on those sunglasses in front of the camera's again. They look like giant spider eyes on ya miss Black Widow."

Susan turned quick to face him, shocked at first. She broke, laughed at the crazy stress of it all. "I shouldn't be so full of myself, I guess."

General Givens added, "Think how ridiculous it all is. People will see it in the end."

But the more Susan thought about it, the less sure she felt. Like climbing out of quick-sand, only to be sucked back down further. "I wish it were true General, but it doesn't work that way in our line of work. Most times, when things go well, nobody ever knows we were there. I doubt I'll ever be able to go in front of the cameras and say, I told you so." Susan drifted away, sat back down, worked on reports, not wanting to look at the news coverage any longer.

Mr. Green wasn't going to let her sulk, but a picture of Amanda Knoxx on a monitor caught his eye. "Hal, volume up on monitor eight."

The station was in the middle of a memorial for the reporter and her crewmates, whose pictures were quickly added to Amanda's on screen.

The smiling photos of all three reminded Susan how deadly this game had become, and how badly she was failing.

A woman co-anchor was speaking. ". . . as the News 5 family mourns the loss. Long time technician Ed Reed, our newer but still beloved cameraman Randy Wilson, and off course, the beautiful and talented reporter Miss Amanda Knoxx. Whose tragic death ended a promising young career just coming into full bloom."

A male news anchor chimed in. "Yes Sally, her cutting edge, in-depth reporting, covering tough subjects we as fellow Americans may not want to face . . . a breath of fresh air in our industry. A Pulitzer awarded posthumously seems fitting? I'm sure, somewhere up there, Amanda and little Juma are in a happier place and giving each other a heart-felt hug."

The female anchor continued, in a spat of anger. "How can some in the C.I.A. possibly think Rehan Al'Camel is involved in the rally bombing? Amanda Knoxx was perhaps his biggest advocate. Some same the two were even forming an emotional attachment. We need our intelligence agencies to wake up and realize there's a much bigger threat out there."

Susan saw it all plain as day. The Chameleon had the news, the public, police, homeland security, federal agencies, the full force and weight of the U.S. Government, military and intelligence, all looking for an international terror network that didn't exist. Susan could see this puzzle as the Chameleon was building it. And no one would ever believe her, even if she screamed it out loud. The President, with all his advisors, and cabinet members, and top brass military drowned her out. At least the President had listened. But the military industrial complex was already gearing up for war. And she'd got run over by a tank in the White House situation room.

Susan couldn't take it anymore, "Please, Pal mute that volume! God, I think I'm going to throw up. They all hated that Amanda Knoxx, the hypocrites. And what in-depth reporting? Rehan Al'Camel fed it too her, and I doubt she had to spread her little legs to get it from him either."

"Susan?" Mr. Green cut in, walking right over to her. "Whatever

Amanda did, or was, she didn't deserve to die, left in that van like that."

Susan couldn't believe what just came out of her mouth? Prayed an apologized to Amanda, promised she'd catch whoever killed her.

Normally that would be easy, since Susan knew exactly who that was.

But it was never easy . . . chasing the Chameleon.

CHAPTER 29: Covering Your Tracks
When Leaving the World

Rehan walked out the front door of his sand-stone house into the bright sunshine of the Kuwaiti village he'd grown up in. He headed towards two young children he could hear playing hysterically around in the side yard. At least a few adults, in burst of laughter, were enjoying whatever scene was unfolding.

The wind seemed loud in his ears as he walked to investigate. It muffled his hearing, but strangely, he couldn't feel it blowing hard at all? His hair and clothes barely moved? He couldn't feel the heat from the blazing sun overhead either. It must be hot?

A thrilled squeal of laughter erupted and two little specters came running around the corner of the house, sliding to a stop, dead still and quiet, just feet in front of Rehan.

Juma took a bloody arm from around her waist and reached to hold the charred hand of her terribly burned friend standing next to her, who was shaking in fear before Rehan.

Rehan froze. Locked by the sight of it. The sound of the wind blew in his ears like a tempest now without the slightest breeze in the dry desert air.

Juma smiled at Rehan then turned to her little friend. "It's Okay, he's my brother. Don't be scared."

Black ash flew from the little girl's mouth in wisp of wind as she mouthed silent words in Juma's ear. The ashes swirled in the air briefly, turning a silvery, glittery-white as they rose. Each spec of ash turned into a bright little white star as they floated up above their heads. The pin-lights were slowly sucked back around the far corner of the house in a galaxy-like whirlwind.

The little girl finished whispering and turned her head down into Juma's puffy shoulder, standing in closer to hide.

Juma looked up at Rehan. She gave him the same sideways, angry, questioning look she'd gave Sargent Jakes. "Why Rehan?"

Rehan sensed depths of sadness pouring over him in waves,

emanating from Juma's soul, hitting and breaking into him. He couldn't talk, he almost retched.

"You hurt my friend? Look, you ruined her dress?" Juma admonished him.

Rehan looked down at the blackened face trying to hide in the puffy shoulder of Juma's white dress. Tears streamed out with the tilt of his head. "I'm so sorry. I didn't realize, you were so close. I didn't think."

An angry voice came from the far corner of the house. "You thought about a lot of things, don't say you didn't realize." Amanda Knoxx stood peering, with her crystal-blue eyes blazing like neon lights, from around the corner. She was holding on to the far sidewall, her hair flying wildly in the wind Rehan could hear but not feel.

Then, all the other ghost Rehan made materialized in swirls behind her. They seemed happy, smiling and laughing, as they came walking up. But, as they peered over and past Amanda, they looked at Rehan with, with . . . pity?

Rehan looked down in shame. Afraid and guilty, he couldn't even look at his Juma.

Amanda called out in a loving voice. "Come on back now girls, you know you can't stay out there." Amanda and the others never came past the corner of the house. Rehan somehow knew they couldn't.

Juma turned to Amanda. "I know my brother's been bad, but can't he come play with us? Just a little? Until Kendall's not afraid of him anymore?"

"No dear Juma, I don't think he can."

Juma turned back and looked up at Rehan. "Why Rehan?"

"I'm so sorry Juma, I'm sorry." Rehan went to hug her.

Juma reached up with her other arm to hug him back . . .

Before her wound could spill open . . .

. . . Rehan regained his conscious mind.

*   *   *

Screaming in his dream until he heard it enough to stop, in a warm damp sweat, Rehan caught a sharp breath, and fell back to his pillow.

Sirens and honking horns blared outside an open window to the sounds of a bustling city street below. Lying on a dingy twin mattress, directly on the floor, Rehan was soaked in what he hoped was mostly his own sweat. It smelled horrible. He didn't want to know.

It took him a second to remember where he was.

"What's up Re-bar? Have a little nightmare?" Sitting across from him, in the cluttered warehouse workshop like space, in a kitchenette area, at a rickety table, a rough looking Asian man with a crack-pipe held to his lips fired up his addiction. He cooked the pipe hard.

Scrawny, and worn out, he could have been sixty something. It was hard for Rehan to imagine his friend was his age. Only the jet-black hair, and the weak, unkept facial patches, gave any clue that he might still be a young man.

"No Zhang, I'm just a little hot and sweaty is all." Rehan said, sitting up on an elbow, rubbing the back of his neck.

"Don't lie." Zhang said, holding his hit. Smoke whiffed out of his nostrils. He sucked in again and again, hoping to catch them. When he couldn't hold it any longer, he let it out in a long, tempered breath. "I was your roommate in college for years, you always had nightmares." Zhang coughed out.

"Have you just been sitting there smoking that crap watching me? Damn, Zhang."

"Don't judge me. You promised if I helped, you wouldn't get on my shit."

"But did you sleep at all?"

"No. I told you. It's got me. I'm not fighting it anymore. An I don't wanna feel like shit about it. We, Agreed!"

"Okay, okay, sorry. Just hot as hell. Isn't this supposed to be the fall?"

"Global warming. The buildings haven't cooled down from summer yet." Zhang fired up his pipe and took another hit. "I finished the sub . . ." Zhang gulped, pointing with the smoking pipe. Blowing out a huge billowing cloud, he made a satisfying exhale out it.

"It's so cool to be hanging out again Re-bar. Remembering all the shit we blew up. The car wrecks. Halloween frat parties, blood and guts, freaking the girls out. Remember?"

"I remember Hollywood studios coming to hire you as the next genius effects artist."

"To hire us my friend, us. You were always the smart engineer one.

The electronics. The controls. My God, the math! I'd've blown myself up in college a hundred times if not for you."

"You give me too much credit Zhang."

"No way Re-bar. You checked shit like, 'the impact acceleration stresses.' Whatever the hell that is. To me, it was just two cars I wanted to smash together. You made it all work, I just made it look good."

"You were the artist Zhang, and the studios knew it. They have a thousand guys like me. The techniques and methods you came up with. They're still using them today."

"Nah, CGI has ruined it all. There's no art left to it anymore. But we did a great job this week, on your little projects, didn't we?"

"Yes, my friend, your masterpiece."

Rehan got up and walked over to Carl's RC sub sitting on a worktable. The top was open, the inside packed with explosive and three shaped charges. "This looks beautiful Zhang."

"Are you really going to use it?" Zhang asked, leaning forward in his chair.

"I'm not sure yet. If they make me. But no credits for you though."

"Ugh, no credits please. Reminds me of Hollywood. They don't do credits here in New York for shooting TV commercials. They just pay me."

"You understand, right? I have to disappear. At least for a while." Rehan asked.

"I guess so, with a freaky huge brain chasing you. The conspiracy theorist would have a field day. And I'd never believe those nut-jobs. Not if you hadn't told me. It's scary shit."

"That's why I needed your help buddy. And once I release your video masterpiece, hopefully, nobody will be looking for me. I'll be free forever."

"But how do you know it isn't on to you right now?" Zhang's facial expression changed as the thought registered. The worst side effects of the crack took hold. He looked around in fright and paranoia. Held a finger to his lips in a near panicked gesture to keep Rehan quiet. He got up and crossed over to his door, looking through the peep-hole over and over as he double checked the locks. Then, he half tip-toed, half slinked and ducked his way over to the side of the windows. He stood glancing out and around nervously through the tattered remnants of some long-ago curtains.

"Don't worry Zhang." Rehan calmed him. "I've got three whole new identities. Top grade. They'll even pass background checks. No way the brain can possibly know I'm here. Relax."

"Okay. If you say so." Zhang sat back down, his eyes darting around in fright as he loaded his pipe. "Helping you screw with that fucking thing is credits enough. I just hope you can get away. Fuck Hollywood."

"I've had plans in place for years in case I had to disappear my friend. Don't worry. You were great in Hollywood Zhang, how many blockbusters did you work on?"

"I don't remember, by the second year, I was hooked on this." Zhang lifted his pipe and fired up another big hit smiling at Rehan from behind the flame.

"Tell me again about these shaped charges. Why not pack in more explosive instead of leaving these three empty, upside down, metal cones in there?"

"There's plenty of explosive in that bad boy." Zhang grabbed Rehan hard by the arm. "Don't be close when it goes off." Zhang choked out, then let go, and blew out his hit to the side. "It's called the Munroe Effect. The three upside down metal cones create a void, that's true. But, the enormous pressure of the explosion drives into the conical void and collapses it upon the central axis. The collapsed metal cone forms a big ol' metal slug, called a "carrot", because that's what it looks like. The tip of the cone, buried at the bottom of the sub," Zhang pointed down into the upside-down metal cones. ". . . is already collapsed, and dense, so it's got nowhere to collapse under the force. The explosion turns it into a high-speed tip full of kinetic energy, which is jetted upwards even as it's reduced to particles. The larger mass, the open end of the cone at the top here," Zhang made a circle with his hands to match the top open end of the upside-down metal cones. "collapses a split second later" he squished his hands together quickly, "and squirts the tip like a hammer up into whatever surface it has all been blasted into. All happens at hypersonic speed, but the end result, you can punch a hole right through thick layers of solid steel armor."

"I just need to make sure it goes through a double-hull if I need it to?" Rehan asked.

"Oh, it will. And once the hull is breached the air void inside the ship will suck in the underwater explosion, the water pressure adding a little kick. The mass of the ship above will force the blast even deeper into the target. It'll be devastating. I wish I could be there to see it."

"It's great Zhang, really. And you got the 'little bugger' attached up front here." Rehan pointed to a little 2-foot by 2-foot treaded vehicle attached to the sub and held on by its grappling arm.

"That 'little bugger' you call it, is totally awesome. I took out all the junk I could from the sub but I left the grappling arm to help hold it in place. So, make sure you release the sub's arm before you power up the "bugger" and try to drive off. "

"My friend Carl designed it as an autonomous spy device. It was designed to creep up on any enemy and just hang out." Rehan said.

Zhang laughed. "Oh, it'll do that. The tank treads are a combination of suction-cups and electromagnets. And whatever that material is inside the cups, I've never seen it before. It can climb up onto anything. Even upside down. Believe me, I tried it on everything in here while you slept. And your friend Carl also designed it to carry an explosive charge, or the military asked him to. I've added a shaped charge to explode downwards, under the bugger, right?"

"Yes, if I'm forced to use it, I'll need the charge to explode down, under the little bugger. The sub will need to explode up, into the hull of a ship."

"I wish I could be there to see that too." Zhang went over to the kitchen table and loaded another hit. Lighting it up and smoking hard.

"Are you sure you could never stop Zhang-man? Are you sure?"

Zhang blew the hit out quickly to the side. "Yes." He paused in a head rush, sat, looking down, in an unfocused wobble. "It's torture Re-bar. I'll drop soon. You promised."

Rehan walked over to his friend. "Well, let's go eat? Get some air? We worked hard this last week. You can show me around a little."

"Nah, I'm good here." Zhang drifted back in his rickety chair, pipe in one hand out to one side, butane lighter in the other.

"Zhang, come on?"

Zhang motioned with his pipe to several small yellowish-white rocks, about the size of a pair of dice. "You don't get it. I got a day or so more here."

It didn't look like a lot to Rehan. The stuff must really be potent.

Zhang pointed with his pipe towards the open window behind

Rehan. "And this ain't no area for us to be 'showing you around' in. You hungry? Downstairs, out the door, one block left is Telly's. Nice little place. Other than that, you take a cab outta here and come back."

"Okay, no last meal. Fine. Be back in an hour or so."

"Take your time. But I'm ready when you are, when you get back."

Rehan made his way towards Telly's in deep thought. The nightmares were weighing in on him. The fitful sleeps made him edgy. Zhang made him edgy. He couldn't release the constant scowl of tension on his brow. The only good thing about his mood was the street hustlers couldn't figure him as a mark as he walked.

As Rehan crossed the street to the entrance of Telly's, a corner newsstand displayed a wall of news pictures on every publication. The 'COLD BLOODED' headline of Events magazine drew him in. The little blond girl from his dreams sat atop her father's shoulders. A frozen, confused look on her face, the split second before she was engulfed. Her father's helpless, knowing look of horror from below clutching at her. A Greek tragedy which could've been carved from a single piece of stone.

Rehan could feel himself bending under the stress of it all. Talking to himself more and more.

Look at it, how can it be? I am just like them.

The right target was hit. A military target. You can't feel true remorse for that?

WHY? Because it happens sometimes in battle? That's what they would say. To justify it.

It became impossible to delude himself. The visual memories flashed in his head constantly. Amanda and her ghost stalked around his Juma time. There was no disassociation like he had with the arms sales all those years before. His stoic demeanor. Logic. Intelligence. Medical works of mercy. None of it helped in this raw reality.

He'd spent days with Zhang building devices in the end he truly hoped he'd never have to use. Knowing, if they forced him to, a part of him, an uncontrollable part, would. That thought weighed on him most of all. They were terrible, horrific ideas.

General McMillian has paid. Perhaps he was the ultimate responsible target anyway.

Rehan worked hard to convince himself, to find an out, pushing his old rage and desire for revenge down deeper and deeper into his subconscious.

Has it come to mass-murder? The news pictures blurred and swirled in a whirlwind, like in his Juma dreams.

Rehan had to push hard. To make all those years and layers fit, and to fold them neatly, one into another, but he finally found a way to close the lid. I'm all exposed now anyway. Any second away from arrest and eternal incarceration. Death? Escape is the only logical option. It has always been the plan in this eventuality anyway.

It's never good when your two minds are at odds. They start playing tricks on each other. Rehan set his resolve. Do only what you have to do from here to escape. Then, fade away to Kuwait forever. Remake yourself, as a devoted family man. A rebirth.

Maybe Susan Figiolli was right after all. The whole mess. Rehan finally talked himself into accepting, that he could let it all go now.

CHAPTER 30: Chasing Shadows

Susan stood leaning with both hands on her console peering out over her control room.

Mr. Green stood with his arms crossed next to her, scanning the various monitors.

"Seven days since the bombing?" Susan moaned. "Did he go down a rabbit hole like Saddam?" Susan shook her head, watching her team work furiously in futility.

"I'm surprised your Pal hasn't saved the day," Mr. Green said sarcastically, and frustrated.

"Why do you always have to?" Susan took a breath. "Every photo and video from the rally was dissected. Not just with facial recognition either. DMV, Fed and State ID's, Criminal records . . . Facebook."

"I bet you're thrilled how fast they let it have access to everything after that rally bombing."

"Once, they thought some terrorist group, or nation sponsor, bombed our political rally, yeah, they opened stuff up to my Pal, so what? Facial recognition only accounted for 78% of the crowd, but, out of all the people at the rally, guess how many are still in question?"

"Don't gloat Susan," Mr. Green said.

"Three. Two are women. The other one could easily be Rehan in disguise."

Her Pal supported her by displaying the photos of a man at the rally from various angles. No clear, head on shots. A few blurry camera-phone pictures. Side views from some of the news coverage. A scraggly bearded man in jeans and a hoody who looked like your average blue collar DC worker, right down to his work-boots.

Mr. Green pointed at the image. "I'd like to talk with the man in person, and both woman for that matter." He turned back to Susan. "Doctor Al'Camel's lawyers are still claiming that they have absolutely no contact with him?"

"Of course. Imagine the retainer. There's an army of people working to find him. Each a little kitten sucking at the escrow teat, dollars streaming in 24/7 to their coffers."

"He's smart. Anyone who looks too hard will be reassigned, or fired, right up until that money runs out." Mr. Green said, then flushed in silence.

Susan looked back at his frustration. "Good legal help is hard to come by and it cost money to provide that level of service."

"Any other leads? People of interest?" Mr. Green said, almost pleading.

"Anyone at, or tied to, the rally, especially with any kind of criminal blemish, was brought in for interviews by the F.B.I. with a live feed to my Pal. Body language, pupil dilations, temperature, respiratory and other improvements my Pal made . . ."

"I get it, your Pal's a genius."

". . . to determine any discrepancy or knowledge of events. No red flags. Not even a yellow one. All other tracts to this investigation seems to be going nowhere."

"The problem remains, nobody's going to believe it's Rehan Al'Camel." Mr. Green said.

Susan and Mr. Green were interrupted by a startled murmur building in her control room. On the monitor wall, TV stations were breaking to Special Report screens like dominoes falling. All programming was interrupted. Everyone sat back in wonder.

"Pal, turn up the main monitor please." Susan said.

Givens was out of the room getting lunch but came running back in with his cell phone in one hand and half a sandwich flopping around in a wrapper in the other. "Well I was just about ta give ya some shockin' news but it looks like were all 'bout to hear."

Susan's gut instinct kicked hard, an instant certainty, whatever this was, it was related.

The volume came up as the 'Special News Bulletin' screen faded to a serious looking news anchorman.

"Ladies and Gentlemen, we have breaking news regarding the mysterious disappearance of Doctor Rehan Al'Camel, the focus of an intense manhunt, and some say, an ill-founded prosecution by the F.B.I and C.I.A. It appears the American people's opinion of the good Doctor has been well founded. Just released to news organizations around the world, a terrorist group is claiming responsibility for the rally bombing, and their leader is claiming to be the real Chameleon."

"Most now know, the Chameleon is a long-time arms dealer who's worked against the interest of the United States around the world for decades. Until today, some in our intelligence agencies believed the true identity of this wanted man was none other than Doctor Rehan Al'Camel. But now, there can be little doubt.

Warning. The video you are about to see is extremely graphic, and shows what appears to be the death and decapitation of Doctor Rehan Al'Camel. I warn all parents, anyone the least bit sensitive, to please turn away now or turn off your televisions. Again, the tape about to be played shows the graphic murder of Doctor Rehan Al'Camel. Parental discretion is strongly advised. . . . Please roll the tape."

A blurred, badly taped video immediately came onto the screen. Seated, tied to a chair, was an obviously shaken and very scared Rehan Al'Camel. Dressed in a dirty suit and white shirt, with a scruffy new-beard face and tasseled hair hinting at days of being held captive. Behind him hung a large black banner with red Arabic writing on it.

Alongside of Rehan stood a man in green camo fatigues wearing a full-face, black ski mask. He held an AK-47 across his chest and stood up straight facing the camera. He began speaking in Middle Eastern accented broken English, with a strong threatening tone.

"Allah Akbar! For over one weeks, we have watched while you have placed credit for our attack on this man. An American dog, traitor to Islam, who deserves no such glory. I am the one they call the Chameleon. My group is responsible for what this man takes credit for."

"I have attacked your leaders. Our attacks continue until our demands are met in full. American infidels, if your leaders are not safe, than what of you? Or you children? U.S. government has brought this terror on to you, but, we know that the American is the one who votes for these evils. All are responsible. We will have no difference in you. Meet our demands or this is what we do to the American dogs."

He paused as he stepped off a little to the side and leveled his AK-47.

Rehan let out a blood curling scream through the dirty rag-gagging him. "Noooooo!"

The sound clicked loud when the terrorist worked the bolt action to chamber a round.

A short burst of automatic fire flew through Rehan Al'Camel just feet away, cutting off his scream in a guttural gasp.

The wooden chair shattered and crumbled as Rehan, blasted sideways, fell with it to the ground. Blood splattered on the banner behind him as he was flung over just out of frame.

The gunman stepped in front of the camera, he slowly set the AK-47 down, then slid a long, serrated bladed knife from a sheath tied to his leg. He paused to point maniacally with it at the camera. He calmly moved over and panned the camera down to where the crumbled body lay on the floor, still tied to pieces of the chair.

Blood poured out from beneath. Wounds on Rehan's chest and abdomen oozed streams of blood, his shirt and waist turned a dark color as it soaked it all up.

The masked terrorist walked into view, knelt, and gruffly grabbed a handful of the motionless Doctors hair, pulling his head back, exposing his neck. He drew the knife back and forth across severing the head after a few sickening strokes.

Blood gushed from the neck and poured out from the head. The assailant stood and held out his bloody prize walking up to the camera. The unmistakable face and half opened eyes of Dr. Rehan Al'Camel stared blankly directly into the lens.

"Allah teaches us to be merciful and we respect His will, unlike the American devil. You have one weeks to meet our demands, or this will be your fate. We will show no more mercy. We are here in your country. We are everywhere. No one of America is safe. Allah Akbar!"

The screen flicked to black, and the news switched back to a clammy looking anchorman who seemed to be holding back tears, and vomit, as he spoke. "Shocking. A truly shocking end to the life of this man who seemed destined for tragedy. I'm sure I speak for most Americans when I pray that Doctor Rehan Al'Camel is finally reunited with his family and, most of all, his little sister Juma in heaven."

He paused for dramatic effect, adjusting to maintain his composure. Clearing his throat. "If you are just joining us, the mysterious disappearance of Doctor Rehan Al'Camel has been solved in what appears to be his horrific death at the hands of Islamic terrorist in a video just released to news organizations around the world. A letter of demands was included. The government has asked us to withhold it for a short time."

"We are going to return you now to your regular programming. Join us at the top of the hour on the 12 o'clock news. This has been a Breaking News Special Report."

Susan's room sat in stunned silence and only a few people managed to start tapping away at their keyboards. A single woman's quiet sobs slowly mixed with the hum of the air conditioning and computer equipment.

Givens was the first to speak, standing slack-jawed with his half sandwich drooping in one hand. "Holy, shit. I fucked up about that guy. Jesus."

Susan slowly sat down, leaning back, gesturing at the monitors with her outstretched hand. "What just happened? Did I just see that?"

General Givens tried his best to be stoic. "Ya just won that dinner bet that's what happened. Looks like yer instincts were right all along Susan, I'm sorry I doubted ya."

Susan felt like the chair was moving around under her. "But? . . . but, it's not possible now? I mean, how can it be? My Pal was up to eighty nine percent probable."

Mr. Green stepped forward. "First, always remember, your Pal could be wrong. Second, don't believe everything you see on the news is my advice."

Susan turned, shaking her head, bewildered.

Givens turned on him. "What the hell ya talkin about? They just cut his fuckin' head off right on camera?"

Mr. Green was undeterred. "I understand that's what you saw, but I'm just saying, let's not jump to any conclusions here."

Givens stood tall and laughed. "Ya lost yer mind. Standin' back there, holdin' it all in, it finally made ya crack. Ya think that guy cut his own head off now?"

Mr. Green answered just as stoically as if he were telling someone how he liked his coffee. "That's what it looked like, yes."

Susan stood, shocked from her chair, weighing the debate between them.

"Pretty damned convincin too," Givens said and looked at Susan. "Somehow he staged all that? I mean, maybe the gunshots, and the chair, and the blood and all, but ya saw 'em pull it back and saw it off? Then, the fucker stuck it in the camera. Sure as hell looked like Doctor Camel ta me."

"Understood, and very convincing, but I'll be more convinced once the Hal, and our team, have had a chance to analyze it. And, once the actual body is found and examined. Then I'll be convinced. But until then, I wouldn't be so sure."

Susan came around. It was the Chameleon after all. "Did you see something we missed?"

Mr. Green looked at her. "I may be wrong my dear Susan but, consider a few things. Given the history, all the slips, tricks and backtracking stunts this Chameleon has pulled over all the years, has there ever been one shred of proof, even an inkling, that he was some kind of Islamic terrorist? Much less a fanatical one?"

Givens conceded the point. "Okay, those guys don't hide their stripes. They scream it from the rooftops every chance they get, an' twice daily fer prayer."

"Exactly. All of a sudden, our Chameleon is supposed to be this big Islamic terrorist, with a network, and agenda. I ask you, does that fit with the man you have been chasing for the last decade?"

"No, no it does not." Susan answered without doubt.

Mr. Green continued. "Terrorist are often quite amateurish but this one, as smart as our Chameleon is, he can't afford a decent quality video camera? Or operate it? Even the cheap ones don't have a picture quality that bad. He said, 'we are here', presumably in the U.S., so why the crappy video image?"

General Givens seemed stunned by the logic. "Holy crap."

Mr. Green stepped up to Susan. "I'll bet you double or nothing on our dinner that your Pal will have trouble precisely because the quality is so bad, like on purpose bad."

Susan smiled in appreciation of his intellect. "No way I'd take your double or nothing bet now, you should have bet me right after I saw that spectacle."

Mr. Green pointed at the screen like he was going to continue his train of thought, but he was cut short by the Palantir. "Mr. Green is correct. The video is not factually accurate in many ways."

A recreation of the video began playing on the main screen from the point where Rehan was shot. Only everything was filtered in a black and white negative exposure, except the wooden chair Rehan was sitting in. The full color of the chair made it pop off the screen in clarity.

"Pal, what are you showing me?" Susan asked, knowing she was about to be awed again.

"Proof Mr. Green is correct." The video rolled in a freeze frame slow motion. "First, the chair explodes in many places, collapsing. But, as you see, the explosive force is outward towards the camera. These are not bullet impacts at the proposed trajectory."

The view zoomed in on the arm of the chair. "Here you see the support on the left arm of the chair explode at the time of execution. However," The view fast-forward to the crumpled body lying on the floor bleeding. "Here, the left chair arm support is shown intact, tied to the supposed body of Rehan Al'Camel lying on the floor. An impossibility if the previous event is factual."

Mr. Green added in. "Of course, I'm not a military man General, and the AK blast was certainly dramatic, but, other than the chair, I didn't see any body parts coming off. And it looked too intact lying on the ground afterwards. Those bullets just zip clean through, do they?"

"Not if they hit any kinda bone they don't. Yer right, it would, or should have, looked more like the pieces of that chair, especially the exit wounds." Givens acknowledged.

"A one hundred percent correct analysis. There are other discrepancies." The Palantir confirmed.

Mr. Green tilted his head towards Susan. Leaned in close. Gave her a deep look in the eyes. Then commanded of her. "It's been a tough couple of weeks, I know. But I want to see my confident, intelligent, top room controller gazing at me with those brown eyes smoldering as she works the case. Move on!"

Damn he could play at her intrigue. And it was working. Susan instantly felt more like her intelligence agent self with something to chew on. She gave Mr. Green a smiled, with a warmth in her look she didn't know she had for him. Somehow his cold, hard, suspicious intellect, or view point, or whatever, it was working on her.

She stood, turned to speak to her room, to her team, knowing her Pal was already listening. "Okay people, you've all heard the first analysis and we should have lots to work on here. I want ballistics to look at each bullet. Trajectory. Impacts. Exits. The way the chair came apart. Forensics and medical review, the impact and motion of the body. Decapitation, blood splatter, wounds, blood leakage, on the ground and coming out of the body, the neck, and dripping from the head. Get firearms to check that

AK stock to barrel. The bullets, powder charges, discharge, bolt action. Run that knife too. What is it? Who's most likely to have one? Where was it purchased? Video techs need to be working on that tape. What kind of camera, why's the picture so shitty? Settings? Light? Speed? Motion stability? Mode? Everything. Duplicate it. Give it all to the computer animation nerds to reverse filter and make it pretty for me so I can see it.

"Linguist? Analyze that banner. What does it say? Is it stated properly? Are the letters written in the right, motion? Is that a real Arabic speaker? If so, where's he from? Country? Down to the village, to the mud brick home he grew up in.

"I'll need an audio specialist too. All the settings. Microphones used? Break it into tracks. Filter it for background noises? Planes. Cars . . . a train going by? If there's a God damned bird chirping in a tree I want to know what sex it is and where it is on its migration path. Was it day or night outside? What time? Look for reflections in the knife blade, or that fuckers belt buckle. I want every frame of that film analyzed by ten different specialists and I want it yesterday. We're on lockdown, you won't be home for dinner. You all know we're using my Pal to help us on this one. Help him. Show him he isn't the only smart brain here at Langley."

Susan felt so good to be back in control, with so much to work on. That video was all just a little too convenient. Just the kind of thing the Chameleon would pull.

Susan turned and smiled to thank Mr. Green, this time, her playful tilt was all too real. "Doctor Rehan Al'Camel is still at eighty-nine percent probable and rising fast. If the good Doctor still has his head attached to his shoulders, I've got him."

"Does that mean we win?" General Givens confirmed.

"Staging his own death? What other possible explanation could there be?"

Susan leaned forward over her own console with a single thought: *You're not giving me this bullshit Doctor, I don't buy it. You just spun a web of your own making.*

Didn't you hear? I'm the Black Widow . . . Now I'm going to bite you in the ass.

CHAPTER 31: New Games, New Rules

Rehan left Zhang's life, and New York, behind. He was headed a few hundred miles north to the suburbs of Providence, Rhode Island. Driving for hours, he switched the radio from station to station to catch the latest angles on the story. Delighted with the huge media frenzy created over the video of his death.

Every imaginable Islamic group was already under scrutiny from the rally bombing. The full power and might of America was coiled to strike at anyone connected to the Chameleon Group, or the bombing murder of an American military hero. Islamic groups and Muslim countries condemned the attack publicly, with statements of condolences, even as their clerics and radical masses openly celebrated.

State sponsored terror groups and extremist all wisely, and in fear, remained silent over the video beheading. None acknowledged any connection to the mysterious "Chameleon Group" as the media now dubbed them. Its deadly leader was a complete mystery.

The logic followed that it must be a wholly new independent cell of Al 'Qaeda. Or perhaps a whole new terror group coming onto the world's stage?

Rehan had no illusions the American government would ever meet the outlandish terrorist demands he released along with the video. He'd thrown in every idealistic cliché he could think of; "Close Guantanamo Bay Prison, leave Iraq and Afghanistan, close military bases in Turkey, the United Arab Emirates, Kuwait and most importantly in the holy lands of Saudi Arabia. Release hundreds of prisoners held around the world by the secret U.S. agencies and allies . . ." The list went on and on. Far, far away from Rehan. Who was dead.

If he could keep stirring the current hysteria, then that brain, and Susan Figiolli, would be running in circles off somewhere else. I just need a little more time to slip away. A final, big diversion when they don't meet the deadline.

The news broke his thoughts. The Federal Government was gearing up for war. But no-one knew who to target? Rehan felt the high at being such an active part of current events. He had to keep watching his speed all jacked up on the adrenaline.

Not the big terrible thing, you can let that idea go. Just do enough to tie up the C.I.A., and that brain.

His current I.D. as Jim Wright was wearing thin. There was always a balance of time with any fake identity. Based on the risk of how much shit you pulled while living in it. He hadn't used the credit cards or ID "on the grid" too much so far. And he didn't want to burn ol' Jimbo yet, if he could avoid it. He would most likely need two more identities to eventually cross the border.

* * *

It was a long drive, digesting the news which repeated itself over and over for hours. Rehan timed his arrival, pulled his non-descript white cargo van into the back-parking lot of the happenstance middle school late Friday afternoon. He only saw two cars left in the entire lot. All the teachers and staff already skipped out, done with work for the weekend.

Rehan swung the van around behind the school, past the ball fields and the giant 'Go Bulldogs' scoreboard. His timing seemed perfect.

He backed into a service dock loading bay with a roll down door. A small set of metal stairs led up to a side door entrance. Rehan pulled on the locked roll-down doors.

He walked up the metal stairs. A buzzer with a sign alongside the locked door. 'Ring for Entry, All Visitors, Deliveries and Contractors MUST CHECK IN AT THE MAIN OFFICE.'

Rehan smiled slightly knowing no one would be there to greet him at this hour on a Friday.

Rehan rang the buzzer over and over. He wore it out. He went back to his van and started honking his horn, incessantly. After 5 minutes, a rickety thin old black man in uniformed blue work pants and a striped shirt appeared at the door. His scowled face set, he fast paced down the side stairs and walked up to the van.

It didn't bode well for Rehan. The man was thin and frail from age but obviously still in good shape. His eyes were sharp and clear with anger. His jaw unlocked as he barked at Rehan.

"What the hell is all the racket mister?"

Rehan decided right away on a strong offense. "I've got a delivery for the science department. A special delivery!" Rehan gruffly shouted back at the man, ignoring him while looking at a clipboard and some papers.

"Well, it is way after school hours so you are going to have to come back on Monday pal, see the sign?" The man pointed with his thumb up over his shoulder behind him. Along the top of the loading dock a sign clearly stated delivery times. They ended at 3pm on Fridays, and it was now closer to 4:00.

"Yeah, the school should have stated that policy before they had me drive all the way from New York with this thing. Our contract with the school board clearly states that any special delivery hours MUST be reported at time of booking, and I wouldn't be sitting here now if they had done that, now would I?" Rehan said, staying strong in his response.

"Well I don't know what to tell ya mister, in case you didn't notice, I'm just the janitor, not the principle, not the school board, so you're barking at the wrong dude."

"Look!" Rehan said sternly and jumped so fast out of the van the janitor moved back to defend himself.

Rehan gave him a sideways glance. "Just look for Christ sakes." he walked around to the back of the van swinging open the two back doors.

The janitor, curious, side-stepped around to look. Rehan was pleased to see his expression instantly change, his eyes bulging in curiosity.

"Yo, what the heck is that?"

"That big one there is an autonomous, remote controlled, deep sea submarine. Well, a model of one anyway. And it's no toy so, as you might imagine, each school only gets three days to use it. If you don't let me leave it inside on the dock, I gotta take it back to New York. Monday they'll figure it all out and, I assume, reissue my delivery paperwork for Tuesday. I'll drive it back up on Tuesday but, then I gotta turn around and pick it up on Wednesday, so I can deliver to the next school in line. Do you see what I'm saying? Are you telling me you're going to deprive those kids a chance to see this thing in action?"

The janitor looked at Rehan and smiled. "No way, dude . . . shit, I'm gonna be the one helping the staff launch this baby. Where they planning to use it?"

"I have no idea, I just deliver and pick-up. Everybody's been absolutely thrilled so far. Look, you don't have to let me in the school, we just set it right inside the door there and you sign that I delivered it. Believe me, the science department will be all over it first thing Monday morning."

The janitor joked, "Well maybe they won't know it was missin' over the weekend then, huh?" he smiled slyly at Rehan ". . . if it went for a dip with my kids and grandkids first?"

Rehan paused and looked the man up and down for a moment. He let the guy want it.

"Yeah, I suppose I could show you how it works. Just promise you'll make sure the batteries are fully charged before you launch it. And you gotta watch the clock too, okay? People get all excited and end up too far out, or too deep, then don't have enough juice to retrieve it. That's the biggest mistake, and I'll deny I ever helped you if you lose this thing at the bottom of some pond."

The janitor smiled broadly. "You serious? Okay man, thanks! The kids are gonna love this thing. I promise, I'll be careful with her."

Rehan paused, looking the man up and down, like maybe he was reconsidering. "Alright, but it's your job if you screw up. All I did was deliver it and you signed for it. What you did after I left? . . . that's on you. Just keep it juiced and use a timer, other than that, it's stupid easy to operate."

"I'll get the door, help you unload it." The janitor turned on his heels and sprung up the steps to go inside and unlock the roll-down door to let Rehan in.

Rehan took out his Golden Terribilis dropper and spread more than enough on the outside loading dock door handle as he heard the janitor inside unlatching things.

Rehan noticed a man in a suit leave the building, get into one of the last two cars left in the parking lot, and drive away.

Rehan was sure he and the janitor were alone, but he wanted to be positive. As the roll-up loading door opened Rehan smiled. "I just saw the only other car leave the lot . . . I'm guessing that's your truck?"

"Yeah, it's just me left."

"Good, I can't have people saying they saw me show you how it works. Close the door and come on down, I'll go over it all with you. Then we'll just load it in your truck for now. You got somebody to help put it back inside later, right? . . . before Monday morning?" Rehan asked with authority, in character.

"Hell yeah." The old janitor reached up and closed the bay door grasping the deadly handle.

He began clutching his chest before they reached his truck.

Rehan tried not to watch, turned away. It wasn't as bad as being stuck in that news-van. He just stood there listening as the nice old janitor died on the ground behind him. Rehan hated that he was more used to it now, to the killing.

He was careful to use a cloth to wipe off any leftover poison on the door to the dock. He loaded the janitors body into his truck and drove it a short distance into the woods beyond the ball fields. If anyone came to the school to check, they'd see his truck was gone, and find all the doors locked. Maybe by Sunday they'd make an interior search of the school, but Rehan doubted it. He'd be long gone by late Sunday morning anyway.

* * *

Rehan worked Friday evening, and the whole day Saturday, to rig the school with what Zhang called a 'chain-of-beads'. A half-stick of C4 each, all tied to a single detonation frequency. You could make the chain as long as you wanted. Controlled by a couple throw away cell phones. Off the shelf deadly.

As he worked, Rehan twisted and turned in his mind more than on the step ladder. He worried about being locked up in that school, all alone, just him and his logic, doing what he was doing.

General McMillian's dead. Susan Figiolli and the C.I.A., exposed. Suffering a living hell in the media.

Rehan found another niche to hide explosives. Frustrating Susan Figiolli, now that he knew how many years she'd been chasing him, was the most fun to think about. "The Black Widow?" It was too perfect. Her and her self-righteousness. If only he could set it up so she'd be demoted, or even fired altogether. He fantasized about finding her at a bar years later, drowning her sorrows, a broken woman. He'd hit on her, seduce her in disguise. How sweet would that be? Only to reveal himself . . . just before he killed her.

The protector, from the jungle, was angry at him. Agent Susan Figiolli, and the C.I.A., are close, and getting closer every day. The enemy's getting smarter.

Smart enough to develop artificial brains to think for them? What could be a better tool for the devil than that? Following a soulless beast and doing its bidding. It's perverted. An abomination. And they're blind to it as well.

Rehan felt older, and wiser. Tired too, after fighting for so long. He was no Martyr. He didn't believe God wanted him to sacrifice his whole life. He'd given up so much already . . . a lifetime, and his lost childhood.

Rehan was trying to convince himself that God had given him this last experience to warn him; to finish his career, and escape.

His battle raged in his head, oblivious to the timers and detonators he was setting.

With a few hundred kids exposed along with his torment . . . Rehan was losing his battle.

CHAPTER 32: Perspective is from the Eyes of the Viewer

Susan was summoned from her control room by an executive assistant of Director Timothy Scott, to appear at a last-minute press conference he'd set-up. No pre-press release or notice. No stoic public relations agent making a statement . . . Director Scott, himself?

The aide that escorted Susan through the hallways at the C.I.A. was little help.

"He just called it at 4pm? To begin at 5:45 sharp? Help a girl out?" Susan pleaded as they walked.

The motherly female aide gave a slight, sympathetic shrug of her shoulders. Of course, she knew nothing, but really everything, that was going on.

Susan looked straight ahead, wondered out loud. "His comments will make the 6 o'clock news, and the weekend papers." She took her debate internal. It won't allow time for the editors to change the context, or final message. No spin, just the story. Timmy's obviously hoping it will come across just the way he delivers it.

Susan turned a corner on a long corridor leading to the doors of the press conference room. She saw Givens standing there, in full dress uniform?

"What the hell is going on?" Susan asked going right up to him.

"I got no idea?"

"No idea? You're dressed for a parade!" Susan snapped at him. Then turned and noticed several of her team members, also all dressed up. "What the hell people?"

Before anyone could answer another aide came striding down the hall towards them. "The director is ready, he asks all of you to file onstage, in line, behind the podium, thank you." The aide opened the door and stood to the side.

Susan felt like cattle in the shoot, letting everyone lead the way. Clicks and whirls of a hundred cameras filled the doorway in an explosion of flash bulbs.

Director Scott appeared as he walked with purpose and motioned with authority for Susan to enter ahead of him. A stern, stone look on his face, his jaw set, looking right past her.

The roar of photographic equipment rose to another level as they both walked on stage. An audible murmur filled the reporters' gallery as the procession settled on stage, forming a semi-circle along its entire length behind the podium. Susan ended standing just behind Timmy's right shoulder as he took position at the podium.

Sounds of the cameras faded off to a more sustainable level.

Susan stood straight, slowly looking out in an arch. Press from all over had sped to be there.

She came to the only conclusion she could think of. Timmy must have finally been placed in a position to ask for her resignation. She looked again at the press. Almost drooling.

Susan hated most that Timmy would be forced to apologize. "Errors in judgement, Mistakes were made." Her stomach roiled with the acid of it.

She could see the anticipation on the faces of the press now. A "humbled" security service, an "official apology", posthumously, to Dr. Rehan Al'Camel, his Father, and little Juma. Maybe some new details about the jungle bombing, or the rally attack, or Dr. Al'Camels death investigation would come out.

But the climax would be the extermination of the Black Widow.

Heads rolling, with a hobbled C.I.A. director wielding the hatchet . . . juicy.

Susan couldn't blame the press for being excited, a big day for them after all. Just a matter of how Timmy worded things. The only little sting was that he hadn't warned her first?

Maybe he couldn't? They liked each other genuinely, so much. Maybe it was a mercy on his part? No politics or being polite. Just a quick, respectful, headshot. There were all kinds of ways that could happen in her line of work.

Susan came around to realizing he was doing her a favor. It probably wasn't easy on him either, putting down one of his favorite dogs.

Director Scott stood center stage, the C.I.A. seal emblazoned on front of the podium, bracketed in honorary flags to either side in the back of the room.

The reporter's area was packed with so much equipment no one could move. The murmurs and nervous laughter of the reporter's gallery was a lot like a viewing at a funeral . . . or right before a public execution.

Without retrieving any notes, Director Scott adjusted the microphone and began speaking, looking side to side, even before the room fell silent.

"Welcome ladies and gentlemen of the press." An explosion of flashes erupted, too many flashes for Director Scott, who raised his hand to shield his eyes. "Kill the flash people."

"It has become clear to me, over the last several weeks, that some hard decisions, and a frank discussion, must take place to move forward. Events sometime get in the way of common sense, but, at the end of the day, we all must take responsibility for our actions. At some point, people need to be held accountable."

The whole room leaned-in towards the stage. Susan felt like a wall was about to collapse on her.

"Make no mistake, as director of the C.I.A., I . . ." Timmy paused, turned and acknowledge all those on stage standing behind him. "We all, have to keep many secrets. I think you'd all agree, at some point, we must protect our trade secrets.

However, ALL of us at the C.I.A. recognize the important role a free press plays in our great nation. We understand your job is to constantly dig and try to uncover a story. Even if it is about secrets, our tricks of the trade . . . and especially if we make mistakes, or, God forbid, exceed our mandates."

A silence fell over the room.

"The C.I.A. works in countries all over the world, places without a free press. Your job is important. A foundation of our constitution. History will certainly bear me out."

Timmy looked serious around the room. "I'm telling you, it's a power with as much force as any we wield here at the C.I.A. Our stated agendas are completely contradictory to one another. But, it's a very good thing in the end."

Timmy paused, "However, with power, comes responsibility. Accountability. When we are wrong, make mistakes, errors in judgment, we must face it." Camera's exploded. The moment before the heads roll always made for interesting photography.

Susan felt her stomach drop as every lens turned to focus in on her. She could sense the millions of eyes behind them. Trying hard not to shake but couldn't tell if she was or not. Waves of energy surged through her. Damned if she'd give them the satisfaction of seeing her be anything but stoic. Susan bit down hard on the inside of her cheek and stood firm.

Director Scott dropped the bombshell. "And I, as the Presidential appointed director of this great nation's finest security agency, sworn to uphold and protect the constitution by that appointment, I, am here today, to state flatly, that YOU!" He pointed a finger at the room of reporters. "The press as a whole, YOU are wrong. You have failed in your constitutional duty as a free press."

The cameras exploded in reflex before anyone started to question the statement. Reporters turned to one another confused? An audible, and building murmur, filled the room.

Director Scott held up his arms to the crowd of riled reporters. "Quiet please, quiet!" He talked over the stragglers. "First, an example of exactly what I am talking about, so that you might see how blinded most of you have become," Reporters were still mumbling to one side, louder now, angry. Director Scott glared over as if to a noisy, spoiled, little child unhappy about being set straight. "Quiet down! Or I'll have you escorted from the room. You people have created a very real and serious threat to our national security and by God you will get it right."

Only a few cameras dared to click off. Each one drawing the stern gaze of Timothy Scott, before he continued.

"Just a few days ago, sent to virtually all of you, a video was shared with the world press simultaneously. Not to the police, the F.B.I. or the C.I.A. And while it was quite sensational, not one of you took the time to question it? Not its motive. Not its message. Not even if it was real!"

A shocked gasp sent the professionals back in the game. Cameras and questions drummed each other out. The director only spoke louder. "Of course, it's our job to do exactly that but, I submit, it was your job too! His scream ended with a disappointed shake of his head.

The roar of questions exceeded the volume of the microphone. As soon as it died down enough, "It has been days, days! No one has even questioned that, that, piece of propaganda?"

Reporters surged forward, shouting questions. Director Scott surged back over the podium, yelled over them in admonishment. "How can that be? It took our analyst a slick second to figure it out. And yet, here we are three days later?"

Reporters seemed to cower, zapped of their power. The mass in the room faded back from the stage. The thought, the realization, of what he was saying hit home. "If you were my agents, I'd fire every last one of you. It's incompetence, a total lack of due diligence. Unacceptable. Since I can't, I will simply say, shame. Shame! Collectively, for not doing your constitutional duty. You've been used, duped, played for fools, and it was done all too easily."

A reported screamed out above the din. "The video's a fake? What proof do you have to say that?"

"YES, that's exactly what it is! A blatant and obvious fake. GO DO YOUR DAMN JOB!" Director Scott jabbed a finger at the reporter who dared question him for emphasis. "Basic video analysis . . . no great secret resource, no special technique or method. I'm not going to just give it to you, so I say again: go- do- your- damn- jobs."

Director Scott let them hang as they exploded again with questions.

"Now, I'll move on to my second example." A few more questions popped out but he stared them down. "I'm moving on, or didn't you hear me? I will call you all to task for your coverage of the jungle bombing some weeks ago, the aftermath, and your ongoing inability to look at that event with the most basic objectivity or journalistic integrity. Wielding power is more than just about sensational ratings. Yes, there was an attempt to bomb and kill the arms dealer known as the Chameleon. Yes, there was a village where collateral damage killed a group of innocent people. It weighs heavily on our minds . . . OUR minds, as a collective agency." Timmy turned slightly over each shoulder to acknowledge the semi-circle behind him.

"I won't make excuses. Sometimes we make mistakes and those mistakes often end in tragedy. We are not perfect, if you want proof, there's a bunch of marbled Stars etched into the wall downstairs in the lobby. Nothing will bring those villagers back. We try to learn lessons, hopefully do better next time, but I stand here today, and I tell you, as the director of this intelligence agency, after in depth review of that mission, if the same exact situation happened tomorrow, I would hope like hell that agents under my authority would act EXACTLY the same way."

Another excited gasp and camera frenzy exploded the room.

Director Scott kept going, "I'm telling you, the press, got it wrong, not the other way around. As soon as you investigate, you'll all see how wrong you were." Timmy shook his head in regret. "Let me ask you, when have our secrets ever stopped you before? You bought a one-sided story and ran it as fact, as the truth? I assure you, IT IS NOT."

The reporters were stunned silent, instinctively listening, none wanted to miss any of this. This, was news.

"Not everything is secret. Facts, FACTS, plain to see, ten brave American military personnel lost their lives. There's no doubt that these American hero's, who made the ultimate sacrifice, neutralized at least six surface to air missiles. Modern, third generation missiles capable, as is clear by the facts, of downing some of our most advanced aircraft and defeating our most sophisticated countermeasures." He raised a finger to make his point. "Missiles, which if left in the hands of our enemies, would posed a very real threat to every American traveling anywhere in the world. They died for all of you. But, instead of being heralded as heroes, for dying in the line of duty, you all have spun this story into the worst case of misplaced blame since Vietnam. I say again, SHAME!"

A dissatisfied rumble spread.

Susan stood there transfixed, trying to focus on Director Scott just feet in front of her.

He took the briefest glance at her over his shoulder. A little smirk, a quick twitch of a wink, it all seemed in slow motion, with a muffled rumble of the press corps.

"Which brings me to the here and now, to the people standing with me, and in particular, Agent Susan Figiolli." It was as if lightning cracked in the air. It snapped the reporters to life, with clicks and flashes, and a zoom at Susan. Timmy turned and opened his arm out to Susan, pulling her forward with a gesture to stand next to him at the podium. The strobe effect made her feel like she was gliding to position. Glad to have something, and someone, to hold on to. Timmy smiled sideways at her, ignoring the reporters.

"Yes, here today, right before you, is an American hero as well. You couldn't' be more wrong about her, and I intend to set you straight. You came here today expecting something else, but you are wrong about that as well."

Susan stared at the side of his face, noticing the stubble of his shave? His words seemed to echo from far off. Timmy turned his gaze away, back to the gallery in anger. "It's ridiculous to me, despicable really, the things you have reported about this top civil servant. You have no right to make stuff up. Sensationalism is not journalism, or the right of a free press. With no verified basis, it's unethical. Immoral. Criminal.

"I tell you all, and listen carefully to me now, her years of service, her entire adult life, has been given freely to protecting and upholding your rights and freedoms. Including freedom of the press. It's an abuse what you have done to this fine young woman and top C.I.A. career agent. 'The Black Widow'? Do you really believe all the propaganda put out by her enemies designed to destroy her reputation?"

Another rumble started to one side. "SILENCE!" Timmy scowled at them. "I'm not finished.

It makes you one of our enemy's biggest weapons, instead of one of our country's biggest assets."

Murmurs spread quietly, but no questions.

"Let me straighten you all out on a few facts, which I can share. This young lady has put her life on the line, for all of you, countless times. Over her career, she has been asked to do things, suspend her own life, given up her freedoms, even any realistic chance to be a wife and mother. We've put her in dangerous and highly stressful situations most of you can't even imagine. Assignments and mission's even other agents wouldn't or couldn't take."

"And never once, NOT ONCE, did she say no. No question of her own safety. She has always followed the rules, the law, and whatever procedures we've asked. Above and beyond her duties. Not a single reprimand or disciplinary action is to be found in her file, not one."

"She has helped countless other agents too, saved their lives in the field, on more than one occasion . . . with her wits and sheer guts. Her service record is stellar.

"AND, for the record, her actions in the jungle operation, and her investigation into Doctor Rehan Al'Camel, has been by the book and stellar as well. Soon you will all see how wrong you have been about her, soon you will know what fools you have been made of.

"And I hope to God the American people are mad as hell at you for it in the end. You've turned the public against us, caused them to unwittingly put themselves in more danger because they don't want to help us. That's damn near a criminal act on your part.

"And so, we come to the real reason for my press conference today. I am officially requesting, as acting director of the C.I.A. that, agent Susan Figiolli, be awarded our highest honor, the Distinguished Intelligence Cross."

Director Scott turned his body and squared his shoulders to Susan. His glance captured her in tunnel vision as he continued. "A medal given for voluntary acts of extraordinary heroism. Involving the acceptance of existing, known dangers. Dangers she took on with conspicuous fortitude and with exemplary courage. It will be my great honor, and proud duty, to award it to her."

Director Scott turned sternly back to the reporters. "But, I won't do that here in front of you here today. You don't deserve to witness an American hero being decorated for service to our country. You, the press, haven't earned that privilege."

He let that hang in the air for a moment. Timmy turned in a broad smile, then reached out to embrace Susan. She couldn't seem to be able to raise her arms to hug him back.

She was trying to make sense of it. The politics of Washington always eroded through? Heads roll. . . . but not this time, somehow? In waves of energy, spinning, her hearing muffled, like being underwater, she could see the reporters screaming questions, nearly climbing over each other towards her. Things were moving funny, not slow, like in a dream, but flickers of film in an old-time movie. A dream? Was she dreaming?

Givens moved up close, all too proud in support, she remembered feeling his warmth.

Several of her female team members, faces teared up, streamed by in support. A few of her male counterparts all but cheered on stage. Standing tall over the reporters as they made their way off stage.

Susan only knew she was awake because she got jostled, and hugged, and moved towards the exit. If it had been the championship football game, they might have lifted her on their shoulders, and carried off in triumph. They really didn't need to, Susan felt like she was floating in the air already.

She didn't realize until later, watching herself on TV, that tears had simply streamed down her face for the entire last two minutes of Timmy's defense. She hadn't even remembered letting them fall at the time.

PART III

CHAPTER 33: A Tormented Beast, The Danger of It All

Rehan listened to the news for so many hours, days, in a row, it was easy to work at the school in silence, in his own thoughts. Late Saturday, he'd fallen asleep early, collapsed really, into a cocoon made out of mats in the school gym.

A grumbling stomach woke him at sunrise Sunday morning. Famished after surviving on the school vending machines.

He packed everything in his van and left it parked at the school. Then walked the couple miles or so to a diner he'd spotted on his way in the day before. A nice breakfast of bacon and eggs, hotcakes, with fresh coffee and juice sounded perfect. His stomach growled as he approached the Silver Coach diner.

'IT's A PIG!' screamed the headlines of a used newspaper on the table top of his booth as he sat down.

Rehan lost his appetite fast. Trying to read the entire newspaper all at once, sweat erupted out of him. He couldn't believe his eyes? How could the story have changed so quickly? Friday evening, to Sunday morning? It was all upside down?

". . . I asked, do ya want some coffee mister?"

Startled, Rehan jumped hard enough to hit his legs on the underside of the table. Silverware rattled, and the sugar dispenser hopped in the air. Rehan almost knocked it completely over grabbing at it.

"Geeze mister, I just checkin' if ya wanted coffee? Okay, you're cut off, de-cafe is all we'll serve ya." The waitress broke out with a hyena-like cackle over her clever little joke.

Rehan's mind was racing on a far-off track. "Ah, no, no thanks. No coffee . . ." Rehan stammered looking back to the newspaper.

The waitress just as quickly stopped her laugh. "Okay, ya ready to order?"

Rehan never registered the question, reading again.

The waitress rolled her eyes and turned to check another table.

His eyes burned through the story in the local paper. It centered around the gory details and forensic analysis of his death video. He and Zhang had indeed used a pig carcass, the most lifelike to the human body. They even pumped their fake blood through its arterial and vascular system. But it hadn't been real enough apparently.

The ballistics on the bullets didn't hold up either. "If the JFK assassination had a magic bullet, then Rehan Al'Camel's death had an AK47 clip full of them." the article read.

Even though Zhang had used a classic magician's diversion, pointing at, then adjusting the camera down to the staged pig. He'd been careful to hold the neck on a downward angle when he thrust the severed wax head in the camera. But the brief shot of the pigs' neck, when the head was first removed, revealed the hoax without doubt. Under frame by frame video review, no magic sleight of hand is real.

Rehan got frustrated with the amateurish local paper. He nearly snapped his fingers in the air as he flagged down the waitress. She broke from a clutch of other girls at the counter.

"Okay, ya ready to order?"

"No, I need change to get the The National Review?"

"It's a dollar-fifty?"

"I know it's a dollar-fifty, I need change for the machine."

The waitress looked at Rehan. "I'll need a couple bucks to give ya change is all?"

Rehan was dripping sweat. "Oh, oh . . . of course." He dug and pulled out a twenty. "This is all I've got, sorry."

The waitress took the bill, slowly turned and walked to get change at the register on the far end of the counter. She talked with a burly looking manager at the cash register, who glanced Rehan's way as he made the change. She couldn't move fast enough for Rehan.

The waitress brought him his change and a used edition of The National Review. "You seemed in a hurry, so here's a copy. It's been read once is all."

"Thank you." Rehan took the paper quicker than he should have. The whole front page, with related side stories and research, seemed to jump out at him in three-dimensions. He burned through it all, turned the front page and gasped for breath. A composite sketch of himself, in his current disguise, was staring back at him. It was like turning on a water spicket compared to how he had been sweating.

Another shock back to reality caused him to jump again, hitting the underside of the table just as hard.

"...I said, you have to order something or I'm going to have to ask you to give up the table mister, what's wrong with you?" The burly looking manager in a white collared shirt and tie said staring down over him.

Rehan hadn't even noticed the man approach. The waitresses all stood a few feet behind at the counter, acting busy, but clearly taking in the unfolding scene. Today's drama was not going to be missed for the gossip sessions later in their shifts. Several customers had stopped eating, and more than a few tables were staring his way.

Rehan felt another wave of panic drawing way too much attention to himself. He looked up at the manager with a smile. Made sure to close the paper as he lowered it. "Oh., oh God, I'm sorry. I've had a three-day stomach flu, or food poisoning, or something. I thought I was feeling better this morning, but honestly . . . well, as you can see." Rehan drew a finger across his slick forehead. "Yes, and, I'm sure your food here is fine, but just sitting here, with the smell, and my, my stomach, a total uproar. I was hoping if I sat for a while and read the papers, maybe, but . . . well . . . of course. I'd be happy to leave, I understand."

Rehan slid from the booth and made a show of pulling out some cash from the change. "Sorry if I was a bother, please, please let the waitress have this for the trouble."

The manager stood erect, his arms crossed.

Rehan dropped a five spot on the table, feeling it was about right to diffuse the situation.

The manager eyed him and another wave of sweat and panic rolled over Rehan, had he been recognized? Rehan started sizing the man up, looking for an exit, when some advice released his tension.

"Pepto-Bismol . . ." the manager billowed. "I know it's been around forever, but some things don't need being made better. It works, trust me, by dinner, you'll be feelin' well enough for some light soup an crackers."

"Thank you." Rehan could only think to say as he stepped aside towards the exit. He looked at the waitress as he passed. "Sorry again, just feeling really rotten. Have a nice day." Tipping his head, holding his stomach, and fast-walking out.

The manager scooped up the newspapers, took a second look at the stories and the strange man walking away down the street. The National Review fell open to the composite photo as he picked it up. The manager did a double take, stared intently, from the picture out to Rehan down the street.

A second later, he shook his head in a chuckle, and turned.

"Table open, table for four!"

* * *

Rehan's whole world was crashing down around him in all out terror. He began to question everything.

His Jim Wright alias had to go. One of the National Review side stories related the tragic discovery of Carl and his "lady friend" dead. It hadn't taken long for the famous MiG-Rig to be recognized. RC Modelers from all over the world called in tips about the owner.

The Press figured it almost as quickly as the police. A picture of Carl's house, and of Carl smiling back from the papers, burned at Rehan's mind. The article hinted that forensics had tied Rehan's fingerprints to the scene? Maybe, maybe not . . . did it matter?

Do I even have a way out of this now?

Rehan's mind was in whirlwind, as he tried to find a way out, and account for every realization.

Surely that Palantir brain has scanned God knows how many traffic and tollbooth cameras, could it have traced me to this small town? They could be here already? Waves of anxiety pulsed through him as he walked. He pictured undercover cops on every street corner. Anyone with a newspaper, or talking on a cell phone, became a secret agent ready to pounce.

Should he run? He felt like it, his brain was screaming at him to just run.

The walk earlier to the diner was pleasant. He'd been thinking to himself how nice it would be to take a long walk back on a full stomach. But now, even with nothing to eat, he just felt like he was going to wretch, and every step felt like a mile.

He quickened his pace when he finally turned the corner, headed back up the road leading to the school.

His thoughts only got worse and worse. Realization after realization tumbled down inside his mind.

Surely the U.S. Government froze his bank accounts before the press conference.

Worry piled on. James Wright? Did he use it here? In this town? God, they could be right on top of him. Think Rehan, think! He was spinning out of control, he could feel it.

Everyone knew he was alive now. And everyone was looking for him. Hot off the press. Getting out of the country and to his primary safe-house was much more risky now. For a man of Rehan's wealth and life-style, being this . . . limited, was as scary as everything else zipping through his mind.

His head hurt. The worries kept mounting. The connection for the fake I.D.'s, could he be trusted to keep his mouth shut? With all that had come out in the papers? Reputation was everything in that line of work. Those scum bastards, no way that guy would take a chance on screwing himself?

Then the worst realization of all crept into his head, and he could feel his sub-conscious trying to delude him from it . . . but it was there. There'd be no denying the biggest terror of them all. His ties to Kuwait were now in serious jeopardy as well, if not already, totally, shattered.

It was always a base foundation to any ultimate escape destination. If he ever had to disappear. In a puff of thought, that safety net was gone.

His distant ties to royal blood just made things worse for him in this new light. Forget that the United States all but saved the royal families ass, handing back their country and wealth by kicking Saddam Hussein's army all the way back to Bagdad . . . that was bad enough. Because surely, they owed a huge debt to Uncle Sam.

But Rehan had tried to kill the people directly responsible for their liberation. It was a dishonor beyond just his direct family. Lying about it all too. It made them all look like fools and it was unforgivable. Family honor and respect is everything in the Arab/Muslim world . . . especially for a royal family member.

"Fuck, fuck, fuck!" Rehan mumbled.

The flow of Kuwaiti oil money was surely turned off, and all his assets there seized as well. But that was nothing compared to his punishment should he ever be caught by the Kuwaiti secret police. They'd surely have him executed without hesitation. It would be demanded of them to decapitate Rehan, to restore honor.

Your dreams of ever going home to start a new life, to raise a family, to be reborn . . . dead and long gone, forever.

He still had that Robin Hood reputation, the 'Chameleon mystique', in certain circles. Even respect and admiration, didn't he? A few friends from his years as the arms dealer . . . but would they chance dealing with him now? Was he a poisoned pill? Probably.

Shit, they might not even recognize him. None of them really knew him. Shit . . . shit . . .

Rehan made it back to the school thinking his way out of the immediate danger. Looking over his shoulder, constantly expecting an army of police cars to descend on him.

All his terrible thoughts ended coming around full circle twisting at his brain.

He had to become, in reality, and forever, this radical persona . . . something Rehan knew he really wasn't. Not fully anyway. His mind snapped under the weight of it all. He was truly all alone now.

Hated.

Despised.

And being hunted . . . by everyone.

Maybe they'd separate his beloved "little Juma" from her "sick" brother.

No way I'm going to hide in some hovel, like Saddam or Bin' laden, waiting for Special Forces to bust in and shoot me in the head. No way!

Rehan was going down fighting. Like he'd always done. Like his Father had taught him; "like a man."

How could he have been so selfish? Thinking he could just walk away, from family honor, and duty? There'd be no rebirth. No wife and kids. No little house tucked away somewhere safe in Kuwait.

The lock he'd placed on history, on his justifications, on his revenge, snapped. His mind slipped so easy from there . . . much, much further.

One thing after another, they just keep coming, your whole life, they'll never stop.

Rehan's rage boiled up like a volcano. The magma chamber had built up explosive pressure, and he wasn't ever going to try and stop it again.

He didn't have a choice anymore? About the things he was doing? Susan Figiolli had to see that? He would fight back. Surely, she knew that much about him. Like he'd always done.

Rehan's emotional acceptance of insanity, in his current reality, made him determined now to be the arch villain. They wouldn't let him escape, left him no way out, so now they would pay. They were turning him into whatever monster they imagined, twisting his mind up in a coil. He'd unleash it soon.

Monday morning, hundreds of kids would be boarding the school buses. By 7:30am, they'd be packed in there. Time was ticking now.

Time for Rehan to change his colors, yet again. "The Chameleon," after all.

Nathan Hopkins. A medical supplies salesman, for a company which, if called, would answer and confirm his long tenure. Neo-Natal specialty. "He saves babies with our advanced nutrition incubation systems." Heavy blond wig, parted smartly on the left. Hi-end, but off the rack, sharp business clothes, properly accented. Glasses to read, and to cover his dark eyebrows in a blend of color. Gay and jovial. Maybe a little gay?

Rehan refocused his intelligent, logical self. Invoked his old jungle habits. Calmed his mind. His breathing. Became Nathan. Took time to think clearly about his next moves.

He drove the van into the woods behind the ball fields, switched everything over to the janitor's truck, and swung the old Chevy north to his next destination. Out of town barely thirty minutes after leaving that diner and all those scary thoughts. Rehan was proud of himself for holding steady under such huge pressures.

Distance between the two identities was key before he first exposed Nathan Hopkins to the world. He started by getting several hours away. Then he'd stop somewhere nice. Get a hot meal. With ever mile, his stomach was feeling much better. A hot shower and good night's sleep, in a real bed, were on his agenda too.

Rehan rubbed a terrible crick in his neck, must be from sleeping on the gym mats for two nights.

CHAPTER 34: Sometimes You Fly Too Close to the Sun

Susan, General Givens, Mr. Green and Dr. Splitzer we're all gathered in a semi-circle around the Palantir tank. The strobe lights flashed up at their faces, they seemed to be in a mental conference with the giant blob. Everyone wanted to put an explanation point on Director Scott's affirmations.

"He's getting closer by the hour." Dr. Splitzer announced. Adding in a decent British accent. "The hunt is afoot."

"Just give us an update Doctor." Mr. Green demanded.

"You are such a kill-joy." Dr. Splitzer moaned, "the MiG-Rig led quickly to the bodies of Carl Perkins and Celeste, a suspected call-girl. And despite what you heard on the news, the Palantir figured out who owned that remarkable jet in about half an hour flat. Not the day or so it took reporters and police. And, in our business ladies and gentlemen, that's night and day, HA!"

"All praise the brain. What else?" Mr. Green asked.

"Rehan Al'Camels fingerprints were discovered on a credit card hidden in the girl's purse. Presumably stolen to use fraudulently later."

Givens laughed. "Yer shittin' me? She lifted a card from the guy?"

The Palantir added. "A highly likely occurrence. The name on the card is "James Wright", an alias Rehan Al'Camel is currently using."

Givens laughed again. "This case breaks wide open over a street hustle he never knew happened? Unbelievable!"

Susan smiled at him. "Identity fraud has never paid such dividends."

Mr. Green was not so chipper. "None of this really pins it to Rehan Al'Camel?"

"The current analysis is reliable Mr. Green." The Palantir said. "Cross checked photos at the Rally bombing and RC airshow, added to Rehan Al'Camels fingerprints on this credit card, confirms he is the person in disguise."

"Great, now just tell us where Hal?" Mr. Green asked.

"James Wright traced back to the rental of a white utility van. Tag numbers on that van, and credit cards used along his route, traced the van to New Hampshire. Using traffic camera and toll both analysis, I have confirmed the same disguised Rehan Al'Camel behind the wheel."

"So where is the joker?" Givens blurted out.

"If he stopped somewhere, as opposed to having switched to a new transport and identity, then we are within a two-hundred-mile radius." A map displayed on a side monitor.

Susan pointed. "Hundreds of law enforcement assets were placed in motion. Converging in a dragnet of biblical proportions. And the net is closing, fast."

"So we got 'em? We know for sure it's him? Doctor Camel and the Chameleon?" Givens asked.

"There is a 97% probability." The Palantir answered.

Mr. Green blustered. "Only 97%?"

"There are rarely absolutes Mr. Green. There is still a chance Doctor Rehan Al'Camel is not, in fact, the Chameleon."

Mr. Green cut him off. "This is where you separate the human from the machine. Rehan Al'Camel is the Chameleon. Yet Hal is still arguing the absurd?"

"Several variables still exist Mr. Green. He may have faked his death to escape law enforcement scrutiny. He may be hiding involvement in some minor way. He may be in fear of, or protecting, an actual third party Chameleon. He may be unstable due to recent events. Even if Doctor Al'Camel admits he is the arms dealer known as the Chameleon, he would have to provide statements, or evidence, of the arms sales that would be known only to the true arms dealer. Otherwise, there would still be a .05% chance he is lying."

Mr. Green just laughed. "I didn't mean to hurt your feelings Hal."

"I completely understand the human in-ability to look at a problem objectively once given a certain amount of contrary data. I do not consider that a flaw in my analysis." The Palantir stated.

"Ouch, I do believe ya just got burned Mr. Green." General Givens joked.

"He was speaking about all of us General." Mr. Green defended.

"Yeah, but I know better than ta' even start with the Hal. Remind me not to go into any cube-rooms with ya' today."

"I'm sure the Hal no longer needs us in there to do away with us

General."

The Palantir came across louder, "I do not believe your comments are consistent with your request that I no longer joke about such malfunctions. I would never contemplate hurting my creators and caregivers. It is against my purpose for being."

Susan came to his defense. "If you guys keep poking at my Pal I'm going to take you to McDonalds to pay off my bet. Play nice."

"Okay, okay, I didn't think the Hal was so sensitive." Mr. Green said.

Susan wasn't letting him off so easily. "You were the one that told him to be so straight-laced, remember? You want more, fluid? Okay. But it's not a fair fight while he's on lockdown. So, just play nice, or take the handcuffs off him."

"Thank you, Susan. You are always very kind and considerate." Her Pal said in her special voice.

"It's okay sweetheart, you just keep tightening the noose around the good Doctor's neck for me. They're just jealous about how smart you are." Susan loved to set the Palantir up above these two. The impending dinner dates added a new dimension to the mix. Two men sparring for her attentions, while tactfully remaining civil and professional. She knew when two bucks were rattling antlers to see who'd come out on top. It'd been a few years since she'd had that kind of attention, and she missed it. A lot to her surprise. When she was new, in her prime, a fit, young, field agent, she had to beat the alpha males off with a stick. Several times in the past . . . but, not so much lately.

Susan shook off the thought. Let herself enjoy the attention. Especially with the affirmation Timmy had given her at the news conference. She felt desirable again. Alive. Sexy.

She flushed thinking, wanting, to put that to the test as well. It had been much, much too long since she had that kind of fun. And catching the Chameleon would be a great aphrodisiac. "We'll show these guys who's the real man around here soon enough Pal." she teased.

"Ouch General, I think you just got burned." Mr. Green shot confidently.

"Like ya said, their talkin' about both of us." Givens gave it right back.

The Palantir corrected them, "Gentlemen, it should be obvious to both of you, at your ages. when a female is using alpha male stimuli in order to determine which of you two might be the best mate in a . . ."

"PAL! For cryin-out-loud!" Susan turned from the group, facing the tank, blushing red.

"Susan?" Her Pal questioned. "I was merely stating the obvious auditory and bio-feedback readings, picked up in the presence of Mr. Green and General Givens, and the fact that you . . ."

"PAL! Button it up already! Jesus! If you know all that then, you certainly must know . . . that women, don't . . . I mean we think, but . . . with a certain . . . we just can't . . . with, with . . . oh, ugghhh. Men!"

In the silence, the Palantir's bubbles noticeably increased. General Givens eyed Mr. Green who returned his gaze, then both men broke out in very satisfied grins.

"I am so frickin' jealous." Dr. Splitzer moaned.

"General Givens." The Palantir finally spoke up. "May I ask you a question?"

"Sure, Hal. What can I do for ya buddy?" Givens asked all too smug, looking directly at Susan, which caused her to turn away, and turn red all over again.

"General, if you could help explain Susan's last comments to me? Perhaps I should rephrase my question, since she is obviously upset with me for talking directly about her, could you please explain her comments about women? After full analysis, there is no clear conclusion as to what she meant that women want?"

"Oh ho! My, my, my!" Givens couldn't help but roar out loud in laughter. "Ooo yer poor, young, brain. I can't imagine the shock to that neural-net muck of yers. Ohhh-ho my dear Hal! Ya stumbled on ta' problem which even yer giant brain could never hope to solve. The mystery of women, Hal. The plague of mankind for ten thousand years."

"That does not sound possible, General?"

Givens laughed even harder. "Let me put it another way, if ya can figure out what their thinkin', and what they mean, with comments like that last one? Yer a hero. Men the world over will come and worship ya like a God. Shoot, we could settle the U.S. debt in a month's time sellin' tickets. Maybe even take over the whole world without firin' a shot . . ."

"O.K., O.K. General, I think he gets the point . . ." Susan tried to interject.

Mr. Green was smirking, "What's her bio-readings telling you right now Hal?"

"MR. GREEN! Don't you dare answer that question Pal! In fact, my bio-readings are hereby off limits. No access. Top secret. Confidential."

"Okay Susan . . ." the Palantir switched to her special Pal talk, "however, both Mr. Green and General Givens have Top Secret and Confidential clearance, so, I assume that I can share that information with them on their personal workstations as requested?"

"NO! Pal? . . . what are you doing to me?" Susan turned back to the tank, reached out and put a hand against the glass. "And I say off limits, top secret, I mean top secret. . . . you know? I don't care about their clearance level? A woman Pal . . . especially in a work environment . . . when she meets . . . gets to know . . . well, we have to be, you know, more . . . womanly. Maybe a little body language, but bio-readings Pal? . . . really? How's that supposed to work?" Susan glanced over to see three smiling males in amused observance. "Honestly . . . ugh, men."

Another silent hum filled the room, obviously the Palantir was doing some serious reflection.

He spoke again. "Mr. Green, may I ask you a question?"

Even Mr. Green laughed out loud at that. "Sure Hal, just don't ask me to explain anything Mrs. Susan just said. Your guess is as good as mine. In fact better, since I've got no bio-readings to even begin to tell you how she's feeling."

Another silent hum. "Okay, never mind Mr. Green" and with that the entire room, including Susan, all burst out laughing. It went on quite a time before the Palantir started in again. "Wait, give me one moment please . . ."

Mr. Green laughed again. "It seems your brain is finally stumped."

General Givens gave Dr. Splitzer a jolt to his shoulder. "We broke yer brain Doc." which caused the room to laugh even more.

". . . One moment please . . ."

Susan's heard it.

". . . One moment please . . ."

Her Pal was on to something. "Okay, okay, quiet down everyone. Let's focus. Fun times' over . . . Pal?"

"Yes Susan. I believe I have something of interest. A call into central communications. A man claiming to be Doctor Rehan Al'Camel wishing to speak with you by name. Voice recognition at 94% probability. Should I patch the call through? He has been on hold for . . . 24 seconds . . . 25 seconds . . ."

Susan walked over to the wall intercom, calling up to her control room.

"Okay people let's get it together! Fish on the line. All possible tracers in play. Narrow it down right off the bat to our little two-hundred-mile kill box. Pal, patch the call through."

"Hello? Hello?" Rehan's voice came through sounding a bit too annoyed.

"Hello Doctor, this is Susan Figiolli. How are you today?"

"Damn it Susan, I call and they keep me on hold for thirty seconds? Now I can only talk for what, another thirty? Maybe less?"

"I'm sorry Doctor, but you've made quite a spectacle of yourself. We get hundreds of Doctor Rehan Al'Camels calling asking for me every day now . . ."

"Stall, deflect, keep him on-line! I'm not stupid Susan, I know how it works, and I'd appreciate you respecting that. Your little brain knows when it's really me, so let's not play silly games . . ."

"Of course, but even that process takes a few moments. Plus, we really didn't expect your call so . . ."

"Enough already! I see you are determined to do this the hard way. Let's try again." Click.

"Damn . . ." Susan knew it was too short. "Anybody?"

Her room gave a collective non-answer. A team member called out over the comm. "Much too short of a trace."

"But we've got him within two-hundred miles? Doesn't that kill his bounce technology?"

"Makes it more vulnerable, still need at least a minute to crack the overseas scramblers back to the states."

Susan groaned. "Pal, is there anything we can do?"

"Yes Susan. With General Givens permission, I can hack into the cell and phone networks. If Rehan Al'Camel calls back, I will send a high-frequency tone over every open line and randomly listen, in sequence, to each possible connection in the networks."

Givens looked serious, asking Susan. "When does this rise ta the level of invasion of privacy? Do ya need a warrant or somethin'?"

Susan smiled. "Thanks for asking. Pal, how invasive are you talking about here, checking every line? How's that better, or faster, then our tracers?"

"The high-pitched frequency is inaudible to human ears. I will need to listen in on each line in the target area for one-tenth of a second. This is an alternate strategy from using tracers. Based on pure chance, the odds to detect an exact location increase with every second Rehan Al'Camel is on the line.

"Well I got no problem tryin' to get lucky on a tenth second listen-in. Go ahead Palantir, make it ready." Givens commanded.

"Rehan Al'Camel has called back in. I've begun my tone search. Tracers are active as well. He has been on hold for 6 seconds, 7 seconds . . ."

"Patch him through Pal." Susan said.

"Hello Susan, let's try again. I'll be talking and you'll be listening. As much as I might like a nice conversation with you, that'll have to wait for another day."

"Sure, I'd love the opportunity to . . ." Susan tried.

"Like I said, another day. You have made things impossible for me out here, you know that? Now, I have to do some desperate things. Things you can stop, or live with, if you decide to screw around with me anymore." CLICK.

"Anybody? Pal?" Susan screamed.

"Too short."

"Tone-checked complete on 27% of the possible lines with no match." The Palantir reported.

"What good is it if he keeps hanging up and we start all over?" Givens asked.

"Unlike the tracers General, I do not have to start my tone-search over for land-lines or a stationary cell phone. Unless Rehan Al'Camel is on the move, or switching phones with each call, the odds of detecting increase with each second he is on the line. . . . He has called again. I will patch him through."

"I've got a sixth sense about these things Susan. Like how long will the old technology of bouncing calls around the world's phone networks to delay a trace still work? Maybe the C.I.A. geeks have figured it out already? And that brain, who knows what it's capable of? You've taken everything from me Susan. My family, my freedom, my wealth . . . and you've left me no escape. That's a very dangerous escalation." Click.

Mr. Green stepped forward to whisper in her ear. "He's careful. Ask about the threat, we need more."

"He hasn't made it this far without being super cautious and even paranoid to various degrees." Susan said. "Pal, how we doing?"

"48% scanned . . . another call has come in. Patching it through."

"Listen up Susan, here are my demands . . ."

"First Doctor, tell me more about what I'm going to regret if I don't meet them?"

Rehan ignored it. "First, go to the press and remind them there's no proof I'm the Chameleon. I faked my own death to get away from your harassment, and I better read that quote from you in tomorrow's papers. Make that Monday morning six a.m. deadline Susan, or suffer the consequences.

Second, I want all of my personal accounts unfrozen. It's my money and not a ransom, so the government can still say they don't negotiate with terrorist. I don't need it, but I want the world to see you give it all back. I did what I did to get away from the C.I.A. tails and constant harassment. Your attempted assassination if you like? None of it means I'm some evil arms dealer. You don't want to test me on this one. Six a.m. Monday. No more calls. No more contact. Non-negotiable." CLICK.

* * *

"Anyone? Tell me we have him?" Susan scanned the room but heads fell in disappointment. "Damn that SOB. How fricking lucky can one man be? Pal, do you have something?"

Always aiming to please he responded in her special voice. "Yes, Susan, I have some good news, although not an exact location. I arranged my scans in a matrix to help narrow our target area. Three old, local phone companies once co-existed there and I eliminate two of them completely using the old phone-network hubs. I eliminated the cell coverage in those old network areas as well.

This matrix has lowered the possible search area to 152 miles. By triangulation of cross covering cell towers, I further limited the possible location to roughly a 128.54 square mile area. The new search area is broken up by county lines, as well as local phone and cell phone coverage areas, represented on the map I am displaying on monitor one."

A map with various odd shaped rectangles appeared. Most clustered together creating the total new search area. Like a county lines map for any given state, with parts of circles where cell towers extended over the county lines.

Susan jumped up and pointed, "Map that up to my control room, the main monitor Pal. That's our focus ladies and gentlemen, right there! Converge all assets from the outlying dead areas and redistribute them within our new target area.

"Let's get the local Sheriffs and Chiefs an update. We've pinned him down to their districts. A direct and imminent threat. Monday six a.m. deadline. Nobody knows an area like the locals so pair them up with our specialist as they arrive. Report anything, ANY-THING which is out of the ordinary. It's the littlest things that break a case like this, let's not overlook something and kick ourselves later for missing it.

"Time to shine people! Show my Pal how much we appreciate his help, our man is there.

"Time to LIC 'em!"

* * *

It was late Sunday afternoon before a tired and weary police officer stumbled into the Silver Coach diner for a quick bite. Police and various agencies were going door-to-door all day in search of the Chameleon. Nothing seemed to be panning out. State Trooper Joe Farley's feet were blistered and sore from walking around all day.

"Hey Joe! Want some joe?" The hyena cackled laugh filled the nearly empty diner once again this day.

"What? Damn Janice, I'm in no mood for your lame jokes today." Officer Farley snapped as he adjusted his belt of equipment to flop in the booth.

"Well, well, I got my second stomach flu grump today. I was just trying to be nice is all. Do you want some coffee . . . sir?"

Farley unceremoniously flopped his Stetson off onto the table in front of him, rubbing his head and temples with both hands. "I'm sorry girl. Been out on a wild goose chase all day, on my supposed day off. I don't even get to go home, and it's my boy's birthday tomorrow." He looked through his hands up at Janice, "My stomach is all tied in knots, how'd ya guess that?"

"I been working a double all day myself, if that makes ya feel any better. Like I said, you're my second grumpy customer, the other guy had stomach problems. That weirdo didn't even order, but he still tipped five bucks, so if you ain't gonna eat somethin, that's the going rate to just sit apparently."

"What weird guy? When?"

Janice looked into her mind's eye up at the fluorescent-lit drop ceiling. "Oh, this mornin, about 7:30 . . . sat in this booth, right where you are now. Reading the paper all bug-eyed. Just a-readin' it, I had to ask him three times if he wanted coffee before I startled him so bad he nearly jumped out the booth." Janice added a few cackles. "Then I'm like, 'you're cut off, I'm only serving ya decaf.' Which I don't care what you people say, it's a funny joke. But he just sat there like he didn't even hear me? So then, I was thinkin that maybe this guy's a junkie or a pill popper or something, considerin' how he's just sweatin' bullets and all."

"What did this guy look like Janice?" Officer Farley asked, sitting up straighter now.

"Oh, he wasn't dressed like no junkie, I didn't mean that. He weren't in no suit or nothin, but you could tell he was clean . . . you know, he didn't smell bad or nothin' like most of those guys do. Although, now that I think about it . . ."

Officer Farley grabbed her forearm, "No, what did the guy look like?"

"Good gosh, I'm telling ya ain't' I?" Janice yelped, pulling her arm away. "Yer acting just like he did when I couldn't get change fast enough for em' . . ."

"Change?"

"Yeah, for the papers."

"Papers?"

"Yeah, like I said, he was reading so intent and all I guess he got through the first one quick enough and wanted a couple more. Like I said too, he didn't even order nothin' he was readin' so much. Kenny will tell ya, he had to ask the guy to leave."

Kenny heard the raised conversation and had made his way over to the table. "Hey there Far, you ain't' ordered nothing yet so I know it can't be the food is bad?"

"Hey Ken, I was just talking to Janice about a guy, in this morning . . . didn't order nothing, reading the papers . . . sweating?"

"Sure, I remember him . . . saying he had a stomach flu or something. Hoping if he could sit and read awhile, he'd settle down enough to eat something. But I had people waiting, ya know, it's Sunday, right after church letting out and all. I told him nice, you gotta order something or give up the table for other customers. I hope he didn't make a fuss about it? He knew even, left apologizing and all, tipped Janice a five-spot."

Officer Farley waved him off. "No, no, it's no problem. I'm just trying to get a description of the guy that's all. What did he look like?"

"That's easy." The manager spun around and went to the far end of the counter, retrieved a stack of used newspapers. Flipping through, he opened the Federal Review composite sketch and slapped it right down on the table staring directly up at officer Joe Farley. "The guy looked a spittin' image to this fellow here."

They all froze when Officer Farley's face paled over in obvious worry. "Ken, this is real important, where did that fella go?"

"Well, he gave a tip and walked out there down the street, a couple blocks, then turned left. Well it's not this same guy in the papers is it?"

"I'm not sure but we gotta check. Stay here, some other folks are going to come by and get your statements. I need to go call this in. Two blocks, then left?"

"Gee Far, yeah, pretty sure? He was a little odd, so I noticed. Last I saw of him. Never seen him before come to think of it."

* * *

Within the hour, Susan had that small town covered. Even underground, when 'spelunker' teams were sent to search a few abandoned coal mines in the area. Word spread quickly throughout the area that Dr. Rehan Al'Camel, the Chameleon himself, had been spotted in their very own little diner.

Helicopters circled with infrared, and snipers, and news crews. The noise a constant din like locust, coming and going in loud cadence as they swirled about.

Every street corner seemed to have at least one car with flashing lights. Every route in and out of the area had manned roadblocks.

Susan demanded door to door searches be started all over again, and this time, to inspect interiors and basements in case someone was hiding or being held hostage.

The school was swept, twice, but no lights were on and no cars found in the lot. Every crevice a man could hide was checked.

* * *

Susan worked her room like a conductor over a symphony orchestra.

Givens walked up beside her. "It's nice to see ya in action, how ya love this job."

"It not much fun for everyone in that little town." Susan said only barely glancing over her shoulder, tapping away at her keyboard. "It's going to be a long, dark, scary night."

"I guess so with riot geared tactical officers roamin' around. Assault rifles at the ready. Fannin' out in back yards an' alleys, checkin' houses for every possible place a person could hide. Not somethin' ya see in everyday suburbia." General Givens mused.

"That's not something I want most people to ever see General. Locked indoors? Huddled with children in interior rooms or sleeping in bathtubs?"

"Not all of 'em will be hidin'. Some'll be loaded for bear, sittin' blatantly out on front porches, darin' that Chameleon bastard ta stick his head up," Givens said.

"Every siren, dog bark or car horn will cause a start. Kids crying as their perceptive little minds sense the fear around them, even in the safety of their parent's arms? I'm as pissed at this asshole for taking that security away from them as anything else."

Mr. Green gave Susan an update as he talked with some source on his cell phone. "Civilian vigilante groups have formed. Exercising their rights to protect themselves, their families, and their community. Evenly matched with the police in arms. They've been dropping hints about heavier weaponry locally available, if needed."

Givens warned. "Special forces and SWAT sure as hell can't have armed men poppin' up 'round every corner, somebodies bound to get shot. Imagine the stress and pressure buildin' with every hour into the darkest parts of the night."

Susan figured that puzzle out fast. She didn't have time to worry about it. "Have the Chief of Police split-up the bands of vigilantes by assigning a few to each SWAT, Federal or Police group. Deputize their asses if you need to get their cooperation."

"Smart. Damn smart way to defuse it." Givens smiled at her.

"Eyes and ears, and brains, General. If the Chameleon is hiding out there, it's only a matter of time before a local boy finds him out."

* * *

Rehan woke Monday morning to a soft, warm glow of sunlight through some shear curtains.

The Luxury Suite's Hotel said nothing about a sunrise room? It's living up to its three and a half stars.

Rehan stretched, rolled out of bed, and grabbed the plush, only $49.95 robe, which would be conveniently added to his room incidentals. The matching slippers were a bit small, so he headed down to the lobby for the complimentary breakfast in his stocking feet. He just wanted his cup of coffee. Once in hand, he checked the time on a cheap wall clock over the waffle maker giving off a burnt batter incense. 5:24am, the second hand seemed to be racing around the dial.

Rehan walked out the front lobby doors, to a line of newspaper stands just outside check-in. The racks we empty, or had a few of yesterday's editions left. Rehan looked around. A young door-man smiled at him.

"Are today's papers here somewhere?"

"No sir. Should be? Usually it's by 5:30 at the latest."

"Okay, thanks." It irked Rehan that he somehow beat the morning papers to this spot at this point in time. But, the coffee was good, so not the hotels fault. Rehan took a sip, smiled at the young valet.

An uncontrolled tire-squeal behind him spun Rehan on his heels. A dark mini-van sped out of nowhere, directly towards Rehan in a long screech of tires as it rounded the check-in lane. The side door slid, slamming open. Two men inside, holding straps with one arm, leaned out, caught Rehan's eye, And Rehan knew, This is it. They found me.

Three huge, brown-paper bundles flew in a thud from the side door and tumble up to the curb. The screeching mini-van never stopped. The men fell back inside as the door slid closed in a slam. A great belch of black smoke from the beaten old exhaust erupted with the stomp of the gas. Screeching side to side, out and down the road.

Rehan's heart was pounding, holding his chest with one hand, his other a cup of coffee with a tremor.

"Paper delivery sir." The valet said as he rolled a luggage cart out. Stacking the bundles, he cut a strap handing Rehan a copy. "Thanks for waiting sir, on the house."

"Four stars my friend. Four stars!" Rehan said and tipped the kid a five spot.

Rehan didn't really expect to find a statement from Susan, or the government, about his money, or anything else. A last glimmer of hope. And a final justification.

Rehan showered and packed quickly. He was scared now. His idea, the one that truly frightened him, seemed in motion all on its own.

On the road headed north, he tried again to talk himself out of it. The school would be his last battle to stop it. His final warning. But that part of him felt weak. The time alone in the truck, was not good on his psyche.

They took it all now Rehan. They are outright hunting you down. To kill you.

A few more days? Scare them with the school, then, I could be long gone.

No Rehan. If you live, we make them pay, for killing everything.

I'm smart, millions in Swiss accounts. Luxurious safe houses, identities, all over the world. Stashes of cash, jewels, stockpiles of gold here and there.

Whose money is now frozen? Stolen! Right before they kill you! Don't you see it yet? They never cared if you were innocent or not.

* * *

As the sun crested that Monday morning, groups of huddled officers stood on every corner for miles, shaking their tense heads. Every inch of that little town and surrounding area had been checked, multiple times, with no trace. No mysterious guest in any nearby hotel. No stores or other restaurants had served him. No credit card used by James Wright.

Susan worried it was all a big mistake. Or a diversion? It was like a phantom came to that diner Sunday morning and then vanished. Susan watched the clock, the seconds ticked by as if in slow motion, everyone a heartbeat of anxiety.

Givens stood close. "Big decision ta call his bluff. I thought maybe ya'd used that to stall 'em?"

"You don't know Washington. The Chameleon would have better luck getting voted President than ever having Congress unfreeze and give back a couple hundred million dollars."

"I see. Already bein' chopped inta pork projects?"

Susan allowed a brief laugh in her tension. "Terrorists have to pay taxes too after all."

Remote camera views all over that little town filled her video wall. Waves of tension radiated off the various groups of officers, building towards the six-a.m. deadline.

By 5:50, Susan felt the pressure cooker building with every ray of sunrise.

Just standing around, waiting for something to happen. Knowing she'd found nothing, done nothing. It has to be a bluff.

At 6:00, 6:01, 6:02, everyone held tense.

6:05 saw a release of pent up adrenaline. Police and agents moved about in agitation.

Susan spoke over the open comm, "Stay calm everyone, we have no incident reports." Susan admonished. "Hold positions. All check clear." Each team radioed in "All clear" in succession. "Everyone relax. Observe."

6:10 a collective sigh of relief and a settling back at their post.

By 6:20 smiles and laughter milled about the relaxed groups of officers. Sitting back on hoods of cruisers and leaning on light poles.

At 6:30 Susan worried it was a little too relaxed. "Stay on alert." Everyone took up a serious stance once again. "Check all clear." All stations radioed "clear" again.

At 6:45 the Mayor called. At 7:00am, he issued the "all clear" to his penned-up residents. He couldn't see keeping people locked down in fear like that without some other solid lead or evidence.

The police and SWAT teams stayed in full force to patrol and add a huge sense of security. As the residents emerged from their bunkers, and the shotguns found their places back over the fireplaces, mugs of hot coffee and Danishes found the hands of officers from grateful citizens.

Everyone had just over-reacted. There was no Chameleon in their midst. Probably never was. The rubber-band wound tight, when let go, unwinds quickly.

Many parents decided to keep their kids home that day but just as many more were determined that the best course of action would be to get everyone back into their normal routines as soon as possible. To show the terrorist of the world that they we're not afraid.

Curious little ones pointed and asked questions about the SWAT equipment hanging off their escorts at each bus stop. Police lifted them up with smiles, letting them play with the flashlights, and cuffs, and badges.

By 7:30 am, the first school buses were rolling out to make their routes.

* * *

When Principal Seals Jackson arrived at school he didn't notice anything amiss. He figured the police had been there and searched, which was confirmed as he was greeted by his secretary, Mrs. Miles. "The school had the twice over Principal Jackson, and no Chameleon was found hiding."

Principle Jackson used his bathroom and noticed right away that the old janitor was slipping up? It was one thing to find trash cans not emptied, but to see toilets uncleaned, and no paper products restocked? The more the principal checked, the more everything looked half-assed at best. A custodian for over a decade, but this was unacceptable. He'd have to give the man a talking to.

Teachers arrived in ones and twos, as the start of a new school week turned the principal's attention away from his cleaning inspection.

The phone rang and Mrs. Miles paged him. "It's Mr. Sellers son on line one . . ."

"Hello, Principal Jackson here?"

"Hello Principal Jackson, how are you sir?" A respectful young man asked.

"I'm fine, the question is, how's your father?"

"I didn't hear from him this weekend, I just assumed he was off on one of his fishing trips. He isn't in this morning?"

"Well to be honest, I thought you were calling to say he was ill. I can't remember the place looking like such a mess on a Monday morning. I don't think he was here the whole weekend, hold on." He shouted to the outer office cupping the phone. "Mrs. Miles get on the P.A. and ask Mr. Sellers to report to the office right away."

"Yes sir." Mrs. Miles was already crossing to the PA system at pace.

"Let me get your number son. If he reports, I'll make sure he calls you. Have you checked the hospitals? And what did you say, fishing? Can you check his spots or whatever?"

"Some of them, that was next. Oh God. Please, I'm plenty worried now, call right back if he's there and I'll call you if we find anything."

"Okay son, don't worry, he's a tough old bird and I'm guessing he just had a bad weekend with the scare last night and all. We'll talk soon, good bye."

The Principle hung-up, mumbled to himself . . . Very unlike the man. Not in touch with his family too?

Mrs. Miles's voice came over the loudspeaker. "Mr. Sellers, Mr. Sellers. Please report to the main office. Mr. Sellers to the main office please."

Principal Jackson's thoughts barely wondered about any possible connection. Maybe it didn't amount to much, but the police ought to be notified. "Thanks Mrs. Miles, could you please get Chief Rowlins on the phone for me."

"The Chief of Police?" Stopping her in her tracks.

"It's nothing to worry yourself about. Just covering all bases that's all. But get him on the phone just the same, right away please." Principal Jackson wasn't sure he was calming her down, or himself. His words sounded phony, wrong in his ears. Something wasn't quite right, he could feel it.

As he spun in his chair and looked out the window the first several school buses were just pulling up parking in line. A steady line of buses followed, as the eager middle schoolers stayed seated until all the buses were parked at a safe stop.

* * *

Susan watched fireballs billow up into the air just outside of town on several of her surveillance screens. A giant rumble from the blast was loud enough to reverberate the audio. The explosion mushroomed, turned to a black cloud full of fire that looked like the devil's own hellish head. It reared up to laugh in Susan's face.

Police, SWAT and federal teams were close enough to feel the massive rumbling explosions when it cracked the early morning sky, flinching in a reflexive crouch to take cover.

The first news helicopters began reporting instantly. Rubble from the flattened school looked like a scene from a direct tornado hit, with a few parts smoking or on fire. A few partial brick walls, and the two far stairwells, were all that stood. The rest was scattered piles of smoldering rubble, I-beams, and red bricks. It looked apocalyptic as the frame widened.

The line of buses sitting out front was horror-movie scary. Each half black, half yellow, scorched on one side. The bus in the front was ablaze, engulfed completely, as a fire truck pulled into view, men jumping out to douse the flames.

The camera panned to the front lawn of the school, with the American and State flags flying their colors on poles overhead. Hundreds of students milled about in shock. Some with scorched, tattered clothing and bleeding from wounds. A few had adults leaning over them, giving what appeared to be more urgent, immediate care. Some kids stood in groups, or sat in stunned circles, crying and holding on to each other.

Emergency vehicles pulled in haphazardly all over, arriving in caravans.

The helicopter news coverage panned suddenly towards the road leading up to the school. Distraught parents began screeching into view, jumping their cars up on curbs, and driving across the lawns to rescue their kids. Emerging from their vehicles only to be held back by police. Several men came to blows. A few broke through, running for the blood-soaked lawn out front. Grief stricken mothers would collapse. Only to recover enough to catch the next mother to arrive, who would collapse as soon as realization dawned.

The sound of the helicopter's circling the scene was all that was heard for several long moments, as the cameraman zoomed in and out on various parts of the carnage. Each view giving the television audience a new shock of terror. A reporter tried to comment.

"There really are no words. You see it, right in front of you, the horror, the senseless horror."

CHAPTER 35: Sermon of the Damned

At 7:50am, right on cue, the media exploded with special reports about the school bombing. Rehan listened intently to confirm he timed the explosions perfectly. His heart leapt at the success, his mind used it as affirmation.

See. This will scare them enough. I can get away.

At 10:30, the special report he knew was coming aired.

"This is a CBC news special report. Delivered by courier today, we have a message from Doctor Rehan Al'Camel. We have forwarded the original to law enforcement, a copy follows, which we now release as instructed to protect our audience from a serious threat."

The tape rolled . . .

"This is Rehan Al'Camel and I am the man accused of being the Chameleon. Many Americans now know my past, and the recent events that have led to this terrible day. I can't believe that this great country continues to operate the way it did twenty-five years ago, when my father and little Juma died for no reason. And now, the C.I.A., and the American government, seems determined to kill me as well. I will defend myself.

This young country has been operating exactly the same way for a hundred years. Certainly since it came to power after World War Two. We as a nation export death, and fear, and horrors of all kinds for supposedly justified reasons, you have all heard them, over and over; National security. To preserve democracy. Human right. Protection against enemies. Threats from nuclear weapons to WMDs.

But let's be honest, it has always really been about money, or oil, or power. The so-called threats that come to America's doorstep are not the result of some evil power rising up to threaten us. They are, and have been for decades, a direct consequence of our pre-emptive actions around the world.

Sadly, there is a long, painful truth written in history that backs up my words today. There for anyone who opens their eyes to see it. The dark secrets they kept from all of us, all those years.

America had a unique opportunity after World War Two, to create a better world. Instead we, and especially our government leaders, have all become corrupted by that power. And corruption breeds evil.

Even the so-called cold war was a direct result of threats against the Soviet Union. We had the atom bomb, and the power to wipe them out, and we demanded they kneel. The President threatened, actually threatened, to rain nuclear bombs down on them. Study your history and see who the aggressor truly was. What did they expect the Soviets to do in response?

And even after billions of dollars spent, and lives lost, and the end of that terrible cold war, what lesson did America learn going forward? None. We just continued on our egotistical, power hungry path.

From all I understand the actions of this Chameleon were mostly an attempt to balance the scales a little. Against America's military industrial monster. The Chameleon has always worked against military targets, in war torn areas, drenched in blood by American agendas and interventions.

Civilians were never targeted. Weapons were not sold or intended to be used for terrorist actions.

It was always about letting soldiers have a decent chance to fight back against an all-powerful American oppressor.

The hypocrisies of the American government, the military, have no bounds. We are the world's leading arms exporter. If you exclude Russia, America exports more arms than every other nation combined, including supposed evil countries like China.

How can the United State use this trade-practice to label people terrorist, or a threat? To single them out for assassination? I say again, hypocrisy!

Under the guise of preserving democracy they have supported some of the world's most brutal dictators. Look at your history. Saddam Hussein, Mummar Kaddafi, the Shaw of Iran . . . many others through time. As soon as these puppets dared be independent, or question their American handlers, they were all simply eliminated and discarded like trash.

Over the last few weeks, I have been pushed into a corner by these same powers. I have made some mistakes, and hurt some innocent people, for that I am sorry. People have died in my escape. Is it justified?

America knows my life's horror. But even that kind of story wasn't enough to make the country listen, to understand, the hypocrisy. It seems

Americans only listen when American lives are at stake. And that's unfortunate.

Recently, I've realized that I needed to show the American people how out of touch it's leaders have become. They have smeared me by calling me this Chameleon, my honor has been destroyed. Honor, my families honor, my Kuwaiti honor, is all that I had left.

Yesterday, I called the C.I.A. and talked directly with those who are hunting me. I made them a simple offer, to just release my frozen bank accounts and clear my name, so that I might return to my native Kuwait and live my life in peace with my extended family.

After they have killed all my direct relatives, I did not think this was too much to ask. Instead, they have dishonored me and taken away any chance for a family. I will never be welcome in my homelands now. I will never have a home. I will never have peace.

You can all hate me now too. I've done terrible things. But realize this, even with your children at risk, they chose to retain their power, and to steal my money, and ruin my reputation. They could have stopped the school bombing. I gave them plenty of warning.

They chose to steal money over protecting your children. Open your eyes America, these are the people running your country. You are now being held accountable for their actions. We, citizens, are always the ones who pay the price.

I don't expect sympathy. I don't expect understanding. But just know that I purposely set those explosives to go off before those students entered the school. I wanted to scare you. I wanted to wake you all up.

Hold them, and realize how close they all came to certain death. Your leaders had plenty of time to stop it, they chose not to.

So now, I'm forced to give one last warning, and the government one last chance. The U.S. Government must unfreeze my bank accounts. I want a guarantee that I will have free access to escape to a country of my choosing. I want a public apology by the President himself, and a full pardon for my crimes.

I understand they will not live up to their promises. They never have. See it as yet another example of why the whole world now despises America and the evil, arrogant country it has become. Which cannot be trusted no matter what it says, or what promises it makes.

You know what I am capable of. If I can place hundreds of children in peril right under their noses. Just imagine what I might do to a whole American city if I so chose? If your leaders put me to the test again, you cannot possibly hope to defend against the thousands of ways I have to attack.

Within the next 72 hours, or I will wreak havoc unlike anything you have seen so far. Hiroshima and Nagasaki will be mere firecrackers compared to the hell I am prepared to unleash. Everything I need to take action is in place and ready, all I have to do is detonate my final plan.

And, it won't be just a few school children in peril this time, it will be all of you.

For my part, I give my word that, should my demands be met, I will leave in peace. I will no longer work against this country. In short, I will retire and hide away where you need never hear of me again.

But, if my demands are not met. If the arrogant agents at the C.I.A. continue their pursuit and persecution, attempted assassination! I will rain terror down on America like never before. All over the world.

Make no mistake, even without my frozen bank accounts, I still have millions and millions. I will fund every group opposed to America. Arm them with weapons to make it unsafe to fly anywhere in the skies, float on any ocean, or travel across any land.

America, this is your last warning. Hold your leaders accountable. Or burn in the hell of your own creation. The choice is yours. We shall see."

* * *

Rehan listened to the stupid reporters repeat over and over what he just said. Questioning it, and making analytical statements, like they were experts. He needed to think for a while and he didn't want to be distracted.

First things first, get rid of this stolen truck. If they hadn't found the van stashed in the woods behind the school already, the bomb investigators soon would. Rehan raced for Boston from . . . that damned brain and its ability to track every move. He needed to get past all the tollbooths, and most traffic cameras, before he rented a new van.

Rehan hid his Nathan disguise for the drive with a cheesy mustache, hoody and dark pair of sunglasses. A cover-up. A disguise for his disguise? Maybe the paranoia was getting the better of him? Hard to tell lately, he was struggling with degrees of sanity taking precedence. The building paranoia on the drive wasn't helping. If they found the van, and fed the brain this truck, everything could be over at any moment.

Rehan checked his rearview. All clear . . . for now.

* * *

Penetrating to the heart of Boston, Rehan used side streets to backtrack, almost all the way back out. He rented a van, transferred the contents of the truck. It was easy enough to find a sea-wall with an overhang. Rehan slipped the truck in neutral and watched it glide down a little slope and dive over into the water. Sinking in a whirlpool of bubbles. Rehan felt the neck muscles let go. The Chameleon changed color and was hidden now by the Boston background. And he knew that brain couldn't see him any longer.

Rehan relaxed, had a day or so to scope everything out. Run some errands, find some dive to rent. He was ahead of schedule.

Next, he checked Craigslist, found a one-bedroom condo for rent, with views of Boston harbor, at a place called Pleasant Bay. Rehan's story was about being in town for a sick family member. All very sudden, last minute. Rehan flashed the man a fake I.D., not Nathan's, and gave him enough cash to remodel the whole place if he trashed it. The landlord was happy to take a wad of cash from the clean-cut mourner.

Paying cash was key to keeping any identity alive longer. "Nathan" had only been exposed twice so far, "on the grid". Once at the hotel far away, and once at the car rental agency inside Boston. Consistent with his identity as a traveling medical salesman.

Rehan dropped off his bags and walked to get some food feeling secure enough in the overwhelming size of Boston. No all-out manhunt in the world could hope to find this needle in a haystack, even if the brain did track him this far.

His next task was to scope out a launch point for Carl's Mini-Sub. He paid a young street hustler to help him carry it off a nearby boat ramp.

It worked flawlessly as he piloted out and around to park it off the dock outside his condo's 5th story patio.

He knew the water and the range out to where he would need to send it next may cause issues with the radio transmission, so he hobbled together a couple booster transmitters by purchasing all he needed at radio shack. He tied it all in with the 240-volt power outlet from the clothes dryer in the condo for maximum range and strength.

Rehan fed the wires out to his balcony, and hung the antenna around the railing. Donning a floppy beach hat and shades, he sat in a lounge chair with a newspaper to cover the remote control.

* * *

At 1pm, right on schedule, a giant ship glided majestically around the point, coming to a stop in Pleasant Bay, directly across from Rehan's condo. A buzz of small boats appeared; coastguard, police and tugs. A helicopter hovered and circled. Rehan waited for the initial sweeps and checks to die down before he powered up the mini-submersible and piloted it across the channel. He stopped a hundred feet from the ship, floating just under the surface. He waited patiently for the security checks and scuba divers to emerge and give the all clear on the hull.

As the tugs moved into position and began to tie onto the Crystal Sun, Rehan used the distraction, moving closer and diving under the ship from behind.

Switching on his lights, Rehan piloted between the two massive propeller shaft housings, back of the rudders. Zhang's magnets attached themselves firmly to the double hull. The mini-sub almost looked like it was a part of the ship, even supposed to be there, between the two propeller shaft fins.

Rehan powered it down to keep it stealthy, and to save its batteries, until the deadline. It might be discovered but, for now, the deadly little arrow had found Achilles' heel.

* * *

Early Tuesday morning on Craig's list, Rehan found the first motorcycle he ever owned himself. He'd rented bikes plenty of times, riding the jungles and backroads from here to Asia. He tried to ride once on the crazy streets of India, but suicide was never his style. Rehan clicked through the pictures of his new ride. A cruiser, not the dirt bike sized ones he was used to. Mid-height bars, nice comfy wide seat. Dark burgundy tank and fins, with tons of chrome. Black leather saddle bags, grips . . . with tassels. Amanda was right, he could be a bad ass biker.

Rehan cruised around on his new ride and made his surveillance run. Everything was right there, as expected, in plain view. The spot he found was inconspicuous, on the far side of the river, next to some warehouses, with a small loading dock, right on the water.

It was all working exactly as planned, well ahead of schedule. Rehan stashed the bike, stocked up on supplies and settled in for a couple relaxing days of rest. He needed it. He'd earned it.

The only question now, would the U.S. Government meet his demands?'

And save the city of Boston . . . from total destruction.

CHAPTER 36: Falling from On-High, Just Gives You More Time to Think

By late Monday evening it was clear the Chameleon was long gone. Again?

Susan's team was beat, discouraged, and going on fifty hours straight.

"Okay everyone, I'm calling it. Unlock. Call home, tell them you're on the way. It'll be a short break people, so get some much-needed sleep. Everyone remains on-call."

A bustle on the floor began as everyone switched to their routine of going home.

Givens walked over to Susan. "Good call. I'm beat. The hour's you people keep . . . brutal."

"You can only push the human brain so far without real rest before it becomes non-functional." Dr. Splitzer said, looking like he needed to heed his own advice.

"It applies to all of us." Susan added. "Get some rest until my Pal catches his trail. No rest for you Pal, you'll keep working, and looking. Right?

"Yes Susan. I am already working several other threads. I will flash alert everyone if there's any actionable intelligence."

"There ya go guys. Go home and rest." Susan said, then turned back to her console watching her team file away.

General Givens came to her side. "You too Miss Susan?"

"Of course. A couple hours of post-work reports and I'm out. We're just sitting around anyway." Susan said typing harder and harder on her keyboard.

"They need this." Givens gestured to her team. "Be with the family, the kids. With the school bombin', on the news all day. Let 'em give each other a big, safe hug."

"I don't want it to be safe." Susan said.

"How's that?" Givens asked.

"When they hug their kids, I want them to think how lucky they are.

This maniac is after our kids now. I want that to sink in."

General Givens stood tall. "Brutal. Just brutal, this work of yers. Hard as anythin' I've ever done. Special forces. Even combat. I'm goin' home ta rest, goodnight."

"I'll be right behind you." Susan assured him.

It was three hours. Before she let herself leave. And only because she was exhausted.

* * *

As Susan drove down the quaint streets of Georgetown to her cozy brick-rowhome, the late-night street lamps seemed to be shimmering under a weight of darkness. A damp mist of rain added to the chill. Susan felt like she was dragging herself through a dark pool to climb her steps.

It felt bad to enjoy a hot shower, bursting in tears twice before the water ran cold.

She absently fixed a cup of tea and flopped in her wet robe into an overstuffed club chair. She didn't deserve a comfortable bed tonight either. How many parents, in uncomfortable hospital room chairs, next to their injured children right now?

Susan hated to be thankful to the Chameleon? To Rehan Al'Camel, for sparing them. Detonating just as the first buses were unloading. Several children suffered serious injuries, but none had been killed or left in critical, life threatening condition.

The worst seemed to be when all those bus windows shattered, cutting and, and . . . Would they ever see again? Have I robbed them of that? Susan sipped her tea and scalded her tongue.

Cut, scarred terribly? Every time they look in a mirror, will they blame me?

Susan fought harder and harder to let herself off the hook, for at least some of the responsibility. She didn't like the answers her thoughts were giving her. Weeks and weeks on this roller-coaster. It took another dip. Near the bottom, the flames of this hell licked at her sub-conscious in waves of anxiety and self-doubt.

How many teachers and staff? 22 so far, with 6 more missing? Rescue crews combing through wreckage. They hadn't officially called it a recovery, yet. I wonder who those families are blaming right now?

Who would she blame in their position?

I'm going to need help with this one, when it's all over. If?

* * *

The American flag flapped majestically in the air. Each time it flapped it exposed another injured and bleeding child . . . Susan bolted awake, sending her cup of tea across the carpet.

She'd dealt with some terrible things from her past. Up-close things she'd seen and done. Let herself be used. Used herself on occasion. There's plenty of psychological training and support as a C.I.A. agent. Dealing with stressors, of all kinds, was a part of her trade craft.

Distracting yourself with an intense case was as good a counter measure to dwelling on negatives as anything. If you weren't exhausted.

She forced herself to sleep. Pal will find him, you'll need your rest then . . .

Her dreams shocked her awake again and again.

Six hours later she was back at work, arriving in the bleak early hours of Tuesday morning. Her control room was dark and lonely, a backup Mr. Green stood watch alone.

Susan made her way to the only companion she could think of. The elevator dinged, and the doors slid open. The lights and bubbles of her Pal bobbing gently in his tank, working away, made her feel better.

She fell to a chair at the first workstation. For a long time, she sat in silence just listening to his bubbles. She made busy work out of reports and emails. An hour passed in the chores of her job.

"Susan?" her Pal asked, in a soft tone of her special voice.

"Hello Pal, what's up?" Came her melancholy reply.

"Hello. Not you apparently? Are you alright, I do not wish to disclose your bio-readings as requested." An amazingly compassionate response in that sweet voice reserved just for her.

"Very perceptive Pal . . . but I bet you didn't need bio-readings to figure out I'm feeling like crap right about now."

"Yes, it is obvious. I want to make you feel better but, after yesterday's conversation regarding women, I am unsure what to say."

Susan laughed a little. "It's okay, you don't have to say anything. I'd rather you use every ounce of energy to keep after that bastard."

"You have to know none of this is your fault . . ."

"No? Did I make the right call Pal? Shouldn't I have just given Rehan what he wanted?"

"It's unfortunate your search for the Chameleon did not lead to the discovery of his explosives. The school was searched twice. But the human mind has a flaw, they failed once focused on looking for a man." Her Pal answered.

"That's not what I asked. After Timmy's show of support, was I too arrogant? Cocky?"

"Susan, there are too many variables."

"It's torture Pal. You can figure out all possible outcomes? Tell me, you think I screwed up? Did I make the wrong move two days ago? Or two weeks ago? Am I right now?"

"Unfortunately Susan, humans do not work like the game of chess, with rules and certainty of motions."

"Good point, all the stress and failures? Maybe my little brain's too crispy from it all, to do my job, what do you think Pal, is that possible?"

"You have to know none of this is your fault."

"Pal please! I'm dealing with it. I know . . . but still . . . just . . . please."

A long silent pause ensued. Susan knew her Pal was confused again. Fighting to understand her. She was barely making sense to herself.

"Would it help to focus on our current task? I could review up to date analysis with you?" The Palantir asked.

"Okay, sure. Thank you for caring." Susan forced a smile knowing he was watching and reading her every . . . output.

The elevator dinged and opened, Givens came in with a fresh hot Starbucks coffee. "Thought I'd find ya here, Good Mornin' Hal."

"Good morning General Givens. It's nice to see you again." The Palantir said.

"Comin' from you in that big tank freaks me out a little Hal."

Givens set the coffee next to Susan. "Couldn't sleep either?" he asked.

"Thanks . . . nope." Susan answered, taking the cup, feeling guilty to enjoy the aroma.

"Pictures of little bleedin' kids dancin' round in those dreams?" Givens sat on the edge of the desk, right next to her, very close.

"Yep." Was all she could choke out. She stared at the wall, unable to make eye contact.

Givens stood, reached over and took the cup of coffee out of her hands, placing it on the table. He grabbed her by the elbows and stood her up, catching her eyes, looking at her the whole way. The chair rolled away from behind her, he stepped in and bear-hugged her, pulling her right in tight.

Susan reflexed to pull away, but he held firm, and she folded. He started turning slowly side-to-side in a great big, strong hug.

Her tears burst again. Letting her head find his shoulder and falling into his embrace. She would have fallen to the floor if he hadn't supported her. Every fiber in her being screamed for her to resist and to be strong . . . but she wasn't.

General Givens reached up and stroked the back of her head. "It's gonna be okay. Not right away, but soon."

She'd always been strong. Intelligent. The "LIC." But right now? She felt weak and stupid, like a little girl crying over some silly adolescent tragedy. But it wasn't. "Those poor kids!" She sobbed out.

"Oh dear, dear Susan, it's gonna be alright . . ."

"It was my job to protect them . . . it's too real! It hurts so bad." The sobs just grew and grew. She knew she couldn't stop now. And, it felt good. Really good, being held, and just letting it all go, if only for that brief moment.

"I know, me too, it's on all of us, I know . . ." Givens stroked and held her, swaying ever so slightly.

It was a huge release, Susan needed badly. Slowly draining out of her, she barely backed away, still in the Generals strong arms. She swiped her face, clearing her eyes and looked up at him. Laughed a little noticing a smear of tears on his uniformed shoulder. She brushed them away, smoothed out the fabric, and gazed back up.

"Thank you" . . . Susan leaned up on her toes and kissed him quite passionately, letting her hand find the back of his neck, stroking his close-cropped hair.

Givens didn't fight, and Susan lingered just as long as she liked. She softly backed away, opening, then dropped her eyes from his.

"That's not why I gave you the hug." Givens said sounding a bit guilty in her vulnerability.

"I know . . ." She answered, looking back up into his eyes, she leaned up and kissed him again, just as passionately. "Thank you . . ." She whispered, her eyes still closed as she pulled away. She turned back to collect her chair, sat, and picked up her coffee.

"Well . . . yer welcome." Givens said. "Damn, I gotta try that compassionate hug thing more often."

It got a nice relief laugh out of both of them. The moment passed and, with some eye contact, they both left anything else unsaid, for now.

The elevator dinged behind them and they both jumped and turned like two teenagers caught making out.

Mr. Green stepped out with his own gift of a Starbucks. Seeing one already in front of Susan, his disappointed look betrayed him, but he recovered quickly. "You damn military guys get up and going way too early in the morning."

Susan didn't want him to feel bad. "Oh, is that for me? There's never too much coffee around here, especially Starbucks, thank you so much." She made a point to get up and cross over to accept it. "It's nice getting presents from such handsome men this early in the morning. A girls gotta love all the attention, right?"

"Sure, you're, welcome . . ." Mr. Green said with curious suspicion. He looked over at General Givens smiling widely, not making eye contact. "Do me a favor though?" Mr. Green said to Susan, ". . . take me out to dinner first, I don't like following this guy all the time."

"You have no idea my boy." Givens shot at him.

Susan whipped her pony-tail around, pleading . . . or demanding, of Givens to be tactful.

Givens covered his comment, "Ah, it's the job of the military ta be one step ahead all the time. Sorry, my friend, old habits n' all, ya know."

Playing it off to Susan's satisfaction, but she could tell Mr. Green perceived there was something more being said, he had his skills too.

"What's going on?" he decided to play, goading General Givens to give more.

Susan took the lead and any chance away from Givens, in case he wanted to toy with Mr. Green. "I was just saying, my Pal is ready to update us on the analysis to date. Pal, if you would?"

"Good morning gentlemen. First, I'd like to say that I'm now 99.75% sure that Doctor Rehan Al'Camel is in fact the arms dealer previously only known as the Chameleon . . ."

"Wait a minute, did I miss something?" Mr. Green questioned. "Didn't you say, even if he admitted it, he'd still be at what? 99.5%, so how in that brain-soup of yours did you come up with 99.75% Hal?"

"It's quite logical Mr. Green. Yesterday's demand statement makes the current analysis perfectly rational. Had Rehan Al'Camel stated matter of fact, 'I am the Chameleon' then he might have been lying. At this stage, a .5% chance. However, if you cross analyze the database of events in the Chameleon's past, with the statement, then you should increase the overall probability by .25%. Does that answer your question?"

"I'm sorry I asked." Mr. Green said looking at the other two.

"Don't look at me, I don't understand half the stuff the Hal spits out . . ." Givens surrendered.

The Palantir clarified more. "Only the real Chameleon would know what type of sales were made. Only the Chameleon would know the targets, or intended use. The history of all the sales he has made. The motive. It is quite telling and informative. There are other statements that also work in favor of this analysis. I could play them as well if you'd like?"

Givens stopped him. "No, please don't for Christ sakes."

"99.75% is close enough for me," Susan jumped in. "I officially declare defeat in our bets gentlemen. But, before I could enjoy any dinner date, I really need to nail this bastard. Pal, please continue with your update."

"Certainly. The biggest news this morning was discovery an hour ago in the woods behind the school of the rented van under the alias James Wright. The body of the school's janitor, whose truck is missing and assumed stolen by Rehan Al'Camel, was also found.

The stolen truck was captured on film at two different tollbooths headed north into Boston on Monday. He was careful to hide his face using a hooded sweatshirt and dark sunglasses, but it seems clear that he has assumed yet another false identity and new disguise.

This theory is bolstered by the fact that none of the credit cards under the alias James Wright have been used since the Friday before the school bombing.

It's probable, but not a certainty, that Rehan Al'Camel intends his next attack in the Boston, Massachusetts metropolitan area.

Most federal assets are moving there now. Local and state agencies have been mobilized as well, all searching for the stolen truck. I would be happy to answer your questions or review other events?"

"Do ya have a search area?" Givens asked.

The Palantir spoke in monotones when providing raw facts and data. "Unfortunately, the last image we have is at a toll booth on U.S. Route 1, which leads through the entire greater Boston Massachusetts area. "Greater Boston" refers to the entire downtown city of Boston, the North and South Shores, plus an area called MetroWest and the Merrimack Valley."

Maps and 3D renderings of the routes into Boston displayed on screens as the Palantir talked, changing in real time. "His route would give him easy exits to the entire Boston Combined Statistical Area of 4,674 square miles."

"Not good news." Mr. Green added watching the infinite number of routes in, out, and around Boston on the displays spreading like a spider's web. "What's the population density Palantir?"

Greater Boston is tenth in U.S. City Population with 4.6 million residents. The entire Boston 'Combined Statistical Area' includes 7.6 million residents.

"Damn, he can easily hide in that mass. Pal, what's the timeline right now?" Susan asked.

"Assuming the 72-hour deadline started at 10am Monday morning, when he demanded it be read on-air, time now Tuesday, 7:43am, leaves 50 hours and 17 minutes."

"Damn." Susan didn't want to ask any more questions. "What's the White House doing about the threat?"

"In response, the White House has asked for all Americans to remain calm and diligent. A Presidential press conference has been announced for Wednesday at 5pm to respond directly to Rehan Al'Camel.

This was designed to placate him, and hopefully ensure that he does not take any action prematurely.

In reality, it is a stall tactic. The President informed law enforcement and federal agencies he has no intention of meeting any demands made under threat of attack. He has issued an ultimatum, 'Find Rehan Al'Camel before that press conference.'

Every imaginable federal and local asset has been mobilized. The F.B.I. and Homeland Security are in full crisis mode and Director Timothy

Scott of this C.I.A. has given his assurance that we will track down and capture Rehan Al'Camel before he has a chance to execute his plans."

"Damn . . ." Susan wished she were so confident. If they failed now, her mentor and champion just signed his resignation papers.

"Why don't they just evacuate Boston?" Givens asked.

The Palantir gave a foreboding answer. "Several reasons General Givens.

First, the panic and chaos of a complete evacuation would cause unknown harm to countless thousands. A complete breakdown of society; riots, looting and lawlessness at severe levels. Which would interfere with, or totally disrupt, the ongoing search efforts.

Second, Rehan Al'Camel would surely know or see the evacuation in progress. He may detonate his weapon early. If it is a nuclear device, as is now suspected, millions of people in their cars, trapped on the highways, would have a lower probability of survival from the blast and radioactive exposure as opposed to staying indoors, in shelters. Prevailing winds should carry the deadly radioactive fallout over the ocean. Therefore, protecting civilians from the initial gamma ray burst, blast wave and intense heat, by keeping them in shelters, is the most logical course of action.

Current casualty estimates assume that only those at ground zero, and within the immediate thermal blast zone, depending on the yield, will perish instantly or within hours.

After detonation, the United States has emergency response, rescue and medical plans in place for just such an event. Since we have an estimated time to detonation, those assets, and many others, are being moved into place to respond immediately. Further increasing survival rates and limiting radioactive exposure and poisoning effects greatly.

Finally, the tollbooth photos show an object that is quite easily transported. Rehan Al'Camel, in the confusion, could simply drive a short distance to any number of other nearby cities and detonate there, causing a double tragedy. All the downside risk of an evacuation of Boston would still be suffered.

Projections clearly show the current course of action will result in a lower inherent risk, with the least fatalities, injuries and subsequent radiation sicknesses and deaths long-term from exposure."

"Damn." Givens added to Susan's chorus. "Ya have pictures of it?"

The Palantir continued. "There was an item or items covered by a tarp in the back of the stolen truck. Analysis shows a main cylindrical object approximately 4 to 5 feet long with several protruding parts, consistent with implosion triggers and hardware found on the exterior of early nuclear bomb designs. It is consistent with what might be expected in a crudely built, implosion type, nuclear device. If the size of this device is indicative of the fissile material used to construct the bomb, estimates of its yield could vary widely."

Susan jumped in, "Help me out Pal, how destructive might this bomb be?"

"The explosive yield of a nuclear weapon is the amount of energy released on detonation expressed in the equivalent of TNT. Kilotons in thousands of tons of TNT, and megatons in millions of tons of TNT. Therefore, a 1-kiloton nuclear blast would be like a 1,000-ton TNT explosion. A 1-megaton nuclear blast would be like a 1-million ton TNT explosion.

"There are even higher measures, in the Tera joules, but it is a virtual certainty that Rehan Al'Camel would not be able to produce and transport any such device.

"It should be noted that the precise nature, and amount of energy, in a TNT explosion has several variables and uncertainties. Therefore, nuclear yield measurements may vary greatly.

Also, the performance of the device itself presents a large variable. The efficient use of the fissile material in the implosion blast can affect the potential yield greatly.

Also, where the blast happens, in the air, on the ground, at sea, in open space, or surrounded by a downtown cityscape, will affect overall destructive forces.

Several unknown variables in this case analysis exist.

First, without being able to see the device, it is impossible to tell what kind of device it actually is.

Most likely, Rehan has constructed a fission bomb using Uranium-235 or Plutonium-239. Materials that could reasonably be available to an arms dealer.

He specifically mentioned Hiroshima and Nagasaki in his demand statement, a possible clue. The device in the truck appears only slightly smaller than the 'Little Boy' or 'Fat Man' bombs used in World War II. If so, max comparable yields would be 13 to 22 kilotons.

I'm displaying the pictures of those two destroyed cities on monitor one as an example of the energy created. A nuclear blast in these ranges creates roughly a one-mile vaporization radius, with severe to moderate damage in a 4-8mile radius and light damage up to a 16-mile radius.

However, a 'Boosted Fission Weapon' would likely double the yields. A 'boosted' design uses high-pressure gases at its core, which compresses and heats the fissile material, causing each neutron to start its own chain reaction when released. A highly efficient design which uses up more of the fissile material, otherwise lost in the blast created.

Causing a 2-3mile vaporization crater, a 6-14mile severe to moderate damage and a 22-mile light damage radius.

The most probable worst-case scenario is if Rehan Al'Camel has managed to obtain highly enriched uranium, and has constructed a thermo-nuclear bomb. Estimated yields vary widely, based on all of the same parameters discussed so far, but are increased beyond Kilotons to Mega-tons. A destructive force that would surely cause the complete destruction of the Greater Boston area.

A thermo-nuclear bomb derives its power from fusion. It is a two-stage weapon, where a fusion process implodes x-ray energy into the primary fissile material. This thermal-radioactive implosion is what causes the second stage, a fission chain reaction, to be much more efficient and many times more powerful. Neutrons are exchanged causing a boost in efficiency for both reactions. Creating significantly greater explosive yields in the tens, to hundreds of kilotons.

The temperatures created are in the tens of millions of degrees. The penetrating radiation from the blast causes all surrounding matter to reach an equilibrium temperature, at a molecular level, with the atomic material causing instant vaporization.

Kinetic energy is created by the chain reaction, and the vaporization, forming a shockwave that reaches speeds of 300 meters per second.

Two pressures are created in this destructive blast wave.

The first, Static overpressure, exerts high-forces per square inch weakening any structure.

The second, Dynamic pressure follows, with winds that exert forces many times greater than the strongest hurricanes. These wind forces are what rip and tear apart the already weakened structures from the static overpressure.

The blast wave is forced outwards for tens of miles in all directions. Obviously, these forces dissipate as the shock wave moves outward and the ...

"Damn it! Enough already!" General Givens stopped the Palantir "What the hell are they doin' ta find this bomb?"

"Under the Megaports Initiative all seaports in Boston have the newest RPMs or Radiation Portal Monitors. These detectors are being used to scan every container in port. Protocols from the U.S. Department of Homeland Security and Boarder Protection as well as the Domestic Nuclear Detection Office have all been initiated.

All container ports have been closed. Ships docked or anchored in Boston harbor, or the surrounding facilities, are being ordered back out to sea at a safe distance. A prudent and potentially lifesaving move.

In addition, several mobile radiation detectors are being flown in as we speak. The Boston area search, working from the downtown and most densely populated areas outward, is proceeding."

"How capable are these scanners Pal?" Susan asked.

"Very sensitive, modern scanners with a good chance to detect a nuclear device should they get close enough."

"I've heard they have false readings?" Mr. Green asked.

"In the past, several faults existed which generated false readings from NORM, naturally occurring radioactive materials. Mundane things like a load of cat litter. Other SNM's, Special Nuclear Materials, such as medical and industrial equipment caused issues as well. The newer, advanced scanners are more accurate with greater ranges."

"How long range Pal? We've got 4,000 square miles to search."

With the newest OCR, Optical Character Recognition scanners, whole stacks of containers, or theoretically whole 15 story buildings can be scanned at once with only a 1 in 1000 false reading rate. Two types of radiation panels are used, a primary RDP and secondary, and it is all driven by remote GPS location software for immediate response to an exact location should a positive reading be generated."

"Damn it to hell, sounds like lookin' fer a needle in a haystack." Givens said.

"The odds are better than that General. A portable or small sized, uncontained, nuclear device given the Boston area with the time we have, and the detectors being utilized, currently creates a 77% probable detection, allowing for an hour to defuse if needed."

"That's the best damn figure you've spit out in the last ten minutes but it's still not very encouraging." Mr. Green said.

"Damn, damn . . . damn!" Susan couldn't take sitting around. "Let's get to my control room, recall the team. We need to find this guy yesterday."

The Palantir had a noticeable increase in bubbles. "I'm sorry to inform you but the President has requested that Susan and her team go to the Boston F.B.I. field office. He believes her team's intimate knowledge of Rehan Al'Camel, combined with the local FBI agents, will give the best possible chance for success.

Two helicopters are being fueled and ready, and are set to leave at 8:30am, 18 minutes from now. Requested team members were already notified and are assembling on the pads now. There is a mobile crisis situation center in route and should arrive in Boston about the same time as you and your team."

The Palantir switched to Susan's special voice, the bubbles in the tank seemed to be boiling. "Susan, you made me promised that I would always watch out for, and protect you. However, if you go to Boston under the current threat matrix, I fear I cannot keep that promise. Please reconsider this request to leave."

"Sorry Pal, I don't believe it was a request. And to be honest, I'm kinda glad. If this shit-head ends up taking out the whole city of Boston . . ." Susan checked her phone for a notice about flying off to Boston? She quickly realized that the Palantir had intentionally delayed that message getting to her inbox, or the alerts to her cell. She got them now, as she was looking. Her Pal had delayed a directive from the President? It scared her, bad. She questioned everything. How could she let Mr. Green know about this huge error by her Pal?

As if reading her thoughts, an ashen faced Dr. Splitzer was just walking up to her holding out his cell phone in bewilderment. She locked eyes with him taking control.

The Palantir was surprisingly agitated. "Susan please! Think. Does it make sense to put more people in harm's way? Especially the people who could best track the Chameleon later if he succeeds again?"

"Damn it Pal, you're not listening!" Susan snapped at him like never before, she strode right up to the tank, staring eye to eye. She didn't say anything out loud, her bio-readings were perfectly clear. She took a deep breath. "We've been ordered to go by our President, but even if he didn't order me, I'd still . . . If I . . . if we fuck this up? I don't want to live with that. You want to save me? Find me that motherfucker, and do it quick."

"But Susan, I really think . . ."

She cut him off again. "That's enough! You are way over the line with this my friend," Susan held her cell up against his glass, the alert on her screen. "You and I have to have a serious talk later. I've got a helicopter to catch."

Susan turned, "Gentlemen, I don't expect that request applies to either of you so I'll understand if you remain here. Do me a favor and stay close in my control room. I'm sure I'll need your help before this is all over."

"What kind of chumps do ya think we are?" Givens asked but Mr. Green seemed even more pissed off. "How can you even say something like that? Damn it Susan,

"We're gonna find this son-of-a-bitch an I'll personally cut his balls off and deliver them to ya for souvenirs." Givens added.

"Please guys, I've got enough guilt on my mind. Save the macho bullshit and do the smart thing. Stay here." Susan said sternly.

"Bullshit?" Mr. Green gave it back to her "You don't tell me remember? I've got a job to do too, Move on."

"Askin' an old soldier like me ta send my lady into the line of fire without backin' her up, ya got some nerve." Givens scolded her.

Susan gave him an exasperated, pleading look.

"I'm a detached military advisor, so I'm pretty sure ya can't order me, yer wastin' yer breath." Givens said standing tall.

Susan shook her head, got up and started for the door, "Fine. Lead the way."

She turned back as they walked ahead, grabbing Dr. Splitzer hard by the arm sitting at his station. Pulled him close to whisper.

"You stay close. And don't you dare hesitate if you have to. Not for a second, you hear me?"

CHAPTER 37: Fabric Stitched in Time

Juma stood at the corner of the house in the side yard. Radiant white, a warm glow, with no scary blood or wounds. The ribbons on her dress glowed in neon pink, her hair flew wildly, in slow motion, in the wind that Rehan could only hear.

Rehan stood in the front yard, smiling and laughing at her vision. A child in pure glee.

"Watch me do it again Rehan!" She screamed and dashed away from him in a white light, forming a shooting star in a big arch up into the sky, coming around in a wide circle, stopping instantly in her own form again at the corner. "Did you see how fast?"

"Yes Juma, it's amazing."

"Do you want to see again?"

"No dear Juma, I've got to go."

"Don't go Rehan! Stay and play with me."

"I don't have time Juma."

"Why Rehan?" Her look of sadness gripped onto him, pulling him to stay with her, into her light.

"I have to try and get away Juma. I have to try? I can't stay here?"

"DON'T GO!" Juma screamed, sounding ominous, her white light increasing in a blinding glow, her hair flying faster. "You'll never come back to play if you go."

Juma reached out to grab him.

As her arms stuck out past the corner . . .

. . . they turned bloody, dripping at the elbows.

Rehan bolted upright in bed. Freezing cold, falling back and grabbing for the piles of covers.

He'd left the balcony doors open before dozing off, letting in the sounds and salt air off Pleasant Bay.

It was much chillier now. And getting dark. He checked the red-LED nightstand clock-radio. 4 pm. Only an hour until the Presidential news conference. His Presidential news conference.

After being holed up for two days now waiting for it, how funny would it have been if he'd overslept?

Rehan put on some sweats and a robe. Cranked up the heat. Brewed himself a strong pot of coffee and switched on the news to catch the latest.

The intensive search for the Chameleon in Boston had started early Monday. With the sudden increase in law enforcement, federal vehicles, and other strange goings-on, people in Boston caught on quick.

When news leaked that Boston might be the target of the madman Chameleon, panic bubbled up. It was subdued by authorities only because the "deadline" was still far off and the news broke slowly, as the story was uncovered.

The police chief held an emergency news conferences. Pulled out all the historic and patriotic stops he could think of; Paul Revere, Bunker Hill, the U.S.S. Constitution along with various other Forts, Ports and Historical sites around Boston. "This isn't the first time our city has been threatened. We need Bostonians to police ourselves. Keep order. Keep off the streets so we can search."

It worked to calm, or at least quell, all out panic.

Until the Black Widow and her team were spotted by reporters arriving by helicopter on Monday a little after noon. If the Black Widow herself was there, so was the Chameleon. How was he planning to destroy them? Then, the nuke leaked.

The roads leading out of town quickly became jammed. Gas stations ran dry. Runs on water, candles, generators, duct tape and plastic tarps, along with anything edible, flew from store shelves and created scenes of mayhem throughout the city and surrounding areas.

Some lootings took place but, with so much law enforcement in town, any real unrest was quickly overwhelmed. Unfortunately, it required a constant quell, and all that manpower was supposed to be searching for a nuclear bomb.

The Governor and Mayor held another emergency news conference Monday evening and patriotically stated that they, and their families, would not be driven from their homes. Pleading for people not to panic. A curfew was set for Monday night at 8pm. "We have to clear the streets so law enforcement can do their job and find this guy. People will be able to leave, if they choose, in an orderly manner, starting tomorrow at 8am."

And while it was true that both the Governor and Mayor, along with their wives stayed, reporters caught their children being whisked away by private jet and cover stories created for their departures.

People hunkered down Monday night and all out, irrational panic ebbed by Tuesday morning. But, the tension of it hung like a static charge in the air.

Outbreaks of unrest continued to be a very real distraction. The police chief held another news conference first thing Tuesday morning, pleading again for "People to police themselves" so law enforcement and federal agents could focus on the job at hand. "We need the people of Boston to help us out here damn it!"

The chief's pleas resonated with most Bostonians. He'd grown up in a tough part of town, took a bullet early in the line of duty, he was one of them. "What are ya doing? Do something! Search buildings and homes. It's your streets he's messing with!"

Bostonians responded and turned out in droves all day Tuesday and did exactly what he asked. Patrolling the streets, helping elderly neighbors and putting down any groups of rough-neck youths looking to exploit the situation. People organized searches for the Chameleon, or his bomb. Ready to kill . . . or defuse. Whichever. Both.

News crews did stories showing groups of unlikely co-patriots; African Americans and Italians and Southside Irishmen working together. Criminal groups opted for being civically responsible, protecting their turf, as opposed to letting it burn in looting, riots and lawlessness.

A reporter was closing the latest feel-good story, "Everyone has a common enemy to focus on, and right now, it isn't one of their neighbors."

Rehan switched off the news with a groan, took his fresh cup out on the balcony, enjoying the view of Pleasant Bay and a setting sun. He leaned around the rail on one side to take in the view leading away to the downtown Boston city-scape. Everything seemed much quieter than days before.

Monday, and all day Tuesday, he watched the coast guard swarm all over the ports. Container ships were turned away, back out to sea. Even those already at dock, but not yet unloaded, were sent sailing into the setting sun by Tuesday night. Rehan worried, and half expected, to see the Crystal Sun float by.

The airport was still open, but he was sure it would soon be shut down.

Commuter trains and mass transit still rolled along, but it had been hours since he last saw a freight train or tractor-trailer leave with a container load from the trucking and shipping terminals.

Police and Government vehicles crisscrossed all over, emergency lights flashed in spots. But no sirens. The chief banned their use to reduce the citywide fear.

You could tell the city was still there, on edge, but it was eerily quiet and empty, like the mall parking lot on Christmas morning.

A 5pm curfew was announced, coinciding with the Presidential news conference, and the whole city seemed to settle down for it while still holding its breath.

Rehan relaxed in a chair on the balcony to read the Wednesday paper he hadn't gotten to.

A front-page picture of Susan Figiolli, coming out of a giant RV command center at the FBI office in Boston was featured. As always, the press made Susan look sexy. Her skirt riding up her right thigh, a fit-athletic leg extended down to the pavement. Her hair caught blowing perfectly in still motion. The headline read, "Spinning Her Web."

Rehan sipped his coffee. Bitter, with that aftertaste of burnt automatic drip he loathed.

The Black Widow was now everyone's little darling. Her persona had morphed to that of a champion fighting against the evils of the world. An example of strength, and how smart and dedicated our secret agents can be. Screw with America? Try and kill our kids? We'll sic' our bad-ass Black Widow on you.

Every story hoping like hell she'd find her prey and inflict her poisonous bite, sooner rather than later.

Rehan tossed the paper aside. He was stiff. Tense. He checked the time, 4:21. It was dragging. He needed to relax. That crick in his neck wouldn't let go.

He stood under the jets of the multiple headed rain shower. Hot water beat through and saturated to his core. Deep warmth, soaking in. Letting some of the pressure vent off in his mind. Rehan allowed for a hopeful, positive outcome. It might all be over. Leave with head held high. Inside, deep inside, it felt good to think it could be true. Rehan stayed until the water started to turn cold.

At 4:53 Rehan settled down, cleaned and refreshed, in front of the T.V. A glass of Scotch on the rocks helped set the relaxation of the wonderful shower.

News anchors talked in circles. A still shot of the empty Presidential podium at the White House filled the screen. Until 5:30pm. Then for five, ten, fifteen minutes more!

Rehan's stress was back to full tilt by the time they announced the President, at 5:50!

How dare they keep me waiting like that? Rehan had half a mind to call and move his deadline up by fifty minutes in response to the insult. But finally:

"Ladies and Gentlemen, the President of the United States."

Doors opened on the red carpeted hall, and the President strode stone faced up to the presidential podium.

"Good evening my fellow Americans. First, our prayers and sincere condolences to the victims and their families. The country mourns and prays, is hurting, right alongside of all of you. I wish my words right now could ease your suffering. I ask all Americans to join me in a moment of silence, to pray for the victims, their families and friends."

The President paused, looking down, mouthing a moment of silent prayer. Then looked back up.

"I also want to thank the first responders and aid agencies who, even now, continue their search at the middle school."

The President paused, jaw clenched, stern as he squared his shoulders. Directly into the camera. "Whether the act of a terrorist group, a radical country, or the delusional acts of a single individual, this country has seen its share of brutal crimes against our civilian population. Defenseless men, women and children killed and maimed for doing nothing more than going about their daily lives. Unfortunately, there is a popular saying of our time . . . Freedom is not free.

For generations, our men and women in uniform have fought in every corner of the world to protect our freedoms. Many have given their lives in that defense, and I would add, many did so with pride and a sense of honor. It was their duty, their calling, and they understood the risk. Making the ultimate sacrifice, for what we all believe in. We owe them a great debt.

But now we, American citizens, have obviously become the direct targets of our enemies. And in today's modern world, with the free flow of information and technology, added to our way of life . . . our freedoms, we cannot honestly, realistically, believe that we can protect ourselves from every possible attack?

IF we gave up our freedoms. IF we curtailed our liberties. Maybe, MAYBE, we could be somewhat safer. But, I submit to you, my fellow Americans, not really all that much. A determined enemy will eventually find a way.

Given those choices, we, all Americans, now find ourselves on the front lines. At home or abroad. Going to work, traveling or on vacation. Out in public, at school, the movies . . . or exercising your right to a political rally.

But, as Americans, we are not afraid. We don't panic. Our forefathers faced it. So must we. My fellow Americans, we have been lucky, for many decades now, but lately, the world has gotten smaller.

I stand here today, as your President, and I tell you plainly, it is your duty to stand up to the evil that threatens us. We must, as Americans, stand united. Even in the face of great danger . . . even, at our own peril. We must be willing to show these terrorist that simply blowing something up will not take away our rights or our freedoms. Paid for in blood, to protect and preserve, for over two hundred years now."

Cameras clicked away. The greatness of this President as an orator never shined as brightly as it did here, as he built his speech to a patriotic fury. "Do not be afraid! Home of the free, and of the brave. We will not back down. We will not cower in fear. We will stand united and come back stronger no matter what they throw at us."

The President had to pause as a spontaneous cheer broke out from the gathered reporter corps and dignitaries. He held up his hand to quiet them and continued.

"I am not going to apologize for the American way of life, nor its government, nor its actions. We are not perfect. But no nation, or religion, or individual on earth is. It is a fact that America has made mistakes, but no other nation on earth, in its entire history, has gone to the lengths this great nation has to at least try and acknowledge our errors, and in many cases, attempt to make amends.

We have the strongest laws, rights, a free press, and a whole system of checks and balances built in to our constitution and government. Is it perfect? No. Is there anything better or more secure in the world in which we live? No.

Some in this world seem to think that we should, or even could, be perfect? Some believe their religion, or their world view, is better, simply because it differs from our own.

But, free peoples, and those under domination, still seek out our country and our way of life. For me, that is the truest test of our system, our rights, our liberties, our freedoms and our government. As long as the poor, huddled masses of the world look to us as I beacon of light, I say we are doing what our forefathers envisioned.

And, like our forefathers, we will defend that way of life with our blood. Is there really any other choice? I ask you, my fellow Americans, what choice do they really give us?" The President let the question settle itself in the minds of the American people. He turned side to side looking for any other possible answer. He collected himself, stared more intensely into the camera.

"Now, on to the matter at hand. Doctor Rehan Al'Camel has asked .. . no, demanded, under threat of mass murder, that I, as your President, do certain things. Here is my response.

No, I will not pardon you for your crimes, and I hope in fact that you are soon held accountable.

No, I will not state publicly that you are not the arms dealer known as the Chameleon, because our security agencies are quite sure you are. I have seen the proof against you. Doctor Rehan Al'Camel, you are the Chameleon, and you must answer for it.

And finally, No I will not unfreeze or ever release your bank accounts or assets because I am convinced that you would only use those funds to further your miss-guided, evil agenda and, given those resources, you would only try to kill more Americans in the future.

Wherever you are know this, if you bomb an American city, we will find you. We will hunt you down to the far corners of the earth.

Any person, group or nation that gives you safe harbor, or help in any way, will be in essence declaring war on the United States of America. All resources and assets will be used to utterly destroy you, and any ally who harbors you.

Let no group or nation say we did not give fair notice. When we find him out, and we surely will, we will give no further warning to you or to him. We will wage an all-out war against him, and whoever helps to harbor, protect or conspires with him.

You can't escape for long. Ask Saddam Hussein, ask Osama Bin Laden, ask Mummar Kaddafi. From a rabbit hole in the middle of the desert, or hiding under the umbrella of some host country, we will find you."

The President paused, the power of his statement commanded silence.

Releasing his stare and glancing around the room of people gathered before him.

"Now, back to my fellow Americans. I must warn you. That was my duty, as your President, to protect and preserve the constitution of this great nation, I am sworn. And, as your President, I call on all of you to hear me now, IT DOES NO GOOD FOR YOU TO PANIC. Please, steady yourself. Stay calm. Uphold the laws of this great land without the watchful eyes of law enforcement. They have a far more important task at hand. That is your duty. As Americans.

"It seems clear this madman is somewhere in the northeast United States, perhaps the greater Boston area, but we cannot be sure. Do not get in your cars and try to leave Boston because you might just as likely drive to wherever he really is planning his attack.

"Be aware that, like the first responders of 9/11, thousands and thousands of law enforcement and government agents have poured into the Boston area. They have come to save you and they are not leaving. I doubt they would leave even if I directly ordered them too. They deserve your respect and cooperation.

"So, I say again, there is no need to panic, no sense to try and flee. Please, stay calm. Stay off the streets, allow law enforcement to do their job.

"After I am done, public service announcements will follow with the best information we have on how you can protect yourselves and your families. Web-sites and toll free crisis lines have been established as well.

"Resources are being poured into the area and staged for your support. We are with you all. Right now, already there, and we are not going anywhere. You are not alone in this fight.

"REMEMBER, this madman only wins if we turn on each other, or allow our society to break down. As the Chief of Police in Boston put it, we

Americans need to police ourselves right now. Keep the streets clear. Follow our emergency instructions.

"I'm declaring martial law in Boston and other nearby cities. There is a curfew that will go into effect at six pm Eastern Standard Time tonight. Anyone on the streets after eight pm will be subject to immediate arrest and detainment. Please, ladies and gentlemen, stay indoors with your families.

"Thank you, my God protect you all, and may God protect the United States of America."

The gathered reporters exploded with questions as the flash of cameras catching the historic moment strobed away. The President stoically turned and shook hands with a couple key congressional and senate leaders, then turned and exited the room.

Rehan exploded out of his seat in rage, launching his drink at the television, shattering the glass across the screen and causing it to black out.

He stood and screamed back at the President, "You're exactly the example! You arrogant bastard, why can't you see?"

Rehan paced the room like a caged tiger, turning at each wall, talking back at the television. Hunt me down? You're gonna hunt me down? You know what happened to the last fucker's you sent after me?

Rehan fumed the entire night. The rage in his brain twisted tight. Every drop of compassion or caring was wrung from his conscience. He talked out loud to himself, and couldn't stop springing from bed, pacing.

There's no choice, and they'll pay for it. This will just be the beginning.

At some point, he crossed to a mental state only the pathologically insane can possibly imagine. Devoid of reason, logic, compassion.

Rehan consciously knew he'd crossed over a threshold, giving up on hope, letting the rage and anger wash through him. The only question, the only thing he kept wondering,

How many people will I kill this time?

CHAPTER 38: Magic Depends on Not Seeing the Sleight of Hand

Early Thursday morning, Susan and her team worked away packed inside the mobile RV command center parked just outside the F.B.I. Office at 1 Main Plaza in downtown Boston.

Since Monday, trash, pizza boxes, and paperwork had overflowed into a giant pile of green, plastic lawn and leaf bags outside the door, under armed guard, until it could be properly incinerated. It was stuffy, cramped, and everyone smelled a bit ripe inside the RV.

The F.B.I. was given the official lead, since it was a case of domestic terrorism. However, the director of the F.B.I. admitted to Susan right away they were way behind the 8-ball in developing a case file on Rehan Al'Camel.

He tactfully asked Susan if a fresh approach, separate from the ongoing C.I.A. efforts, might uncover something they had missed by attacking the problem from a different angle.

Susan readily agreed. After working the same case for years, a fresh set of eyes sometimes sees something that has been right in front of you the whole time. Susan was deathly afraid she might be missing something that would haunt her even more than the school bombing. She could taste that fear, from all her years chasing the Chameleon.

There was no animosity, pulling rank, or fighting over resources. The C.I.A. shared everything . . . opening an access portal directly to the Palantir for any support, advice, or background information "it?" might have. The F.B.I. fed it right back to him, allowing unprecedented access to their databases.

Only one thing mattered . . . I've got to find Rehan Al'Camel before his deadline.

* * *

A group of bipartisan congressmen and senators held an emergency press conference directly after the president the night before.

They debated publicly nonstop all night since then. Defiantly questioning the president. Some were indignant, not sure the president was justified, or even legal, in seizing Rehan's accounts? "In the United States of America, a citizen, is innocent until proven guilty." They "certainly hoped that Doctor Al'Camel would give the Congress and Senate a chance to respond to his . . . request.

A near majority of congressmen and senators came out publicly in favor of granting Rehan's demands. Calling for, then demanding, a vote on the House floor. After all, "This country is a democracy, not a dictatorship, and even the president can be overridden with a three-quarters majority."

Susan shook her head, bewildered at the news coverage and interviews of phony senators and congressman play-acting. "I wish it was this easy to tell when they're lying all the time." she commented.

Givens looked on in wonder. "I gotta play poker with these jokers. What the hell's the point?"

"The point General," Mr. Green answered from behind, "is to get Doctor Al'Camel to extend his deadline if possible. They will play act, call, then delay a vote, argue more, call another vote, going past his deadline. Who better to filibuster than a group of seasoned politicians?"

* * *

It played out just the way Mr. Green had said it would. Motions flew, were debated, voted on. Got, approved.

A resolution was floated. "Unintentional Inflicted Mental Duress", would absolve Rehan of any crime or liability. America had been the unknowing "Inflictor" of duress, operating in a dangerous and unpredictable world. And Rehan, the inflictee, from his past to present, committed actions caused by that "Mental duress."

The politicians took Rehan's side and cast blame back at the C.I.A., especially that "artificially brain," which seemed to be the source of everything against Dr. Al'Camel. "Ban any 'artificial intelligence' work product from legal prosecutions" was attached to the 'UnMenDuress' motion. If passed, the resolutions would tear to shreds any legal case against Rehan. A senator on TV openly pleaded with Rehan to contact his lawyers' for verification. "Our message to Doctor Rehan Al'Camel is clear. Representatives have heard you. We're working hard to make a firm agreement, under the law, within the short timeframe, we just needed a little more time."

Givens released a gruff breath. He turned to Susan. "I respect ya, Susan. Ya know that, right?"

"You respect me General?" She hadn't heard that statement directed her way in years.

"Yes. The old soldier in me can't take this. Waitin' ta be attacked? Play-actin'? We're not movin' quick enough."

"Stick around. I have a feeling you'll be wishing for a breather soon enough."

Givens grabbed her, up close, "Ya seem . . . concerned 'bout somethin' What am I missin'?"

Susan looked at him and smiled at his perception. "C.I.A. and F.B.I. have been working-over every informant, snitch, junkie, drug dealer, prostitute, gangster, and criminal organization on the planet. If Rehan has somehow constructed and smuggled in a nuclear bomb, some shady character or group somewhere knows something."

"If they hate America, I doubt they'll fess up?" Givens asked.

"We've threatened, bribed, blackmailed, harassed, and, interrogated, intensely. F.B.I. has been putting the squeeze on every known member of this distinguished social class in cities across America. I didn't expect we'd get the whole story, but . . ."

"But?"

"We've been working that angle since Monday, and there's, nothing really."

General Givens' concern was evident. "That don't surprise me. Bad guys went deep underground until this shit-storm blows over. Ain't surprising crime the world over paused with the tickin' time bomb in Boston."

"That's true, the Chameleon's poking the beast hard. Anyone remotely screwing around with the investigation is bound to get burned. But, we know the bad guys who'd have the capability to help him pull this off, and we know where they hide, who their connections are. If the worst happens, especially if the worst happens, they'd be scared about blowback. They'd at least set us off in the right direction, you know? My gut says they simply told the truth."

"Nothin'? Not a single lead? So, impossible?" Givens asked.

Susan worried. "They haven't found the stolen truck. It's like he vanished off the face of the earth again. After what? Setting the timer on a nuclear device he built all by himself before leaving town?"

Mr. Green advised, "More likely, he's hiding in plain sight, the Chameleon after all."

Susan was struck by a thought and drifted right past both of them down the aisle of the RV.

General Givens and Mr. Green picked up on it and followed her as she jumped in a seat and logged in with her Pal.

Mr. Green leaned over. "Are we working on something?"

She mumbled, barely audible, "It's not right. Nobody's that good, no way. Parts? Material? Logistics? It's gotta be near impossible. The search we did? Maybe before, but with the search we did?"

Givens leaned in to watch her screen. "Yer not makin' sense again, little lady. What's up LIC'em?"

Susan glanced up, smiled at his use of her nick name. "The Chameleon never does anything we've predicted. It's always been different. What we're thinking is wrong. He's pulling something else. He's a master at it."

"Sound tactics, but I don't see how all this attention helps him?" Givens asked.

"What's more scary than a nuclear bomb, right? Everyone would be focused on it and missing something else. Hey, Pal, you there?"

"Susan? I do not have any data from the international sweep operations. Not a single thread or lead." Her Pal was using her special voice, but it sounded very . . . stressed? . . . and worried?

"That's because it didn't turn up a single lead, Pal. Now what's the odds of that?"

"Very remote. Either the sources are lying or . . . or . . . or . . ." Her Pal seemed momentarily stumped.

"Or there's no God damned nuclear bomb. The one thing we know, he always seems to be doing something other than what we think he is doing, isn't that right?" Susan knew she was on to something, but what?

"Absolutely correct analysis. His misdirection in virtually every case is well documented. Your intelligence is quite unique, Susan, in this way." Her Pal gave her credit, somehow sounding a bit too hard in his shortcoming.

"It's okay buddy, that's why we're a team. And, I bet now that you are on the right track, you can give me other options the Chameleon might use to destroy a whole city like Boston?"

"One moment . . . one moment please . . . one moment . . ." Susan loved when she knew her Pal was digging deep, it always meant results.

They were back in the game. The key to the whole thing. Still one step behind, but closing fast to pull up alongside this maniac in his marathon of death. How apropos, after all these years chasing him, in a city like Boston, with its world-famous marathon.

"He's burning up those brain cells of his," Mr. Green said, his eyes glued to Susan's monitor.

"Come on Hal," Givens encouraged.

"Thank you. I have four viable possibilities. First, he does have a nuclear device and our efforts to find it have simple failed. But, Susan is correct, a probable diversionary tactic. Supporting this theory is the lack of results from the worldwide, intensive search for accomplices and a sixty-five percent scan of the city, including a predicted ground zero location for maximum results, also not having discovered even trace elements of nuclear materials. The search continues, so considering alternatives is prudent.

"A second option, as a medical doctor, he could be planning a chemical or biological attack. Certain biological agents, if already disbursed, would already be terminal, and there is nothing we could do. Chemical agents would be less likely to 'destroy a whole city'.

"Rehan indicated he would 'detonate' his plan. It would take several hundred devices to cover the greater Boston area. Countermeasures in place would be deployed. In addition to law enforcement, the citizenry has privately searched most buildings looking for a nuclear bomb. Any suspicious devices would have likely been detected.

"In addition, the international sweep of undesirables would have produced some tip or lead regarding such a massive undertaking of this nature as well.

"Third, he is planning to somehow attack a nuclear power plant or plants. There are four possible targets in the general geographic region, surrounding the greater Boston area. One north of Boston, Seabrook Station, Seabrook, New Hampshire. One south of Boston, Pilgrim Power,

Plymouth, Massachusetts. One further south-west, Millstone Power, Waterford, Connecticut. And one north-west of Boston, Vermont Yankee, Vernon, Vermont.

"None are close enough to destroy Boston even if they experienced a complete catastrophic failure. The biggest risk is a total meltdown, causing the release of a massive radioactive plume into the atmosphere, with Boston being downwind from prevailing jet streams and weather patterns. The fallout and radioactive cloud would cause the Boston area to become contaminated, uninhabitable, for decades afterwards. Rehan's claim to destroy a city would be accomplished.

"However, this option is a known terrorist target. There's a high likelihood of failure or detection, especially with the current heightened level of security and awareness. Implementation of Part 73 of the Nuclear Power Plant Safeguards Contingency Plan is in effect. Whole sets of protocols by the Nuclear Regulatory Commission are in effect. In conjunction with Homeland Security, all four local reactors were placed in a type of secure lockdown and are running in a safe mode.

Contingency plans in case of an accident or sabotage are highly regimented and comprehensive. A complete sweep has been made every day since Monday. In addition, rotating pairs of Air Force F-15E fighters are preventing any type of air intrusion or attack.

"A final fourth attack scenario exists, and I compute that it is the most likely based on the Chameleon's methods, ability, and desire to remain undetected. To attack the Liquefied Natural Gas imports and storage facilities located in Everett, Massachusetts, just upriver from Boston.

"These dock terminals, power stations, pipelines, and storage tanks are all highly regulated with strict security protocols in place. With advanced warning and heightened security levels, the risk that any conceivable attack would be successful is quite low. Planted bombs or explosives would have already been found in one of the many ongoing searches.

"A complete no-fly zone has been created with Air Force F-15E fighters on patrol augmenting armed security helicopters at lower levels. The air cover is currently double normal operations and runs twenty-four hours a day.

"Also, security sweeps for miles in all directions limit any chance of a conventional arms attack. The LNG facility is well up the Mystic River, inland from the ports and the dock areas, and has a five-mile fenced security perimeter.

"Mortars, RPGs and missiles would all pose a threat, but require Rehan Al'Camel to be inside the perimeter fence, and much closer to the LNG storage tanks. Otherwise he would be outside the operational range of most conventional weapons.

"Perhaps the biggest conventional arms risk would be a long-range artillery strike. As an arms dealer, we must assume the Chameleon would have access to such a weapons system. This threat must be taken seriously.

"However, he would have to be extremely lucky to make a first round, direct hit on a storage tank or vital area. Long-range artillery is very difficult to man and operate alone. Delays between a first, or second, 'ranging shot' would expose his position via triangulation and the F-15E's would quickly neutralize the threat.

"I do not perceive any other possible threats that would result in severe damage to a city the size of Boston. However, several smaller threat options are possible should his statement to 'destroy a whole U.S. city' be unfounded. I can provide more information on the smaller threats."

"No Pal, that's good. Thanks." Terrifying, but Susan felt good about being in Boston. Finally, felt it in her bones, they were close.

"Okay, team, listen up! Have nuclear search teams switch over to chemical or bio delivery systems. Search downtown buildings and rooftops, and concentrate on the air conditioning and ventilation for some kind of a mist dispersant. Make sure they understand how creative this little bastard is. It might not be a bomb with a ticking clock. Think outside of the box. Anything amiss? The sewers? Or water supply? Gas lines to deliver a chemical or biological agent?

"Get the chemical and biological sniffers out in force. Times short. Give a heads up to FEMA and Health and Human Services. Prepare new warnings and safety instructions. But, don't release them. The public is already hunkered down for a nuclear blast, so they're protected as much as we might hope. When it's safe, we'll release to the press simultaneously. No other network will get the scoop. Go to the top of the food chain, not some desk reporter looking to make a name for themselves. Tell those editors if they break it early, any blood will be on their hands. Remind them how Director Timothy Scott likes to hold them all accountable.

"Where are my infrastructure folks? Okay, contact the utilities and have them prepared to do whatever it takes to initiate an immediate shutdown of service. If an actual attack is launched, we can minimize any dispersal.

"Counter-terrorism team? Alert the NRC and Homeland Security at the nuclear power plants up and down the coast."

Susan turned her eyes ablaze in her thoughts at Givens. "Liaise with air command and remind them this guy likes little toys too, so they can't be watching for full size aircraft way up in the blue yonder. He might have a mortar, or hidden artillery piece, looking to take a few pot shots at the reactors or LNG terminals. He's an arms dealer, help me think." Susan clutched General Givens forearm, "Some kind of high-powered rifle? Exploding rounds or something? What's he going to use to screw me?"

"Lots a things, dear Susan. I'd recommend the Marine rapid deploy units on standby. MEU Composite helicopter squadrons." Givens answered.

Susan was on a roll. "Good, let's make it happen. Okay, special liaisons team, or maybe Mr. Green, the White House should call it, go ahead and shut down air traffic in case he's got some 9/11-type plan in play. Get everything that could reach Boston grounded. Better safe than sorry. Clear the skies so the military can take down anything bigger than a Tweetie Bird."

Susan turned, commanding, "General Givens, please, make sure they do this in steps, coordinated with air traffic control and the FAA. Let's not shoot down any civilian aircraft by accident. Ground 'em all, give them fair warning, double check, then, sweep the skies."

"Roger that." Givens confirmed.

"Mr. Green?" Susan turned a bit pleading. "Anything you can add? Chemical or bio detection secret assets? Counter measures? I know you don't like to offer stuff, so I'll say I asked for, whatever. Please, is there something I'm not thinking about?"

"No, Susan, you've made all the right calls. My counterparts are already with the various agencies and law enforcement detachments. Any assistance is already in play. You and I know what's left, it's what that bastard is really up to."

"Great minds think alike my friend." Susan smiled, turned to her mobile command room full of hope.

"Okay, folks, that leaves us the Liquefied Natural Gas threat. I want everything you can think of uploaded directly to the Palantir. Let's feed the brain. Pal, you still there?"

"Yes, Susan. I'm listening and have already begun my analysis."

"Great. What's our current timeline?"

"Assuming a 10 a.m. deadline, we have three hours and fourteen minutes."

"There it is people, I don't need to remind you what's on the line. Upload everything you can find in the next fourteen minutes. My Pal's is going to cover most, if not all, of the basic. Think outside the box. Show him how creative our little brains can be.

Susan turned to Mr. Green and General Givens. "I don't have time to argue, I'm taking one of the SUVs down to Everett. He's there. Let's go."

Susan turned on her heels and went bounding out of the RV.

CHAPTER 39: Ride of the Dark Chariot

The armored SUVs thick doors and windows sounded like a spaceship air-lock when Susan slammed the passenger door shut, followed by two more sucking-thuds behind her.

It looked like a spaceship as well from her passenger seat, crammed with navigation, computer equipment and three big monitors. The dash area extended around the driver halfway over to Susan. "I hope the power and suspension are as good as this thing looks. Get me to the LNG plants at Everett." Susan commanded.

"She'll get up and go," the driver said, looking over at Susan. "How fast do you really want me to get you there?"

"I'd rather die in a horrible crash than not be there in the next five minutes."

The driver gave a wide smile as he looked in the rearview. "Gentlemen, I'd buckle up if I were you." In the second it took to don his aviator shades, the SUV launched forward.

Susan put her phone on speaker. "Pal, what do you have on the potential LNG threat? Explosive yields? Catastrophic spills? Casualty estimates?" She asked and buckled up.

"Unfortunately Susan, officials in Boston have requested for years to have updated threat assessment reports. The last one was completed in 1977 . . ."

"1977? Yer kiddin' me!" Givens blurted out from the back.

"No, General. The push has been to get the LNG threat out of the harbor to an offshore facility with a pipeline to the terminals. But that option creates other risk and problems for power plants. LNG provides nearly forty percent of the Boston area's heating, more during the peak winter season, and viable alternatives are hard to come by."

A sudden swerve through an intersection to avoid traffic caused everyone to shift sideways and hold on. Tires screeched the other way, the heavy chassis rocked in swings like a boat. "We're still alive," the driver announced, accelerating forward.

Givens seemed oblivious to the scary ride, glancing out the window, clenched jaw, shaking his head. "Stickin' their damned heads in the sand since frickin' 1977? We're doin' one every damn few months or we'd get tanned, what's wrong with these people?"

The Palantir supported his case. "Yes, General. I'm currently running a threat matrix of my own and have already come up with several glaring weaknesses in current protocols."

A sudden braking, tires screeching, to a near stop, threw everyone forward, before a jerk of the wheel to the side, then a correction sprint onward. The smell of burning rubber and heated brake pads filled the cabin.

Givens sat shaking his head, looking out the window. "Ya might just drive us into a brick wall fer all they done." he mumbled at the driver.

Mr. Green sat next to him, belted in and holding the hand strap with every twist and acceleration. "I'd rather make it there in one piece, thank you, General."

Givens looked over at Mr. Green having lost all his normal jovial tone. "I'm pretty sure I could Google frickin' maps the range and distance to that LNG facility, smart as that S.O.B. is? An artillery round or somethin'?"

"Look out!" Mr. Green screamed, grabbing the shoulder of the driver from behind. Causing a sudden brake, swerve and startled glance around, before a jolt forward again.

"Look at me!" General Givens screamed, grabbing and turning Mr. Green to face him. "Don't distract the driver! Ain't nothin' you can do. Hold on and ignore the ride."

Mr. Green internalized the advice and adjusted himself in a ridged pose.

Susan worried out loud. "If he hits his target Pal?"

"The Everett Marine LNG terminal has two main cryogenic storage tanks, which hold a combined 974,000 barrels of liquefied natural gas.

"Assuming only one tank was hit, holding seventy-five percent capacity, it would result in a catastrophic LNG exposure to the environment, overwhelming the current containment and run-off safety measures, designed to handle a heavy leak or pipeline rupture only.

"LNG spilling out, exposed to the warmer air, would create an ever-expanding gas cloud of monumental proportions. Super cooled, the LNG cloud would stay close to the ground, pushing out rapidly past the facility.

Models I'm displaying on monitor two show it flowing down the cooler waterways to the Boston city area. Wind direction and current weather analysis predicts several communities would be directly enveloped by the fog bank like LNG cloud. Including; Everett, Revere, Chelsea, Charlestown, East Boston, Winthrop and the entire east coast shoreline from the Jacobs-Sullivan Park area south to Deer Island Park, including Logan International airport."

The white cloud on monitor-2 billowed across the map with the Palantir's words.

The driver braked hard to a stop, coming up on traffic, stopped at a light. A few cars, blocking both lanes in either direction. His air-horn blared and lights flashed when he spotted and opening and climbed the curb onto the sidewalk to get past. Jumping back down to pavement and stomping the gas again.

Susan urged him on from the passenger seat. "Okay, okay . . . go, go. Pal? No explosion? Or fire? Just a cloud?"

"The initial weapon used in the attack is unknown and may cause a fire or explosion. It would be quickly suffocated by the super cooled LNG cloud. However, as the gas warms, eventually, a spark or ignition source around its outer perimeter will ignite ten to fifteen percent of the outer ring, where it is directly fed by the surrounding oxygen. This ring of fire would grow rapidly, sucking in more oxygen from the surrounding air, fueling the ever-expanding LNG. It would burn hotter and bigger in a chain reaction, as the LNG climbs and burns high into the atmosphere, eventually growing to an inferno, with a blow torch like effect in the center. It would only end when the entire tank of LNG burned off."

"Would that be it? A huge fire?" Susan asked, hopeful.

"No Susan. The other LNG tank, as well as three 25,000-gallon nitrogen tanks, used for cooling, would eventually add to the conflagration.

"LNG is compressed to 1/600th its actual gaseous volume, at 75% capacity, calculated to 730,500 barrels, it would expand to a burning cloud of over . . ."

"Stop Pal! Oh my God, it's millions of times. What happens in and around this building gas cloud and what plans are in place to fight such a blaze?" Susan asked, truly frightened now.

Her Pal didn't use her special voice when he reported. "Everything in or under the cloud of gas would eventually be incinerated. The intense, relentless heat would cause buildings and structures up to 3,000 feet away to ignite as well. Exposed people as far as 1.5 miles away would suffer second degree burns almost instantly on exposed skin. The intense heat would set clothing, hair or any other readily combustible material aflame as well.

"Variables such as water flows, winds and building densities will alter the effective radiuses given.

"Many other secondary fires and explosions would take place in the immediate vicinity of the Everett LNG facility. Numerous storage tanks and factories for other petroleum-based products from oil to asphalt exist within Everett. Based on the current weather conditions, I predict a fire-storm would be created, any one outcome cannot be realistically computed. However, every outcome is a catastrophic event."

The Palantir displayed a map of the Everett facility and a chain reaction of fire spreading like cancer across the entire Boston area. Different scenarios played out in video loops. Unlike the LNG cloud display, which mostly spread downstream and out to sea with prevailing winds, the fire seemed to eat its way back over the land, spreading over huge distances. Spreading in vast tentacles.

"Boston is a densely populated, built-up area, with urban sprawl for hundreds of miles in all directions. With nearly inexhaustible industrial and highly combustible fuel sources, a chain reaction seems inevitable. The inevitable conflagration is enormous."

"Is there any hope to stop it? Contain it to let it burn off?" Mr. Green asked.

"Local fire and rescue officials' only train for small spills or pipeline leaks of LNG. They readily admit that, in a worst-case scenario, there is little anyone could do to stop it. Therefore, they do not plan for, or attempt to simulate such a disaster. Evacuation and escape would be the only hope of survival for those caught anywhere near such an event."

"Just stickin' their God damned heads in the sand!" Givens went to slam a fist, but caught himself instead as the driver had to brake hard and fishtail around a couple crossing the street.

"I can provide more details on any aspect of my summarized response?" Her Pal asked in her special voice.

"No Pal, that's quite enough for now." Susan was in deep thought, blocking out the possible horror of it all at a certain point. If Rehan managed to set off the LNG storage tanks at Everett, it was game over.

The driver looked over at Susan as he made a final fishtail turn and headed straight toward a gate with tactical armed men in numbers all around. "That's four minutes forty seconds ma'am. If you give me permission to crash the gate coming up, I'll make your 5-minute mark, but they might shoot us all dead if we don't check in?"

*　*　*

Susan got trapped at the gate by her own security precautions longer than she wanted. Glad they were careful. On the other hand, she knew this was just the kind of procedural rule the Chameleon would use to slow her down.

They assigned her a guide and as soon as she cleared the gate, the question became, "Where do you want to go?"

The Boston Everett Industrial complex was truly massive. It was a couple miles from the entrance gate to anything sensitive, another fenced gate, then a never-ending sea of industry, huge tanks, and pipes, and box-like warehouse buildings with some sparse office space. Storage yards and a railway inter-change, and every manner of production smokestacks jutting from various-sized buildings. Separated and fenced off from each other by what seemed like a quarter-mile distance of open space, ditches, culverts, and layers of barbed fences. Mile after mile Susan looked out at the grayish-brown dirt and industrial smell of the worked over landscape. It took fifteen minutes just to get close to the LNG facility.

When Susan finally pulled up it was no more impressive than most of what she'd just driven through. She got out of the SUV. The early morning sun cast a glow of light off the sides of the giant LNG twin tanks. Industrial street lamps ringed the tops of the cylindrical tanks a hundred feet up. A chilly, dewy mist hung in the air. Susan walked right up to the massive cylinder, touched the cold steel with her bare finger-tips. Looking aside toward the other tank, she couldn't see around the radius. The LNG tanks were bigger than any of the others she'd seen, and perhaps that should have felt ominous, towering over her.

But Susan knew ominous, even abject fear while looking at some situations in her past. But not here, she didn't feel it at all. The complete puzzle hadn't fallen into place yet, or she'd be able to see it. Sense it. Had the Chameleon led her off in circles again?

Givens walked up beside her. "Umm, if he's gonna blow these things, ya think we oughta' be standin' right here?"

Susan turned, allowing the briefest of smiles. "I still don't feel it. The Chameleon doesn't take chances. One, being caught, or two, being blown away. Hail Mary pot shot at those LNG tanks? With F15's and helicopters flying around? It's not his style."

Susan turned to her escort. "Excuse me. Is this all the LNG here at Everett?"

"Is that all? That's a shit ton is all."

"So, Mark was it? Help me out here. How might an evil dude blow this up?"

"Jeez lady. I don't know. Never thought of it."

"Come on, kid. I'm not going to tell on you. 'It's a shit ton,' you said. Never thought of what might cause it all to blow?"

"Maybe, but since I work here, and I'd be cooked . . ."

"Mark please! Don't bullshit me. What? Set off one of the nearby tanks of whatever? Blow that up. Acts like a fuse, and the whole place goes?"

"I doubt it. You saw driving in. Everything is way separated. And nothing, nothing else here, has the expansive pressures and energy volume of the LNG. All the rest could explode and burn and we'd contain it. But honestly, it don't matter. Everything's under tight ass security protocols. Super tight right now as you'd imagine. Anything even close to Everett LNG is on lock-down."

Susan pointed around. "All these pipes, the maze of joints, and transfers. No way to reverse back flow something?"

"The LNG is a closed system. In from the ports, out to your stove. It all goes one way."

Susan's phone vibrated. She looked at her screen. A message from her Pal appeared. May I break your conversation?

"Yes PAL!" She said out loud to her phone still on speaker. "You can politely interrupt and add to any conversation. Always. Right? I'll let you know if I don't want you to. What do you have for me sweetie?"

Her guide Mark gave a puzzled look.

"Thank you Susan, you are always so kind. Your idea, about setting something off nearby to trigger an event, added with your idea of using the LNG systems to cause failure, led to the discovery of an LNG Tanker docked at the Everett off-load facility on the Mystic River. Five miles of pipeline lead to that docked tanker."

"BRILLIANT! Simply Brilliant Pal! That's got to be it!" Susan screamed.

Susan turned to her driver. "Let's go, get me to those docks!"

* * *

As they flew along the maze getting back out and around, much faster than her Everett complex guide approved of, Susan pushed the driver on. "Go! Go, go . . ."

Her Pal was working too. "Susan, I have the LNG tanker threat analysis complete," her Pal announced less than two minutes later.

"Great Pal, thrill me?"

"Strict protocols are in place to control transit of LNG tankers. The deepest part of the channel runs very close to the downtown shoreline and the draft of these tankers requires they follow the channel. Passing perilously close to the downtown cityscape of Boston, before making their way up the Mystic River to the LNG off-load docks and storage facilities.

"Safety protocols require LNG carriers to announce their pending arrival while still four days out to sea. Coast Guard and the LNG terminal operators run back-ground checks on the entire crew. The manifest is confirmed, and the tanker must report to the Coast Guard again at 24, 12 and 5 hours outside the Boston seacoast harbor entrance.

"Two certified Coast Guard officers board the ship for safety checks while still at least 5 miles out to sea.

"Many ships are subjected to random security sweeps by teams of Coast Guard personnel, especially those tankers originating from high-risk countries such as Yemen.

"Once cleared at five miles out, a certified Boston Harbor Pilot takes command of the vessel, performs safety protocols, and thoroughly rechecks the ship's systems before he enters the harbor.

"Just outside Boston harbor itself, at a place called Pleasure Bay, near the old ports, the LNG tanker slows to a stop, where four heavy tugboats are lashed alongside. They are used to help steer the ship, as a guide, or for emergencies in case of engine malfunction or unforeseen maneuverability needs.

"LNG tankers have the latest maritime maneuvering drive-jets, independent of the drive shaft propellers used to power the ship across the ocean. These drive-jets can turn the LNG tanker in any direction, while at a dead stop, or under way. The giant ships are so maneuverable they can spin in place if needed. These drive-jets enable control of the incredible mass, especially at slow speeds and when docking.

A higher security zone is implemented for the final transit to the Everett dock facility. On shore police vehicles are stationed along the coast and on most piers. At least one MH-65C Dolphin Coast Guard helicopter under HITRON, the Helicopter Interdiction Tactical Squadron, flies overhead armed with the 'airborne use of force package' which includes an M240 machine gun as well as specially trained airborne snipers equipped with the latest Barrett M107 precision rifle.

"Up to four Coast Guard Defender-C fast boats compliment these escorts. Called Response Boat Charlie, they fall in the TPSB or Transportable Port Security Boats category. 25-foot-long, with a center lookout cabin, they include one M2-Browning fifty caliber heavy machine gun on a modified forward mount and two M240 Browning forty caliber machine guns just aft of the cabin on each side.

"Once security is in place, the all clear is given. The LNG tanker is then maneuvered past Pleasure Bay, up into the harbor and follows the channel past the downtown Boston skyline and up the Mystic River to the Everett LNG off loading dock. It must be a clear day with low winds. Once the ship has entered the north channel it is considered 'committed to dock' and proceeds at a slow, steady ten knots.

"Maritime traffic is kept a minimum of five hundred yards away in an exclusion zone which falls under a 'use of deadly force authorized' enforcement order.

"High-security personnel oversee the maneuvering of the LNG tankers while in transit, carrying various small arms in case of external attack, or internal rogue agent sabotage attempt. Even the harbor pilot is observed by three different armed escorts in case of sudden mental instability or attempted sabotage."

Givens stood up straight. "How can he pull somethin' off? Seems damn near impossible, once it's allowed anywhere near Boston, all the way ta the LNG terminal docks."

Susan wasn't deterred, willing the SUV to career along. "He's here General. I'm close. Pal? Get the U.S. Coast Guard C.O. on line for me. Let's update them on the threat. Tell me about this LNG tanker. Any others currently in port or scheduled to arrive?"

"None have been cleared to approach the coast since Monday. However, this new generation LNG super tanker was allowed to proceed to dock because it was well past the commit point by late afternoon Monday. It was deemed safer to secure the vessel at dock than to allow such a potentially dangerous target to pass back through the harbor, or to remain close to shore out at sea.

"The fear was it would be more vulnerable to being commandeered and used as an attack vehicle away from the tight security in port and at the LNG docks. The crew was evacuated and a port security team has taken complete control."

Mr. Green unclenched his jaw. "Susan, I don't like this, not one damn bit. Hal, have they checked that super tanker out thoroughly?"

"Yes Mr. Green. The 'Solenil Cristal', French for the Crystal Sun, was subject to all normal safety protocols. At Pleasure Bay, it was re-inspected from stem to stern by specially trained teams, inside and out, including two complete underwater hull searches. Pilot tugs were latched on. Absolutely no threat was detected. All equipment is functioning normally. Complete safety checks and test of the emergency systems were performed. No problems were detected."

"I don't like it one bit," Mr. Green said again.

"Me either," Givens confirmed.

"Me three," Susan added to make it unanimous. "But how is the question? What could he be planning? Pal, what's our timeline?"

"There are two hours and twenty-three minutes left to our assumed ten a.m. deadline."

"Damn. I just need a little more time."

CHAPTER 40: Humpty Dumpty Floating in a Boat

Rehan tossed all night Wednesday into his Thursday morning deadline, watching the TV he hadn't shattered in the condo bedroom. He laughed out loud several times at the congressmen and senators as they play-acted. What do they think, I'm a total imbecile?

The U.S. government had no intention of dealing with him honestly.

They're forcing me to do it. For no reason? Don't they realize what I'm capable of?

No! They just threatened more! After all they've already taken!

Juma didn't come to him in his dreams when he finally drifted off for an hour or so around four a.m. Rehan felt the hardness set, like a bug stuck in a piece of amber in Jurassic Park.

Not like them. Of course you feel bad, for the innocent, who inevitably get caught out in the open as a sacrifice. As dawn broke on Thursday, Rehan was packed, getting ready to go try and kill millions of them.

He watched the city stir with the sunrise. The thought of a ticking nuclear bomb eventually got the better of them. At seven a.m., an hour before the official curfew ended, the floodgates opened like someone kicked an anthill, pouring forth from the center of town in a growing mass.

Trying to climb over each other, the traffic jams solidified and stretched for miles within the minutes. Medians and shoulders were the first to become extra lanes. Without any incoming traffic, fathers soon opted to chance a head-on collision rather than sit in a nuclear fireball watching their kids melt away before their eyes.

By seven thirty it was an all-out free-for-all, with accidents and deaths mounting. Chain reactions in the panic resulted in multi-car pile ups. People pulled out directly into motorist coming up from behind way too fast. Several cars were forced into bridge abutments, off the road, down steep embankments, into trees or light poles. The news helicopters couldn't capture them all.

People abandoned vehicles only to be plowed into by crazed drivers out of control coming up from behind, cascading one on top of another, causing smoking gridlock and mayhem. With thousands of now stranded motorists out in the open. Soon, herd-mentality and panic set in, and it looked all too much like stampeding cattle running headlong over a cliff.

By eight a.m., survival instinct took over and the news helicopters began capturing the worst of human nature unfolding below. Rehan flicked off the TV and left on a survival instinct of his own.

*   *   *

He had no problems driving towards downtown and along the waterfront, to his stakeout spot at the warehouse docks on the Mystic River. Traffic was light, especially around the harbor and up the Mystic River. A few cars and some sturdy, stubborn citizens milled about. Rehan passed easily by the few preoccupied police, who were searching for a nuclear bomb. Most had been called out to the highways of death, and nobody wanted to be trapped down here along the harbor and docks on the waterfront.

He made his way up the access road to his spot. His target came into view floating across the Mystic River. The Crystal Sun, a 5-sphere LNG super tanker, at the Everett LNG off load dock, just up river from Boston. A fully loaded example of man's arrogance, of his greed. Blind to the dangers it created right in the middle of a modern city.

Rehan had done his research. The new Q-max LNG super carriers were five times the size of the original ones. Like everything else, once a certain technology was proven, and all the kinks worked out, the smartest thing you could do was build up to economies of scale. Once out on the open seas and up to speed, the transit across the waves could carry 50,000 cubic meters of LNG, or, just as easily, 266,000 cubic meters. The excess amount of revenue created was irresistible. Just a little added fuel cost. Of course, LNGs carry their own inexhaustible supply of fuel, a "boil-off" that would otherwise be a waste product. With free fuel, it became a zero-loss game, they built these super tankers as big as anyone could imagine.

An eight-story high "office building" control tower bridge and crew's quarters sat on the back end of these great ships. Then five huge spherical LNG tanks, almost as tall, running in a line to the bow of the great vessel. Mighty and strong it grew, as Rehan got closer.

He didn't agree with their safety assessments. The shipbuilders blinded themselves to the sheer magnitude of the massive amounts of material they were dealing with, and how quickly and effectively they could possibly cope with any real crisis. Like the fabled Achilles, in all their thinking and safety planning, they had been too focused on the main body and the LNG tanks. They failed to watch out for their exposed extremities.

Rehan parked alongside his little warehouse hideout. A typical industrial area in any port city, surrounding the harbor and waterways. Lots of import export companies. Plenty of other vans and box trucks parked in front, all idle, adding good cover. Well away from the security at the Everett dock terminal, which was clear across on the other side of the Mystic River. No police this far down, coverage in the area was thin at best.

Rehan slipped his seat way back, tilted out of view, scoping out the Crystal Sun with his binoculars across the half-mile wide expanse of the Mystic River. Everything had fallen into place perfectly. The Crystal Sun sat anchored at the Everett LNG docks, out from the far shore a thousand feet, tied to a huge pipeline unloading platform. Rehan was plenty close enough on this side of the river, in a perfect spot, just a hundred yards from the rear of the massive ship.

He scanned along the docks to the far side with his binoculars. A black, unmarked SUV pulled up, jerking to a stop. A shock hit Rehan when Susan Figiolli stepped out the passenger side and walked onto the dock, heading directly towards the Crystal Sun. Rehan felt her gaze pass right over him, watching her scan all around.

Hello Susan. Just an hour or so, to honor my deadline.

. . . You should have just let me get away.

CHAPTER 41: Fleets of Time

Susan jumped from the SUV, walked straight out onto the dock, headed a thousand feet out toward the huge Crystal Sun floating on the Mystic River.

Susan realized the commanding officer of the Coast Guard in Boston, Rear Admiral Lawrence Mortimore, was probably a busy man at the moment, but it was taking too long for her communications team to reach him, and she knew she needed his professional help. Right now.

General Givens walked up beside her. "I've known a few Coasties. Fearless on the water. They relish the idea of flyin' head-long inta the worst storms. Frickin' crazy-ass rescue swimmers jump inta seas only Poseidon himself could conjure up."

Susan smiled and teased. "I'm surprised, Mr. Army Ranger, sounds like you'd be scared to jump?"

"Yer damn right. Our motto's, 'Ya never leave a man behind.' The Coastie's is, 'Ya have ta go out, but ya don't gotta come back.' We don't think shit like that where I come from."

"Pal, give me a quick update on the Coast Guard. Overall duty, history, what assets they might have locally."

"Formed in 1790, America's oldest continuous seagoing service, the United States Coast Guard currently operates under the Department of Homeland Security. The president can have it conduct military operations directly or transfer control to the navy at any time. Congress can transfer it during wartime.

"Maritime duties extend into international waters. In peacetime, the Coast Guard's primary law enforcement function is protecting U.S. shores and ports. A massive fleet of Coast Guard vessels has descended on the northeast U.S. coast, concentrating on the Boston area ports, sea lanes and the ocean directly offshore. Smaller vessels are patrolling Boston's many rivers, bays and up into streams and estuaries.

"It is a large armada of boats and ships including Cutter class up to four hundred twenty feet. Various aircraft assets for search and rescue, port security and drug interdiction provide considerable air cover. Small arms with thousands of trained personnel and ships' hands.

"Since 9/11, the Coast Guard has been upgraded in all areas. Including a state-of-the-art, isolated, and hardened communications network, including secure dedicated satellites. One moment please . . ."

Her Pal changed tone. "We have Rear Admiral Lawrence Mortimore, commander of the local Coast Guard online."

"Patch him through. Hello, Rear Admiral Mortimore. This is Susan Figiolli, C.I.A. agent in charge here in Boston."

"Well hello, Mrs. Figiolli. I thought they were BSin' me when they said the Black Widow was on the line. I've seen you on the news, quite a bit of you in fact." He laughed good-naturedly.

"Yes, Rear Admiral Mortimer, well, I was quite exposed," Susan said.

"Call me Mort. Or Rear-Mort, my nick-name, due to my rather large posterior. I tell my cadets . . . your rear-end swells to that size as you get kicked in it so often on your way up the ranks in the Coast Guard."

Susan allowed a small laugh. "Okay, Mort. If you'll call me Susan."

"Most of us never believed the B.S. the media was spewing. And don't worry, you look good or they wouldn't have pulled that crap. Nice to see Director Scott stand up for you guys too."

"Well, I'm really beginning to love you military guys. Our thanks to you, the whole Coast Guard. Unlucky draw to get this assignment, I guess? It's not lost on us that you've all come running directly into the line of fire. Oh sorry, I guess I'm supposed to say, came here all-ahead-full speed?"

Rear-Mort laughed at her wit. "The admirals in Washington, and any vice-admirals are riding desks close to retirement, but I'm not un-lucky, I'm the luckiest bastard I know! Most guys go a whole career and never get a moment like this. I can't imagine not being right here, right now. Not just me either, we had to beat the volunteers off with a stick after that school bombing. Honestly, I thought a few of our reserve captains might mutiny when we ordered them to stand off out to sea."

"That doesn't surprise me Mort, the Coast Guard is full of brave men and women."

"Yeah, well, someone had to stay away. Who's gonna clear the harbor of all the balls of molten lead when we get nuked?"

"We're not going to let anything like that happen, Mort."

"I'd say it's a pleasure to be speaking with such a patriot, but I have a feeling I'm not going to like what you have to say." Mort said.

"You would agree that the ports and containers have all been scanned, without finding any trace of a nuclear bomb, correct?" Susan confirmed first.

"Boston is our water, so we kinda took the Chameleon threat personally. What we didn't ship a hundred miles out to sea has been scanned twice and you are correct, not even a trace amount of any nuclear material. The surrounding city, buildings and all, have been cleared as well. Why, what are you thinking?"

"Our Chameleon has always seemed to lead us one direction, while his plans were something else entirely."

"Smart little lizard," Mort added.

"Yes, I'm worried about a possible threat with the Liquefied Natural Gas infrastructure in and around Everett."

"Well, if he could attack those facilities it would make for a very destructive ka-boom." Mort said dryly.

"Maybe you can give us your assessment and the nickel tour of what's out there, and how you might go about setting it off for maximum effect?"

"Sure, the basics? LNG, Liquefied Natural Gas, exactly what the name implies, take the gas, freeze the crap out of it, minus 260-degrees below, like negative 162 Celsius. Either way, it's damned cold. It shrinks in volume six hundred times as it liquefies. That's the key to shipping the stuff all over the world, and to transport it via ports like ours, through pipelines, to terminal conversion centers, where it's converted back into a gas and piped out so you can make some nice hot tea. If it stays cold, it's just a liquid sloshing around in storage tanks. Some of it naturally 'boils-off' back into a gas. They convert that boil-off in a few nifty ways,

"On land, and in the tanks on ships, they keep the LNG at atmospheric pressure so when some boils off, the phase exchange helps to actually cool the remaining LNG. I think they called it auto-refrigeration, something like that. LNG ships pump some of the boil-off gas to the engines. It's very efficient. I mean, the stuff's turning back to a gas anyway, might as well use it to fire the engines, right?

Same process at the off-loading facilities, the pipeline pumping stations, storage systems, and converter supply centers. They all use the natural boil off to create the power that runs the various systems. It's almost like a parasite living off its host or something. In the end, all very efficient, safe, and reliable."

"Safe you say?" Susan asked.

"Very safe, especially in the liquid form. In sixty some years of shipping and handling the stuff there's been one major tank explosion back in the 1940's, in Texas. But those were older systems, a new technology, the rough-neck Texas boys hadn't worked out all the kinks yet."

"But it's flammable? Explosive?" Susan asked.

"In a liquid state, not really. Not as much as you might imagine. There's a demonstration in training where the instructor puts out a lit cigarette in a cup of LNG. No explosion. No fire. If it spills out in the ocean, on open water, it would just create a giant boil off, nothing more than a fogbank-like cloud which would simply dissipate in the air."

"Rear Admiral, this is Special Assistant Green. Where's the big threat?"

"We go back to the super-cold condensing of the gas part. You don't have to super-heat the stuff with those types of compression differences, just bring it up to room temperature. The expansion would be too much for the relief systems to vent off. Those giant LNG spheres explode like a pressure cooker you don't want to imagine. And, it's still a petroleum-based product. Turn that much of it into a giant vapor cloud, with all kinds of secondary fires burning after the pressure explosion, and it's only a matter of time before it warms up, ignites. When that happens, the pressure explosion will look like a firecracker in comparison. The fire would burn for maybe days, and we're talking hell-fire temperatures, secondary fires, collapsed buildings, over most of the Greater Boston area. Upwards of a million lives, maybe a few million. If the whole Everett complex goes? The blast wave alone would wipe out . . . a few hundred thousand instantly.

"Mort, tell me about this tanker you've kept in port I'm staring at?"

"It's a Qatargas Q-max class, the Crystal Sun, one of the newest super carriers. Five sphere tanks holding sixty thousand plus cubic meters of LNG each. Modern technology. All the latest safety upgrades. Onboard reliquification plant, which recycles the boil-off back into the tanks. It's a big S.O.B., if you'll pardon my French."

"How big? How safe?" Susan asked.

"The ship itself is built like a tank. Thick armored steel. Double-hulled, compartmentalized, insulated. Rip open the outer hull on a coral reef, an iceberg, or a collision with another ship from stem to stern without worry. They don't use the term 'unsinkable' in the shipbuilding business anymore."

"He doesn't have to sink it though, just damage the LNG tanks," Susan debated.

"The LNG tanks are built inside of that shell and are even more robust. Five massive spheres in a line from the bow back to the eight-story tower and bridge at the stern. Carbon-composite, armored steel, several inch-thick outer shells. Then several feet of durable, protective, super-insulating foam with a metal foil membrane to keep it all dry and cool. Redundant safety and cooling systems, relief valves, fire suppression. Each tank is completely isolated in a cocoon of metal supports directly tied to the superstructure of the ship. Add a ballast layer of extra insulation, ballast tanks fore and aft, plus a spacer between the outermost walls of the insulated LNG tanks and the ships double-hull."

"But at sixty thousand cubic meters per tank, expanding to six hundred times, he only has to get one tank?" Susan looked for the flaw, worried.

"In any conceivable accident, even if two of the massive LNG tanks were damaged, they could vent off gas from all other tanks, while pumping LNG from the damaged tanks into the sound ones. With a reliquification plant on board, and the ability of the engines to burn off massive amounts of gas, plus safety controls and mechanisms. The whole ship works like a giant safety relief valve."

Susan confirmed, "So, it's a constant balance between containment and what you can vent off if you had too?"

"That's the cause for concern and tight-ass security. Is this sounding like your guy's M.O. or what?"

"Yes, it sounds exactly like him. Mort, I know you've checked that tanker. Do me a favor, check it again."

CHAPTER 42: Walking the Plank

Rehan's heart gave a little jump as he watched Susan push through the far gate. She seemed to glide as she strode out onto the dock toward the Crystal Sun, her hair flowing along with the flap of her overcoat. He could see the wind but not feel it. He checked himself, wondering if maybe he'd fallen asleep dreaming.

He barely finished the thought when two men on the far dock came fast walking up alongside her. Givens and that weird special agent from the C.I.A. All three walked together right up to the Crystal Sun.

Onboard, armed men appeared on deck and walked along its sides, looking around, over the edges.

Did they discover the mini-sub? Rehan spied on the scene, focusing in and out with his binoculars. More men appeared on deck, the docks, talking and pointing in agitation.

He took out the RC controls to the sub and the "little-bugger," switching them on.

Two Coast Guard Defender fast boats came flying down the channel, right up alongside the Crystal Sun, before arching around wide in the water taking up observation positions.

Rehan scanned intently, focusing the lens to get a clear look at the boats. He didn't notice anything at first but, when the little boats circled, something hit him. Wait, weren't there six guys on each?

Rehan dropped the binoculars, turned to his laptop, fired up the "little bugger," used the sub arm to release it on the hull. Sent it on its brief journey crawling away.

The onboard camera view was terrible as Rehan adjusted the settings on his laptop. Damn Carl, you know the military would have paid for the best HD camera, what were you thinking putting this piece of crap on there? Rehan piloted the "little-bugger" and climbed up the side of the giant ship's hull.

When he came out of the water the camera view was suddenly much better. And the little thing was fast. He gave ol' Carl a reprieve. Good job on the faster motors my friend. Smart.

A crewmember on one of the Coast Guard Defenders did a double take. With binoculars gave a closer look, his training kicked in, pointing, reporting the sighting of the strange device.

His commander barely had time to register it before it topped the side and disappeared onto the deck of the Crystal Sun. But he'd seen it, grabbing his radio and sending out the alert.

All alarm hell broke loose almost instantly. Loud speakers came to life. In the confusion, it took precious seconds before anyone realized what the man on the radio was saying.

By the time security and dock crews started to look, Rehan was already sprinting the "little-bugger" up the backside of the eight-story bridge tower on the rear of the Crystal Sun.

The men on the Coast Guard Defender boats watched and pointed. They swung their 50-cals, but hesitated, being told to hold their fire. No one ever thought to train them about shooting at the LNG tanker to protect it. The commander tried frantically to report what he was seeing over his radio.

Rehan took a second to glance across, looking for Susan, spotted her running across the dock pointing. Security crews scrambled about, screaming and pointing, looking over the sides of the ship, trying to locate the threat. But there was no real vantage point on the LNG tanker to view the back-side of the bridge tower. It was too late anyway. Rehan sprinted up those eight stories in no time flat.

At the top, on the side closest to him, he quickly climbed right around on the front windows of the main bridge. He lost sight and worried someone might take a shot from inside the ship, or from one of the bridge overlooks, and blow the device off into the water,

Rehan flipped the switch.

Ka-boom!

CHAPTER 43: Wheels in the Sky Burning

Susan thought her eyes were playing tricks on her. It looked like a giant bug crawling around the side of the ship? Far enough away to be safe, but she flinched with the crack and flash. A debris shower of flame and sparks boiled outward. Half of the windows on the bridge platform shattered, blowing out in a crystal waterfall below the mushrooming orange fireball.

Sailors and security personnel near the blast were thrown backwards. One man was flung over the railing and fell thirteen stories into the water below. Susan instinctively moved over to the dock railing, pointing down, even as another man, less fortunate, lost his desperate grip, and fell eight-stories, hitting the much harder deck in a sickening thud.

At the rail, Susan watched the Coast Guard Defender fast boats on the water below take a heavy shower of flaming metal and glass. Their crews trying to hide and dive to get out of the way.

Bells clanged and new alarms began blaring on shore, adding their own urgency to the chorus.

Susan turned, looking up at the eight-story building sitting on the end of the giant ship. A whole corner of the bridge over look was gone. With fire licking out of the jagged hole into the sky above. Exposed to the prevailing winds, it whipped and sucked in as much oxygen as it needed, stoking it hotter and hotter, making a dense orange glow clearly visible in the side windows that remained.

Susan watched as the port authority and Coast Guard regrouped, attacking the situation.

A fireboat came flying down the river channel, Boston has three fireboats, but only one had been left on-station, to save the other two from nuclear destruction, they had been sent out to sea. "Old Chugger Joe" fire-boat arrived on scene with three bold arcs of water-jets spraying and hosing down the bridge tower. Sucking in and spraying out as much water as it needed from beneath its own hull.

It was a challenge to reach the thirteen-story inferno from the water level below. The water-jets weren't spraying into the base of the blaze and attacking the fire with force, as they would have liked. A lot of their spray was splashing off the tower, falling harmlessly back into the river below.

The bridge fire grew more intense. Flames and smoke poured out, clawing up into the sky, the wind whipping and feeding it relentlessly.

Splashing water on it is not going to put that fire out. Susan knew. She got back on her phone.

"Admiral Mort? Are you still there?"

"Yes, Susan. Report?"

"He exploded a device on the bridge tower. Took out a whole corner. Fire intense and growing. That bridge looks like a total loss. Is this going to cause a failure of those LNG tanks Mort?"

"No, the bridge is not vital to the tanks' integrity."

"Pal? Susan asked out loud, "What's he up to? How's this fit?"

"If he wanted to disable the ship, and put the LNG tanks in peril, the backup systems in the engine room would have to also be attacked."

"Mort? You got guys in the water when the Defender's came in?"

"They've already completed a hull search from the bow back to tank four."

"Look under that engine room Mort!"

CHAPTER 44: Ringing the Bell

'So far, so good' Rehan mused. Upset he didn't have time to enjoy the view. He was sure Special Forces divers were in the water, off the Defender boats, searching the hull for a threat. And they would soon find it, partially hidden between the two propeller shaft housings and rudders, but it was obvious to anyone who looked.

Rehan expected the divers would concentrate on the areas directly under and around the LNG tanks first. They were missing the Achilles heel.

Rehan turned on the mini-sub, switching on its powerful underwater cameras and lights.

He was shocked to see a scuba-masked man looking directly into the camera. A sudden burst of bubbles from the man's mouth let Rehan know that he was just as shocked at the sudden illumination.

Rehan had a second or two as the camera rotated and caught a glimpse of a knife held in another divers' hand, furiously working at the magnetic connections. The knife was pried under the magnet, but it slipped out and the magnet reattached itself. The last thing Rehan saw was the other diver moving in position, so he could hold the sub away with his legs as his partner pried with the knife.

Rehan flipped a switch and the camera instantly went dark.

There was a huge rumble, like muffled thunder. The water churned, turning white, before it exploded from around the entire stern section of the huge tanker. Jets of spray shot hundreds of feet into the air, fanning outward, deflected by the contours of the ship's hull.

Erupting with the massive spray of water, the sound of the huge explosion followed and filled the air with a deafening rumble-like, Boooomm! Followed by a groaned billow, like a wounded elephant, reverberating across the water off the hull. Rehan's side window vibrated from the low-pitched moan.

* * *

The entire vessel dipped, ever so slightly, into the water at the stern. Rising back up with the shower of water from the explosion, as if a waterfall had been opened up in the sky.

Two of the Coast Guard Defenders were too close, were blasted and capsized, sending crews flying into the waters beyond. The men inside the cabins were trapped in the overturned boats. Stunned crews dove to their rescue.

A third Defender boat, a little farther off, was swamped by the massive wave created, and then doused further by a torrent of the falling water. One crewman was swept overboard, but the others managed to hang on, all looking like soaked rats clinging to a flooded life raft.

"Yes Zhang! That was beautiful!" Rehan screamed.

Smoke started venting from lower port windows, proof the shaped charges had done their work, penetrating the double hull, directly below the engine room, generators, auxiliary diesel fuel tanks, and boilers. Which were all now a raging inferno.

As if in confirmation, black smoke started pumping hard out of several lower engine room vents up on the deck.

Burn baby burn.

A few minutes later the ship went dark, alarms onboard stopped, their echoes across the river faded to silence for a second or two.

Emergency battery backup lights, alarms kicked on and took over.

In quick succession, two smaller, secondary explosions rumbled from deep inside the Crystal Sun. Each causing blasts of smoke to shoot from vents and openings, climbing higher and higher within the bridge tower.

The port security, having replaced the ship's crew, were slow to manually try and close the various emergency hatches leading upwards. Rehan wasn't sure if it mattered. The living facilities, galley, dry storage, supplies, crew, and officers' quarters were all feeding the flames. Three or four stories of ignitable material already all ablaze. It would have been nearly impossible for anyone to descend into the thick smoke and heat to close those hatches.

And like a huge bonfire being cooked by a hot starter fire below, it was a quickly building inferno.

On shore firefighters began to concentrate on dousing the first LNG tank in line in hope of keeping it cool. But Rehan could see the emergency relief valves atop all five LNG tanks already venting pressure with large, white plumes of smoke, billowing into the air.

Right on cue, two harbor "heavy-tugs" could be seen barreling up the Mystic River. With powerful engines and Z-drive thrusters, they're highly maneuverable. Known as a Kort nozzle, the thrust-to-power ratio of a Z-drive is enhanced for moving huge ships many times their size and mass into dock positions. While they are perfect for ship-docking, they are not nearly as efficient for towing operations.

Rehan counted on them bringing lots of energy and punch to the fight. The Q max-sized Crystal Sun was way beyond their operational limits, and like the fireboats, most of the other Boston tugs were far out to sea for protection. The Crystal Sun was sitting low at the stern, heavy in the water. They needed a lot more help.

Ka-Blam!

A huge explosion rocked the bridge tower. A large hole was blown out, this time in the port side, about half way up, right in front of Rehan from where he sat. A chunk of exterior wall, a four-foot jagged square, swung dangling, as it tick-tocked side to side in flames, before breaking off and dropping in a smoke-filled splash into the river. There goes the galley. A plume of flames and smoke found an escape. The interior glowed white hot in the exposed hole. The fire obviously massive and totally out of control.

Rehan crawled through the van, opened the rear doors, and hid from view behind it across the river. He quickly prepped the two remaining RC airplanes.

With both engines running, Rehan climbed back in through the back of the van, leaving the rear doors open so he could watch the planes take off down the street. Unlike the other models so far, neither of these had a pilot cam, so Rehan had to use visual flight rules to take off and steer them into their targets.

He threw the throttle forward in excitement and jetted across the pavement down the street. The speeding plane veered and weaved sideways, caught air under a wing. Rehan over corrected the steering and nearly crashed into the curb, just before it lifted away.

Once airborne, the four-channel radio control made flying a breeze. Rehan made a wide climb away in an arching loop and approached from the opposite side of the waterway.

It's always easy for a Chameleon to hide his true location.

CHAPTER 45: Incoming

Susan's wits were just coming back around to full. The shock wave from the blast knocked her down. She bumped her head a bit when she fell back. Givens knelt next to her with a worried look, casting a concerned eye around at the scene. Mr. Green seemed composed and stoic, except his hair was tosseled and out of place. The sting of her scraped hands confirmed she took a little spill.

Two tug-boats arrived, honking horns, casting lines, pulling hard to try and get the great ship away from the dock. The Crystal Sun didn't budge. The mass dwarfed the power of the puny tugs.

The tugs cast off the lines and positioned themselves, one at the bow, one at the stern, trying to angle in between the dock and the ship, to create leverage at each end, trying desperately to get the massive ship off the dock, so they could spin it, then tow it back down the Mystic River and out to sea.

But without power assist from the ship itself, it sat heavy as the tugs revved at top RPM's.

Susan's ears whined with the engines and smell of diesel smoke as she leaned over the rail directly overlooking the tug at the bow below. Almost willing it to push the ship away.

Over all the noise and confusion, Susan's eye caught something, up in the air, approaching the bow. A Corsair World War II fighter making an attack run? Susan screamed in her phone to Mort, and yelled frantically at the closest Coast Guard Defender down on the water. Waving her arms in fury. To their credit, they were instantly aware of her pleas, looking to where she pointed.

Within the last hundred feet, one of them spotted the incoming plane. The spotter didn't even bother to point it out to the machine gunner, it was too close. He jumped in place, shoving the gunner to the side, pulling the bolt action as he swung around and opened fire.

Brapt-brapt-brapt-brapt-brapt-brapt-brapt. Brapt-brapt-brapt-brapt.

The plane came in high, but cut power at the last moment to dive, causing the gunner to over-shoot. He was a little too late to hone in on the small, fast moving target.

EEEeennnnnnnnnnnnnnnnnnn

At the last second, Susan heard it throttled up to full speed. An instant of fear gripped her as the kamikaze was diving right at her. Rehan was going to take her out the same as General McMillian.

She could almost reach out and touch the plan when it screamed past over her head, diving to the water below.

Eeeeeennnnnnn

Ka-Boom!

It smashed into the back of the heavy tug, directly at the base of its smokestack, near the back of the bridge-cabin. The explosion, debris, and fuel from the model split in two streams around the smokestack and sprayed forward into the open rear door of the pilothouse, like a giant Molotov cocktail.

The interior cabin of the tug was instantly engulfed in flames. "Get out! Get them out of there!" Susan screamed as she watched in horror. The two men clearly visible through the unbroken front windows, dancing inside the flaming box. Instinctively, they both managed to spill out the side door overboard into the water.

A Coast Guard Defender immediately moved to help. Coastie's diving to rescue the two burned men, swimming to pull them from the water. The other crewmen tried to attack the flaming tug but the intense heat kept them at bay. Their handheld extinguishers worthless from a distance on the blazing tug.

The creased smokestack on the tug crumbled over at a weird angle. When it crimped over completely, back pressure built up and black smoke belched out in heaps. The tugs' engines were still revving at high speed in a terrible, growing whine, with no pilot at the controls.

Bravely, the Coast Guard Defender boat captain gunned the engines and attempted to charge in on the blaze, to try and board her and attack the fire up close. Just as they reached the rear of the tug . . . *Ka-Purrchhhh . . . Boom!*

Susan remembered a split second screaming mad at Givens who grabbed her hard from behind, forcibly pulling her away from the railing.

Then the boards under her feet seemed to float upwards in slow motion, splintering, filling with fire. Next she was spinning backwards, sliding across the dock in that weird dazed reality, like the boards were made of ice. The exact same sensation she had fifteen years ago, sliding across the tarmac of the airport hangar outside Cairo.

He's done it again.

CHAPTER 46: Situational Awareness

What Rehan was hoping to hit directly had finally caught fire; the fuel lines leading to the tugs' forty-thousand-gallon tanks of diesel fuel.

The rear of the tug and pilothouse shattered in a splatter of wood, glass, and fire. The brunt of the blast blew the approaching Coast Guard Defender boat to pieces, along with her crew, who disappeared in the flash of parts across the dock and out into the water. What was left of the Defender dead floated back away from the blazing tug. A half sunk, six-man burning funeral pyre.

The front part of the exploding tug was blown forward, like a giant shaped charge itself, and was now jammed firmly into a giant hole created in the bow of the Crystal Sun. Wedged in on the underside of the splintered dock like a giant, flaming tikki-torch sticking up out of it. Right where Susan had been standing before she disappeared in a flash of fire and splintering wood.

A slick of flaming diesel fuel and hundreds of gallons of oil bled out from the burning tug. It oozed outward, causing the size of the blaze to grow, engulfing nearly the entire bow of the Crystal Sun, and cooking the pipeline dock.

Emergency lights further on shore began rotating and whole new sets of alarms went off. Emergency vehicles and fire crews on land moved as close as they could to help keep the flames at bay, trying their best to keep the fire from spreading further onto the dock and LNG pipelines.

"Yes!" Rehan couldn't help but scream as he tossed that plane's remote aside. He turned to take off his last flying bomb. Knowing surprise was lost and hoping all the new confusion would help as a diversion, Rehan immediately turned the plane in a quick loop and flew it directly over his van and across the river. Aiming towards the other tug, which was still pushing at the stern of the LNG tanker, trying desperately to get the great ship away from the dock.

Rehan had a direct view on this attack run, coming from behind the tug, toward the chugging smokestack, just a few hundred yards away across the river. Low and faster this time, confident, making a direct bee line for the stationary tug, and the base of the smokestack aim point.

This is perfect . . .

Rehan didn't noticed the other Coast Guard Defender moving in, anticipating an attack on the second tug. The crew had been watching their side of the river, where the first plane had come from. But a sharp cadet turned to scan the warehouses along the opposite shore and spotted the incoming plane, a Cessna fixed-wing beginner model.

The gunner was grabbed hard and spun around, not needing to be told why. He quickly spotted the plane against the backdrop of warehouses and condos along the opposite shore and opened fire.

Brapt-brapt-brapt-brapt-brapt-brapt-brapt . . .

His raking shots impacted along the buildings beyond, helping him track his target like tracer bullets. He adjusted his fire, led the plane just enough.

Brapt-brapt-brapt-brapt-brapt-brapt-brapt.

POP! . . . -ennn-ennnnnn-ennnnnnnnnnn . . . Boom!

At the very last second, he managed to shave off the tailfin and vertical stabilizer with a single hit.

The jolt caused Rehan trouble controlling the plane and not enough time to adjust. It spun down, striking the dock wall and exploded. Some of the wreckage and flaming fuel leapt forward onto the back of the tug, but it was far from a direct hit. The tugs crew emerged immediately with fire extinguishers in hand, and quickly doused the flames.

Rehan cursed the lucky shot but used his binoculars to survey the scene. Smoke on the Crystal Sun was pouring from the base all the way up the bridge tower, mixing with licking flames coming out of every port and window on the first five stories. A fully involved eight-story building sat burning on the deck of the super-tanker Crystal Sun. They won't put that fire out anytime soon.

Rehan scanned forward. The tug at the bow was also blazing intensely, with the flaming diesel fuel and oil slick spreading out over the water. It made the whole river look as if it were ready to catch fire.

The fire boat had switched to a foam retardant, making little progress towards the flaming, charred, tug wedged into the hole at the bow under the docks.

Firefighters spilled across the dock, their hands full keeping the flames from spreading to the off-load pipelines, creating an immediate catastrophic hazard. Concentrating efforts to secure the on-shore facilities for now.

Achilles has an arrow sticking out of his ankle. Floating there, crippled by his wound, docked to his destiny. The fate of the Crystal Sun is sealed.

Then he saw her, Susan, a little farther down the dock, looking ragged, up against the railing. He was instantly glad she hadn't perished. She held her own binoculars now. And she was looking right at Rehan, pointing at him, screaming out to someone.

Rehan scanned the water to see who she was screaming to. Terror grabbed him.

The commander of the last Defender fast boat pointed across the river directly at Rehan's van. Two spotters with binoculars sprang forward, falling to corner spots, one on each side of the bow. A 50 cal gunner standing between them at the ready. He worked the bolt action and pointed the barrel with intent.

Rehan saw the commander screaming orders. The powerful engines dug deep into the water, jetting the small craft forward. Without another warning . . .

Brapt-brapt-brapt-brapt-brapt-brapt! Ting-ting.

Bullets tore through the side door of the van and climbed up the building overhead. The boat's acceleration caused the burst to go high. The building façade next to, and just above Rehan, exploded in chunks. The 50 cal opened up again, sending round after round downrange at Rehan.

Brapt-brapt-brapt . . . ting-ting-ting.

A jolt of adrenaline caused Rehan to fumble with the ignition. He nearly flooded the engine pumping the gas violently in a reflex. Move!

He was parked facing the LNG carrier, to make his escape, Rehan had to drive toward the incoming Defender or make a dead still three-point turn.

Every flash of the fast approaching.50 cal made his head tingle. Anyone could send a slug through his brain . . . he was seeing way too many flashes.

He slammed the van in gear and it lurched forward just a couple feet in a flood of gas hesitation.

Brapt-brapt-brapt . . . Brapt-brapt-brapt-brapt . . . ting-ting-ting.

Just in time. The aim trailed him by inches. Bullets passed through the van right behind Rehan's seat. Every ting in the metal sides sent an electric shock through him. He should have surely died right there. But the engine finally caught and he peeled off down the street.

Brapt-brapt-brapt . . . Brapt-brapt-brapt-brapt . . . ting-ting-ting.

A few rounds found the rear-door windows, which shattered in an explosion of glass. Still open, the doors swung wildly on their hinges, then slammed shut as Rehan swerved side to side up the street. He watched in terror out the front windshield as the gunner adjusted his aim and let out another burst.

Brapt-brapt-brapt-brapt . . . Brapt-brapt-brapt-brapt . . . ting-ting-ting.

Rehan desperately zig zagged, making a screeching left turn up a side street, checking his mirror. The flash of the 50 cal fast boat closed in on him. Glass corners of buildings on both sides exploded, taking hits.

In half a block Rehan was momentarily hidden from direct-fire line of sight. He floored it another block before he could make a side-slipping, tire-screeching left to go back towards his stashed motorcycle. Just as he made the turn an ear-splitting sound roared in.

Ssssscccrrrrrullllllllll . . . Blam! . . . Blam!

Two Hellfire missiles screamed right past the rear of his turning van and exploded up the side street just beyond the intersection he'd just turned off. The deadly explosions lit up three stories of the buildings on both sides in fiery vengeance, as glass shattered out of the lower level corners.

The fireball and blast waves buffeted the van, shaking Rehan into another fish-tail, almost losing control. He managed to straighten out just in time as he nearly slammed head-on into a parked car. It took a final swerving screech of his tires to correct and center his van.

An F-15 Eagle screamed by overhead a split second later, his two missiles having missed Rehan by mere seconds.

Rehan floored it and flew through the next few intersections, the whole time checking his left window, worried the Defender fast boat might be waiting out on the water between the buildings at each crossroad.

Rehan knew the jet was circling around for another pass too. As he listened for it, he picked up on the sound of an approaching helicopter, and an army of police sirens screaming in louder and louder from all over.

His heart pounded so hard in his ears he couldn't tell what the closest danger was.

Rehan, adrenalin pumping, made a quick, reflex decision, and jerked the van into a raised parking lot under a vacation condo complex, still two blocks from his motorcycle.

Pulling around the opposite side of the elevator column, he slid to a stop, sweating and shaking in terror. He heard the jet come screaming over-head again. Rehan held his breath, knowing a bomb could be falling on top of him. When he didn't explode, he let out the breath only to tense up instantly, hearing a helicopter coming in from the river, loud, right on top of him. Screaming sirens closed in from every direction, getting louder in a chorus.

"GO REHAN! GO!'" He screamed out loud to himself in desperation.

In a flash, the helicopter dropped down free falling from the sky directly in between the buildings. Coming into view, it stopped, hovering just a foot or two off the street, looking directly at the van parked against the wall of the elevator column. It unleashed a torrent of lead. Bonnie and Clyde style.

Bullets shredded the van, hitting the gas tank, which exploded blasting outward from under the condo. The helicopter hovering feet away, in the confined space, got blasted backwards. The tail rotors cut into the building behind, shattering in a shower of glass and pieces.

The helicopter whipped into a wild spin. The pilot shut down the engines and came down hard, spinning, with plenty of torque. The landing gear on the right wrenched in a sideways motion and collapsed.

The helicopter kept spinning as it tipped over on its side. The main rotor blades chopped into the street, shattering with chunks of blacktop, shooting off in pieces in all directions. Cutting into the buildings on all sides, blowing out more windows, exploding glass rained down in burst.

The cockpit was sent skidding, spinning like a top, as parts came off, ricocheting across the pavement.

It finally rotated and slowed, as their scary slide and spin across the pavement mercifully ended. Their cockpit made a final, slow rotation to a stop, facing the burning van under the building fifteen feet away across the street. They could feel the heat through the cracked and broken cockpit glass.

The two men held their breath as the last of the glass rained down from the buildings around them. Still strapped in, hanging sideways, the two pilots grabbed each other's hands in a power shake, knowing they had just cheated death.

But not that fucker in the van, the pilot thought.

CHAPTER 47: All the King's Horses
and All the King's Men

Susan screamed in the air as she watched the van make its escape across the far shore, disappearing into the city beyond.

She turned to notice Mr. Green, who was a bit more tosseled than before. Blood dripped here and there from a small cut on his right cheek, making his eye twitch. Maybe he wasn't happy about his now ruined suit.

Pain made her look down, to her scraped and bloody knees. Her left elbow and forearm stung with burns and blisters, scorched marks mixed with the bright red blood from fresh scrapes, and her right hip had a deep, dull ache that radiated through her pelvic bone. She looked up to see General Givens' ashen face, and Mr. Green's worried look from behind him.

"Okay, General, we all know you Special Forces guys are tough, but let's get you looked at," Mr. Green said, delicately approaching his back shoulder.

"I'm fine. Did they get the fucker?" Givens leaned awkwardly, as he asked Susan.

"What's wrong? Are you hurt?" She asked.

Mr. Green spun him around. The back of his uniformed jacket was peppered with burnt marks and bloody spots, but the three-inch long wood shard sticking out of his back shoulder, bleeding well enough to form a blackened patch and run at its base, caused her memory to come back. He had thrown her down, in the middle of an explosion, managed to cover her from the worst of the blast.

"Oh my God, are you okay? Get an ambulance!" Susan screamed.

"It's just a splinter, and I'm not goin' anywhere."

Susan turned him to look, knew not to argue, but was mad as hell. "Fine, MEDIC!" she screamed. "Get a damn medic to look then, like it or not."

Givens reached over his shoulder, grabbed the wood shard sticking out, and yanked it free, tossing it over the rail into the water. "There, all better. Bring me a Band-Aid. Did they get the fucker?"

"I think he got away." Susan spun, turning back to the ominous backdrop behind them, pointing absently across to the far shore. "He drove off."

An apocalyptic firefighting effort around the Crystal Sun and the Everett Dock facility surrounded them. An army of fire trucks poured in and collected onshore, but it was a thousand feet out to the dock. Men hauled hoses, making extension, bringing more waterlines into the fight.

A swarm of little boats circled in the waters below, approaching the smoldering Coast Guard Defender. Looking for survivors, retrieving bodies from the Mystic River. Adding to the fire suppression efforts.

It felt like the mass of firefighters and equipment closing in from all sides would smother the entire area.

Black smoke billowed from the bridge tower on the Crystal Sun. Flames jumped out, licking at the sky from every opening in the eight-story tower.

The tugboat fire at the bow still covered a wide area, a thick column of black smoke pumping into the sky. Flames spit around the curves of the bow. The fireboat dumped foam retardant on the burning slick, coating the surface of the water, closing an ever-tightening semicircle to contain the spread. They were far from reaching the burning tug itself, but turned their high-pressure water jets at it and the underside of the flaming dock, knocking down the flames considerably.

Susan looked up to pray, thankful the fire seemed to be getting under control, and the true terror grabbed at her. Columns of white smoke were venting, pumping, from the tops of all five LNG storage tanks.

"Susan!" Mr. Green yelled out. "Rear Admiral Mortimer on the line. On speaker."

"Hello, Susan, this is Mort?"

"Mort. I'm so sorry, the SEAL's? In the water . . . they . . . ?"

"It's a tough business. We didn't have time to get their wet-sub here. Just rebreathers disguised as life jackets. Dropped them without their head gear too. We must have spooked the Chameleon on the way in."

Susan knew they were gone with the giant explosion and shower of white water. Two more hero's . . . she thought. How many more before I can do my damn job?

"Their heads were exposed in those cold waters. Well, warm by SEAL standards, but, it's cold water and it sucks the heat out of an exposed human head. Their strength was sapped. The murky water didn't help."

"I'm so sorry Mort. I've always been one step behind this asshole. Now it's cost your men too."

"What? No way! We were just a little too late getting to that son-of-a-bitch."

"Welcome to my world Mort."

"This one's on us. You gave us plenty of warning. We slipped up sending those SEALs in like that. He must of saw something, why else detonate early?"

"I'm, Mort, I wish . . . I wish . . ."

"Now damn it Susan, you don't take the blame for this one. IT's ON US! This is our water, our responsibility, period. General Givens you still there?"

"Right here Mort?"

"I'd like your officers' witness."

"Of course."

"Very well, for the record, let it be known that Mrs. Susan Figiotti . . ." He got her name wrong, but Susan didn't mind. ". . . is one smart ass lady. She figured out what that Chameleon asshole was up too and pointed us right to him. Nobody could expect more unless you people want her to come down here and jump in that water herself which, is-not-her-job. She got us the intel. We tried, we failed."

"Thanks Mort, but . . ." Susan said.

Mort cut her off. "But, that's not why I called. I thought you'd like to hear this yourself. Patch Spit-ball One in. Spit-Ball One, Spit-Ball One, Rear-Mort here. Repeat and confirm last transmission?"

"Spit-Ball One here. Confirmed. Van destroyed. Suspect neutralized. Over."

"What?" Susan asked, not sure if out loud, so she confirmed. "What'd he say?" Maybe she had gotten knocked in the head harder than she thought?

"I'm happy to be the one to tell you Susan, your Chameleon is a flaming, bar-be-cuing lizard as we speak. The van was trapped under a condo complex and exploded while eating forty cal rounds until the gun emptied. The Chameleon, is dead."

A spontaneous cheer erupted in Susan's peripheral.

Givens scooped her up and swung her around in a full circle. "Yee-haa!"

Mr. Green met her as she landed, both hesitated, before breaking out in huge smiles and a hugging swing of their own.

"LIC'd him! LIC'd him! LIC'd him!" Givens danced out loud.

"One moment. One moment, please . . ."

Susan leaned against the dock railing. Her hands felt tingly holding out her cell. She stared in shock without seeing, lost in waves and reflection.

"LIC'd him! LIC'd him! . . ." General Givens' chant seemed muffled.

"One moment. One moment please . . ."

Anything else might not have registered, but Susan heard it. She'd been here before with the Chameleon. Felt this exact same way before. She put her hand up to quiet everyone, pushed off the railing. "Hold off! Pal's onto something?"

"Yes Susan. The Chameleon's plan is still in motion."

"Come on Hal, he's toast?" General Given's questioned.

Mr. Green placed a hand on the general's forearm with a serious look. "Explain fully Palantir. Immediately."

"The current efforts to extinguish the fires on and around the Crystal Sun would be effective given enough time. The LNG dock and pipeline are already secured. However, there will not be enough time to extinguish the fires."

"Pal? He's going to win from the grave? How's that possible?" Susan asked.

"Rehan Al'Camel's plan is brilliantly simple. As Coast Guard Admiral Mortimore explained, LNG tankers and the LNG storage spheres are hardened and virtually impervious to attack. The safety features and fire suppression systems, including backups, reliquification, engine burn-off, and cross tank transfers, were all designed to deal with any conceivable threat.

"However, it's clear Rehan Al'Camel's bomb was not intended to sink the ship. The ship is not sinking. The attacks on the bridge and tugboats were not a direct assault on the LNG storage spheres. They remain undamaged."

"What the hell?" Givens blurted out.

"Rehan Al'Camel is using the nature of the material itself to attack the overall ship design. He has purposely left all five spheres intact."

"How the hell is not sinkin' the ship and not attackin' the spheres a good thing?" Givens asked.

"First, he destroyed the bridge and ship's controls, except for backups or manual controls located in the engine room.

"Second, he blew up the engine room, its backup controls, the reliquification plant, the engines to burn-off LNG, and the transfer pumps. Rendering the ship immobile as well. In addition, he ignited an inferno of extra backup diesel fuel, oil and LNG stored there. No amount of firefighting effort will extinguish this blaze until the combustible material is exhausted.

"Third, he exploded the heavy tugboat at the bow. He must know, like the hijackers of 9/11, that these heavy tugs carry 40,000 gallons of diesel fuel, plus lubricants and oil in quantity. By setting off the energy potential of the tugboat, instead of using his last two flying bombs in a futile attack on the LNG tanks, or on the Coast Guard Defenders, it was clearly an intentional act."

"Scuttle the ship, sink her right there, put the fire out an' cool the LNG too?" Givens suggested.

"It would only cause further damage and a quicker failure of the tanks," the Palantir answered.

"Son-of-a-bitch!" Susan screamed. "And if that tanker blows at the dock, how bad?"

"The Crystal Sun is near capacity at 245,000 cubic meters of LNG. A total explosive force more massive than any nuclear bomb Rehan Al'Camel could have ever hoped to deliver. The dock pipelines lead the five miles inland to the Everett LNG storage tanks. Like a long fuse, the destruction of Boston scenario we discussed earlier seems highly likely."

"Come on Hal. Can't we contain it at the docks? Take the blow somehow?" Givens asked.

"No General Givens. Leaving the Crystal Sun anywhere close to port, or the city, puts the entire on-shore Everett facility, terminal, and LNG storage tanks in certain peril."

"Pal, give me options. What should we be doing?" Susan asked.

"Immediately tow the Crystal Sun as far offshore as possible. Unfortunately, Rehan has destroyed the port jet maneuvering engines, main drive shafts and rudders. Every system on the ship with the ability to help move the tanker away from the terminal ports is compromised. Four heavy tugs are required to move the Crystal Sun, with only two on scene, one has been destroyed. No others are within an hour's distance. Three smaller tugs are enroot, but the mass of the Crystal Sun is far beyond their operational limits. I do not see any possible solutions to this dilemma. It is only a matter of time before the LNG heats up beyond relief pressures."

"What happens next, if we can't tow that tanker away Palantir?" Mr. Green asked.

"The Crystal Sun has lost all power and went onto emergency backup shortly after the attack began. Battery power will last two hours maximum, on a single LNG tank failing."

"And if it's working on all five tanks?" Susan asked.

"Under such a heavy load, the batteries will last less than one hour."

"Why not just plug her in at the docks?" Givens asked.

"It is currently attached to the dock's auxiliary power. Unhooking and towing to a safe distance will take at least an hour, well past the battery life of the backup cooling systems. Regardless, emergency cooling systems will soon fail no matter what is done. It is only a matter of time before the metal super-structure of the Crystal Sun heats the LNG from within beyond cooling or venting safety measures."

Susan looked up at the Crystal Sun burning . . . from both ends.

CHAPTER 48: The Saints Come Marching In

"Susan? This is Mort. I don't much like your little computer nerd's analysis. If we thought like that, we'd hide under our bunks."

Susan still had her phone on speaker, in conference mode.

"Thanks Mort!" Susan replied. "If you don't have any better ideas, why don't we get your people out of there?"

"Oh, I got a better idea. Just watch little lady. Tell your scientist geek friend the Chameleon ain't won shit yet. We're still in this fight."

"Mort please, I really think . . ." Susan said.

Givens stopped her, grabbing her arm. "I told ya, they relish the idea. You'd think, 'It's hopeless? Not a chance?' They think . . . Fuck 'em, we're Coastie's!"

"Amen General." Mort chimed in. "The mighty seas don't rattle us, the Chameleon sure as hell don't."

A long, ear splitting airhorn blast cut through the scene, drowning everything else out. Susan turned startled to look up river. Steaming, bow-first cutting through the water directly at her, with its white and blue markings, was what looked like a warship. The 110-foot Coast Guard Island Class Cutter commanded by Rear Admiral Mortimer himself came barreling up the Mystic River. Susan dropped her phone to her side, stunned, slowly crossing back to the dock railing to hold on in awe. Three more loud airhorn blast announced her witness.

In that tight space, with a flaming, ticking time bomb off his port bow, the man performed a three-point turn like he was riding in a little powerboat. The very tip of his bow coming within inches of the far side channel before the full reverse engines caught, and he spun her hard around. With a quick burst of forward power, he cut the engines, "all stop" causing his 110-foot Cutter to drift right up next to the burning LNG carrier.

Susan wasn't sure if he'd bumped into the side, or if ol' Rear-Mort simply side-slipped in, leaving a foot or so to spare. It was a masterful display of ship piloting.

Coasties jumped to action just as determined. Men from shore scrambled past Susan, crawling onto the burning tanker, throwing and catching towlines to the Cutter.

Susan could see them being buffeted by the intense heat, bending and shielding themselves, burning, as they found the cleats and aft capstan attach points. One after another, backing away, holding up their scorched hands and arms with sleeves, -what Susan prayed was only their sleeves- hanging down, smoldering. Some collapsing as soon as they got far enough away. It doubled her over watching the impossibly tragic ballet that ensued, as man after man sacrificed himself.

Three small tugs arrived tooting horns, speeding in. They, and the one remaining heavy, latched on to try and finally get the giant tanker pulled away from the dock.

Susan listened to Rear Admiral Mortimer over her speaker. "Come back up dead slow. Keep those tow-lines from snapping." It was another feat of piloting mastery, as he gently coaxed the tanker away from the dock.

Once moving, he pulled the giant tanker with just a little extra momentum, making it swing out by the bow, doing a complete 180-degree turn. Cutting in reverse to slacken his lines without over turning the mass, it spun perfectly around in the current facing the right direction back down the Mystic River.

Then gently, gently, Rear-Mort began to pick up speed, coaxing the lines taunt, going for Boston Harbor, and the sea beyond . . . if they could just make it.

The hole in the right-side bow of the Crystal Sun immediately sucked in a torrent of water. The sinking weight of the flooded aft sections caused the ship to behave wildly under tow. The two issues stopped Mort dead in the water, like dropping a giant anchor, which kept pulling to the right, dragging him down, whenever he tried to get up to speed.

Susan worried the towlines would all snap like twigs under the pressure, whipping wildly in the process, killing scores of his gallant crew on deck.

In another masterful display of piloting, he reversed to a stop, radio positioned the three little-tugs on the left side and the remaining heavy tug directly in front of the hole in the bow. Reducing the drag while the three little tugs kept the Crystal Sun straight and true. "Rear-Morts Cutter" provided the pull.

The crew quickly cut lines to reposition, with no time to latch back on properly, it was a dangerous improvisation. With every uptick of speed, the ropes strained and frayed.

Susan watched the little tugs alongside take a beating from the mass of the Crystal Sun, even though they had wide, inflated rubber skirts to cushion contact. Every bump threatened to swamp or smash them beneath the towering hull. Like some giant, smoking sea creature trying to suck them under to the depths.

However, slow and true now, the Crystal Sun began making way at speed, a dead, dark, sinister hunk of steel trailing columns of black and white smoke away from the LNG terminals toward downtown Boston.

Every yard of progress was a stressful moment of suspense,

Ka-Blaaammm! . . . fivvvvzzzz-Uuuuuuuunnn . . .

The aft LNG tank's relief valve blew completely from its housing shooting like a toy rocket out of sight arching into the sky. Releasing a high-pressured stream of white vapor shooting hundreds of feet into the air.

Is this it? Susan wondered. It's over?

But it wasn't. The Crystal Sun continued to smoke its way downriver.

Susan turned to her driver. "Let's go. Follow that tanker!"

She had to side-hopping down the dock to the SUV on her throbbing hip. Everyone piled in behind her.

"Susan?" her Pal asked immediately. "May I access the SUVs systems to provide news video of the towing operation by Admiral Mortimer."

"Yes Pal! Right away."

The entire dash blinked in a reset. The SUVs center monitor switched over instantly.

Heroes were being made right in front of the cameras. Men continued to send extra towlines across to the Crystal Sun. It bucked and pulled back hard in the waves as the speed increased.

At least one sailor was seen flung overboard in the efforts, and a few more were spun across the decks as the lines slipped and tightened unpredictably with every crest or fall.

One sailor toppled over shooting streams of blood. Helicopters zoomed in as he was grabbing for his sliced off leg, caught between one of the tow ropes and its makeshift tie down point. A couple other sailors dragged him off, blood streaming in a trail, until he was out of view.

The Crystal Sun started listing heavily to its port side, water being forced into the hole at the bow during the speedy tow. The tugs were having a tougher and tougher time keeping the ship on course, the massive vessel tipped ominously over top of their little boats.

The slightest roll of the great ship smashed the lead tug. The top corner cabin was crushed in, blowing out windows, breaking off into the water alongside in chunks. It looked as if the crew were crushed, but the brave pilot stood back up in the open air of broken windows and wood, fought to correct his boat, staying in the fight.

"Go Mort. Get away from the docks and Everett," Susan urged them on.

"The inflow of water has killed the flames in the bow. Maybe it's bought him enough time," Mr. Green added.

"Unfortunately, without the auxiliary power from the docks, the emergency batteries have quickly drained, failure is imminent," the Palantir reported.

"You don't know shit," General Givens shouted back.

Susan watched out the front windshield of the SUV at the Crystal Sun as it was being towed away back down the Mystic River out of sight. Emergency vents atop each tank were shooting jets of white gas high into the sky, the front sphere, without it's housing, leading the way. Susan imagined one of the old luxury steam liners going at full steam. They always looked so majestic, but this was no steam boiler exhausted, it was the emergency vents reaching their maximum output.

Susan screamed at the driver. "Get this thing moving!"

The SUV made a screeching turn to pull away but the engine jerked, and died completely. The driver worked the ignition hard. Cranked on it. "I don't understand?"

Givens called Susan's attention back to the news footage. "Mort's approaching downtown."

Susan froze at the site. The channel hugged the coast right up close to the downtown Boston skyscrapers. If the Crystal Sun blew there, whole buildings would fall. Worse, the curves and turns of the channel, caused everything to slow way down. It seemed impossibly slow, drifting past the fragile cityscape wall of glass.

Rear Admiral Mortimer coaxed and maneuvered, and finally cleared the last downtown channel curves. With the city skyline directly behind him, Susan heard him command. "Bring her up slow, ALL AHEAD FULL!"

"That crazy son-of-a-bitch got 'em past the city." Givens cheered in awe.

Susan wanted to call out, scream at Mort to cut the tanker loose in the middle of Boston Harbor and get the hell away. But she'd met, known, lost, these hero types before. Like most, Rear Admiral Mortimer was going to tow that hunk of metal out to sea, if he could, or as far as he could, ignoring the danger. How, if, he'd get away, was an afterthought. Other countrymen had this courage, but it was an American bravado somehow. Damn the torpedo's! Take that hill! You're either with us, or against us!

The fire in the bridge tower was being stoked by the wind created under full speed tow. It reached blow torch like temperatures and spewed angry flames and smoke back into the sky.

Givens leaned into Susan's phone. "Fuck 'em, Mort! Ya just saved the city of Boston, ya crazy Coastie bastards!"

In response, a sickening crack, like a high-voltage zap, split the sky open with thunder.

The aft LNG tank, beyond relief pressure, blew and instantly set off the other four tanks in quick succession like a string of firecrackers.

The tugs vaporized with the creation of the shockwave ring. A brief view of the Coast Guard Cutter was captured as the pressure wave jetted the entire ship forward, driving the bow straight down into the water, causing the entire backend of the ship to be peeled open and flip over into the air. It cartwheeled in half, the stresses snapped the keel, breaking the ship in two, sending the stern pan-caking on top of the submerged bow. Scattered parts of the disintegrating ship went shooting out, skipping across the water ahead of the destruction and massive billowing white cloud, which mercifully engulfed the scene, sparing viewers the world over the final realities.

The Cutter, the tugboats, would never be found. But something was added to Coast Guard lore that day: The Story of "Rear-Morts Cutter."

More hero's? Susan knew, sinking with the weight of it.

Reality shook her head back to consciousness. A rumbled explosion enveloped and rocked the SUV, it bounced on its suspension. Everything, including the pavement, seemed to ripple outside. Everyone grabbed hold to keep from being tossed around. Slowly it past as everything seemed to settle.

"Susan. you are in great danger in your current location!" her Pal screamed through the speakers of the SUV. Please have the driver proceed at all speed on the route I am displaying."

The SUVs engines started on their own. The driver held his hand clear of the ignition, holding out the keys in wonder, looking at Susan.

Susan felt a click in her mind. The blood drain from her face.

"Driver! This is the Palantir. DRIVE the route I am displaying immediately. Everyone is in danger from the impending explosion. You must obtain a safe distance."

The driver instinctively peeled away, glancing over at Susan for approval.

Then she heard Mr. Green in the back on his cell phone. "I want Doctor Splitzer, now!"

Susan looked at the driver. "I trust him. DRIVE! Go! Get us away!"

The driver shot forward. Susan looked back at the TV newsfeeds. Stations switched to grim anchors in studio. Switching to other coverage feeds around Boston. "Ladies and gentlemen, we are sad to report that many news helicopters around Boston Harbor have been blasted from the sky . . ."

Within a few seconds, tape from onshore, long-range cameras showed their falling colleagues. Exploding, catching fire, or smoking in a spin on their way down. The shock wave and intense kinetic pressures broke them like toys, dropping them from the sky.

Ships, tugs, Coast Guard vessels, and pleasure-craft on the water vanished from video footage all around the immediate harbor. The pressure wave blasted and pushed everything close in under the surface. A few hulls floated. Shattered, smoldering wrecks.

News stations switched to brave, or late arriving helicopters as they came on scene. "Downtown Boston has not escaped unscathed, although it could have been much worse, had the super tanker not been so far out in the harbor." Came the dramatic report from the lucky, young, rookie reporter flying in from his backup assignment covering the interstate traffic horrors. "Buildings facing the direct onslaught have their windows blown out, raining deadly shards of glass down on the city streets below, into anyone foolish enough to be out."

Susan shook her head. *What have I let him get away with?*

The devil himself answered her. The very heavens opened in an apocalyptic shower of smoldering chunks of metal. Flung from the Crystal Sun's LNG-armored tanks when they exploded and disintegrated. It had taken several seconds for the smoking pieces to start falling back to earth.

The inland news coverage showed the trails of meteors crashing down onto the crowded gridlocked highways. It was a lottery out in the open. Some, the unlucky ones, would have to live with their decision to flee that day. Large pieces fell first, then smaller and smaller, setting off fires and explosions in and around Boston for miles away.

"HOLY SHIT!" The driver screamed slamming on the breaks. A whistling frisbee sound cut in front of the windshield, as a jagged, twisted piece of metal, four-foot around, flew over top of them. It stuck with a thump on impact, the back half sticking up like an eclectic art sculpture. As they drove past, Susan thought how ironic it would be if one of these huge pieces were to hit a main LNG tank after all of this.

CHAPTER 49: The Devil's Due

"Driver, please drive faster!" Her Pal simply took over the interior SUV communications as needed.

Susan was transfixed on the TV monitor, amazed to see the Crystal Sun still afloat in Boston Harbor. The mangled hull, bobbing in the water, with a blowtorch of fire at the control tower stern. A huge, billowing, white cloud roiled from its center length. The bottom quarter remains of each jagged LNG tank formed five witches' caldrons. The evil white cloud didn't just spill out, it dropped and roiled into a tumble, then seemed to be clawing its way along the top of the water towards Susan as they sped away from the docks. It pushed across Boston Harbor in all directions. A nearly inaudible swishing rumble as it grew and grew. Billowing upwards, hundreds of feet in the air as it expanded.

The inside of the SUV suddenly glowed orange, like someone had turned a spotlight on them from behind. The explosion sound followed, booming like a jet hitting the sound barrier. A shockwave hit a split second later, tossing the SUV into a swerve, hopping it forward down the road. The waves intensified, Susan could feel the heat build with each buffet.

She caught the glow behind them in the side mirror. A huge ring of fire rolled like a donut under itself in the air over Boston Harbor. The hull of the Crystal Sun sat spewing a stream of white cloud at its center. Above it, a massive fireball climbed into the sky and looked every bit as big and hellish as any nuclear bomb going off, but it never stopped. It mushroomed and mushroomed in a blazing ball. Soon, the entire sky above all of Boston Harbor was on fire.

"Oh my God." Susan mumbled.

As they made their way further away from Everette the video feeds came back online. The in-sucking winds were feeding the fire but keeping it far from shore. It was a delicate balance between the input of air and the amount of LNG billowing out. It prevented destruction from spreading further into the city blocks and surrounding areas.

Helicopters pushed in, flying away and back in again in a brave dance to get closer. The news was nothing if not blindly brave to capture the story. The downtown skyscrapers facing the harbor were blasted and scorched top to bottom, but all managed to stay standing, saving countless lives. Unlike 9/11, their fire retardants and sprinkler systems were left intact, and kept them from burning to the ground. The wall of skyscrapers along the harbor helped save the rest of the city from even more destruction, acting like so many shields, absorbing most of the blast waves and intense radiating heat.

The video feed in the SUV cut, blacked out screens. Everyone heard the sound outside instantly. The rumble, and grumbling, barreling right at them. An angry tornado, growing louder. A roaring wind tunnel formed, deafeningly loud. Then it got even louder, scary sounds mixed with the howl.

The SUV fought the reverse in-suck of air feeding the billowing LNG fireball behind them. A gust raised it up on its suspension. Susan knew how much an armored SUV weighed. It scared her bad.

Looking out the window didn't help. Debris was flying past at sickening velocity.

"Driver! Veer right, alongside the upcoming concrete culvert drainage." Her Pal demanded.

The driver swerved off-road into a culvert backed up by a concrete drainage causeway. The SUV scraped alongside the concrete wall."

"Driver, pull up to the drainage tunnel."

"There's no way we can fit in there?" the driver asked. "It's too small, we won't fit up that pipe."

"Driver, pull up to the drainage pipe as far as you can and stop. You do not need to enter."

The driver tucked the SUV right up against the drain tunnel, the front hood and engine fit up inside and the rest of the SUV was surrounded on three-sides by the concrete abutment.

"Pal. Why are we stopped here?"

"Susan, the vehicle is protected from the radiating heat by the surrounding concrete abutment. The culvert drain pipe is feeding oxygen to the engine of the SUV over a distance which is cooling the air slightly. There is a seventy-eight percent chance you will survive until rescue crews arrive."

Susan twisted to look out the back windows of the SUV. The buildings Susan could see around her seemed to sway like trees in a storm.

Heat and wind built up in waves. Hotter and hotter. Louder and stronger.

A tire exploded in a bang, and a scream of fright. Then another a couple minutes later. One by one. The anticipation of the last one to go was unbearable.

Mercifully, in half an hour, what was left of the Crystal Sun finally sank and the intensity of the fire storm dropped off considerably.

Her Pal had kept her alive, protected her. But Susan worried he was doomed. He had over-reached, multiple times.

* * *

The LNG boiled-off for a few days, seeping to the surface, feeding the fire above. Burning a hole right through the center of Boston Harbor. Like a torch from hell had been thrust up through the middle of it.

When the fire finally began to burn down, cool off, enough to get anywhere near the harbor, Susan set out for the van.

She stood there with an F.B.I. forensic team at the site of the Chameleon's smoldering demise.

The condo had ended up fully involved, a burnt-out shell, after being cooked for days. No firefighters came initially, because at the time, they were all working on the Crystal Sun at the docks. Then everyone was pulled away with the impending explosion of LNG.

When they finally got down to the van, it had been reduced to a molten puddle. A steel splat of wax re-hardened into the blacktop. White-suited techs scraped for DNA samples out of a chunk of blackened steel. Susan was hoping they'd somehow find a tooth, or a piece of fused bone. Maybe if the cross cut it in sections.

A young female F.B.I. agent, assigned to Susan as a liaison, approached with phone in hand.

"I'm sorry, I know we aren't supposed to put these calls through, but this guys called like ten times. He's using a voice filter to disguise himself. I told him we don't put those calls through, but, well, he said you'd know him. He has your personal card, direct number, or I wouldn't have bothered you."

"Know who?" Susan asked.

"Says his name is James Wright? An old friend of Carl Perkins? Does that make sense?"

Susan saw her own shock register on the girl's face like she was looking in the mirror. A cold, damp chill clamped around her throat as she took the phone.

"Hello, Susan Figiolli, who the hell is this?"

"Hello Susan! I was glad to hear you survived . . ."

The devil himself was on the line, boasting about the souls he'd claimed.

Susan decided to sell hers to get the Chameleon, no longer interested in catching him.

Rehan Al'Camel must die.

# # #

Made in the USA
Columbia, SC
24 July 2018